LEITH, 1850

D0688365

NO LONGER PROPERTY OF
SEATTLE PUBLIC LIBRARY

RECEIVED
NOV 12 2021

SOUTHWEST BRANCH

A Corruption of Blood

Also by Ambrose Parry

The Way of All Flesh
The Art of Dying

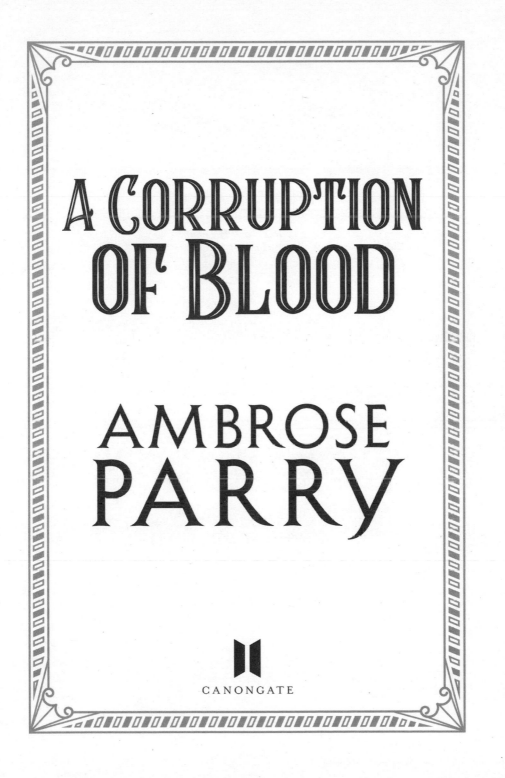

A CORRUPTION OF BLOOD

AMBROSE PARRY

CANONGATE

First published in Great Britain, the USA and Canada in 2021
by Canongate Books Ltd, 14 High Street, Edinburgh EH1 1TE

Distributed in the USA by Publishers Group West and in Canada by
Publishers Group Canada

canongate.co.uk

I

Copyright © Christopher Brookmyre and Marisa Haetzman, 2021

The right of Christopher Brookmyre and Marisa Haetzman to be identified as the
authors of this work has been asserted by them in accordance
with the Copyright, Designs and Patents Act 1988

British Library Cataloguing-in-Publication Data
A catalogue record for this book is available on
request from the British Library

ISBN 978 1 78689 985 9
Export ISBN 978 1 78689 986 6

Typeset in Van Dijck by Palimpsest Book Production Ltd,
Falkirk, Stirlingshire

Printed and bound in Great Britain by Clays Ltd, Elcograf S.p.A.

MIX
Paper from
responsible sources
FSC
www.fsc.org FSC® C018072

For our parents:
Grace and Jack, Alicia and Gerry

1850

EDINBURGH

ONE

book is already written before the reader casts an eye upon the page. Its tale creates the illusion of uncertain outcome and myriad possibilities, when in truth all of its events are predetermined, unfolding in an ordered sequence that cannot be altered, only observed. Was this also true of each human life? Were our fates decided even before we were pulled screaming into the world: dictated by provenance and circumstance, by what our forebears could or could not grant us, and by what they were unwittingly forced to pass on?

Such were the thoughts of Dr Will Raven as he ascended a squalid staircase in Leith. His surroundings did not augur well for the child whose birth he had been called to assist. He wondered too what his own blood might harbour – a recurrent preoccupation – and what the implications might be should he ever father a child himself.

The address he was looking for was in Old Sugarhouse Close, a ramshackle building situated beside the candle works. The air was full of the smell of tallow, the meaty stench of rendered animal fat. There were other, rawer scents too, with the flesh, fowl and fish markets abutting the factory. The last was always on the breeze, fish being a pervasive aroma this close to the port, as much a constant as the cries of the gulls.

Raven found the door that he was looking for and was about to knock when he heard the sound of crying. He paused. It was not the tormented screams of a woman in labour but the lusty bawling of a healthy new-born.

He sighed. Leith was a long way to have come for this. It did happen, of course. *Uti veniebam natus*: born before arrival of the medical attendant. It was a common enough entry in the outdoor casebook. The professor liked to say that he too had escaped the intervention of the local doctor in this way. Then, as always, Simpson had been in a bustling hurry to get on.

Raven rapped upon the door. He heard the scuffling of hasty footsteps and then it opened, a grey-haired woman standing before him cradling a naked infant in her arms, its skin still smeared with blood and vernix.

Raven held up his battered leather bag to identify himself.

'I'm here for Mrs Corrigan, though I don't suppose I need to ask if this is the right place.'

'You took your time,' the woman said.

He wondered if she was a local midwife. They had a tendency to resent the intrusion of doctors upon what they considered to be their territory. The meddlesome accoucheur with his forceps.

He smiled in what he hoped was a placatory manner.

'Dr Raven. At your service.'

The woman stood her ground for a moment before stepping aside to let him enter. A short passageway led to two closed doors.

'Where is the mother?' he asked.

She nodded towards one of the doors. 'In there. Afterbirth has still to come away.'

'How long since the birth?'

'A while.'

'Could you perhaps hazard a guess as to the precise time?'

'Not long.'

'Has there been any bleeding?'

She looked at him askance. 'There's always a bit of blood when a child is born.'

'I mean brisk bleeding. Flooding.'

'I'd hardly be standing here talking to you if that was the case.'

He noticed a nautical chart hanging on the wall.

'The father is a sailor?' he suggested.

The woman frowned, giving the tiniest of nods, perhaps conveying that this was hardly a complex deduction given they were in Leith.

'He is at sea now.'

'When does he return?'

She rolled her eyes. 'More of an if than a when, if you ask me.' She lowered her voice. 'It is *Miss* Corrigan,' she added archly.

Raven pushed open the door and entered a small room containing a bed and not much else. It was a familiar sight: a household that would struggle to feed another mouth.

He had often heard the voices of churchmen and politicians railing against the poor for having children they could not afford to feed and clothe. Ignorance was always fertile soil for the sowing of moral indignation.

The air had a clammy feel to it, humid and oppressive. There was a small window set into the wall above the bed but throwing it open would require scrambling over the patient lying in it. A thin sheet lay over her and the still prominent mound of her belly. Raven did not like what he saw. The uterus should have contracted more than that by now.

He put his bag down. Miss Corrigan had her eyes closed but her colour was good and her breathing steady. He gently lifted her hand and felt for the pulse at the wrist. Rapid but strong. Reassured, he spoke her name and introduced himself. She opened her eyes. He explained what he was going to do. She nodded.

Raven took off his jacket, rolled up his sleeves and then gently laid his hands on her swollen abdomen. Aware of the old woman's eyes upon him, he opened his bag, took out his stethoscope and listened. He felt the uterus harden and then relax. He completed his examination by assessing the maternal passages and the cervix.

There was no other sound in the room. The baby, now consoled, was quiet.

The old woman tutted loudly. 'Have you not done this before? Do you even know what you're looking for? It's like a bit of auld rope. Give it a tug and the afterbirth will likely come away.'

Raven looked at her and arched his brow.

'Probably best if I deliver the other child first,' he said.

The second twin, another girl, proved to be a straightforward delivery, and Raven required no assistance to deliver the afterbirth. The old woman was still hovering, only briefly cowed by what she had missed and rapidly returning to her previous attitude of barely tolerating his presence.

Her surprise was as nothing compared to that of the mother, though. She seemed overcome, the shock of a second, unexpected child evidently not a welcome one. For those of narrow means, children could be a blessing or a curse. Additional mouths to feed could be offset by the ability of the youngsters to work and contribute to the family coffers should they survive early childhood. But two at once, with their mother's ability to work hampered by having not one, but two babes to care for? Raven could not but fear for these little girls if this was their start in life.

At such times he consoled himself with the thought of Simpson's humble origins, the seventh son of a Bathgate baker. Nobody had a choice over what they inherited, into which home they were delivered or what would greet them there: riches or poverty, love or cruelty, nurture or neglect. But Simpson proved that a man did not have to be defined by the start he was given.

To Raven's mind, the corollary also held true. If you were born into wealth, it was not difficult to make your mark, and thus your achievements ought to be measured accordingly, but this was not a perspective shared by the rich. With a smile he recalled his friend Henry, back in their university days, speaking of a wealthy student given to diatribes condemning 'the lowborn' as somehow deserving of their fate: 'He has the right to judge harshly, for he chose his parents well.'

When Raven emerged once more into Old Sugarhouse Close, the early summer sun was high enough to find him between the buildings. He put a careful hand to his pocket watch, mindful of the press of bodies he would have to navigate as he got closer to Leith Shore. There were subtle hands at work down here with a dexterity that would be the envy of any surgeon. The timepiece was the only thing of value that his father had left him, though he could hardly call it a bequest.

The crowd was thickening with every yard as he made his way along Tolbooth Wynd towards the Shore, indicating that a ship had recently docked. This had troubling implications for his chances of hailing a cab. He would probably have to walk. It was a pleasant enough day for it, but time was against him. Raven's trip to Leith had left his new colleague, Dr Morris, to cope with the morning clinic on his own.

As he was calculating how quickly he could cover the distance on foot, and how much the extra time taken would add to the hostility of his reception back at Queen Street, he noticed that a small group had gathered at a quieter part of the quayside. They were looking over the side at something in the water. A man at the centre of the crowd was using a fishing pole to retrieve whatever it was that had fallen in.

It was a parcel of some kind. The fisherman's rod bent as he raised it up, water pouring from its underside.

'It looks heavy,' someone said as it was carefully lowered to the ground.

'Well, it'll no' be full of sovereigns if that's what you're hoping for,' the man with the fishing pole replied.

'Ye cannae know that until ye take a look.'

The fisherman snorted and shook his head. 'As it was floating and no' sunk to the bottom of the Forth, I can tell ye now it's no' full of gold coins.'

They all stood staring at the parcel. No one made a move to open it.

'Smells a bit ripe,' a woman's voice said.

'That's cause you're standing down-wind of auld Geordie,' came the reply, producing a few titters of laughter from the crowd. The old man in question volubly cursed his accuser, provoking further laughter, but still no one seemed willing to approach the salvaged object, let alone open it.

'Let me take a look,' Raven said, holding up his bag. 'I'm a doctor.'

As a physician he was well used to taking charge of a situation and dealing with things others found distasteful. The onlookers seemed happy enough to defer, parting to let him through.

As he reached the front, he caught a whiff of the odour leaching from the package and understood the hesitance of the crowd. He knelt down beside it, pulled a knife from his bag and carefully cut the binding. There were audible gasps from around him as he peeled back an edge of the paper, revealing a tiny hand. Reluctantly he peeled back some more, enough to disclose the head and torso of an infant: a human child wrapped up and tossed away.

The fisherman sniffed and wiped his nose on the end of his sleeve. 'Told ye it wasnae treasure,' he said.

Raven was seized by a surge of pity. As an obstetrician he had seen enough tiny corpses to be inured to the sight of another dead baby. He had held them while they were still warm, knowing no breath would ever issue from their lips even as their mothers looked on in hope. Yet something about this caught him unawares. Perhaps it was simply the fragility of the twins he had helped deliver that morning. He had feared for their start in life, but this served to remind him that for some there was no start at all.

TWO

aven's return to Queen Street was delayed by having to wait for the police to arrive. Most of the onlookers had drifted away, leaving him to find a spot far enough away from the parcel that he was no longer disturbed by the smell. Without the distraction of conversation, he was left with his own thoughts for company. His mind returned to an earlier concern, and to the reason it felt imperative.

He had found the woman he wished to marry.

Raven had surprised himself with the strength of his feelings for her, feelings that for a time he had suppressed because he did not think their match would meet with approval. Of late, however, he had resolved to overcome whatever obstacles might lie in his path and allowed himself to truly contemplate the prospect of marriage. What he had long wished for was now within his reach. She was a woman with the knowledge and experience to assist him in his professional life, to help in the running of his medical practice, and she would wish to do so. She would not be content to be merely wife and mother. Nonetheless, he knew she would want to be both of those things too, and though Raven wanted children, he worried what he would pass on to them. Because every day he worried about what had been passed on to him.

You have the devil in you, his mother used to tell him. She had first said it in jest, later in worry. For they both knew where the devil had come from: whose blood ran in his veins.

You're a useless mouth at my table, his father had been fond of telling him, *a grasping hand forever in my pocket*. He had seldom been content with verbal recriminations alone. At times Raven wished that his father could see what he had become – a doctor and assistant to the famous Dr James Young Simpson. More often he was grateful that he would never have to set eyes upon the man again.

Would his father have been impressed by his career thus far? A medical degree from the University of Edinburgh, furthering his education at some of the greatest medical institutions in Europe, and now assistant to the man who had changed the world through his discovery of the anaesthetic properties of chloroform? No doubt his father would have found a way to denigrate each and every one of these achievements. A bitter and disappointed man who would have been threatened by his son's success.

Raven knew that his situation sounded impressive when spoken aloud, but he also knew this was mainly because proximity to Simpson placed him in the corona of the great man's glow. Day-to-day practice was altogether less grand. Reality for Simpson included aristocrats and even royalty: patients travelling from around the world to stay in fine hotels on Princes Street, where they would wait for days or even weeks for a consultation. The reality for Raven was a trip down to Leith to deliver ill-starred twins and stand guard over a dead baby.

In time he was joined by a pair of constables tasked with transporting the little corpse back to the police office on the High Street for examination by the police surgeon. Raven gave his statement, which proved a prolonged task as the constable taking notes was excruciatingly slow in doing so. He struck Raven as the kind of fellow whose lips moved as he read.

'When do you think the post-mortem examination will take place?' Raven asked.

The constable shrugged his shoulders as he continued to scribble in his notebook, the tip of his tongue poking out between his teeth as evidence of his intense concentration.

Raven looked to his colleague, who was circumnavigating the parcel as it lay on the quayside. He had his hands clasped behind his back as though reluctant to touch the thing for fear it was dangerous in some way.

'Up to McLevy, isn't it,' he stated.

Raven felt himself stiffen at the mere mention of the name. It was a common response, and one in which McLevy revelled. His reputation inspired fear throughout the city's streets, except for those in the upper echelons of Edinburgh society who would be unlikely to ever feel the detective's hand upon their collar.

Raven anticipated that McLevy would take charge of this latest grim discovery, unwilling to delegate such a matter to a junior member of his team. Nonetheless, Raven decided that he would like to be present at the post-mortem, his curiosity piqued. Unfortunately, he was not acquainted with the police surgeon, Dr Struthers, but his old friend Henry Littlejohn was now assistant pathologist at the Infirmary and assisted him on occasion. Raven was sure he would be able to prevail upon him for both introduction and invitation.

Raven arrived at 52 Queen Street damp with perspiration, a result of his brisk walk back from Leith in the strengthening sunshine. As he rushed through the front door, he very nearly collided with several bags piled up in the hallway.

He enjoyed a moment of elation, thinking that Sarah had returned despite her last letter indicating an extension to her travels – London, Paris and now Grafenberg. Then he saw Jarvis, Dr Simpson's butler and general factotum, pick up one of the bags and take it into the professor's study. He remembered that Dr Simpson had been off in the countryside somewhere, delivering the heir to a grand estate. No doubt the larder would benefit from gifts received in addition to the hefty fee: the largesse of a country laird grateful for the safe arrival of his child. The promise of game pie helped dispel thoughts of dead children and grudge-bearing detectives.

Lizzie, the housemaid, appeared at his side to take his coat and hat. She tutted loudly as she passed the garment onto Christina, the new girl standing at her side. Christina had not been with the household long, but was as diligent as she was uncomplaining, in contrast to her frequently simmering and occasionally terrifying colleague. Not that Christina was a cheery soul. The girl seemed burdened by a constant pall of melancholic gloom, which was unlikely to be lifted by working alongside Lizzie.

Lizzie pointed at the mud on his coat, acquired when Raven had knelt down to examine the parcel on the quayside.

'You'll have to take a brush to that,' she told Christina. 'Dr Raven has a tendency to pick up a great deal of dirt when out on his rounds. I've had to take that coat out the back with the carpet-beater before now.' She gave Raven a stern look, daring him to contradict her.

'What would I do without you, Lizzie?' Raven replied. He had learned from experience that arguing with her seldom did much good.

She snorted and turned round, colliding with the luggage cluttering the hallway.

'Don't know why he bothers unpacking those bags,' she said. 'The professor is off again at the end of the week.'

'Is he?'

'London.'

Raven found it hard to keep up. Staying abreast of the professor's activities was an impossible task. Simpson had at one point employed an amanuensis to order his affairs, but that had not ended well.

'London,' Christina repeated. 'I'd love to go.'

Lizzie snorted again. 'The only chance of you and me getting much beyond the outskirts of Edinburgh,' she said, 'is if we're transported.'

As far as Lizzie was concerned that might well be true, Raven thought. He looked again at the new girl, who was now studying her shoes, possibly regretting that she had opened her mouth at all. She was young to have her modest hopes extinguished, yet how likely was it that her life would amount to much more than this?

Raven had just begun to flick through the pile of correspondence on the hall table when Hugh Morris stuck his head out of his consulting room. Dr Morris was also a recent addition to the staff at Queen Street. He was a decent sort, but a quiet, industrious type, always working, reading, writing papers, performing experiments in his room. He was not much for revelry or conversation. To Raven's mind, occasional light-hearted distraction was essential when one was forced to contend with the diseased and the dying on a daily basis.

'Difficult case?' Morris asked, by way of acknowledging how long Raven had been gone.

'Cases plural, as it turned out. Twins in the first instance, both delivered safe and healthy, but the next infant was not so fortunate. Found floating in the water at Leith.'

Dr Morris's eyes bulged briefly. 'And the mother?'

'Currently being sought by McLevy.'

'How thoroughly unpleasant. I wish I could offer respite, but . . .'

Raven nodded. There were still groups of patients clotted together at the door to the waiting room, a low hubbub of muted conversation from within.

Raven went into his consulting room and called for his first case of the day, which turned out to be an older lady full of gripes about the condition of the roads and the conduct of young people.

'They do not show the proper respect for their elders any more,' she grumbled, settling her ample posterior down on the examination couch like it was the assertion of a claim. 'I had to wait an age for someone to give me a chair in the waiting room.'

Raven listened to her grievances as attentively as he could, before manoeuvring the conversation back to medical matters. He knew that sometimes the best medicine was a listening ear, that loneliness and isolation could contribute to a patient's complaint, but this was not something at which he considered himself to be proficient. He could hear Simpson's voice in his head as he struggled to concentrate: *An unsympathising physician is a physician bereft of one of the most potent agencies of treatment and of cure. He knows not, and practises not, the whole extent of his art, when he recklessly neglects and eschews the marvellous influence of mind over body.*

Simpson's mantra had been repeated so frequently Raven could recall it without effort. He agreed with the principle but found its application a little more problematic.

He finally managed to coax from the woman the reason for her visit, asked the relevant questions, and made his examination of the crusted, scaly lesion that extended in patches from forearm to shoulder. He wrote out a prescription before applying a dressing and then a bandage to the worst affected area, congratulating himself on his patience and fortitude.

He handed her the prescription with a smile. It was not returned, the woman evidently not as impressed with his performance as he was himself.

'When is Sarah coming back?' she asked flatly. 'I generally prefer to be looked after by her. A lady is naturally more comfortable being treated by another woman.'

'Perhaps Sarah should obtain a medical degree then,' Raven replied.

The lady looked askance at Raven's handiwork, which he had to admit was not nearly as neat as Sarah's would have been.

'Yes, perhaps she should.'

As he watched her amble to the door, Raven knew that his

patient was not the only one who was missing Sarah. It had been a month since she had gone, and the house did not feel the same without her.

Or was it simply that *he* did not feel the same without her? Aye, he would have to own that too.

There had been a time when he intended to make Sarah his wife, but he had not been sufficiently resolute until it was too late. In that respect, he had proven himself to be unworthy. He had let slip his chance through cowardice, concerned that marrying a housemaid would be injurious to his prospects. It took the pain of losing her to understand what she really meant to him: first when she married someone else, then when she had come so close to death.

As she recovered from her episode of ill-health, he had cast his plans. He would ask her initially to join him in setting up his own practice; then in time, once the appropriate decorum of widowhood had been observed, he would ask her to become something more. But on the very day he was preparing to broach the issue, she returned from visiting her husband's grave and told him she wished to follow in the footsteps of Elizabeth Blackwell, the first woman to obtain a medical degree.

That was when a true epiphany struck him. Her circumstances were profoundly changed. She was a widow now, with her late husband's resources at her disposal. She was embarking upon a voyage of discovery, both physical and metaphorical, trying to find her place in a world that had suddenly become much larger.

Raven realised he could not make his offer: not because he feared she would reject it, but because he feared she would accept it. He could offer her a good life, far better than she might have dreamed only a few years ago, and she might well settle for that, but she deserved better. Sarah wished to be something more than a woman was usually permitted to be, and if he truly cared for her, he could not be the man who stood in her way.

The nobility of this often felt like small consolation as he watched her make her plans, and the hardest part was that he could not tell her any of it. But quite unexpectedly, by the time she was packing her cases, it had become easier: paradoxically because things had become more complicated.

He still cared for Sarah a great deal, but his feelings for her now had to be accommodated alongside his feelings for someone else.

THREE

London, three weeks earlier

arah could see nothing but a cerulean blue sky and the type of pristine, bleached white clouds rarely encountered north of the Tweed. Not typical of London either, she would wager, given what she had witnessed thus far. Smoke and dust seemed to hang in the air, great plumes of it obscuring any view of the firmament above. Perhaps that explained why their hosts had painted the ceiling of their dining room with a view that could not be obtained by simply stepping outside. A reminder of what the sky was supposed to look like.

The décor was at least providing some distraction from the monologuing gentleman to her left, who seemed intent on describing, in its entirety, his collection of microscopic slides. He seemed wholly oblivious to the fact that Sarah had been staring at the ceiling for a full five minutes.

'. . . the lung of a frog. A piece of shark skin. The wing of a horse fly . . .'

Sarah regretted that their meal had ended some time ago, or she might have feigned a choking episode as a means of bringing this interminable, one-sided conversation to an end. She looked

across the table at Mina, who had evidently been more fortunate in the seating arrangements. She had been placed beside a
handsome young man with an intelligent face and a full head of
hair which moved about as he did, a great strand of it breaking
free from the rest and sweeping across his left eye as he came
to the end of an amusing anecdote that Sarah could not hear.
Mina laughed discreetly behind her hand as the other men in the
vicinity guffawed loudly.

'. . . a piece of goat's horn. The scales of a freshwater trout . . .'
the slide man droned on.

Perhaps she could attempt a faint. Or stab herself in the eye
with her cake fork.

Lady Montague, fortunately, came to her rescue.

'Let us all move through to the drawing room,' she announced.
'We shall have a musical interlude. My nephew Geoffrey will play
a piece by Mendelssohn on the piano.'

They had left Edinburgh three days before, stopping in London
en route to Paris. Sarah had been excited to see the great metro-
polis that she had heard so much about but had quickly tired of the
place. It was too crowded, the atmosphere oppressive. Everything,
even the most palatial residences, seemed begrimed with filth.

Their great expedition had been instigated by Sarah, but it
was Mina – Mrs Simpson's sister – who decided the route they
would take, the invitations they would accept and the sights
they would see on the way. Mina's brother Robert, being the
accompanying man in their party, was nominally in charge, but
he generally followed Mina's lead and did what was asked of
him without complaint. Barring his attendance at a few business
meetings, there was no specific agenda he wished to pursue, and
he presented no impediment to Mina's grand plans.

Consequently, Sarah had little say in how they spent their
time and had been strictly instructed not to go off by herself.
Even at her most frustrated she would not have done such a
thing, intimidated by the scale of the place and worried that

she would become hopelessly lost. She had enjoyed their visit to Westminster Abbey, never having seen anything on such a scale before. St Giles in Edinburgh could not compare. They had viewed the new Houses of Parliament and witnessed the great morass of the Thames crowded with boats.

She had a list in her mind of the places she would have preferred to visit but she did not wish to seem petulant or ungrateful. She would have loved to walk the wards of one of the great hospitals – St Bartholomew's, St Thomas's – or wander around the displays of morbid anatomy at the Hunterian Museum. The British Museum would have served at a pinch, and Sarah had suggested it, but Mina declined. The weather was much too fine to be indoors, she said.

Sarah was impatient to get back on the road to their next and ultimate destination, but Mina was enjoying sightseeing and socialising too much for that. Being the sister-in-law of James Young Simpson, Professor of Midwifery and discoverer of chloroform, guaranteed a steady supply of invitations to luncheons, dinners and parties.

Sarah felt out of place at all of them. Her modest wardrobe was insufficient for such a variety of gatherings and she was obliged to wear the same dresses in short rotation. Initially she worried that people would notice and then she decided that she did not care. As a consolation for the endless round of social engagements that she was compelled to attend, she thought she might at least meet persons of a scientific bent with whom she could converse on matters that were of interest to her. Instead she found that she was forced to endure the same inane discussions about clothing – the latest fashions from Paris (rather scandalous, apparently) – and the relative merits of serving dinner *à la russe* compared to the more traditional *à la française*. It was becoming increasingly difficult to fathom when the French were to be emulated or shunned; approved of or disparaged.

Sarah moved away from her dining companion with relief and

walked around the expansive table towards Mina, who seemed disinclined to leave. As Sarah approached, Mina held out an empty wine glass which Sarah accepted without comment and then headed towards the decanters lined up on a sideboard to fill it.

What am I doing? she thought as she poured the wine. Sarah was unsure who she was more annoyed with: Mina for treating her like a servant, or herself for behaving like one. Mina, she realised, was experiencing great difficulty in recognising Sarah's altered status. She had been a housemaid once, but marriage and then widowhood had changed that. She was now a woman of independent means, however modest.

As Sarah followed the rest of the guests out of the room, she lost sight of Mina in the crowd. There was a slow procession between the rooms, the most eminent guests leading, those of a more moderate standing bringing up the rear. The drawing room was as large and ornately decorated as the dining room, hung with huge paintings of severe-looking men in military attire and a large tapestry depicting an ancient battle.

The playing of the piano was delayed as the sheet music had been misplaced. Lady Montague swept around the room to offer effusive apologies to her assembled guests, clutching at the jet beads which adorned her neck and then adjusting a lace headdress that had somehow been knocked askew.

'You'd think she had poisoned someone rather than mislaid a concerto,' said a voice at Sarah's shoulder. She turned to see the man with the resplendent hair who had so entertained Mina throughout dinner.

'Mr Cadge,' he said, 'at your service.' He smiled and made a bow. A lock of hair fell across his face and he tucked it behind his ear as he straightened up again. 'I am given to understand that you work with the great Dr Simpson.'

'I do,' Sarah said, returning his smile.

'And what is it that you do?'

'I'm an assistant. Of sorts.'

Mr Cadge frowned.

'I help with the patients and administer chloroform on occasion,' she clarified.

'You have an interest in anaesthesia?'

'I am interested in medicine.'

'Then our Miss Gillies would approve of you.'

'Miss Gillies?'

'She is an artist.' He looked around the room. 'She is here somewhere. Ah, yes. There she is. Deep in conversation and gesticulating wildly as though having a fit of some kind.'

He indicated a woman on the far side of the room, dressed extravagantly in brightly coloured silk, an explosion of colour in an otherwise drab corner.

'She thinks that women should find themselves a useful occupation away from hearth and home. Work is good for the soul, apparently.'

That rather depends on the work, Sarah thought. Scrubbing floors was not perhaps the kind of toil the good lady had in mind.

'She was very much taken with Dr Blackwell who was here last summer,' Mr Cadge went on. 'You will have heard of her, I suppose.'

'Of course.'

'The first woman to acquire a medical degree. Quite an achievement.'

'We are hoping to meet her in Paris,' Sarah said, although the truth of the matter was that it was only Sarah who wished to meet her, the very reason she had embarked upon this trip in the first place. Mina had declared herself impressed with Dr Blackwell's success but unlike Sarah had no desire to emulate it.

'Is that where she went. I had assumed she had gone back to America,' Mr Cadge said, taking a sip of his brandy. 'I consider myself to be something of a pioneer in the field of anaesthesia,' he continued, his interest in Dr Blackwell seemingly exhausted. In Sarah's limited experience, men vastly preferred to talk about themselves and shifted discussion in that direction at the earliest opportunity. 'I was present when Liston performed the first operation under ether. I was his house surgeon at the time. Do you know this story?' he asked.

'Not the details,' she said. At least this was a story she wished to hear.

'A butler from Harley Street needed his leg off and was somewhat reluctant to undergo the procedure. Could not be persuaded even when told that Liston could complete an amputation in about thirty seconds. He jumped at the chance to have ether. Funny thing was – and few people know this – before Liston arrived in theatre that day, it was thought prudent to try out the ether on one of the hospital porters, a big man who agreed to participate in this experiment for a fee. Took a few breaths of the stuff and then leapt off the table, rampaged round the room, cursing at the top of his lungs. Took four of us to restrain him until he recovered his senses. If Liston had witnessed that he would probably have abandoned the whole thing and lost his place in history.'

'Does Mr Liston use chloroform now?'

'He does not.'

'Why?'

'Died shortly after it was discovered. Hit in the chest with a yacht boom. Led to a thoracic aneurysm which subsequently ruptured.' Mr Cadge mimicked an explosion with his free hand.

'Tragic.'

'Messy.'

Sarah was confused by this and briefly considered asking for more details, but further enquiry was forestalled when they were approached by another guest, an elderly gentleman wearing thick spectacles, his rheumy blue eyes magnified by the lenses. He seemed to be a little unsteady on his feet and failed to introduce himself. This lapse was perhaps explained by his excessive consumption of Lady Montague's claret, some of which had spilled onto his shirt.

'Lady M tells me that you are on your way to meet the lovely Miss Blackwell,' he said, standing so close to Sarah that she could smell the alcohol on his breath.

'Dr Blackwell,' Sarah corrected him.

'Yes, yes. The lady MD. I met her when she was here last summer. Delightful little thing. Something of a surprise.'

'That she had succeeded in obtaining a medical degree?'

'Well that, yes. But we were all expecting someone, you know, more physically robust. Broad-shouldered. Brawny.'

'Masculine?' Sarah suggested.

'Quite.' The old man shook his head. 'I applaud her achievement and all of that, but it is not really a profession suitable for the fairer sex, is it?'

He smiled at her as though this was a self-evident truth. 'I mean, who in their right mind would consult with a lady physician?' he continued, oblivious to Sarah's growing irritation.

Sarah could feel her face flush. She looked again at the crimson stain on the gentleman's shirt front. It reminded her of the blood-spatter seen after a dental extraction. Or a punch to the face.

She heard a titter from Mr Cadge and wondered if he would say anything in reply, something that would atone for the other man's remarks, but he seemed amused rather than appalled and Sarah was left with the impression that he shared this view even if he would perhaps have put it a little more delicately himself.

She desperately wanted to say something pithy and devastating that would change the minds of those around her, but in her anger was struggling to find the right words. What words would possibly change the minds of those so entrenched in their views? Mere rhetoric would never be enough. Action would be required. A clear demonstration of their misapprehension.

She saw Mina coming towards them at speed, clearly unhappy about something. That Sarah had failed to deliver her wine? Or that she had commandeered her dining companion? She was welcome to them both as far as Sarah was concerned.

She had to remind herself, not for the first time, that she was indebted to Mina. Without her, she would never have been here at all.

'I think it's time we took our leave,' Mina announced, a tight smile on her lips. She did not wait for introductions or proffer any explanation for her sudden need to depart. 'Get the coats, will you, Sarah?' she added as she turned and made her way towards the door.

FOUR

ith Dr Morris having been left short-handed for so long, the clinic had overrun, though in truth it would have been more remarkable had it not. Raven went to the kitchen and grabbed a leftover chicken leg by way of lunch, Mrs Lyndsay's admonishments ringing in his ears as he ascended the stairs to the front hall. He needed something he could eat on his walk to the Maternity Hospital, a consideration she seemed unprepared for, despite its regularity.

He was on his way to the front door, narrowly avoiding collision with one of the children, when he heard the professor's voice. Simpson was descending the stairs at his usual rapid clip. He was a man in a permanent state of hurry, as though every moment was already allocated to a task, but he had forgotten to account for the time required to transport himself from place to place.

'Will, I'm glad I caught you. Do you have plans for this evening?'

The unspoken answer to this question was always 'Not any more'. Raven had been intending to seek out Henry in one of their preferred taverns to enquire about attending the post-mortem on the Leith baby. He would have to send a note instead.

'I am at your disposal as ever, professor.'

Simpson was an impossible man to say no to, and not merely because he was Raven's employer. As his long-term mentor, Raven felt a constant need for the man's approval and a desire to impress him. Nor was this an entirely passive compulsion. Simpson had an energy about him that was as inspiring as it was addictive, like a fuel that made one burn all the brighter, though it could be utterly exhausting.

'Is it an evening consultation?' Raven asked, hoping there might be some rich patient lodged at a Princes Street hotel. Raven was always looking to make an impression so that his own name might come to mind should the professor not be available in future.

Jarvis appeared with his unfailing stealth and handed the professor his familiar hat, one that would drown a lesser head.

'No,' Simpson replied, giving Raven a conspiratorial look. 'I should warn you that it is not your clinical assistance I wish to draw upon. My duties tonight require me to traverse dark and treacherous straits, wherein I would feel better knowing I have able reinforcements.'

'Of course, professor.'

Raven had occasionally wondered how much Simpson might suspect about his experience of violence. This request confirmed that, as in most matters, it was wise to assume the professor knew all. But what such a man might be fearful of was a matter of intrigue and, Raven would have to concede, some concern. Simpson was respected, even beloved in the grimmest and most disreputable parts of the Old Town, having interceded so often in the homes of the poorest without taking a penny in payment. Ever recognisable in his hat and coat, Raven had assumed there was nowhere the professor could not walk unmolested even on the blackest night.

As Jarvis held open the front door, Raven observed that Simpson's carriage had been summoned, his trusted coachman Angus at the reins.

'I would offer you a ride, but I am bound for Newhaven and thus headed in the opposite direction.'

Raven was not sorry. He was already late enough for it to make little difference, but more importantly he had a reason why he would prefer to walk. His journey to Milton House was becoming one of the highlights of his day, because it was a chance to see *her*.

He finished the last of the chicken leg as he turned on to George Street, cleaning his fingers on a handkerchief before checking his reflection in the window of a gentleman's tailor. He was looking presentable enough, but his eye was drawn to the scar on his cheek. He had been considering growing a beard to cover it, as he had done when he first received the injury. First impressions were an important consideration for prospective patients, and Raven remained fearful that it made him look like the kind of man who got slashed in a back alley as a warning from a money lender.

He had desisted because *she* said she liked the scar, and because it held a certain significance between them. Raven nonetheless remained concerned about the significance it might hold for her father.

He pulled out his pocket watch and saw that it was almost two o'clock. Some days she contrived to be out walking in St Andrew Square around the time he was on his way to the Maternity Hospital. Other days she would simply arrange to be at her bedroom window so that they might see each other as he passed. That was as much as he could hope for today, but he would treasure it all the same.

Raven had reconciled himself to not marrying Sarah, but that did not mean he had been looking elsewhere for a wife. If so, he would not have wanted for prospects, albeit none that were particularly tempting. For some time, oblivious of his feelings towards Sarah, Mrs Simpson's sister, Mina, had been casting about on his behalf. Raven took it as an indication that Mina had all but given up on finding a spouse for herself that she was pouring boundless enthusiasm into procuring one for him. He felt pity for her, which was why he tolerated it, pretending not to notice that she was arranging 'chance' meetings with those she deemed suitable candidates.

Raven had sought to build a career longer than he had sought a partner to share it. He knew it was expected of a doctor that he be a family man with a wife who appeared and behaved according to certain standards. This was particularly true in the field of obstetrics: Simpson freely admitted that he had asked Jessie to marry him in part because it would improve his chances of securing his professorship. Being a bachelor was considered an insurmountable impediment.

As in many things, he looked enviously towards the professor and the relationship he enjoyed with his beloved Jessie. As second cousins, they had corresponded for years, trading confidences, worries, observations, aspirations, and sharing a profound love of books. Consequently, they were two people who truly knew each other's minds, each other's souls, long before they knew each other as husband and wife. But for that, Raven did not think they could have endured some of the tragedy and heartbreak that had befallen them.

Mina's prospects were all pleasant girls, doubtless more than happy to assume the role of wife to a doctor and mother to his children, but it disappointed Raven that these were the only roles they wanted. They were sweet, pretty and eager to please, but they were raised to be acquiescent. Compliant. Guileless.

The very properties that supposedly made Sarah an unfitting wife were now the attributes that he had come to most value in a woman. Perhaps fittingly, then, it was no machination of Mina's that led to his good fortune. Rather it was the request of the professor that he attend the house of Dr Cameron Todd, who wished to observe the effects of chloroform on one of his patients suffering from intractable neuralgia.

It had been a crisp spring morning, a little over six weeks ago, when Raven presented himself at the St Andrew Square address. Dr Todd was one of the richest practitioners in the city, a man whose inherited wealth meant that he had no need to supplement his earnings with income from teaching at a hospital.

When Raven pulled the doorbell, he had marvelled at how the sound echoed within. The maid who answered directed him to a capacious drawing room, where he was left to admire the oil paintings which adorned the walls. He was contemplating a dramatic landscape full of brooding clouds, crags and waterfalls when he realised that he was not alone. A young woman was reclining on a sofa by the window, an open book on her lap. She was staring at him and continued to do so for far longer than was strictly polite, as though appraising him in some way.

'I'm sorry. I thought the room was empty,' Raven said.

'And who might you be?' she enquired.

'My name is Dr Will Raven.'

'A medical man, then. I had assumed something else. Something more exotic and interesting.'

She still made no attempt to stand up and introduce herself properly. Raven wondered if she was an invalid of some kind, though she lacked the pallor associated with the chronically sick and was fashionably dressed for someone who spent all their time indoors. The more he looked the more he realised that she was possibly the healthiest-looking invalid that he had ever come across. In fact, she was not merely healthy, she was truly striking, though he could not gaze long upon the beauty of her face with her eyes so unflinchingly fixed upon him.

Before he could ascertain who he was speaking to they were joined by an elegantly dressed gentleman who introduced himself as Dr Todd. He was a thin man with a full head of grey hair and neatly trimmed whiskers. He was clad in a black frock-coat and trousers, starched white collar and necktie. His clothes exhibited neither stain nor crumple, suggesting a man whose practise of physic was presumably of the old-fashioned sort where the physician rarely made physical contact with the patient. There was a precision and a meticulousness to his attire that engendered an aura of sleek professionalism, something that Raven hoped one day to emulate. He looked down at his own coat and trousers, well used and weather-beaten. He did not compare favourably and struggled to find anything about his appearance that had caused the young woman in the room to think him exotic.

Given the strangeness of his interaction with the woman thus far, Raven was grateful for the interruption, but Dr Todd looked far from pleased at having found them together.

'Eugenie! What are you doing in here? I was told that you had gone out.'

'Well, quite evidently I did not.'

Todd ignored this remark and turned to Raven.

'Dr Raven, I presume,' he said, shaking Raven's hand. 'Do please forgive my daughter. Her manners frequently desert her.'

He then addressed his still-recumbent offspring.

'Leave us, would you, my dear? We have important matters to discuss.'

Eugenie closed her book and rose slowly from her chair.

'Important matters that I wouldn't understand, or indelicate matters not to be spoken of in front of a fragile creature such as myself? You must be careful, Dr Raven. Say the wrong thing and I will faint clean away and you will be forced to revive me.'

She sashayed across the room in a swirl of mazarine silk. The scent of rosewater hung in the air as she passed. She took her time, in no hurry to leave. Then as she reached the door she halted and looked back.

'That is quite a scar, Dr Raven. How did a respectable man such as yourself acquire it?'

Raven was taken aback by the directness of the question but did not have the time to answer before Dr Todd chastised his daughter and sent her from the room.

'My apologies once again for Eugenie's lack of decorum. Please understand that her impertinence was not intended as a mark of disrespect towards you but towards me. It amuses her to torture her father sometimes.'

'It is truly of no matter,' Raven assured him.

'How you came by such a scar is entirely your own business.'

This last was intended to sound like polite sensitivity, but Raven could not help detecting a certain judgment to it. It was not the kind of thing you said if you suspected a scar had been sustained falling from a thoroughbred while riding with the hunt. Rather, back alleys and criminal associations were what Todd wished to spare Raven from acknowledging.

It was once his business was concluded and Raven was about to leave that Eugenie reappeared in the hall. She had evidently chosen her moment, waiting until her father had retreated back into his study.

'Do you have an answer for me?' she asked.

It took a moment for Raven to recall what she meant. His fingers went automatically to his cheek.

'It is a sabre cut,' he said. 'I sustained it in a duel.'

'Defending the honour of a wronged woman,' she responded, indicating how seriously she took his answer. A game of sorts was underway.

'Did you win?'

'Nobody ever truly wins a fight, Miss Todd.'

'So you lost. Hence the scar.'

Raven thought of the alley, the blade, the criminal associations.

'Oh, I most definitely lost.'

'You are assistant to Dr Simpson, are you not? I have heard many a rumour.'

Raven shook his head. 'Pay them no heed. For when it comes to Dr Simpson, the truth is always more remarkable than anything the New Town gossips might dream up.'

She fixed him with a lively gaze, her smile playful, albeit in the way a cat plays with an injured bird.

'I wasn't talking about Dr Simpson.'

These two fleeting encounters had cumulatively lasted only a few minutes, but over the following days, Raven had been quite unable to stop thinking about Eugenie. He caught himself daydreaming as clinic patients droned on about minor symptoms, straining to remember the curve of her jaw, the smell of her, and the glint in her eye as she spoke. There was a tantalising promise of misbehaviour about her, a hint of mischief in refreshing contrast to Mina's insipidly acquiescent young ladies. Eugenie seemed spiky but not cruel, amused but not scornful.

He began speculating about how he might engineer another meeting with her, but she beat him to it, presenting herself under circumstances that seemed even more contrived than one of Mina's stratagems. Eugenie appeared at 52 Queen Street with a letter for the professor from her father. She said she had offered to bring it as she was on her way to visit her aunt in Randolph Crescent, and would therefore be passing. Raven did not for a moment imagine she was in the habit of delivering post amidst her perambulations.

And that had been the start of something quite unexpected.

It had also been the start of something necessarily clandestine. They arranged to meet in St Andrew Square two days later, Raven's eager anticipation of the rendezvous heightened by a frisson of danger. The choice of location lent plausibility to why they might have happened upon one another, but it also added to the likelihood of their being seen by someone from her household.

He had felt an exquisite anxiety as he walked along George Street that day, uncertain whether she would be there, there being so many reasons why she might not. This gave way to a surge of exhilaration as he saw her waiting for him.

He asked her how she had spent her morning, forestalling any enquiries about his own. He had no desire to spend this precious time discussing sores and rashes.

'I was reading a book,' she replied, 'a novel translated from the German. It is called *Elective Affinities*.'

'By Goethe.'

'Oh, you have read it?'

'No,' he confessed. 'But I often heard his work discussed when I studied in Prussia.'

Her eyes widened in surprise. 'Where did you study?'

'Berlin. Among other places. I spent a year travelling Europe.'

'So I was right: you are indeed more exotic than an ordinary medical man. Did you live among artists and bohemians?'

Raven thought he had best steer away from this topic. Tales of his association with a fugitive aristocrat-turned-artist might delight Eugenie under other circumstances, but it would hardly strike the right tone to discuss a past affair with an older woman.

'You find medical men uninteresting?' he asked, trying not to sound concerned for the implications.

'Not as a rule, but the problem with medical men is that their conversation is often too much of one thing: and by that I don't mean medicine – I mean themselves.'

'I assume that through your father you have been exposed to more of them than you would care.'

She had given him a curious smile, the look of someone confessing a sin of which they did not repent.

'Father likes to show me off at social gatherings but has to balance that with the risk that I might give offence. It is amusing to watch his trepidation.'

'Are you in the habit of giving offence?'

'It is tempting. The number of eminent men in Edinburgh is greatly exceeded by the number who consider themselves so, and the latter tend to be the more thin-skinned.'

Raven could attest that the former could be thin-skinned too.

'They speak to me like I am a silly girl, so I disparage them with subtleties they assume beyond me. They treat me as guileless and so I respond as though it were true.'

'What do you mean?' Raven had asked.

She gave that unrepentant smile once more.

'I will not be so indiscreet as to name him, but for instance, there was one gentleman who availed me of the time he treated the visiting Princess Marie Amelie of Baden. I told him, "How I envy your wife, for she must get to hear that wonderful story over and over again."'

Raven laughed.

'My father worries that they will belatedly realise the insult on the carriage ride home, or when they sober up the next morning. I contend that he credits them with too much introspection.'

'That poor woman, though.'

'His wife?'

'No, Princess Marie Amelie. She must have been dangerously ill, for half the physicians in Edinburgh claim to have treated her during her stay.'

Eugenie had liked that. Her laughter was joyous and unrestrained.

'What is this Goethe novel about?' he then asked. 'Elective affinities sounds like a scientific term.'

'It is. The book postulates that the relationships between human beings are comparable to the relationships between chemicals. That when you bring certain combinations together, a reaction is inevitable.'

They stopped in the north-east corner of the square and looked into each other's eyes.

'I think I know what he means,' Raven had said.

Over the coming weeks they had met again and again; all the while the question of whether Dr Todd would welcome Raven's attentions hung ever heavier. Edinburgh medicine was like the European courts of centuries past, as powerful men constructed alliances and fortified their positions through the marriages of their children. Dr Todd was diligently protective of his only daughter, whose mother had died giving birth. Hence their secret meetings: brief walks and surreptitious appearances behind glass.

Although discretion was warranted Raven was beginning to wonder how much longer they would be satisfied with meeting in this way. It felt like so much more than a dalliance, more than a flirtation, but he was unsure what their next move should be.

Raven tamed some stray hairs and smoothed down his jacket, then resumed his progress east in the direction of the square. As he approached the house, he glanced up expectantly at the first-floor window.

Eugenie was not there.

Instead he saw her father standing with his arms folded, looking out with the vigilance of a sentry. Their eyes met briefly, then Dr Todd withdrew, as though satisfied he had seen what he expected to.

FIVE

impson's carriage rolled between the fields of the Grange, the cobbles of the south side long having given way to a dusty track beneath its wheels. Though it was almost seven o'clock in the evening, the sun remained as warm and bright as though it were the middle of the afternoon, which caused Raven to realise he should have anticipated Simpson's mischief when they spoke at lunchtime. There was literally nowhere dark that he could have been heading on a clear June evening, not even in the Old Town, and they were far from its putrid labyrinth. At that very moment, the brougham was approaching Crossford House, wherein lived Sir Ainsley Douglas, one of the wealthiest and most influential men in the Lothians.

'Have you had the pleasure?' Simpson asked, referring to their host. Something about the professor's tone indicated that he was using the word euphemistically.

'I have not, though I did encounter his son, Gideon, at university. He was a medical student too.'

Raven said nothing more, knowing his brevity was likely to convey enough. Gideon Douglas was the arrogant and detestable individual he had recalled that morning, whom Henry had complimented on his choice of parents. If it was true that the apple seldom fell far from the tree, then Raven could well understand Simpson's subtle warning about Sir Ainsley. What was less clear was why the professor had accepted his invitation.

Such thoughts of fathers and their influence prompted a resumption of the uncomfortable reflections that had troubled Raven throughout much of the day. His mind kept returning to how Eugenie was not to be seen at her window that afternoon, and more significantly, how her father had been all too visible there instead. He had argued with himself back and forth over what he might reasonably extrapolate from a single passing moment. He had been later than usual, after all, and there were many reasons why Eugenie might have been indisposed. However, there seemed fewer reasons why Dr Todd would be loitering at his daughter's bedroom window, and that look of vindication Raven had glimpsed upon his face was an image he could not erase. It felt like the end of something.

He only needed to look at himself to see why. He was dressed as smartly as he was ever likely to manage, and yet his appearance served merely to emphasise why he would never be considered good enough by the likes of Dr Todd, for he was conspicuously wearing borrowed clothes. Mrs Simpson had dug out an evening suit for him, one her husband had purchased at least three stones and a dozen years ago. It was as short in the sleeves as it was loose around the middle, and given Simpson's indifference to sartorial aesthetics, Raven doubted it had even been fashionable in 1840.

The carriage rattled past the gatehouse and into the grounds of the estate, the track narrowing as it wound through aged woodland before emerging onto a grand avenue flanked by verdant lawns and lovingly tended flowerbeds.

'There is a smell of cooked meat upon the wind,' Raven said approvingly.

'Indeed. And the hospitality will be unsparing, but to a specific end. Sir Ainsley hosts this summer soirée every year to call for funds towards the several hospitals on whose boards he sits.'

As the carriage stopped to discharge its passengers, Raven could not help but observe that the proceedings were very much underway.

'Are we . . . late?' he ventured.

'I may have misread the time on the invitation,' Simpson said with a casualness suggesting that his habitual tardiness for social engagements was not always the result of his clinical caseload.

They stepped down onto the drive and began strolling towards the throng. There had to be two hundred people here, standing in groups next to tables laden with food and wine. Raven searched in vain for someone as poorly dressed as himself. Even the staff looked smarter.

Simpson placed a hand lightly on his arm as they approached.

'From here on in, we must imagine that we are on a fever ward.'

'How so?'

'In that duty obliges us to make our rounds, but in so doing, it is imperative that we do not expose ourselves long enough at any station as to be infected by the poisons borne on the miasmic ether.'

Simpson was hailed by a member of a nearby gathering, one of whom was distinguished among companions in evening suits by the garb of a church minister.

Raven immediately recognised another of the group as James Syme, Professor of Surgery, and as Simpson made introductions, he was grateful that Syme did not in turn recognise him. While studying under him, Raven had once vomited during an operation, overcome by the heat of a crowded and unventilated theatre. Syme had picked on him mercilessly thereafter.

Simpson and Syme were seldom on good terms either. Syme was constantly militating against Simpson's intrusions into surgical territory that he deemed forbidden to the physician-accoucheur. Raven wondered whether his role here was to restrain his mentor should their ongoing disagreement come to blows.

As well as Syme, the group comprised Professor Malcolm

Eustace of the Royal College of Surgeons, Charles Dymock of the Society of Writers to the Signet, and the Reverend Lochlan McLean, all of whom served on the board of the Royal Infirmary, as did their host.

The hostility that Raven was anticipating did not come from the expected source. Simpson was perfectly civil to everyone and Syme was his usual taciturn self; it was the Reverend McLean who emanated a distinct froideur towards Dr Simpson whenever he made a contribution to the conversation. He had the haughty air, common among senior churchmen, of individuals unused to being disagreed with. Simpson lived for disputation and the free exchange of ideas, so it was not difficult to imagine from whence derived the reverend's displeasure.

'Am I to infer that you and the reverend are in dispute in some way?' Raven asked as soon as they had extricated themselves.

'Our differences derive from when I was a visiting physician at the Lock Hospital, which as you know is largely concerned with the treatment of venereal disease. As a charitable institution, its ostensible mission to keep young girls off the streets has always come with an unwelcome dose of piety. My position there became untenable after I publicly criticised the trustees for heaping on the moral and religious instruction at the expense of the medical help.'

'Lizzie was a patient there, was she not?'

'Yes. As was the new girl, Christina. In each case, a colleague discreetly brought them to my attention, seeing potential in them.'

'And the Reverend McLean was vocal among these trustees, I assume.'

'Passionately so, though one might say he was merely a willing and enthusiastic piper. But he who *pays* the piper calls the tune.'

Raven was about to ask the obvious question when he realised Simpson meant none other than the man they were approaching.

Sir Ainsley Douglas was the wealthiest and therefore the most powerful member of the many hospital boards on which he sat.

He was holding court, attended by no less than Austin Mansfield, provost of Edinburgh, and Auberon Findlay, Dean of the Faculty of Advocates. Also present was William Sanderson, editor of the *Edinburgh Evening Courant*, and a gentleman Simpson evidently did not know, introduced by Sir Ainsley as his nephew Teddy Hamilton.

This last sparked the realisation that Raven had not seen Gideon, but as it had been three years since they last met, there was no reason to believe he might be here. He would have graduated by now, and for all Raven knew could be practising anywhere from Glasgow to Galashiels.

'Dr Simpson!' Sir Ainsley greeted the professor. 'Congratulations on your growing renown. I am told the discovery of chloroform is truly transforming the practice of medicine throughout the world.'

'There are still pockets of resistance, particularly in the field of childbirth, but I believe we are prevailing.'

'Who could possibly object to such a boon?' asked Teddy, genuinely incredulous.

'There are those who believe that pain in childbirth is divinely ordained and that to prevent it is in defiance of God's will,' Simpson replied. 'This largely derives from a mistranslation in Genesis. The verse states: "In sorrow shalt thou bring forth children," but the Hebrew word in fact means *toil*.'

A stern-faced butler replenished Sir Ainsley's glass but did not offer anyone else a refill from the same bottle. There were lesser members of the household staff charged with dispensing refreshments to everyone else. It was an unsubtle assertion of status, not that Sir Ainsley needed such attentions to emphasise his importance. He was an imposing enough presence, tall and sharp-featured, a severity about his face that conveyed formidable strength of will. Raven estimated him to be in his late fifties, but suspected he had always looked much the same, finding it difficult to picture him as a younger man.

'An important distinction,' Sir Ainsley agreed, 'though unfortunately there are legions who regard toil itself as a source of sorrow. It is why idleness is the cause of such misery among the poor, as I have been *toiling* to explain to my nephew. His mother sent him to study the law in London and it appears he has fallen in with radicals. Before you arrived, he was questioning the benefits of the new Poor Law. I fear his cosseted existence has shielded him from the slothful and slovenly ways of the underclasses.'

Teddy had developed the flushed look of one who knew he had no choice but to patiently endure his uncle's patronising manner. He looked to be around Raven's age, though he carried himself with the certainty of an older man, evidently not shy of holding forth in esteemed company.

'My concern is that the law provides insufficient support for abandoned women, leaving mothers to shoulder the burden of child-rearing alone,' he countered, directing his explanation towards Simpson and Raven in the hope of finding allies in the newcomers. 'And so, the only public aid she might receive is conditional upon her submitting herself to the poorhouse.'

'You are talking of *unwed* mothers,' Sir Ainsley clarified with open distaste, 'to whom the infant at her breast is rightly her stigma and her punishment for the sin of fornication. Abstinence and self-discipline are the desirable qualities demonstrated by those who refrain from relations outside wedlock. If women lacking such virtues are not made to atone for their wickedness, then what kind of example is set for our daughters?'

Raven was rapidly appreciating the truth behind Simpson's jest: this was indeed a dangerous place, one that had to be navigated with a care for neutrality. Any allegiance one might make would also garner corresponding enemies. This was why he had preferred the route of trying to establish his own practice rather than seeking a position at the university. Such reflections made him think again of Eugenie, but that in turn made him think of Dr Todd, and he feared he had most definitely garnered an enemy there.

'Poverty is the product of idleness,' chimed in Sanderson, the newspaper man. 'And children born out of wedlock inherit the wickedness of their mothers. This is why it is imperative to discourage such moral laxity, lest it multiply.'

'It is not idleness that prevents an unwed mother from being able to fend for her child,' Teddy argued. 'How is she to work and care for an infant at the same time?'

'These are the very questions we would want young women to ask themselves *before* they contemplate temptation,' Sanderson responded.

In his exasperation, Teddy looked towards the provost.

'I would have thought I might find an ally in yourself, Mr Mansfield. I was under the impression you had been an opponent of the Poor Law.'

Mansfield looked uncomfortable, suddenly red around the ears.

'Mr Mansfield has lately overcome the folly of his previous position,' Sir Ainsley said.

Mansfield cleared his throat, a contribution clearly expected of him.

'Just as the prostitute in the street serves as a warning to a housemaid, lest she become insolent or shiftless, harsh consequences serve to inculcate good morals.'

His tone was flat, indicating his reluctance to get involved. Nonetheless, Sir Ainsley seemed pleased enough. He placed a hand on the provost's shoulder.

'Well spoken, sir. And I am sure the provost would also agree that each woman who makes herself the occasion of sin makes herself the instrument of a good man's downfall.'

He stressed this with a significance that Raven did not follow.

'But none of this addresses the issue of the children,' said Teddy. 'They should not be damned for the sins of their mothers.

Who is to care for them when their mothers are not provided with the means to do so?'

For a moment it appeared no one had an answer. But Sir Ainsley was merely biding his time.

'Perhaps Dr Simpson might suggest a solution,' he said.

The professor's face remained impassive, but Raven had known him long enough to recognise what passed silently beneath the surface of his expression. Simpson was involved in the fostering of children, finding good homes for the unwanted offspring of the upper orders. In this matter, discretion was paramount, so by even alluding to it Sir Ainsley was being gravely disrespectful.

Evidently Simpson's outspoken dissent over the Lock Hospital's policies several years before had been neither forgotten nor forgiven.

Teddy looked expectantly towards the professor, but before he was obliged to speak, their host intervened.

'But this is not the occasion for such disputations,' he announced cheerily. 'Duty obliges me to say a few words, and I have happy news to announce, so please, eat and drink. Have your fill.'

With that, he took his leave, headed in the direction of a small platform that had been erected on the western edge of the lawn, where the sun would be at his back when he addressed the assembly.

The group dispersed immediately thereafter, as though Sir Ainsley was the only force strong enough to hold such disparate individuals together.

'That felt . . . delicate,' Raven ventured. 'I have sympathy with Mr Hamilton's sentiments, but I confess I was too cowardly to voice them.'

'Sometimes discretion truly is the better part of valour, Will. Poor Mansfield had the look of a man humiliated.'

'Quite. For a fellow whose position requires oratory, he did not sound convinced of his own words.'

Simpson nodded. 'There are those who are happy to enjoy Sir Ainsley's patronage and do his bidding because they are in concord with his beliefs: the Reverend McLean for one, and Sanderson for another. Sir Ainsley owns the *Courant*, and Sanderson is his placeman. Sir Ainsley appreciates their fealty, but I believe he derives greater pleasure from the corruption of those who previously opposed him. He revelled in Mansfield making a display of his enforced *volte face*, no doubt the price exacted for his assistance in some private matter, financial or otherwise. I fear Sir Ainsley has bought the provost, as he has bought many others before him.'

SIX

Paris, two weeks earlier

arah followed Mina down an echoing corridor, the sound of their footsteps reverberating off the vaulted ceiling. The floor was of polished brick, both uneven and slippery, causing her to look carefully at where she placed her feet, much as she had been doing in the street outside. Evidence of the building's former life as a convent was everywhere – a cloistered courtyard, images of saints and angels carved into the plasterwork.

Mina was initially reluctant to come – 'A maternity hospital holds no interest for me,' she had said – but Sarah knew only a few words of French and needed her to act as translator. Yet here she was now, striding ahead, with Sarah following a few paces behind, much as they used to. Mistress and servant.

Sarah was trying not to be overly sensitive about these subtle demonstrations of status. She doubted that Mina was even aware of them. Without conscious thought Mina slipped back into their outdated roles, like putting on a comfortable old coat, reassuringly familiar yet in need of being thrown out.

They were led through a series of labyrinthine passageways which linked various buildings to one another, Sarah doubting

whether she would be able to find her way back to the front
door without assistance. Eventually they were shown into a little
parlour belonging to Madame Charrier, the *sage-femme*-in-chief.
Sarah had been expecting something purely functional, akin to
a monastic cell, but the room was stuffed full of all manner of
things – chintz sofas, china figurines, crucifixes, paintings and
embroideries. Mme Charrier, a stooped, wizened old lady who
stood to receive them, seemed dwarfed by her surroundings.

Formal greetings were exchanged, everyone sat down and then
Mina launched into rapid French. It was impossible for Sarah to
understand any of it. She had to resort to examining hand gestures
and facial expressions to estimate whether Mina was making any
headway in her request for information. She was left with the
impression that things were not going well. Mme Charrier shook
her head repeatedly, shrugged her shoulders and then spread her
gnarled hands wide as though fending off Mina's entreaties. Then
she pointed to her left eye, frowned and shook her head again.

Sarah looked at Mina, hoping that she would translate the
gist of the conversation thus far, but she merely paused before
launching into another incomprehensible torrent. Sarah gave up
trying to follow and sank into her chair. She looked around the
room again, marvelling at the clutter, a profusion of mismatched
items.

What would they do if they were not permitted to see Dr
Blackwell after travelling all this way? Sarah had not considered
this until now. The sole purpose of her journey had been to
meet the woman who had achieved the seemingly impossible:
storming the citadel, gaining entry into the exclusive gentleman's
club that was medicine.

Initially Sarah had planned to pursue her quarry across the
Atlantic, to track her down in America where Dr Blackwell had
obtained her degree. She had the financial means to do so, however
when she announced this intention, strenuous attempts had been
made to dissuade her: it was too far, too dangerous, she was not

strong enough for such a journey after her illness. In the end a transatlantic voyage became unnecessary because Dr Blackwell was no longer there. As with many a medical graduate looking to expand their practical experience, she had gone to Paris.

Mina had volunteered to be travelling companion and translator, a role that she was now relishing a little too much, as it provided yet another means of demonstrating the gulf that still existed between them. Sarah may have married up, but she had not achieved equivalence, not in social standing or in education. Sarah's parish-school achievements could not compete with those who had been blessed with more expensive and comprehensive instruction.

Sarah became aware that Mme Charrier was nodding now and sat up a little straighter in her chair. Some progress had evidently been made. The old lady then stood and shuffled from the room.

'Where is she going?' Sarah asked.

'To find the intern. Monsieur Blot.'

'What about Dr Blackwell?'

'She is no longer here.'

'What? Where is she?'

Mina shrugged. 'Madame Charrier thinks that she may still be in Paris but cannot be certain. She believes that Monsieur Blot may know of her whereabouts. He and Dr Blackwell were on friendly terms when she left.'

They heard footsteps in the corridor outside and a young man entered, followed by the ancient *sage-femme*. He bowed low and introduced himself – in English, much to Sarah's relief.

'I understand that you are looking for Dr Blackwell.'

'We have a letter of introduction from Dr Simpson of Edinburgh,' Mina announced before Sarah could say anything. 'My friend and I are great admirers and are keen to make her acquaintance.'

The mention of the Simpson name had the intended effect.

'Ah, Simpson of Edinburgh. Chloroform,' Blot said, smiling.

Then he frowned, passing his hand through his hair and causing it to stand up in untidy tufts. 'Unfortunately, Dr Blackwell is no longer with us. She has . . .' He paused for a moment, searching for the appropriate word. 'She is . . . departed.'

'What happened to her?' Sarah asked, the words coming out in a rush. She imagined Dr Blackwell falling from a great height or crushed under carriage wheels, a nascent career ended before it had a chance to begin.

Monsieur Blot took in their shocked expressions and hastily explained.

'She has left the city. Has gone to Grafenberg to seek treatment.'

'Grafenberg?'

'There is a famous spa there. She has gone to take the water cure in the hope that it will help her eye.'

'What happened to her?' Sarah asked again.

'Purulent ophthalmia,' Monsieur Blot replied. 'A bad case. I . . . we, did everything that we could but the vision in the eye is not what it was. She could not continue her studies here.' He looked down at his clasped hands. 'I am not sure that she will be well enough to continue her studies anywhere.'

SEVEN

aven watched Sir Ainsley make slow progress towards the platform, being stopped and greeted by every group he passed. The ostensible purpose of the evening was to raise funds for the Royal Infirmary, but Raven suspected that Ainsley's principal incentive was the opportunity to bask in the glow of his own importance.

He was currently being glad-handed by Professor Henderson, who a few months back had falsely accused Simpson of causing the death of a patient. Henderson had been part of a clique spreading rumours in person and in the press, motivated by fury at Simpson's ridiculing his belief in homeopathy. Raven turned to warn the professor of his presence, but Simpson seemed to have vanished. Instead he found that he had crossed the path of someone he was altogether less pleased to see.

'Gideon,' Raven said, striving to keep surprise from his voice.

Though he was younger than Raven, Gideon looked the more mature, perhaps because of the bespoke cut of his suit and the air of being in an environment in which he belonged. Standing before him, Raven's borrowed clothes felt all the more conspicuous, his very right to be here also borrowed from his employer.

Gideon gazed upon him with a pronounced puzzlement

intended to convey irritation at being importuned by someone with no such right.

'You have the advantage of me. Have we met?'

His skin was darker than Raven remembered, sun-kissed in a way that suggested he had not wintered anywhere near here.

'I am Will Raven. I knew you as a student.'

Gideon continued to look blank. Bored, even.

'University feels like such a long time ago. I recall little of it.'

Something burned in Raven that this man could choose to erase him from his own record. He did not wish to rise to the insult, but nor was he going to indulge Gideon in the convenient fiction that they did not know one another.

'I was your personal tutor for a month. Are you honestly telling me you don't remember?'

Gideon gestured across the lawn, to where staff in black uniforms were replenishing platters.

'Servants come and go. I seldom have reason to remember their names.'

Raven took a moment, swallowed.

'I understand. It was perhaps this limited capacity for recollection that so caused you to struggle in your studies.'

There was a satisfactory flare of outrage in Gideon's eyes before their attention was drawn by the ringing of a bell. The butler was sounding it to call the assembly to order as Sir Ainsley finally ascended the little stage.

It took a few moments for everyone to fall silent, then Sir Ainsley began to speak, at a lower volume than Raven had been expecting. It was not the booming projection of one used to addressing crowds or even raucous debating chambers, but the even register of one used to being heard.

'I want to thank you all for joining me here this evening, in some cases for your ongoing generosity, but as importantly for your shared commitment to the health of our city. I have always been a believer that the health of one is the health of all, that the health of the individual and the health of society are inextricable. What corrupts one of us, corrupts *every* one of us.'

He took a moment to receive the calls of 'Hear, hear!' that rose in response, then resumed.

'Immoral behaviour is a blight upon our city, which is why I am proposing an ordinance regarding certain contagious diseases, and I am pleased to have the support of the provost in pursuing this. Such infections are the physical manifestation of a moral corruption, which is why I contend that any woman found to be spreading such disease should be put in jail, where she can do no further harm.

'We are all of us here tonight good people, decent people. But if we shrink from imposing our will, then the will of the indecent will surely prevail, and that will be a judgment upon us all. So, let us work tirelessly that the will of the decent should define our great city.'

This precipitated a round of polite applause, during which Raven turned to take in some of the responses. He spotted Simpson and observed that he – perhaps strategically – happened to be holding a glass and was thus impeded from all but a cursory gesture generating no audible percussion. More conspicuously he noticed that Gideon was standing with his arms folded, a look on his face Raven was singularly qualified to recognise. It was the simmering gaze of a man who despised his father.

Sir Ainsley gestured as though to damp down the applause, a technique Raven had witnessed from showmen on the stage, one actually intended to emphasise the adulation.

'We are all looking towards a bright future together, so it seems appropriate that I share with you some news of coming brightness in my own future. As you all know, I lost my dear wife, Margaret, mother of my children Gideon and Amelia, these ten years ago now, and I have mourned her every day since. The burden of the widower must be borne alone, but in recent times I have found it eased by the acquaintance of someone who shares my grief in having lost a spouse. I have been blessed with the companionship of Mrs Lucille Chalmers, and it is perhaps the worst-kept secret in Edinburgh that we are soon to marry. We ask you all this evening to join us in celebrating this happy news.'

A woman ascended the platform to stand alongside Ainsley. She was striking both in her appearance and in that she had to be half Ainsley's age. Twenty-five at most, Raven estimated. The lawn erupted in another round of applause, this time accompanied by the chink of glasses and calls of congratulation. Raven was interested to observe Gideon's response to the announcement of an intended stepmother only a few years older than himself, but he had moved away. As Raven searched the crowd, he was arrested by a sight that instantly purged all other thoughts from his mind. Smiling at him from but a dozen yards away, amidst a throng of excited chatter, was Eugenie.

His heart soared for precisely as long as it took the person next to her to investigate what had suddenly captured her interest, placing Raven for the second time that day in the stern gaze of Eugenie's father.

EIGHT

s the evening wore on, Raven found it difficult to pay close attention to what anyone was saying. His eyes flitted surreptitiously about the throng, seeking another sight of Eugenie, whilst always mindful of where her father might be. Every glimpse of her was to be treasured, but with it came the tantalising sense of being so near and yet so far.

Having long since lost track of the professor, he found himself in the charge of Mrs Winnifred Beaumont, who was delighted to introduce him as the young gentleman who had administered chloroform while Simpson delivered her third child. Raven only vaguely remembered the woman, but her recollection of the encounter was understandably more vivid. 'A miraculous experience, incomparably preferable to its two predecessors. Dear Simmy is known to us all, but it is this young man's face that I think of dearly when I recall that confinement. It was the last thing I saw before I drifted off, only waking to see my wee Ronald being placed into my arms.'

Raven had no sooner been approvingly presented to the other ladies when Mrs Beaumont's face lit up as she beckoned someone over Raven's shoulder.

'Amelia, do come and join us.'

He assumed this was Sir Ainsley's daughter, Amelia Betten-court. Simpson had pointed her out earlier, informing Raven that her husband, a cavalry officer, had been thrown from his horse and killed while she was pregnant with their first child. Amelia was dressed in the black of first mourning, rendering her distinct amongst so many ladies in bright summer colours.

As she approached, disengaging from another group, Raven observed with a combination of delight and mild alarm that she was accompanied by none other than Eugenie. Moments later they found themselves finally face to face, but having to act as though they were being introduced to each other for the first time.

It was frustrating that there was no opportunity to converse alone, but there was an unexpected intimacy in their being complicit in this deception. They shared secret glances, all the more exquisite for being covert and fleeting.

Inevitably, talk soon turned to the happier of Sir Ainsley's announcements, a subject on which Amelia was conspicuously noncommittal. It was as though she was tolerating such discussion out of an understanding that it was of interest, but did not share everyone's excitement. Perhaps it was difficult to think of nuptial joy when you were recently a widow.

It turned out she was not the only one. 'I'm told Mrs Chalmers' late husband died of a sudden illness,' Mrs Beaumont remarked. 'Something he was thought to have contracted in India, or possibly on the sea voyage home.'

'They were married for only a year,' said someone else.

'She is very handsome, is she not? Youthful,' Mrs Beaumont suggested, delicately but inquisitively broaching the issue most likely to be troubling Mrs Chalmers' future stepdaughter.

Raven watched with interest to see how she responded.

'Indeed,' Amelia said. 'Of child-bearing age.' She wore a thin smile, a subtle tartness to her expression.

'The poor thing lost her first husband before she had the chance,' Mrs Beaumont ventured.

Eugenie flashed Amelia a smile. 'She might soon bear your young Matthew an uncle or an aunt,' she said.

There was knowing mischief in this, which told Raven there was a rapport between them.

'And won't that be lovely for all of us,' Amelia replied, a statement from which each listener derived a different meaning.

Moments later, Amelia made her apologies.

'You are not staying overnight?' asked Eugenie, disappointed.

'No. Matthew did not travel with me as he was poorly this afternoon, and I could not rest under another roof if I did not know he was well.'

'Of course you must go,' agreed Mrs Beaumont. 'I heard the poor lamb was terribly ill in the spring, which must have given you such worry.'

Amelia swallowed before speaking, troubled by the memory.

'After losing Hilary, the fear of losing our son too was intolerable. Thank the heavens, though, he rallied. But now I am anxious whenever he is out of my sight.'

'It is a pity you cannot stay,' said Eugenie. 'We have not spoken in so long. I haven't seen young Matthew since he was but a few weeks old.'

Amelia nodded sincerely. 'As I recall you were quite overcome. I was moved to see it.'

'Who could fail to be. He is such a beautiful child.'

'You will have one of your own in good time.'

A look of uncertainty clouded Eugenie's face for a moment before she masked it with a smile. Raven thought she had looked almost tearful. He wondered what her father had said to her today, what hopes might have been dashed.

Was this evening to be a symbol, the essence of their relationship from here on in? Occasional glimpses from afar, and encounters in which they were forced to disguise that they knew each other, all the while haunted by the memory of what feelings they might once have had?

'You two are fast friends, then?' Mrs Beaumont asked Eugenie, once Amelia had departed.

'Yes. Since we were children. I used to come here frequently, my father being Sir Ainsley's physician.'

'Oh, of course. Dr Todd.'

'It is such a beautiful house, is it not?' Eugenie said. 'I haven't visited for such a long time. I may take a turn around the grounds before the light fails.'

She briefly eyed Raven as she spoke. He gave the gentlest of nods to acknowledge that he understood. He felt his pulse quicken, a sensation immediately followed by the thought that her father's eyes might be upon him. He was unable to look around for the man without it being conspicuous, so he would have to ensure they were not seen leaving together.

Raven made his excuses, saying that he had to catch up with Dr Simpson to check when his carriage was leaving.

'Of course. But we must talk further,' said Mrs Beaumont.

'And soon,' said Eugenie.

Raven slipped through the crowd and onto a path at the edge of the lawn, where he asked one of the staff where he might find the water closet as a pretext for proceeding towards the house. It took fortitude not to glance back to check whether Eugenie was following, a fortitude he turned out not to possess. He did not see her. He reasoned that for the purposes of discretion she was likely to wait a few moments before following. He opted to take a circuitous route, around the stables to the east of the house.

As he approached the nearest of the outbuildings, he spied Gideon just inside. He had his back to the door, but there was no doubt who Raven was looking at; nor who he was listening to. He could hear Sir Ainsley's voice angrily berating his son: 'Did you think some enchantment had rendered you invisible as you stood there with your arms folded and that sour look of childish pique writ so vividly upon your countenance? I saw you plain as day from the stage, and if I saw you, then so did everyone else.'

'I thought their eyes would have been on you, father. That, after all, was the purpose of the evening, was it not?'

Raven saw a hand reach out and strike Gideon about the head, Sir Ainsley briefly leaning into view as he put his weight behind it. In observing this act of violence, Raven was made conscious of the disparity in their statures. Gideon was shorter, slighter, and seemed to shrink further in the face of his father's ire.

'You would make a show of your disrespect before all those people, when I have seen to it throughout your life that you should want for nothing. You seem determined to fail as though to spite me.'

Gideon's voice sounded halting, fearful. There was a trace of defiance in it, but it was a dim ember of a fire long since doused.

'I should have thought you happy to see me fail. You have told me often enough that I am destined to do so. That I will never be worthy of the name that has been conferred upon me.'

'I have handed you every advantage, granted you boundless opportunity, only to watch you squander all that was within your grasp through your feckless indolence. You are living proof that some are born to fail regardless of how straight and clear their path to success. I hate to consider that such weakness must have come from your mother, but as the years go on, I have to concede that this must be the case. It could not have come from me!'

'My mother's only weakness was her blindness to what you are. But in time the scales fell, and that was why she—'

Ainsley lashed out again with a long and powerful arm. The open-handed blow struck Gideon across the jaw, the report of it enough to make Raven's teeth rattle.

'Do not speak of her! It is my consolation that she did not live to witness your manifold disgraces.'

Gideon put a hand to his mouth, wiping away a smear of blood.

'I will speak of her, for I am her son, as I am your heir.'

'You are an inconvenient remnant. A parasite, a leech, and I will no longer fund your dissolute ways. It is decided. I have spoken to Admiral Whitelaw, and soon we will see whether the Navy can make a man of you where I have failed. I hope you enjoyed your voyage home from Tobago, for you will be seeing a great deal more of the ocean from here on in.'

'I will not go.'

'Then you will starve, for I will not give you another penny.'

NINE

here had been a finality to Sir Ainsley's tone that warned Raven to leave. He slipped away on quiet feet, anxious not to be seen. Neither of them would forgive a witness to such an exchange, however inadvertent.

Raven walked swiftly in the direction of the house, eager to gain some distance from the stables. Eugenie had not been able to specify where they might meet, so he would have to walk a circuit and hope to encounter her coming in the other direction, or perhaps she would be waiting for him somewhere out of sight of the lawn.

Raven was excited to hear footsteps as he approached the corner of the house. He quickened his pace in impatient anticipation and all but bounded around the edge of the building, where he found himself face to stern face with Dr Cameron Todd.

'I would speak with you privately, Dr Raven,' Todd said, his voice quietly imperative, that of a man who did not expect argument.

'Of course.'

He had chosen his moment well. They were alone, unseen, just as he and Eugenie had intended for each other. Raven wondered if the man's eyes had left him the entire evening.

Dr Todd looked him up and down, as though only just noticing his attire.

'What are you wearing?' he asked with mild bemusement.

'It is an old suit of Dr Simpson's,' Raven replied, thinking it might as well be rags.

'It is not a good fit,' Todd observed, redundantly. He paused, as though his previous thoughts had been shunted, but when he spoke again it was clear that they had not. 'A good fit is important, is it not? Standing in another man's clothes, one cannot help but feel an impostor. In this world, one ought to have a strong sense of what one is rightly cut out for, whether that be clothes, or . . .'

He allowed his words to trail off. If he was being invited to respond, Raven did not see any advantage in doing so. Nothing he said would alter the man's purpose here.

'I am aware you have taken an interest in my daughter. And that you have sought to conceal this from me, engaging in clandestine rendezvous.'

It was folly to deny it. The only dignity here was in honesty.

'I meant no disrespect to you, sir. Your daughter and I spoke when I visited your house some weeks back and found that we enjoyed a rapport.'

'Yes. I recall Eugenie being particularly indecorous on that occasion. Am I to deduce that you admire such a quality in a young woman, or that it was merely something you were prepared to overlook?'

'On that occasion, sir, you assured me her lack of decorum was aimed at you, not me. But either way, I prefer it to obsequiousness.'

Todd took a moment to consider this. He had, once again, that look of having found what he expected.

'I am hearing of your intention to set up your own practice.'

Raven was unsighted by this change of subject. Why was he waiting before bringing down the axe? Unless he considered his message sent.

'Indeed,' Raven replied, too unbalanced to offer anything more.

'Dr Simpson speaks highly of you. His association will be beneficial.'

'Most certainly. I could not ask for better.'

'As a physician-accoucheur, being a married man would be beneficial also, would it not?'

Raven felt a rushing in his ears, his mind racing to take in what he was hearing. Once again, it had not been a change of subject. He stared blankly, quite unable to respond, partly from fear that he might have misinterpreted.

Dr Todd looked at him with uncertainty for the first time.

'Are these your intentions by Eugenie, or have I drawn a false conclusion?'

Raven found his voice. 'These are my intentions. I was not expecting to find you receptive to them. I thought we were about to have a very different conversation.'

The first hint of a smile played upon Todd's lips.

'I would caution both of us that the question of whether Eugenie is receptive has yet to be broached,' he said.

'I would make no assumptions in that regard. But I am delighted that you should consider our match an appropriate one.'

Dr Todd wore an unexpectedly arch look.

'Do not thank me too soon, Dr Raven. As a father, Eugenie has often given me pause. I would be remiss if I did not disclose that she is not without . . . complications. But for that reason, I do believe you and she are a good fit. I therefore wish you well.'

Dr Todd ended their exchange with a curt nod and retreated in the direction he had arrived, leaving Raven to stand with his head spinning, wishing there was some independent witness to confirm what had just transpired. The vertiginous feeling was not entirely rooted in incredulity. All at once he was confronted with a possibility that had hitherto been abstract.

As he steadied himself, Sarah came to mind unbidden. For the first time he felt an unexpected sense of disloyalty in his pursuit of Eugenie. He realised that this was also the moment to ask himself whether he was truly reconciled to letting her go.

And then finally he saw Eugenie emerge from a doorway at the rear of the house, and all doubts dispersed. He saw within his grasp a future that he and Sarah could not share. It was a future he hoped Eugenie might be satisfied with, but one he knew Sarah would not.

He hastened towards her, but she remained where she was. As he drew closer, he saw that she was beckoning him to follow her inside.

She led him down a wood-panelled corridor and beneath the vaulted gallery of the entrance hall. Raven sensed movement above and glanced up. He saw Mansfield, the provost, ducking out of sight as though concerned at being seen. Perhaps he was not the only one sneaking inside for a secret assignation.

Eugenie pushed open a door and led Raven into a grand drawing room hung on three sides with paintings, many of them portraits: Sir Ainsley's relatives and forebears.

'What kept you?' she asked.

He was about to answer when he was distracted by a section of the wall unexpectedly swinging out and revealing itself to be a concealed door. A housemaid, dressed in a black uniform and cap, stepped through. Upon seeing the pair of them, she immediately vanished back the way she had come. Eugenie had her back to the door, and the maid was gone before she could even turn around.

Raven noticed the maid had bowed her head and shielded her eyes with her hand as soon as she noticed guests, as though the mere sight of them would dazzle her. He knew it was for fear it would be regarded as insolent to meet their gaze. This was the practice in some households, where servants were even required to turn their backs when members of the household passed them on the stairs. Raven had only caught a glimpse of the maid, but she seemed familiar. He assumed he had seen her out on the lawn, and yet he felt that he recalled her from somewhere else. Perhaps she had previously worked at another house he had visited, on duty with the professor.

'Where did she appear from?' Raven asked.

Eugenie laughed in a way that was uncharacteristically girlish. For a moment he was able to picture her here as a child, playing with Amelia.

'There are servants' passages so that the staff may come and go unseen. Let me show you.'

Eugenie pressed the panel in a practised way and it unlatched, gently swinging out from the wall. She proceeded into a narrow passage and glanced back with a conspiratorially inviting look. He realised they had never been alone together unseen.

Raven stepped inside and glanced back and forth. He saw light spilling in further along, only for it to be shut off as the housemaid exited and closed another door behind her. The only light now was from the drawing room, barely enough for them to see each other.

Raven felt close to Eugenie in a way he had not experienced on any of their walks together. He would have attributed this to the conversation he had just had with her father, but that could only account for his own feelings, and he got the sense that Eugenie felt it too. Neither of them had spoken since they stepped into the passage, yet something profound and complex was being communicated between them, something older than language.

He leaned closer and found her already turning her face upwards to his. They met in a kiss that began delicately, then quickly became something deeper, mutually urgent as they pressed their bodies close.

Raven broke away, mindful that if he did not, things might go very far, very fast.

'I have longed to do that since the moment I caught sight of you in the crowd tonight,' Eugenie said. 'I had not expected to see you here.'

'Your delight was not tempered by the sight of this old suit?'

'I will not lie, it is not flattering. But that is not chief among my reasons for wishing to see you out of it.' As she said this, she placed her fingers between the fastenings of his shirt, touching the skin of his chest beneath. 'I thought we would never get the chance to be alone,' she continued. 'I am sure my father has been watching you all evening. I fear he suspects.'

'He does not merely suspect,' Raven told her. 'He knows. He accosted me not five minutes ago. He told me he was aware I had taken an interest in his daughter.'

Eugenie gasped. 'We are discovered! And yet you defy him.'

She sounded both worried and pleased. And though she did not say so, Raven inferred that she was prepared to defy her father too. He smiled, recalling Dr Todd's words. *She is not without complications.*

'I have no need to defy him.'

'What do you mean?'

'He did not seek me out to warn me off.'

There was absolute silence in the dim passage. Raven could not even hear Eugenie breathing, realised that she was holding her breath.

'I had not hoped or planned to do this so soon, but . . .'

He did not get to make his proposal. She was already kissing him again. He took that as a yes.

TEN

Rotterdam, two days earlier

re you going to eat that?'

Robert's enquiry interrupted Sarah's contemplation of the rain battering against the windows of the inn.

'I don't think so,' she admitted, pushing her plate towards him. 'You can have it if you like.'

Robert speared the sausage with his fork and began chopping it up and shovelling it into his mouth.

Sarah was happy to abandon her meal. The odd-looking sausages that had been served to her revealed themselves upon closer inspection to contain intestines rather than meat. It brought to mind the tripe her grandmother would boil in milk, claiming it had healing properties for something or other. She could no longer remember what boiled sheep's stomach was supposed to cure. What did linger, what she could recall without effort, was the appalling smell of the stuff as it cooked. In truth she had been disinclined to eat much since leaving Grafenberg. What she found there had suppressed more than her appetite.

The thought of her grandmother induced a deep sadness, as it always did. She had been the village howdie – healer and wise woman – and Sarah missed her. She was loved and respected, providing care and compassion in addition to herbal remedies. Perhaps Sarah was wrong to aspire to more than that. What was good enough for her grandmother was surely good enough for her too.

She felt foolish. She had pursued Elizabeth Blackwell seeking vindication for her ambitions, a route map to a summit drawn by someone who had already made the climb. Instead she had found the foothills littered with corpses, her ambitions revealed as naive and deluded.

What did that leave her with? What was she supposed to do now? She wished to return to Edinburgh but was no longer sure she wanted what awaited her there. Should she just accept the role she had been assigned, the role that she had fallen into? She had done it thus far because she told herself it was the beginning of something else. Now that she knew otherwise, could she be happy spending her days as a doctor's assistant when she had envisioned so much more for herself?

'Back to Auld Reekie tomorrow,' Robert said, wiping his mouth on an already heavily stained napkin.

'How I yearn for my own bed,' Mina said in a plaintive tone.

'Anyone would think we have been setting up camp in the wilderness, Mina, rather than staying in the best hotels the Continent has to offer.'

'As you well know, Robert, one of the joys of travelling is the renewed appreciation it engenders for hearth and home.'

Sarah traced the route of a raindrop on the window with her finger, leaving a long trail in the condensation on the glass.

Auld Reekie.

Edinburgh.

Queen Street.

Home.

For the first time Sarah was no longer sure she could call it that.

ELEVEN

here is an unfamiliar air about you,' said Henry. 'Something strange and disturbing.'

They were hurrying across the North Bridge on their way to the police office, where the police surgeon was to carry out his post-mortem examination of the baby found in Leith.

'Strange and disturbing? What are you talking about?' Raven asked. 'There is nothing wrong with me. I am perfectly content.'

'Precisely,' Henry replied. 'What has become of my glowering and combustible companion? Who is this doppelganger that has taken his place?'

'Perhaps he has gone to Selkirk to await you,' Raven said.

He knew that Henry was considering quitting the city and taking up a post as a medical practitioner in the Borders, believing that the pace of life there might suit him. Raven had been vocally sceptical about this, arguing that Henry could do more good staying where he was. This had been neither selfless nor objective advice. Henry was a close and valued friend, Raven's better angel who had helped him suppress what Henry called his 'perverse appetite for mayhem'.

'You won't let this go, will you?' Henry replied. 'Or rather, perhaps you will not let me go. Are you so afraid of the mischief you might become embroiled in without me being here to hold you back?'

'You don't have to worry yourself on my account. I now have a strong incentive to rein in the less reputable aspects of my character.'

Henry's eyes widened. 'Is that so? A strong incentive, you say.' He rubbed his chin in mock contemplation. 'Could this perchance have anything to do with a woman?'

Raven grabbed his friend's arm. 'I can assure you that this is quite serious. We have reached an understanding.'

Henry stared at him for a moment, taking in what had just been said. A grin spread across his face.

'Congratulations. An announcement may be a bit premature though.'

'Premature? How so?'

'Well, she's still in mourning, is she not?'

It took Raven a moment to realise his friend's mistake.

'It's not Sarah.'

Henry stopped in his tracks.

'Oh, I'm sorry. I just assumed . . .'

'Sarah and I are friends. No more than that.'

Henry looked at him for a little longer than was strictly comfortable, then resumed walking.

'Well, who is this secret woman that I know nothing about?'

'I have been discreet because I feared her father would not approve. Happily, I have been proven wrong on that front.'

'Then who is this father, whose good judgment I must now question, and who cares so little for the welfare of his daughter?'

Raven looked about, as though afraid of being overheard. He did not want to risk breaking whatever spell had facilitated all of this, and yet he felt he had to tell someone.

'Dr Cameron Todd.'

'You are to marry Eugenie? Well done.'

Henry looked both surprised and impressed, though Raven was wary that he appeared to know of her. What had brought her name to his attention? Dr Todd's words about Eugenie being complicated were suddenly preying on his mind, fuelled by the instinctive unease that if Dr Todd was happy to let his daughter marry Raven, then there must be something wrong with her.

'I suspect my association with Dr Simpson will not have harmed my standing,' he offered, both by way of explanation to Henry and reassurance to himself.

'Do not underestimate yourself, Raven. Joking aside, Cameron Todd would not marry off his only daughter merely for the sake of a profitable alliance. He was always known to be vigilantly protective of her well-being. In fact, it was my understanding that he sent her overseas for her health, at some expense.'

'She was sickly?' Raven asked. He could not think of anything about Eugenie that gave the impression of enfeeblement. Robust and combative were the adjectives that most readily leapt to mind.

'I don't know what the supposed ailment was, though some suggested Dr Todd was merely keeping his daughter away from a number of eager suitors. It seems he was reluctant to part with her. Evidently both have recovered from their afflictions. There will be much interest in this news.'

Raven felt a pang of concern, still anxious about protecting that spell.

'Henry, you must keep this to yourself for now. There has been no formal announcement. I have not yet told Dr Simpson.'

'So no to a proclamation in the *Scotsman*, then. Or the *Courant*.'

'Definitely not the *Courant*,' Raven said as they turned onto the High Street. 'I was recently introduced to the editor – and its proprietor.'

Henry gaped. 'You were at Sir Ainsley Douglas's grand soirée? You truly are moving up in the world.'

'Merely travelling on Dr Simpson's coat-tails.'

'A pleasant evening?'

'I spent much of my time terrified of saying the wrong thing to the wrong person. Oh, and I was briefly reacquainted with Gideon.'

'I trust he had lost none of his charm,' Henry mused.

'He is entirely unchanged.'

'I often wondered what became of him after he abandoned his studies.'

'I didn't realise he had,' Raven admitted, having assumed Gideon was already in practice somewhere. He recalled what he had witnessed at the stables. 'I believe his father fancies him for the Navy.'

'I hope it's a better fit than medicine. Hard to imagine that there was ever anyone less suitable for a career in the healing arts. He regarded suffering humanity as a lesser species.'

The police office came into view and they quickened their pace to get out of the rain.

The door squeaked on its hinges as they entered. There was a familiar smell about the place: sweat and damp wood. It made Raven uneasy, recalling the last time he was in here. At least McLevy was not to be seen.

Henry nodded to the sergeant on the desk and led Raven through to the back of the building, down a bleak, unadorned corridor.

'Thank you for clearing this with Struthers,' Raven said.

'Don't mention it. Though it would have been easier with his predecessor, who would probably have been too drunk to notice you were there.'

'So, what is Struthers like?'

'Seems to know his stuff,' was Henry's frugal reply.

They entered the cramped room which had been assigned for post-mortem examinations. Struthers was standing behind a table, his jacket off and his sleeves rolled up. Unlike the

Infirmary's mortuary with its tiled walls, multiple sinks and cabinets full of instruments, this room felt as though it had been cobbled together at the last minute with furniture scavenged from unsuitable sources. There were no marble-topped surfaces here, just a standard wooden table that would not have looked out of place in any dining room, apart from the knife marks that scarred its surface and the various stains that had seeped into the grain.

The smell hit them full in the face, but Henry had come prepared. He pulled a small bottle of Friar's Balsam from his pocket and liberally sprinkled some onto his handkerchief before allowing Raven to do the same. The pungent aroma of the tincture would not neutralise the smell completely – nothing could – but it would certainly make the proceedings more tolerable.

Struthers looked to be around forty, of slim build with a neat beard and white hair, his eyes blinking expectantly behind a pair of spectacles. His arms were braced on either side of a small bundle covered in white calico. It seemed incredible that such a small specimen could be responsible for such a stench. Had something even worse preceded this? Some maggoty, partially decomposed body perhaps? Raven sniffed again at his infused handkerchief. A strong stomach and a poor sense of smell were certainly prerequisites for a career in pathology.

Henry made the introductions, and Struthers stepped around the table to greet him. He had an awkward gait and steadied himself with one hand while extending the other for Raven to shake. The reason became quickly apparent. His right leg had been amputated below the knee; the shortfall made up by an elaborate wooden prosthesis.

How typical of Henry not to have warned him.

Struthers noticed where Raven's eye had been drawn.

'You like it?'

'I have never seen anything quite like it,' Raven answered.

It was a quite remarkable piece of work. The polished wood had been intricately carved to delineate the muscles of the calf.

'Tibialis anterior, peroneus, gastrocnemius, soleus,' Struthers said. 'Useful for reminding medical students of their anatomy. I am fortunate to know a skilful artisan who supplied me with this, shaping it to my precise specifications. The only problem is that I am hostage to the weather, as it expands and contracts in response to temperature and humidity. There are times in the winter when I can walk for an hour and find I have merely gone in a circle. On the other hand, on such days I am very nimble around a hillside.'

Raven smiled but silently cursed Henry. He should have warned him that the man was somewhat unto himself.

Struthers hobbled back round the table and whipped the sheet from the little body lying in the middle of it. Its chest and belly had already been opened, its tiny ribcage spread apart.

'Gentlemen, I'm afraid you are a little late. As you can see, I have already completed my examination.'

'That's my fault,' Raven volunteered. 'My duties at Queen Street delayed me. My apologies.'

'Not at all,' Struthers replied. 'I will summarise what I have ascertained so far. As you can see, we have a male infant. Size suggests the child was several months old when death occurred, so it's not a stillborn babe we're dealing with here.'

'I suppose it could have been abandoned while still alive,' Henry mused. 'Left in the hope that someone would find it.'

Raven wondered why Henry had made such a suggestion. He thought it indicated wishful thinking rather than sound reasoning but then remembered that Henry had not been party to the details surrounding the discovery.

'There are two problems with that hypothesis,' Dr Struthers said, peering over the top of his spectacles at Henry. 'The first is that the body was found wrapped in parcel paper – presumably as a means of concealing it. Unless the original plan was to post it somewhere.'

Struthers took a moment to laugh at his own joke. Nobody else did, though this did nothing to dampen his mirth. He really was a strange character and Raven thought it a blessing that he had pursued a career in pathology. He was perhaps best suited to dealing with the dead.

Henry reddened with embarrassment at his error, but he had not known about the paper. Raven had not told him.

'The second,' Struthers continued, evidently enjoying himself, 'is that the child was almost certainly dead before it entered the water.' He looked at them expectantly.

'Not drowned then?' Raven asked.

'No.'

Raven wondered how he could be so sure.

'Was there no water in the lungs?'

Struthers sighed. 'Just because a body is found in or close to water does not necessarily mean death by drowning. Drowning as a cause of death is a diagnosis based upon the exclusion of other potential causes.'

Raven knew then that Struthers had found something to explain the death, but he was not going to tell them just yet. This was a performance, a demonstration of his skills of obser-vation and deduction. He had an audience and he was going to make the most of it.

'There were no marks of external violence upon the body. The lungs were collapsed, no froth in the trachea. A small amount of farinaceous food in the stomach, partially digested. Vessels of the brain mildly congested.'

Struthers paused for a moment. Raven wondered if he was inviting suggestions as to the diagnosis. He looked to Henry, who merely shrugged his shoulders. They both stared at the dissected chest, as though doing so would offer up answers.

'Do you see it?' Struthers asked.

Raven shook his head but then noticed that Henry was smiling.

'This child died of asphyxia,' he said with certainty. 'May I?' He pointed at a pair of fine-toothed forceps lying on the table beside the body.

Struthers nodded, now looking distinctly less pleased with himself.

'This baby', Henry said, 'has been strangled.' He pulled a length of white tape from the folds of mottled flesh around the child's neck.

'Murder then,' said Raven.

'Indeed,' Dr Struthers confirmed, pushing his spectacles further up his nose. Raven felt sorry for him. Henry should have let him make the grand revelation himself. Probably be the most fun that he had had in a while. But Henry had the bit between his teeth now, keen to make up for his earlier mistake.

'Where is the paper that the child was wrapped in?'

Dr Struthers pointed to a small desk in the corner.

Henry marched over, picked it up and took it to the window. Raven followed, intrigued. It was heavily stained, a rusty discolouration blooming over large parts of it.

'Looking for a return address?' Struthers asked. 'You won't find much. It has been thoroughly examined already.'

Henry turned the sheet over delicately in his hands. It was stiff in parts, where the salt water had dried out. The paper had been written on in several places, but the ink was now so faded as to be indecipherable. The only visible inscription was two letters: M and O.

'Part of a name, perhaps?' Henry suggested.

'McLevy already has his men out scouring the city for any woman bearing those initials,' Struthers said. 'Or their inverse.'

'Bit of a long shot,' Raven said.

'Oh, you know McLevy. Always gets his man. Or woman in this case. Some wretch by the name of Mary O'Reilly or Olive

Watson will have her appointment with the rope. Appropriate I suppose, given the method by which her son was dispatched.'

Struthers covered the body and began tidying his instruments away, his good humour finally extinguished as the grim reality of the situation bore down upon them all.

TWELVE

aven cursed the rain as he made his way along the High Street, the downpour having failed to abate while he was inside the police office. It had come on so rapidly that it had quickly filled the gutters, flooding the cobbles with a ghastly slick of diluted muck. Henry would have had something to say about it, had he not remained behind with Struthers. He was grimly fascinated by the inadequacy of the city's drainage.

Raven shoved the newspaper he had just bought beneath his jacket to prevent it getting any wetter. It had been a foolish purchase under the circumstances, but he preferred to arrive bearing gifts of some description. And if its intended recipient was feeling morose in his infirmity, then at least Raven would have something to read.

He cut along an alleyway at the side of the Ship Tavern, through an open door and up to the first floor. He knocked briefly, calling out to identify himself as he did so. He was expected, but the man he was visiting was not an individual it was wise to startle.

There was a rumbling grunt of acknowledgement from within and Raven entered. He sat himself down in his usual seat, an upholstered chair that had seen better days, presumably sometime in the last century. Stuffing was escaping from various holes in the fabric, a material so worn it was impossible to tell what its original colour had been. It matched the rest of the furniture in the room, equally shabby, much like the householder himself, who was seated opposite in an oversized chair.

'What have you brought?' his host asked. The man's name was Gregor, but Raven could only ever think of him as Gargantua – a term of endearment now, though it had not always been. He was a giant of a man, grossly oversized and strangely proportioned, as though certain parts of him kept growing when others had naturally stopped.

Raven pulled his copy of the *Scotsman* from inside his jacket, earning him a scowl. Then from his pocket he produced a bottle of whisky, which was greeted more favourably.

'That's more like it.'

Gregor grabbed the bottle and pulled the cork out with his ramshackle and widely spaced teeth, more robust than their appearance would suggest. He declined to pour but drank straight from the bottle, neglecting to offer Raven any.

Raven had not come expecting hospitality. He watched as the man glugged down a good portion of the bottle's contents without pausing for breath. He was drinking too much, more than was good for him, but Raven was there as a companion, not as a doctor. Even if his medical advice had been sought there was nothing that Raven would have been able to suggest. Temperance was unlikely to add much to his limited span. 'Won't live any longer, it'll just feel that way,' was how Gregor had put it himself.

Gregor was aware that his great size and strength came at a terrible price. He had an understandable interest in the life of Charles Byrne, a fellow similarly afflicted who had been known as the Irish Giant. Raven had seen a sketch of him on his visit to Edinburgh: it depicted the man lighting his pipe from a street lamp on the North Bridge. Byrne had lived a mere twenty-two years.

'Right,' said Raven, opening the damp newspaper and scanning the pages for something informative, entertaining or preferably both. Gregor could read well enough, but his eyesight was failing, and he was troubled by the small print, especially indoors. In addition, Raven suspected that he enjoyed being read to. Raven didn't grudge it. He knew the kind of stories to look out for.

'Sheriff Court, Thursday last,' Raven said.

'Magistrate?'

'Boyle.'

Gargantua snorted, evidently familiar with the man. 'Go on.'

'William McInnes. Found guilty of assaulting a woman near the Grassmarket. Six months' imprisonment.'

Gargantua nodded.

'Peter Cannon. Convicted of stealing two top-coats from a house in Comely Green Crescent. Six months' imprisonment.'

'Harsh,' Gargantua stated authoritatively. 'Must have had previous convictions. Will have been in front of Boyle before.'

There was a wistful, faraway look in his bloodshot eyes. He looked so much older than he was. And it was not merely his appearance, but also his manner. Gregor had the weariness of a man who had already experienced more life than he cared to.

Raven decided to change tack, scanning the pages for something less perplexing.

'"Leopard Chloroformed at London Zoo",' he announced, confident that this would be appealing to his listener. '"This magnificent beast, a gift from the Pasha of Egypt, sustained a serious injury to one of its limbs following an accident in its cage. Professor Simmonds of the Royal Veterinary College considered amputation necessary to save the animal's life. The animal survived the surgery and seems set to make a full recovery."'

'Don't fancy that job much. Wrestling with a wild animal.'

Raven did not think the animal in question would stand much of a chance against Gregor.

'"Chloroform was administered using a sponge on the end of a long stick,"' Raven read.

'A very long stick, I should think,' Gregor mused, taking another long swig from the bottle.

Raven turned the page, wondering if there would be anything of interest in the intimations, always Mina's favourite section. He tried to imagine her reaction to the news that he was to marry Eugenie.

As he scanned the page, a name caught his eye.

'What?' Gregor asked. 'They've treated a shark for toothache?'

'Sir Ainsley Douglas,' Raven said. 'I was at his house two nights ago.'

Raven stared at the page, remembering the man holding forth to the gathered crowd; causing his son to cower before him in the stables. Strong, clamorous, formidable.

'Rubbing shoulders with the quality now, are you?' Gregor said. 'Sir Ainsley Douglas, no less. There's a man who doesn't have to worry where his next bottle of whisky is coming from.'

'You have that much right,' Raven replied, pointing to the newspaper. 'He's dead.'

THIRTEEN

aven was taking off his sopping coat in the hall when he was intercepted by Mrs Lyndsay carrying a pile of plates towards the dining room.

'You'd best come through. Dr Simpson says we have a special guest for dinner.'

He quickly ran up to his room to change into a dry shirt, fastening the buttons as he descended the stairs. He was propelled both by a desire not to keep everyone waiting and by curiosity as to who would be joining them. The professor was wont to invite upon a whim any remarkable individual who happened to be visiting the city, often giving little or no notice to the cook.

Raven entered the dining room to find the professor and Mrs Simpson already seated at the table, together with Dr Simpson's brother, Sandy.

'Ah, Dr Raven. Are you to join us? Excellent,' Sandy said.

He looked like an older version of his brother: a little more rotund with substantially more grey hair on his head and in his whiskers. He had the same open face, ready to laugh at the slightest encouragement. Sandy was welcome company but his presence here would not be regarded as remarkable by anyone, least of all Mrs Lyndsay. Raven remained intrigued.

Raven sat down and realised how hungry he was. He had

missed lunch entirely, a recurrent hazard in his chosen line of work. A meaty aroma was emanating from the large tureen that Lizzie had deposited in the middle of the table, provoking a grumble from his empty stomach. He would have to be patient though, as the special guest had yet to arrive.

With this thought, Raven glanced around the table and noted that there were no spare place settings. At the same time, Sandy helped himself to a warm bread roll and slathered it with butter. He seemed to notice Raven's surprise.

'Something amiss?' Sandy inquired.

'Mrs Lyndsay said we were expecting a special guest.'

'Am I not special enough?' Sandy asked, laughing.

'All I said to Mrs Lyndsay,' Dr Simpson explained, 'was that we would be joined by a young man who has news to announce.'

Mrs Simpson reached across the table and clasped Raven's hand.

'Warmest congratulations, Will. We are all delighted to hear it.'

'Cameron Todd has a very lucrative practice, has he not?' asked Sandy. 'That is bound to be a profitable association.'

Clearly a formal announcement was unnecessary. It was not news to anyone present.

'How did you find out?' Raven asked the professor.

'How could I not? It is the talk of the town.'

Raven stiffened, then realised Simpson was relishing his discomfort.

'Don't torment him, James,' his wife chided.

'Of course, there is no such gossip. I happened to encounter Dr Todd outside Duncan and Flockhart's and he told me. He seemed quite delighted, had the air of a man unburdened. It's no secret that he has long worried over whether a suitable match would ever be found.'

'Nobody ever good enough until you came along, eh?' suggested Sandy, smiling at Raven. 'That's a fine endorsement.'

'Undoubtedly,' agreed the professor. 'Will here is quite the catch by anyone's standards. But I believe Dr Todd's concerns were on the basis that Eugenie might be the one considered unsuitable.'

'Really? Why would that be?' Sandy asked.

Raven hoped that he already knew the answer to this, though he was beginning to wonder about the contradictory perspectives he had heard regarding Dr Todd's concerns: overprotective and thus reluctant to let his daughter go, and yet concerned that a suitable spouse would not be found to take her off his hands.

'I think that the problem has been a perceived lack of meekness and deference in Eugenie, attributes that many a gentleman would prefer to find in his wife,' Raven said. 'These, however, are the very qualities that drew me to her.'

'Ah, meekness and deference. The cornerstones of our relationship, Jessie,' said the professor, sending an adoring glance towards his wife.

Mrs Simpson snorted. She rose from her seat and lifted the lid from the tureen. 'Mina will be disappointed to have missed this,' she said. 'She was convinced that she would be the conduit through which you would meet your match.'

Raven smiled, thinking of all the wholly unsuitable women to whom Mina had engineered introductions.

'When does she return?' he asked.

'She sent word from Rotterdam that she wanted to go back to London again before returning home.'

It was easier to ask about Mina than what he really wished to know, which was when Sarah would return. He missed her, and yet felt a vague discomfort at the prospect of having to face her. Normally she was the first person he wanted to share news with, but this felt like something he would have to admit to rather than happily announce. Why did he fear that she would be hurt by it?

'You're bound for London yourself, James, are you not?' Sandy asked. Turning to Raven he added, 'Did you know he is to take tea with Prince Albert?'

'I did not,' Raven said, taking a bread roll himself while waiting for whatever was in the tureen to be ladled out.

'Well, I'm to meet the man,' Simpson said. 'No one has said anything about tea.'

'Does he want to talk to you about chloroform?' Raven asked. He wondered if the Queen was pregnant again and considering its use in labour. Wouldn't that be something! The London medical establishment had been demonising its use in natural labour and would be appalled, which in turn would delight Simpson.

'The Prince Consort is planning a great exhibition of industrial technology and design,' Dr Simpson explained. 'He wants to discuss scientific exhibits and presumably chloroform will fit in there somewhere.'

'I should think so,' Sandy interjected. 'It is the most significant discovery of our generation. Do you know, Dr Raven, whenever clients at the bank find out that I am related to the professor here, I become fairly elevated in their esteem. Such is his reputation. Greatness by association and all that.'

'And how about yourself, Sandy. What news from the world of banking?' Simpson asked, deftly changing the subject to deflect attention from himself. Raven noticed that though the professor was proud of his achievements, he was reluctant to revel in them. He did not seek, nor did he seem to enjoy, unfettered adulation.

Sandy took a mouthful of wine and swallowed.

'To be plain, we're all still reeling from the news about Ainsley Douglas,' he said.

'Yes,' said Raven. 'I read about it in today's newspaper. Found dead in his bed the morning after we visited.'

'Shocking, out of nowhere,' said Sandy.

'What was the cause of death?' Simpson enquired. 'Do you know?'

'I have no idea. I didn't think to ask.'

'For it to be so sudden and without any preceding illness, I assume it must have been his heart,' Simpson suggested. 'Which is remarkable in itself for being proof that he had one.'

'James,' Mrs Simpson admonished. 'He was a generous donor to the hospitals of this city.'

'Indeed, indeed. A philanthropist and a man of piety. He will have gone to heaven, no doubt, though I don't believe he'll like God much, and I can't imagine he will approve of Jesus either. Talk of redemption and forgiveness for sinners never sat well with Ainsley.'

'This will mean a great deal of upheaval for his family,' Mrs Simpson suggested, trying to reassert some decorum.

'The consequences will be considerable,' replied Sandy. 'Almost all will be inherited by Ainsley's son, Gideon. It is not anticipated that he will be a steady hand on the tiller.'

'And Sir Ainsley was due to be married,' said Mrs Simpson. 'How unfortunate for Mrs Chalmers, widowed once already.'

'I feel for her in particular,' Sandy said. 'Had they married, she would be entitled to something, the widow's part of his moveable property. But that will now be divided between Gideon and his sister, while Gideon gets the heritable property outright.'

Raven did not understand the details of this but grasped the gist. Gideon was now an extremely wealthy man. All of this reinforced Raven's professed agnosticism. He was prepared to accept the possibility that there was a God, but nobody could make the case that He was a just one. Gideon was a thoroughly callous, arrogant and selfish individual, and now, finally faced with the potentially chastising fate of life at sea, he had instead been granted unfettered access to his father's fortune.

The thought had Raven reaching for more wine when the sound of the doorbell reverberated around the walls. Everyone at the table fell silent, waiting for Jarvis to arrive with the inevitable emergency summons to some distant location. Raven fervently hoped that whatever it was would not entail a return trip to the Old Town.

Jarvis duly appeared a few moments later, an oddly amused expression on his face. His look was directed at Raven, making him immediately wary.

'Dr Raven, there is a young woman to see you.'

As he spoke, Raven heard a commotion from the hall, a cacophony of excited voices. His heart leapt as he thought he recognised one of them as Sarah's.

He hurried to the door to confront the stramash on the other side of it. The first thing he saw was a trunk, Christina and a coachman carrying it between them and placing it down awkwardly. Guiding their efforts while trying not to get in their way was indeed Sarah, evidently having parted ways with Mina.

Raven had always wondered whether Jarvis knew there had been something between them, and took his words and amused expression as confirmation. That was until he stepped fully into the hall and saw that Sarah was not the only arrival. Standing against the wall in an attempt to remain clear of the clutter, hands clasped and an anxious expression upon her face, was Eugenie.

FOURTEEN

efore Raven could decide which one to address first, let alone summon the words to do so, the professor bowled into the hall, Mrs Simpson at his back.

'Sarah, what a surprise! You are returned.'

'I was impatient to get home.'

Then Simpson noticed Eugenie.

'And Miss Todd. We were just talking about you, my dear. Your father told me the good news. Jessie, this is Dr Raven's wife-to-be, Eugenie.'

At these words, Raven's eyes went to Sarah, who was staring back in astonished confusion. He had thought about how he might break the news to her but had not yet settled on any particular strategy. This scenario was likely to have been close to the bottom of the list.

'Will, I must speak to you urgently, and in private,' Eugenie said quietly.

'Come away through,' he urged, guiding her past Simpson, who was embracing Sarah in one of his bear-like hugs.

He led Eugenie into his consulting room where they might have some privacy, but closing the door did not erase the scene he had just left. His head was awhirl, the look on Sarah's face etched on his mind, transforming from confused to accusatory in his imagination. That uncomfortable feeling of disloyalty had returned tenfold.

'It's about Sir Ainsley,' Eugenie said.

Her eyes were beginning to fill, which took him by surprise. Raven could not imagine she and Sir Ainsley had been close, but then he remembered that Eugenie had been a regular visitor to his house since childhood. He cautioned himself that it was not always accurate to judge someone's character solely on their public face, though what he had glimpsed of Sir Ainsley's private face had done little to elevate the man in Raven's esteem.

'Yes, I heard. Such a terrible shock.'

Eugenie was shaking her head. 'You don't understand. Because his death was sudden, my father insisted a post-mortem be carried out. The pathologist has discovered arsenic in his stomach. They are saying he was murdered!'

'Murdered?'

She swallowed. 'They have accused my dear friend, who I have known for most of my life and who could not possibly have done this. It cannot be so. I know that Sir Ainsley was not always easy to love, but murder?'

Raven's mind was running to catch up.

'They have arrested Amelia?' he asked, further confused. He recalled that she had been among the first to leave the party, when her father was still very much alive.

'No,' Eugenie corrected, 'Gideon. A policeman by the name of McLevy has taken him to Calton Jail. Because he stands to inherit, it is assumed that he must have poisoned his father.'

Raven had to admit that on this occasion McLevy probably had a case. He thought it wise to keep this to himself, however. He was still processing the fact that Eugenie regarded Gideon as a 'dear friend'. He should have made the link, he realised. She had been close to Amelia growing up, why not her brother too?

'Gideon swears he had nothing to do with it. He is distraught.'

A tear rolled down her cheek and she wiped it away with a gloved hand. 'The tragedy of it is that Gideon only ever wanted to please his father.'

Raven moved towards her, his arms outstretched, thinking to comfort her. She put a hand up, holding him back while she looked for something in the small bag she was carrying. She produced a crumpled envelope and thrust it at him.

'I have received a letter from him. He asks for your help.'

'*My* help?'

'Yes. He wants you to go and see him. As soon as you possibly can.'

'So, he remembers me after all,' Raven said, the words issuing before he could stop himself.

'What do you mean?'

Raven realised that Eugenie had known Gideon a lot longer than she had known him, and that in her eyes such petty enmity would not reflect well on either of them. In the current circumstances he had the more to lose by bearing a grudge.

'Gideon and I have not always been on the best of terms,' he explained.

'You would refuse him?' she asked, incredulity and disappointment mingling in her voice.

Raven considered his options. Was he mistaken about Gideon Douglas or was he indeed the kind of man Raven believed him to be? It struck him that if he still wanted to marry Eugenie, he had no choice but to find out.

FIFTEEN

ell, isn't this lovely news.'

Sarah put her hand out, pressing it against the nearest wall to steady herself. She found that she could not speak, did not trust herself with a polite response to Mrs Simpson's assessment of the situation. She had been unsure about her future, what might await her on her return to Queen Street, even whether she still belonged, but she had not expected this.

She looked at the consulting room door, closed now, Raven and his intended in conference behind it. She felt tears form and blinked rapidly, trying to hold them back.

'Is everything all right, dear? You've become very pale.'

Mrs Simpson approached, taking Sarah's free hand and rubbing it vigorously between her own warm palms. Somehow her kindness, her concern so earnestly expressed, just made everything worse.

'I think I'm merely a little overcome. To be back home and amongst you all again.' She tried to smile in defiance of her true feelings. Which were what? Shock. Surprise. Confusion. Disappointment.

'You must join us for dinner,' Dr Simpson said. 'We could ask Eugenie to join us too. Give us all an opportunity to get to know her.'

The thought of facing everyone was overwhelming. Sarah knew that she could not tolerate making conversation with the woman Raven was now betrothed to. It was not something that she could possibly endure. Not now. Not yet.

'You are both so kind, but I am tired from my journey,' she said. 'What poor company I would be in my current state.' She forced a laugh. It sounded hollow and false to her own ears and she wondered if her true sentiments were obvious. 'Perhaps something could be brought to my room,' she added as she made her way towards the stairs.

'Of course, of course,' Mrs Simpson said. 'I will send Lizzie up with a tray.'

Sarah closed her bedroom door and leant against it for a moment. She tried to slow her breathing. Tried to calm herself. Tried to work out what she was feeling. Horrible, mainly. She was finding it difficult to be more specific than that.

She took off her hat and sat down heavily on the bed. She had only been away for a month or so. How could he have formed an attachment so quickly? The problem, she realised, was that their relationship seemed to be in a constant state of flux. She had once thought that she and Raven could have a future together, but he had made it clear that a suitable wife needed to improve his social standing rather than diminish it. His ambition had stood in the way of what she had imagined to be love. He had disappointed her, and she had married Archie, a marriage that had come with its own complications.

Why did it feel like such a blow to learn this news? He had made her no promises, had not expressed his feelings explicitly. And yet she knew that he still cared for her and she knew that she still cared for him too, and not merely because he had saved her life. She thought that her being a widow, still in first mourning, would have granted them some time to come to terms with what they felt for each other, allowing whatever it was that existed between them to blossom into something solid and secure. She had thought that he would wait for her.

She had been greatly mistaken.

Were the feelings that she harboured for him deeper than she imagined them to be? She was aware that having something snatched from you could make you want it all the more, so perhaps she was simply falling prey to that. Did she really want to be married to Raven? She had not thought that she did. Just as he had done, she had decided to put her own ambitions ahead of matrimony. But that was before she went to Europe. Now, she wasn't sure *what* she wanted any more.

A knock at the door roused her from her introspection. She felt her heart flutter in her chest at the thought that it might be Raven on the other side, come to explain himself. Why he had chosen another woman over her. Perhaps there had been a mistake, a misunderstanding. Her hope was short-lived.

'Get the door, will you Sarah? I've got my hands full here.'

It was unquestionably Lizzie.

Sarah sighed, got up off the bed and opened the door.

'You're really supposed to call me Miss Fisher now, Lizzie.'

'Right,' Lizzie replied, swooping past her with a heavily laden tray, her tone giving the distinct impression that Sarah would be waiting a long time to hear herself addressed as such. She put the tray down with a scowl. 'Mrs Lyndsay's sent up enough to feed three people. Nearly wrenched my arms out of their sockets carrying it up here.'

Sarah smiled despite herself. It was at least some comfort to know that certain things had not changed. Lizzie was as unpolished and irascible as when she left. As Lizzie began pouring tea Sarah realised that there was someone else standing on the threshold. Lizzie noticed her looking.

'Christina,' Lizzie explained. 'You remember her, aye? She started here just before you left.'

Sarah looked again at the girl hovering in the doorway. Quiet, unsure of herself, in stark contrast to Lizzie's brashness. She looked as though she or her forebears hailed from warmer climes: olive tones in her unblemished skin, dark hair and eyes.

She stepped tentatively into the room. 'I've to help with the unpacking,' she said.

'Well, get on with it,' Lizzie said. 'I need to go down and help with the dinner. There's more of them than usual tonight.'

She clattered the teapot back down onto the tray and took her leave, all jutting elbows and indignation, in high dudgeon at the prospect of having extra guests to serve. This caused Sarah to smile again. The thought of Lizzie brandishing a ladleful of stew at Raven's intended . . .

Sarah took a sip of tea, the warm fluid easing the tightness in her chest. She examined the food piled up on the tray, a selection of Mrs Lyndsay's finest cooking that would tempt the most reluctant of appetites. A large slice of game pie with pickle. Bread thickly sliced. A wedge of cheese. A fruit scone with raspberry jam. She tore off a small piece of bread and put it in her mouth. She chewed slowly, tasting nothing.

She became aware that Christina remained rooted to the spot just inside the doorway. Sarah pointed to the trunk sitting at the end of the bed.

'You can start with that if you like.'

The girl still did not move. Then, without warning, she started to weep. Silent tears spilled down her cheeks. Sarah put her cup down.

'Whatever is the matter?'

'I don't know what to do,' Christina said. She looked so miserable, Sarah's own feelings writ large on her young face. Sarah felt compelled to stand and hug her, to comfort her as she would a child. As she held her, the girl began to cry in earnest and Sarah wondered what on earth Lizzie had said or done to provoke this degree of upset. Unpacking a trunk was hardly a demanding task.

She fished about in her pocket for a handkerchief and pressed it into the girl's hands, giving her a moment to compose herself. Sarah poured some more tea and offered her the cup.

'Why don't you take a seat and tell me all about it.'

The girl cradled the cup in her hands, looking a little unsure. She took a sip of the tea, then drained it. She sat down on the bed beside Sarah with a shuddering sigh.

'Is it Lizzie?' Sarah asked. 'Or Mrs Lyndsay?' The cook was volubly intolerant of shirkers.

'What? No.' Christina shook her head vigorously. 'Everyone has been kind to me here.'

'Then why the tears?'

She looked at her hands. 'I can't find my baby,' she said, her voice a whisper. Sarah thought that she had misheard.

'Your baby?'

Christina nodded, sniffed, wiped her nose with the handkerchief.

Sarah tried to recall what she knew about this girl, a former resident of the Lock Hospital as Lizzie had been. Dr Simpson had for a number of years been in conflict with the management there. Too much religious instruction and not enough medical care, prayer being of limited use in the treatment of venereal disease. The hospital rescued these girls from a life of vice and then he rescued them from the hospital. Or so he liked to say.

'I had a baby,' Christina continued. 'That is why I had to leave my previous employer.'

'And the father?' Sarah asked.

Christina shook her head, beginning to tear up again. 'I cannot tell you.'

Sarah put her arm around the girl, squeezing her shoulder. She knew that there was probably no point in pressing her for this information. She had perhaps been taken advantage of, seduced and abandoned. Or forced: a common enough occurrence in certain households. To some, domestic staff were disposable, easily replaced. But then again there were many ways in which a man could so disappoint a woman that she would not wish to be reminded of him.

'You were dismissed when your employer found out?'

'I tried to hide it for as long as I could. As soon as it was discovered that I was with child, that was it. I was told to leave.'

'Who was your employer?'

Christina shook her head again.

It hardly mattered. There was nothing that could be done about it now.

'What did you do then?'

'I was taken in by someone. A respectable woman by the name of Mrs King. My employer paid for her to look after me until the baby was born. Or that's what I was told.'

'But the terms changed,' Sarah suggested.

Christina nodded. 'By the time he was born I had run up a debt. Mrs King told me I had to find the money or my baby would be given away. She said she wasn't looking after him for free, and she knew of many couples who were desperate for a healthy child, especially a boy. She often found good homes for unwanted babies, she said. But he *was* wanted.'

'What happened?'

'I earned the money the only way I could. Ended up in . . . a house of . . .'

She could not finish, but nor did she need to.

Sarah was neither shocked nor surprised by the revelation. Dismissed with no prospect of reputable employment, with debts to pay and a child to support. There were not many other options for a girl in such a position.

'I kept up the payments for a while,' Christina went on. 'But then I got sick and couldn't work any more.' She started to cry again. 'I told her to wait, that I would get the money. I went back with my first wages from here, but my baby was gone.'

'Gone?'

'Yes, gone. Mrs King wouldn't tell me where he is or what

has happened to him.' She sniffed and wiped her nose again. 'She said it's for the best. Maybe she's right. What kind of life could I give him anyway? When I was offered the job here, I began to think I might be able to redeem myself. Earn my right to be a mother to him. But even here, where I have a decent job among good people, it's not like I could have him with me. How could that possibly work? And now he's gone, likely given away and I didn't get the chance to say goodbye. I just want to know he is all right.'

'When did you last speak to this woman?'

'The last few times I went there, there was nobody at home. I'm worried now that she's gone too and that I'll never find out what happened to my wee boy.'

'What did you call him? Your son?'

'Jamie.'

'And how old would he be now?'

'About six months.'

Still just a baby. How heartbreaking it must be for this poor girl, blamed and shamed. Dispossessed. Bearing the brunt of all this alone. Sarah clasped her hand.

'I wish there was something I could do to help.'

Christina looked at her beseechingly. 'Mrs Lyndsay says you're smart as a whip. Maybe you could find him for me?'

Coming from Mrs Lyndsay this was praise indeed, but Sarah doubted she was likely to have much success. If this woman had absconded, she would have made sure to cover her tracks. Finding her would be no mean feat, never mind uncovering what had happened to the child.

'Would you know him, Jamie, if you saw him again?'

The girl looked horrified. 'Of course I would.'

Sarah evidently did not look convinced.

'I would know him,' Christina insisted. 'He has a mark on his left arm.'

'A mark?'

'Birthmark.'

Sarah looked at her tear-streaked face. She squeezed the girl's hand.

'I'm not promising anything,' she said. 'But I'll see what I can do.'

Christina sniffed, smiled and hugged her.

Sarah realised that she had just agreed to a near-impossible task and briefly wondered why she had done so. Probably because she needed someone to have faith in her right now, even if it was this poor girl, because after Grafenberg she had lost all belief in herself.

SIXTEEN

aven stood outside Calton Jail, its silhouette picked out against the slowly setting sun. It was an occasional source of confusion to visitors from other parts who had a tendency to confuse it with Edinburgh Castle. With its gatehouse, battlements, towers and crenelations it looked more like a castle than the castle itself. Why such external embellishments had been deemed necessary when building a prison was anyone's guess. Within the mind of whoever had designed the thing there seemed to have been some doubt about its purpose, whether to keep prisoners in or invaders out. The pouring of boiling oil over the battlements was unlikely to be necessary anytime soon. It had been built to replace the Old Tolbooth jail, a medieval structure described by Lord Cockburn as 'an atrocious place, the very breath of which would fell any stranger who had the misfortune to cross its threshold'. Raven hoped that the air had improved since the jail's relocation.

He was grateful for the late light and clear skies. He could not have been prevailed upon to visit the place at this hour during any other time of the year, and even in daylight the sight of it tended to make him shudder when he thought how close he had come to ending up here only a few months back.

Having established his credentials at the gatehouse, Raven was escorted through a series of corridors and shown into a small room where Gideon lay sprawled on a bed, staring at the ceiling. Raven noted that he was the sole inmate. These were not the accommodations to which he was accustomed, but they afforded considerably more privacy and security than Raven had enjoyed in the Night Asylum for the Houseless when it was used as an overspill for the police's holding cells. Evidently when you were the son of Sir Ainsley Douglas you were entitled to better treatment, even when you stood accused of murdering him.

Gideon climbed languidly to his feet, almost as though Raven's visit was an inconvenience. Raven guessed it was for show. Gideon would not wish to admit even to himself that he was the supplicant in this scenario.

He had a bruise beneath his eye. Raven wondered if he had earned it at the hands of McLevy's men, or perhaps one of the guards here. Then he remembered seeing Ainsley strike him there and on the jaw – mere hours before Ainsley was supposedly poisoned.

'You don't seem surprised that I responded to your plea,' Raven said, choosing his words deliberately.

'I conveyed my summons through Eugenie for a reason,' Gideon replied. 'I knew you would be disinclined to assist me and would doubtless derive some satisfaction from seeing me hang. But I also knew that failing to help would jeopardise your good standing with your intended bride.'

'Summoned, was I? Perhaps I came merely to see you caged, knowing only one of us could walk out of here tonight.'

'Were that the case, you would at least have waited until you had an idle hour. You came running immediately, though you were probably at dinner. There is no shame in it. Doing something you find unpalatable merely to stay in your betrothed's good graces strikes me as perfect training for marriage.'

Though it was not what Gideon meant, Raven thought of his mother, walking on eggshells, always taking care not to do or say anything that might precipitate his father's rage. He thought of what he had seen in the stables and wondered whether Gideon had witnessed the same.

My mother's only weakness was her blindness to what you are, he had said. *But in time the scales fell, and that was why she . . .*

'Make yourself comfortable,' Gideon invited, gesturing towards a careworn chair that looked likely to collapse under his weight. Raven descended gingerly onto it while Gideon perched himself once more on the bed. He looked oddly childlike in his posture, arms wrapped around his knees. Raven suspected that he was afraid; worried but determined to hide it.

'How are the servants looking after you in your new home?' Raven asked. 'Do you think you'll remember *their* names?'

'Only if it turns out that I need something from them,' Gideon replied.

Raven could not decide whether this brazenness was actually a form of contrition. Or maybe his pride was all he had to cling to right now.

'Did one of them give you that?' Raven asked, pointing at his face, curious to hear how he would answer.

Gideon took a moment to grasp what he was referring to, his fingers briefly touching the bruise.

'No. This was . . . an accident. I have been treated well, other than the trifling matter of being wrongfully accused of poisoning my father.'

'The bump has certainly jogged your memory, given that you now recall my name and presumably that we knew each other as students. How has your medical career progressed, by the way? What field did you choose to specialise in?'

Having noted his previous evasion, Raven wondered what else Gideon might lie about if invited, and what truths he might inadvertently reveal.

'Cane-fields, mostly,' he replied. He fixed Raven with a stern eye, conveying his suspicion that his interrogator knew he did not complete his studies. 'My father sent me to the Indies to oversee his interests there.'

'You were forced to abandon your medical degree?'

'You could say I studied at my father's pleasure. When he needed my help, I had little choice but to oblige.'

'It is difficult to imagine a man such as your father needing help,' Raven suggested. *Still less him turning to you*, he left unsaid.

'He has . . .' Gideon paused for a moment before correcting himself. 'He *had* several business interests in the Indies, the largest of which is a plantation on the island of Tobago. It was being poorly managed locally and my father needed someone to go over there and sort things out. For such a man of parts, he always had trouble delegating. He could not be in two places at once, so the next best thing was to send his own blood.'

'Wasn't that a little beyond your area of expertise?'

'I had visited the plantation before. Amelia and I went there with our father after our mother died. But yes, it was not a task I was particularly well-prepared for. I think it was a test.'

'Did you pass?'

Gideon appeared to think about this but did not answer. Or at least, did not answer directly.

'The estate had sustained considerable damage during a hurricane a couple of years ago and was slow in recovering the losses accrued, mainly because the rum-soaked overseer was by that point failing to do much of anything. Merely by remaining sober during daylight hours I represented a considerable improvement.'

'A test with a low bar, then.'

Gideon gave him an odd look, not so much irritated by the comment as by how little Raven understood.

'Within six months I had arrested the decline. I diversified, planting cacao as well as cane. The sugar business is not what it once was.'

'Something to do with emancipation, I imagine,' Raven suggested. He knew that the Douglas family's fortune had been built upon the backs of slaves and felt a desire to point this out.

Gideon ignored the jibe. 'It was not the life I had imagined for myself, but I found the climate suited me. I would have stayed on, but my father relieved me of my duties and summoned me home. I failed the test, you see.'

'I thought you said you had arrested the decline.'

Gideon gave him that look again. 'When it comes to my father, there is no such thing as good enough. He tells me that I will fail, and he is continually proved right because it is always in his gift to define what constitutes success. Thus he is permanently disappointed in me, in an unending cycle of self-fulfilling prophecy.'

Leaving aside Gideon's use of the present tense, his words were doing little to support his claim of innocence.

'You are making a strong case for the prosecution here in the event that they do not already consider you to have motive enough,' Raven observed. 'What is it that you think I can do for you?'

Gideon shifted uncomfortably on his bed, sitting up straighter and unclasping his arms. It was as close as Raven was likely to get to a gesture of openness.

'I feigned not knowing you when last we met. An evening dedicated to my father's self-aggrandisement did not make me well-disposed. But I did remember you. I had heard stories, in fact. Your investigations exonerated your employer a few months ago.'

'You spoke to Eugenie.'

Raven hated the thought of her having been in conversation with Gideon unbeknown to him, and no doubt without the need for secrecy.

'She talked of little else but you,' Gideon said, then gave him a crooked smile. 'But I also heard rumours about you from altogether less respectable sources. Whispers in taverns. I was given the impression that you are a man who could search this city's underbelly should he need to.'

'And why might I need to? What would I be looking for?'

'You met my father two nights ago. You must have got a measure of him and the spheres in which he moved. Powerful men accumulate powerful enemies. Do you really believe I could be chief among them? The most ruthless?'

'Greater enmity borne towards your father by others is immaterial. Arsenic has been found in his stomach. You stood to gain the most from his demise and were the one best placed to carry out the deed.'

At these words, Gideon had a look of satisfaction about him, as though Raven had finally stumbled upon what he wished him to.

'And that is precisely what proves my innocence,' he said. 'I was conveniently placed to take the blame, but whoever actually did this has failed to take into account that I studied medicine.'

'Or perhaps they simply knew of your examination results.'

Gideon glared. He had no more patience for sparring.

'Even I attended enough classes to know that arsenic is a metallic poison. It is easily detectable in the body and can be found in the tissues long after death has occurred. If I were going to poison my father, arsenic is the last thing I would use.'

Raven had to concede that he had a point. Gideon had always struck him as vain, callous and dissolute, but he was not stupid.

'Who else stood to gain from your father's death?' he asked.

'I do not know, and nor am I in any position to find out. That's what I need you for.'

SEVENTEEN

aven was crossing the courtyard, eager to put the environs of the jail behind him, when his path was blocked by none other than James McLevy. One of his officers was pulling up the rear, his hand gripping the arm of a young woman clearly in their custody.

They all stopped at a signal from the detective, dashing Raven's hopes of passing unrecognised, or at least ignored.

'Dr Raven, what about ye?'

McLevy always seemed shorter in the flesh than he loomed in Raven's memory. His intimidating presence did not derive from physical stature, nor entirely from his office. There was an unshakeable confidence and certainty about the man, a sense as he stood before you that no matter how hard you might push him, he would not, could not be moved. Raven had once heard him say that 'a bold front is the best baton'.

'This is one for you,' the Ulsterman added, indicating their prisoner.

Raven did not follow.

'The dead baby you found down in Leith,' he explained.

'I didn't actually find it, I merely—'

'Struthers said you attended the post-mortem. You'll have seen the initials on the parcel paper the corpse was wrapped in.

This one's name is Mary Olsen, a prostitute. According to my man Wilkie here, she was an unwed mother: except that one day she had a little baby and then all of a sudden she didn't.'

'It's not true!' the young woman screamed at McLevy. 'How many times do I need to say it before you'll listen. I'm no whore, and my wee boy died of fever. He's buried in Hope Park kirkyard. This bastard Wilkie is having his revenge because I refused him.'

'We'll find out the truth of it when we dig up that grave then, won't we,' McLevy told her.

The woman broke down at this announcement, doubled over as Wilkie dragged her away with rough hands.

McLevy's knowing expression indicated that he believed her crushed by the inevitability of her lies being exposed. Raven suspected she was more likely disconsolate at the prospect of her lost child's remains being disturbed. She had been arrested on the basis of two initials on a piece of paper – letters which could as easily be OW – and the word of a man who might very well be holding a grudge.

McLevy remained in the courtyard, the black shadow of the building stretching ever longer about both their feet. There was still light yet, but not for much longer.

'What brings you here of an evening?' McLevy asked.

'Gideon Douglas,' Raven stated.

McLevy's eyes widened in surprise and amusement. 'What have you to do with him?'

'More than I would wish. We knew each other as medical students. He has appealed to me to find out who poisoned his father.'

McLevy let out a rumbling chuckle. 'Aye, I suppose when you're rich enough, you don't merely plead your own innocence. You can pay someone else to create a bit of theatre: make it look like you sincerely believe it and there's a secret to be found. You're a fool if you make yourself his puppet.'

'He isn't paying me anything.'

'Then you're even more of a fool. You're doing this because you believe him?'

'I don't have sufficient information to make a judgment either way.'

'I do. Enough to see him swing.'

'You had me all but hanged for Archie Banks,' Raven reminded him. 'Until you were shown that things are not always as simple as they appear.'

McLevy liked to boast that he always got his man, but it was more accurate to say he always got *a* man. Though his testimony and evidence invariably proved compelling to judges and juries, those who looked more carefully spotted that there were often steps missing in his logic. Raven was still chilled in the night by thoughts of how close he had come to the gibbet mere months ago, when McLevy fixed his sights upon him as a murderer. It had taken the professor's intervention to demonstrate that the death concerned had not been by his hand, and indeed had not even been murder.

McLevy had been content to defer to a man of Simpson's standing, aware that the professor was a useful ally. Raven enjoyed no such status, however, and had the strong impression that his exoneration was a mark in McLevy's debit column: one that could only be redeemed when he nabbed him for something else.

'The case against Gideon Douglas is entirely as simple as it appears. He's a layabout who stands to gain untold riches from his father's death.'

'He maintains his father had enemies who were more powerful and more ruthless.'

'I don't doubt it, but did he have enemies who were more foolish or more desperate? He acted in anger and haste. According to Admiral Whitelaw, he was about to be shipped out at his father's request and against Gideon's wishes. The physical evidence shows that he poisoned his father's supper with arsenic.'

'Gideon studied medicine and knows that arsenic is easily detectable. He might have acted in haste, but he is not an idiot.'

McLevy gave that rumbling laugh again. 'The jails are full of men who thought they were too clever to make a mistake. I would caution you not to waste your time.' McLevy gripped Raven's arm and leaned in close. 'And I would doubly caution you not to waste mine either, Dr Raven. One of the wealthiest men in the country has just been murdered. People are expecting justice, and that is what Gideon will get, on the gallows.'

As Raven endured the fury of McLevy's gaze, he asked himself why he would invite the ire of a man he so feared by advocating for one he despised. But it was also in those eyes that he saw the answer, and it was nothing to do with pleasing Eugenie. It was the man's immoveable certainty that troubled him.

It was entirely possible McLevy was right. Raven knew better than anyone what a rash individual might do when he was consumed by rage. But if there was more to this, he could be sure McLevy would make no effort to find it. Gideon's arrogance stemmed from never having faced the consequences of his failings, but if he was innocent he did not deserve to die.

EIGHTEEN

he next morning, Sarah entered the dining room to find Raven already sitting at the table scribbling in his notebook. She had not seen him since her retreat to her room last night. She had skipped breakfast so as not to have to face him in front of everyone else, but she knew she could not put it off for ever.

He did not look up, either because he had not heard her come in or because he was ignoring her.

Part of her wanted to leave him undisturbed, to just stand quietly and watch him. Part of her wanted to throw the ledger she was carrying at his head. She noticed that his hair was longer than it had been before she left, curling a little around his ears. His jacket seemed a little too tight, the material strained across his broad back. There were a few stray threads hanging from the shoulder seams. He needed someone to take care of him. She had thought for a time that role might fall to her. But she had been usurped.

She sighed, approaching the table and throwing the ledger down with a little more force than she intended. It shook the inkpot and the glass of water by Raven's right hand. He finally looked up at her, a little warily.

'Is there much today?' he asked, referring to the mail that

they were about to sift through. During the summer months, when there were no lectures to be given at the university, they had fallen into the habit of discussing medical correspondence before lunch. It had been Sarah's idea, an attempt to impose order onto chaos and ensure that nothing was missed. This was particularly important given Dr Simpson's imminent departure to London. No patient should be kept waiting, she had said, alluding to the professor's tendency to make appointments and then fail to keep them.

'The usual.' A terse reply. She was finding it difficult to keep a certain tetchiness from her voice.

Raven put his pen down. 'How was your trip? You haven't told me much about it.'

'Opportunities for conversation have been limited,' she said. The formality of this response sounded wrong to her own ears. Raven gave her a quizzical look.

'Are you angry with me, Sarah?'

'Angry? Why would I be angry?'

'I realise that you have returned from Europe to find circumstances somewhat changed.'

'I assume by circumstances you mean your sudden engagement. You didn't need to wait for me to leave to start courting.'

Raven cleared his throat. 'It started before you left.'

'Why didn't you tell me?'

'In the earliest stages I wasn't sure there was anything to tell, but in truth—'

'Of course. It was private. Why *would* you tell me?'

'Why should it bother you that I did not?'

'It bothers me that I had barely stepped over the threshold on my return from Europe when I found out that you were engaged.'

'I had barely stepped over the same threshold upon my return from Europe when I found you were *wed*.'

Sarah had no reply to this.

'Who is she, this Eugenie?' she asked, her tone a little milder.
'The daughter of Dr Cameron Todd.'

'I have heard of him. Physician with a large practice. Good
for you. She will require minimal training. Probably already well-
versed in the duties expected of her as a doctor's wife.'

'You make that sound like a condemnation,' Raven said. 'Was
that not what you once wished for yourself, when you married
Archie?'

His comment felt pointed, intended to injure. But perhaps it
was merely her own sensitivity at work. She reminded herself
that she didn't know what she wanted any more.

She was saved from further chastisement by the entrance of
the professor bearing his post clinic cup of tea, followed by
Jarvis carrying a silver platter piled high with letters and tele-
grams. Sarah opened the leather-bound ledger and dipped her
pen in the inkpot, ready to begin. Dr Simpson assumed his place
at the top of the table and took a sip of his tea. He looked at
them both, one and then the other, as though sensing something
was amiss. A frown creased his brow briefly then he nodded to
Raven, who took the first letter from the top of the pile.

'From the doctor treating Lady John Russell, requesting
advice regarding a female complaint,' Raven said.

Dr Simpson indicated that the letter should be passed over
so that he could read it himself. Raven and Sarah exchanged
a look. It said something about Dr Simpson's reputation that a
letter regarding the health of the prime minister's wife was
a routine matter. Sarah wrote the name in the book, a reminder
to ask later if an appointment should be scheduled. Perhaps
this would be one of the patients he saw when he went to
London.

Dr Simpson read the letter in silence then folded it up and
put it in his pocket. Sarah frowned at the sight. The doctor's
pockets were a realm far beyond her control, a repository for all
manner of things put there on a whim and frequently forgotten.

She would have to hope that the status of the patient ensured that the letter would be retrieved at some juncture and then suitably acted upon.

Raven picked up another letter from the pile. He scanned it quickly then snorted. 'This one comes with a request,' he said. 'This patient would like you to send some more of the white powder you gave him last time. It was in a big, wide-mouthed bottle and you emptied it out onto a sheet of paper.'

'Any other clues?' Dr Simpson asked. 'Nature of the complaint being treated perhaps?'

Raven shook his head. 'I'll write back with a request for more details.'

Several more letters were dealt with in quick succession and appointments made, one for a Lady Furness who would be at the Caledonian Hotel just before Dr Simpson left for London. Sarah noted the dates down in her ledger.

Raven reached for another. The quality of the paper suggested an aristocratic source. Sarah recognised the handwriting.

'It's from Lady Mackenzie,' she said as Raven opened it.

Dr Simpson and Raven groaned in unison. Lady Mackenzie was a frequent correspondent, writing at regular intervals to complain about Simpson's reluctance to visit her.

'What does she say?' Dr Simpson asked.

'She starts by stating that she is still awaiting a reply to a letter sent two and a half months ago. Your response to a previous query as to whether she should use mustard baths or leeches to relieve back pain was somewhat cryptic. "Three baths, three leeches" was all that it suggested and was furthermore sent to the wrong address. She states that she has continued to take mustard baths three times per week and wonders if she should persist. In addition, her son Harry has begun complaining of queer sensations and you are requested to attend. She has moved him south to the milder air of Bridge of Allan and can see no geographical impediment to your coming.'

Sarah sat with her pen poised, waiting for Simpson's response. He considered for a moment.

'Dr Raven and I will head up there at the end of the week.' He held up a hand to stem Sarah's protestations. 'I can fit it in before London. A visit will be just the thing to appease her and we'll see if we can't cure poor Henry of his queer sensations at the same time.'

Raven looked like he was about to protest too but any argument against such a journey was forestalled by a knock at the door. Jarvis entered, carrying a small wooden crate.

'This has just been delivered,' he said. He placed the box on the table beside Sarah and left the room.

Sarah took a look at it. 'It's from Dundee.'

Simpson glanced up from the letter he was reading, having helped himself from the pile.

'Oh, I know what this will be.' He got up from his chair, leaned over to grab the box and then recoiled, shaking his hand.

'What happened?' Raven asked, concerned.

'Just a splinter. A skelf.' He showed them his hand and laughed. 'I think I'll live.'

'Shall I open it?' Sarah asked.

'Please do.'

She prised the lid off with a letter opener and looked inside.

'It's a pelvis,' she said. 'Someone has sent you a pelvis. Through the post.'

'It will be from Dr Nimmo,' Dr Simpson stated, completely unperturbed. 'An obstetric case he presented at the Medico-Chirurgical Society not so long ago.'

Raven lifted it out of the box and placed it on the table.

'Mollities ossium. Adult rickets.'

'Surely the dining room table is no place for such a thing,' Sarah suggested, a little alarmed at the sight of it. Raven seemed surprised at her vehemence. She wondered about it herself. She was certainly no stranger to anatomical specimens.

Raven began to explain the interesting features it displayed, as though trying to justify its presence on the table.

'This is an extreme example of the condition and will be useful for teaching. See how contracted the pelvic aperture is?'

'How on earth did they deliver a baby through there?' Sarah asked.

'They didn't,' Dr Simpson said. 'If I recall the details correctly, the patient was a forty-three-year-old woman in her fourth pregnancy. Visibly deformed. "Decrepit" was the word Dr Nimmo used.'

Sarah stared at the specimen, finding it difficult to equate the jumble of bones in front of her as belonging to a living, breathing person, decrepit or not.

'On examination, the sacrum and the rami of the pubis were so approximated that a finger could scarcely be introduced between them. There was no possibility of delivery by that route.'

'They delivered by Caesarean section?' Sarah suggested.

'That is correct.' Dr Simpson looked at her and smiled.

This would normally have pleased her – getting something right, demonstrating her knowledge and understanding – but today she felt nothing. Grafenberg had left her hollow.

'It didn't work, did it?' she stated, indicating the bones sitting in front of her.

'The child lives,' Dr Simpson said gently. 'That is something. And it was the only chance for her too. Unfortunately, the initial incision cut through part of the placenta. There was considerable haemorrhage.'

They all stared in silence at the bony remains of the person they were discussing.

'She was given chloroform. That, at least, would have eliminated any suffering at the end.'

Sarah realised that she had placed her hands over her abdomen, where her own, well-healed scar was a constant reminder of how close to death she had come herself. She felt suddenly hot, perspiration beading along her hairline.

'Excuse me,' she said and left the room without further explanation.

She stood in the hallway, breathing in the slightly cooler air. 'Sarah?'

Raven was standing beside her.

'I'm alright,' she said. 'Or I will be.'

She moved away from him and sat down on the stairs.

'It just felt wrong to be staring at those bones while hearing about the woman they belonged to. How do you manage to remain so detached?'

She realised that her tone sounded harsh, accusatory.

'You learn to be,' Raven answered softly. For some reason this annoyed her. As though he felt he had to coddle her in some way.

'Can anyone learn to be so? Could I? Although I suppose the real question is, do I want that for myself? Do I want to become hardened to the distress of others?'

Raven looked a little injured. 'I do not consider that I am impervious to the suffering of others. Although I would argue that a certain detachment is necessary. You have to learn to suppress your own emotions in order to do what must be done in a crisis. But that does not mean that there is no room for feeling.'

He moved towards her, but she did not want him to comfort or console her.

'I need some air,' she said, brushing past him.

She was out of the door and a good way along Queen Street before she realised that she was without coat or hat. She continued anyway. What did she care what anyone thought of her now?

Not so long ago she had been so sure of herself. She had a plan, a sense of direction. But perhaps her desire to be a doctor had been misplaced from the beginning. She did not want to change who she fundamentally was, to become someone else. She did not wish to suppress her feelings or moderate her compassion. She thought again of Elizabeth Blackwell, the sacrifices she had made in order to fit into a world controlled by men.

She did not need to be like Raven.

Sarah stopped walking for a moment as something else occurred to her.

She did not need Raven.

She let this last thought seep in. It was true though, wasn't it?

She was a woman of independent means, free to live her life as she chose. She did not need him. She did not need anyone.

NINETEEN

aven was aware that his footfalls were heavier than normal as he strode east along Queen Street. It was an excess of energy born of frustration, the stamp in his gait a substitute for screaming as a means of venting his pent-up emotions.

They said absence made the heart grow fonder, but perhaps absence also made you forget someone's less endearing qualities: in Sarah's case, how high-minded and self-righteous she could be. She had an unfailing talent for putting him on the back foot: morally, intellectually and sometimes both.

As he looked back over their history of disagreements, he recalled a litany of apologies from him to her. He did not recall her ever apologising to him. Sarah was never in the wrong, at least in Sarah's mind.

She had met and married Archie while he was abroad. After Archie died, she had expressed her desire to travel and educate herself, and despite Raven's own desires, he had chosen not to stand in her way. But now that *he* had found someone else, someone he might be happy with, she was acting like he had been selfish and deceitful.

He had always harboured strong feelings for Sarah, and had believed them reciprocated, but he was starting to wonder whether those feelings were not quite what he had imagined. Had she instead drawn him into constantly seeking her approval, and mistaking that for true affection?

Eugenie did not belittle him. She did not constantly give him the sense that he had let her down and had making up to do. Quite simply, she did not make him work so hard to feel that he was good enough. She did not make him strive so hard for her approval.

He did not need Sarah's approval, he counselled himself. He did not need Sarah.

Eugenie looked up from the table as Raven was shown into the drawing room. Her expression of intense concentration was replaced by a look of pleasure as she saw who her visitor was. She strode across the room and took both his hands. He wanted to kiss her, but privacy was precarious in this place.

'Did you see Gideon?' she asked.

'I went straight there last night.'

'How is he?'

Raven took a moment to consider his response. He decided that the phrase 'Still an arse' would not serve him well, for all its veritas.

'Defiant. There may indeed be more to this than meets the eye.'

And it may be *entirely as simple as it appears*, as McLevy put it. In truth the only real question over Gideon's guilt was the imprudence of the use of arsenic, but Raven preferred to keep it vague for now. Despite his earlier musings, he had to admit that he did crave Eugenie's approval. He wanted to please her.

Eugenie was not easily fooled, however. She was worryingly adept at reading what he left unsaid.

'After we last spoke, I realised that your impression of Gideon must be very different to mine,' she told him. 'I know what he can be like. Selfish and conceited. Callous too, though I think he uses it as a shield. There is a side of him you've never seen. He can be considerate. Tender.

'When he was younger, he used to escape to the summerhouse by the river at Crossford, and I sometimes went to talk to him there, in his own private world. He was a different person in that place, away from his father. He said he wished that could be his life.'

Eugenie looked away, suddenly wary, as though concerned her remarks may have been unguarded.

Raven was instinctively prompted to wonder whether there had ever been something between them. It certainly did not sit well with him that she had a lingering affection for this person, and just as troubling was what it suggested about her judgment. But perhaps Gideon had always been on his best behaviour around Eugenie, presenting a different face to that seen by others. Raven, after all, had never shown her any glimpse of his own dark side.

He supposed Eugenie's impression stemmed from having first got to know Gideon when they were both children, meaning that beneath everything else, she still saw the child he once was. Perhaps Raven needed to see the child in Gideon: the scared and fragile boy who was cowering before his cruel father. Raven had once been that child too. The problem was that this only made it seem more plausible that the cowering child had finally fought back: in anger and haste, as McLevy had said.

'What were you poring over when I came in?' Raven asked, eager to change the subject.

Eugenie led him to the table, upon which was laid a large sheet of paper bearing a detailed monochrome image. Some kind of heraldic carving. A knight's helmet, a crown, a hunting dog, with a Latin inscription beneath.

'It's a brass rubbing. I made it at St Giles' Cathedral.'

'The detail is remarkable. How is it done?'

'Affix some paper to the brass and rub with shoemaker's wax. It's amazing how much detail emerges.'

Raven looked closer. 'Unexpected detail. "A pound of carrots, a shank of mutton",' he read.

Eugenie examined the paper. 'I'm not convinced that was part of the original coat of arms. The cook must have been leaning on this when she wrote her shopping list, and left an impression.'

'As do you,' Raven replied.

He was about to lean closer when he heard footsteps from the hall, and a moment later Dr Todd opened the door. He greeted Raven with a warm smile.

'I trust all is well at Queen Street.'

'For now. Though we are bracing ourselves for Dr Simpson's imminent departure. He's off to London to meet Prince Albert.'

As soon as these words were out, Raven felt a little embarrassed by both his eagerness to impress Dr Todd and his resort to greatness by association.

'What a privilege. For the prince,' Todd added, smiling.

'The professor told me you had already informed him of our happy news,' Raven said.

'Take it as a compliment that I could not hold my tongue. I appreciate no announcement has yet been made, but as Dr Simpson is to be family, as it were, I took the liberty. In fact, with regard to that, we ought to discuss certain formalities. Eugenie, would you excuse us?'

'At once, Father,' Eugenie replied.

She carefully rolled up the brass rubbing and left the room.

Dr Todd gave him an amused look. Raven suspected he was recalling that first encounter, when Eugenie had made an altogether less gracious exit.

'You have bewitched and enchanted her. I sometimes wonder of late whether she is the same young woman. I have seldom seen her so carefree.'

'Though she did seem rather upset by recent events,' Raven observed, feeling it would be indecorous not to acknowledge it.

'Of course,' Todd agreed, thin-lipped. 'A terrible business.'

'You and Eugenie were close to the Douglas family, I gather.'

Todd looked slightly uncomfortable. 'Well, I was Sir Ainsley's physician. I would not presume to describe myself more than that.'

'I merely mean that you must have known him a long time. Eugenie said she visited the house as a child.'

Todd nodded rapidly, sincere but keen not to dwell. 'Sir Ainsley was my patient for many, many years.'

'Were you the one called, when . . .?'

'Indeed. I was roused from my bed as soon as he was discovered. I went there without delay. He had clearly been dead since some time in the night. I insisted he be taken to Struthers at once to perform a post-mortem, though Sir Ainsley's butler tried to object. He maintained his master had often expressed revulsion at the notion of his remains being "butchered", as he put it, but I brooked no such nonsense. Struthers carried out his examination and I escorted the stomach contents to Christison myself.'

There was no greater authority on poisons than Robert Christison.

'So you immediately suspected murder?'

'You saw him yourself. He was a quite indomitable specimen, in perfect health, and making plans for his wedding.'

'No physical concerns at all?'

'He suffered a touch of dyspepsia, for which he was taking bismuth, but nothing beyond that, unless you count insomnia in a man who tended to view sleep as a waste of valuable time. For that I prescribed a glass of brandy last thing at night, which I confess I recommended less for any medicinal purposes than as an incentive to go to bed. It is true that most any man can be struck down without warning, but simple inspection indicated that he had suffered. My instinctive impression was that he had been poisoned.'

'Were there the remains of a meal to be investigated? Contents of a bedpan?'

'Those had all been cleared away by the time I got there, unfortunately. Though that in itself pricked my suspicion.'

'Was it you who first fixed upon Gideon as the culprit? I mean, was there any particular reason he should stand accused?'

'Only he and Mrs Chalmers were in the house overnight, besides the staff. And of the two, his future wife stood to lose all by Sir Ainsley's death, his son to gain by it.'

Todd eyed Raven with a growing wariness. 'What is your interest in this matter?'

'Eugenie has asked me to look into it. She cannot believe this of Gideon.'

Todd seemed exasperated, as though unsure where to look in an appeal for strength.

'After everything, she still . . .' He sighed.

'What?' Raven asked.

Todd paused, long enough for Raven to wonder if he intended to dismiss the subject. Eventually he spoke.

'Are you personally familiar with Gideon Douglas?'

'Our paths crossed as medical students.'

'What was your impression of him?'

'Nothing that I would wish quoted back to your daughter.'

'Delicately put. A troubled young man. He is . . .'

Todd let it trail, unable to find the words, or perhaps allow himself to speak them.

'His father's son?' Raven suggested.

Todd met him with a grave look. 'Aye,' he said, his voice low. 'And for that reason I would caution you, though it pain Eugenie, not to look too deeply into this. These are dark waters that you do not know how to navigate.'

Raven nodded his acknowledgement, but continued, 'I

would happily leave the matter to others but for one question: Gideon asked me why he would use arsenic when he knew it was so easily detectable.'

Todd issued a bitter, mirthless laugh. 'I can think of two reasons. The first is that he wanted his father to suffer. And the second is that Gideon did not think so far ahead because he has never learned to anticipate the consequences of his actions. There has always been someone to clear up his messes for him.'

'He suggested his father had greater enemies than he. Would you say that was true?'

'Indubitably. I am sure many a man wished him ill. But none stood to reap so much from his dying.'

TWENTY

arah looked again at the address Christina had written down for her: Dickson's Close, off the Cowgate. She was in the right place and yet something about it felt very wrong. Christina had spoken of a respectable woman, which had conjured up the image of a more salubrious residence. No woman of any means would choose to live here.

The Old Town had its share of desirable places to stay. It was built bridge upon bridge, layer upon layer. But the further you descended from its airy heights the worse it became: buildings more dilapidated, ancient constructions repeatedly subdivided and poorly maintained. Generations of the same families crowded into single rooms.

Sarah had walked past many dark alleyways on her way here, concerned about what or who might be lurking within. She had begun to question the wisdom of her venturing out alone long before she got this far. Walking unaccompanied through any part of the city was ill-advised if you were a woman. It was a fear she had long since learned to accommodate. Otherwise how would she ever get anything done? But the deeper, darker parts of the Old Town were another matter entirely.

She remembered attending a church service near here

with Raven once. She had to admit she felt safer in his company. Raven had a dangerous streak in him, but why should you need a dangerous man to protect you from the deeds of other dangerous men? Why was it that women were forced to alter their behaviour, when it was men whose conduct was at fault?

Sarah took in the folk passing on the street, working men and women with their carts and baskets. She drew reassurance from the thought that someone might come to her aid should she be accosted. But there was a difference between a busy street and its shadowed tributaries.

Dickson's Close was a narrow lane, the buildings four storeys high on either side. In the middle of the passage, an additional apartment had been added halfway up the wall, like a carbuncle held aloft by wooden beams. It looked as if a stiff breeze would bring the whole thing crashing down. She thought about Daniel in the lion's den and hoped that divine intervention would not be required.

The sun briefly broke through the clouds overhead, illuminating small sections of the passageway and making it seem momentarily less foreboding. Then it darkened again. Sarah could see a woman at a high window beating a piece of clothing against the wall beneath it, sending a shower of gravel down into the lane below. A woman with a child carried on her hip emerged from a doorway, walked a little further down the lane and then disappeared.

Sarah took a deep breath and proceeded into the close, looking for a name or number beside each dwelling. Thirty yards along she found the address Christina had specified, a peeling blue door up a short set of steps. There was a smell of food coming from somewhere. Not appetising. Like fish several days past its best.

She climbed the steps; found she was counting them for some reason. Five. Uneven. Well worn. A means of distracting herself from what she was really afraid of, which was what might lie beyond the door. She felt both disappointment and relief when her repeated knocking went unanswered.

The smell of cooked fish was stronger now. It seemed to be coming from a doorway further along the lane. Sarah decided to ask a few questions of whoever was home.

She stood for a moment on this second doorstep and paused before knocking. She should have asked Raven to come with her. It would have been the sensible thing to do. But that would have meant confiding in him, asking for his help, and she had already decided she was better off on her own. She would have to get used to it.

Sarah knocked the door hard, as though trying to convince herself that she was unafraid to do so.

She felt the tension ease from her shoulders when a woman answered, wiping her hands on her apron and not best pleased at being disturbed. She had a livid rash across the bridge of her nose. Sarah tried not to stare.

'I am looking for Mrs King. I was told that she lives here in Dickson's Close. Do you know her?'

The woman paused for a moment as though considering how to answer.

'Haven't seen her for a while. Not sure she even lives here any more. Not sure why she ever did to be honest. Always looked as though she had the money to live somewhere else.'

'What do you mean?'

'Good coat. Good shoes. Better than the rest of us can afford round here.'

'Do you know anything about her business? About her looking after . . . infants?' Sarah asked tentatively.

The woman looked wary. 'I don't know anything about that.'

'I was told that she takes in babies. Cares for them when their mothers are unable to.'

The woman's eyes went immediately to Sarah's midriff.

'It's not for me,' Sarah said. 'I'm looking for a friend.'

'Aye, that's what they all say,' the woman replied. Her eyes widened briefly as she realised that she had let slip more than she intended.

'So, you do know a bit about it then.'

The woman sighed. 'There's no end of rumours about what went on behind that door, but she didnae take well to questions. I asked her once, just in passing, about the crying I heard, and she put me against the wall: right there. Told me it was none of my business. If it so happens she's done a moonlight flit, then I'm glad she's gone.'

She closed the door.

Sarah turned and headed back to the entrance to the close just as a woman with a basket of washing was entering. She had a plaid shawl wrapped round her shoulders, the ends tucked into her waistband. The bright colours of the tartan caught Sarah's attention, standing out as they did against the drabness of the alleyway. The woman took no notice of Sarah, too intent on the task in hand, and Sarah had to manoeuvre around her. A little behind, previously hidden by the woman and her washing, came a well-dressed lady in a fitted green jacket with matching hat, voluminous red hair swept up beneath it.

Better than the rest could afford round here.

'Excuse me, are you Mrs King?' Sarah asked instinctively, without pausing to think.

The woman glanced up quickly, and upon seeing Sarah turned and fled, splashing her fine shoes through muddy puddles in her haste. Sarah gave chase but her quarry had a start and was quickly along the lane and out onto the street. Sarah emerged onto the Cowgate in time to see the woman climbing into a cab, and it was off down the road before she could get anywhere near it.

As Sarah stood at the mouth of the close, she was aware of the scent of perfume lingering in the air. It was cloying, so thick it caught in the throat. Sarah had never been much of an enthusiast for fine fragrance; the result of an over-developed sense of smell perhaps. She vastly preferred the clean smell of soap and water and found overpowering scents to be worse than the body odour they were frequently employed to smother. They often made her suspicious of what else the wearer might be trying to hide.

Good coat, good shoes.

She was reminded of something that her grandmother used to say: 'Fine clothing is an affectation and often conceals a great deal of dirt.'

TWENTY-ONE

he tangy, putrid stink of raw meat mixed with the metallic smell of blood assailed Raven's nose as he opened the door to the police surgeon's room. He found it hard to believe he was back here again so soon. He generally preferred to conduct meetings with Henry at a local hostelry, or if time was pressing, the Infirmary mortuary. Admittedly, the latter rarely smelled much better than this place, but at least there was less chance of encountering McLevy into the bargain.

Beyond the door the stench intensified. Henry was standing at the sink, washing his hands.

'Anything interesting today?' Raven enquired.

'Trauma to the head. Blood in the brain. Not difficult to assign a cause of death in this one.' Henry noticed the look on Raven's face. 'He was lying a while before he was found.'

'That would explain the smell.'

'Horrible way to die.'

'Is there a good way?'

'There are certainly better ways than being bludgeoned to death in an alleyway,' Henry said, drying his hands. 'I think I'd prefer to die at home in my own bed.'

Raven thought of Ainsley Douglas. Not all deaths at home were peaceful ones.

'Didn't make it to the Infirmary then?' Raven said of the corpse on the table.

'Probably for the best. Nothing that they could have done for him there and you know how much Syme hates to lose a patient. Uncontainable rage when they have the temerity to die on him.'

Henry scribbled something in a notebook then put his pen down.

'I presume this is not a social call. What can I do for you?'

'A couple of things. First, why are you always here helping Struthers? I would have thought that the Infirmary supplied enough work for a pathologist.'

'Assistant pathologist,' Henry corrected him. 'The work is interesting. I learn a lot from it. And if truth be told, I have one eye on Struthers' position here.'

'Police surgeon? Really?' Raven smiled at the implication that his friend might not be leaving Edinburgh after all.

'You said that there were a couple of things,' Henry reminded him.

'The Ainsley Douglas post-mortem. Do you know anything about it?'

Henry arched his brow. 'More than I would care to. Struthers has been talking of little else.'

'Even in death, the wealthy make a greater impression,' Raven suggested, making his way to the cabinet in the corner.

'Struthers says that he has been hounded by your Dr Todd throughout the whole examination, which he did not much appreciate.'

'And what of the findings?'

'Initially Struthers thought the diagnosis was dysentery, but Todd badgered him into sending off the stomach contents for analysis. Todd seemed to consider that this was a suspicious death from the outset, although he failed to enlighten Struthers as to why he thought this was the case. Not only did Todd insist on being present for the duration of the dissection, he then arranged transport of the stomach contents for analysis himself, conducting the jar of fluid in his own carriage. This enraged Struthers no end. Thought that his competence was being impugned.'

'And what was found?'

'There was a small amount of arsenic in the stomach contents, but none was found in any of the organs. Enough to satisfy McLevy, though what he doesn't have is proof of who administered it.'

'Why was Todd so certain from the outset? Any idea?'

Henry looked wryly amused. 'None, but you can be damn sure he was relieved. When your wealthiest and most famous patient drops dead in the night, you do not wish it to emerge that the cause was something you failed to diagnose or anticipate. That is why he was sticking to Struthers like a limpet. If he had missed something, he wanted to be the first to know. Incidentally, what on earth are you doing?'

Henry had belatedly noticed Raven's activity. He had retrieved a box from the cabinet and was fishing about inside. He extracted what he was looking for and began working at it with a piece of black shoemaker's wax which he had purchased on his way here for this very purpose.

'All will be revealed. Or nothing will. It is too early to say. You know it's Gideon who stands accused?' Raven added.

Henry was hovering, trying to see what Raven was up to.

'Yes. I have to confess I am surprised, given all I observed of him when we were students. I would not have thought him capable of carrying out such a deed.'

'How so?' Raven asked. Following his discussion with Eugenie, he was curious as to whether Henry also had a deeper impression of the man.

'Because he would have had to do something for himself. It would be far more Gideon's manner to pay a flunkey to take care of it for him, and I cannot imagine such services are so easily procured.'

'You'd be surprised,' Raven observed.

Henry examined his fingernails and frowned. 'Joking aside, though Gideon was spoiled and conceited, I never considered him capable of actual harm. Cruel of tongue certainly, but cruel of deed is something else. Though that is the advantage of poison: it allows one to fell a physically stronger foe. It does not require the same fortitude as stabbing or—' Henry jabbed a thumb towards the body on the table '—beating one's enemy to death. That is why it is the preferred method of murder by women of their husbands. Betrothed persons take note.'

Raven did not respond to his friend's jest, too intent on what he was doing and upon the repercussions of what Henry had said. Nothing in it augured well for Eugenie's hopes. Poison would be the perfect means by which Gideon might murder a more powerful man he could not face down.

Even the first part of his musings held no comfort, for Henry's impression of Gideon as physically harmless was based on limited information. In an alley outside a tavern not far from here, Raven had once glimpsed an aspect of Gideon that he kept hidden from the world, perhaps even from himself. Only one other person might testify to what Gideon was truly capable of, and he would likely remember little, between the drink, the damage and the darkness. It would be fair to say, however, that this individual was the very definition of an eyewitness.

Raven heard the creak and scrape of the room's heavy door. He had not recognised Struthers' inimitable gait, each footfall alternating with the sound of wood upon the boards. Instead it was McLevy who filled the frame.

'Dr Littlejohn, if you have a wee minute, I was—'

The detective took a moment to notice Raven. It did not appear to be a pleasant surprise.

'Dr Raven, I'm after telling you to stay out of my way, and yet here you are.'

Raven lifted his hands, ostensibly in a gesture of submission. His true motive would reveal itself as soon as the detective proved himself appropriately observant.

'Merely conversing with a friend,' he said.

'Oh, really? Conversing about Sir Ainsley Douglas, perchance?' He looked to Henry. 'Did your man here tell you his grand theory that Gideon must be innocent on the grounds that he was incapable of doing something that would get him caught? Because there's a wee problem with that logic.'

'I won't lie to you, Mr McLevy,' Raven said. 'I have made enquiries, but the harder I look, the clearer it appears you are right. Nothing I have discovered contradicts your conclusions.'

McLevy looked satisfied, if a little surprised.

'Aye, that's the way of it in detective work. Much the same as in medicine, I'd wager. As long as you follow where the evidence is pointing, you'll usually get to the truth.'

'And what of the evidence that was pointing to Mary Olsen? How will you feel if you find she was telling the truth, and you have dug up her dead child on little more than the say-so of a slighted man?'

The policeman did not react with his usual ebullience. The look on his face told Raven that this possibility had weighed on his mind.

'Following the evidence sometimes requires a distasteful course, though if it is the course that leads to the truth, we do not shrink from pursuing it. But we have more to go on than one man's say-so. Mary Olsen had a baby of approximately the right age, and her initials were written on the parcel.'

With these words McLevy became aware of two things: that Raven was holding that very sheet of parcel paper, and that the fingers of his right hand were stained black.

'What are you doing with that?'

'Most of the ink was washed away by contact with water, but the impressions of the pen nib remain. It says "D. McCabe, 49 Candlemaker Row".'

McLevy snatched it from his hand, looking at the lettering that had emerged as tiny grooves in the wax. He could see for himself that there had never been an 'MO', or even an 'OW'.

'We follow the evidence in medicine too. But I have learned the hard way to be doubly sure of what it's telling me before I proceed.'

There was a flash of warning in McLevy's eyes, but it was quickly replaced by something close to gratitude, and not merely for being given a valuable lead.

TWENTY-TWO

arah walked past the Assembly Rooms on George Street, avoiding the crowd milling around the coach-stand on the opposite side of the road. She stopped to read a poster advertising an evening of musical entertainment. The list of names meant nothing to her, but she thought perhaps that she should attend. So much of her time had been focused on serious pursuits – work and study – that it would no doubt do her some good. She would have to find someone to accompany her, however. There was a limit to what she could reasonably do alone.

She thought of Raven, but immediately dismissed that notion and was annoyed at how readily he still came to mind. Mina then, when she finally tired of travelling and returned home. Old maids together.

As she resumed walking she caught a whiff of scent on the breeze and realised that she was approaching Mina's favourite perfumier, a place they had visited often when she was still a housemaid. She took a moment to consider how much her life had changed since then. And how little. Her own aspirations had not come to much; while Mina, who desired the more traditional role of wife and mother, had also been disappointed. Sarah was unpleasantly reminded of a certain Dr Beattie, at one time Mina's intended, who had favoured a distinctive cologne. She hoped that he was still sufficiently far from civilisation to be deprived of it.

The smell grew stronger as she proceeded, reminding her of the residual scent in Dickson's Close. It had been such a strange, unique mix, unlike anything she had smelled before. It suddenly struck her that if she described it to the perfumier, he might be persuaded to tell her to whom he had sold such a scent. He always had a good memory for his customers' names.

Through the shop's front window, she caught sight of a lady with auburn hair standing behind the counter. Sarah was halted in her tracks. The green jacket was absent, but the woman was of similar height with that same, distinctive colour of hair.

Sarah cursed herself for not making the connection before. She could so easily have missed this had she taken a different route home. Working in a perfume shop would certainly explain why the woman in the green coat had left such a strong spoor of clashing scents behind her. An occupational hazard, or perhaps she willingly doused herself with the shop's merchandise.

Sarah entered the shop and made a show of perusing the elegant bottles on display, silently scoffing at the ludicrous prices attached to them. She was perfectly happy with her own rose soap and lavender water. She made them herself. These products seemed to be aimed at those with more money than sense.

She risked a surreptitious glance at the flame-haired woman, satisfying herself it was the same person she had pursued in the alley. Then she picked up the most expensive bottle to examine, a time-honoured manoeuvre guaranteed to summon the nearest assistant.

'Can I help you with something, madam?'

She was aware that she was being appraised. With a quick look the woman had scanned her head to foot, trying to ascertain her likely wealth from her apparel.

Sarah made her own assessment in return. Though she was

sure this was the woman she had seen, she was less convinced that she was the one who resided behind the blue door in Dickson's Close. Why would Mrs King be working in a perfumier's? Sarah needed to talk to her nonetheless. She decided a direct approach was probably the best.

'I was hoping that we might run into each other again,' she said.

Several emotions registered on the woman's face in quick succession. Confusion. Recognition. Concern. She tried to bluff her way out of it.

'I'm sorry but I don't believe we've met.'

'It is true we have not been introduced but we have seen each other before. At an address down in the Cowgate only yesterday.'

Concern quickly turned to alarm.

'I'm afraid that you are mistaken.'

'I can assure you I am not. I would like to talk to you about what you were doing there.'

The perfumier emerged from the back of the shop. He did not appear to recognise Sarah, though she must have been in here dozens of times. Maids were not to be noticed.

'Everything alright?'

The woman smiled. 'This lady is interested in a bottle of the Mille Fleurs,' she said, spritzing some into Sarah's face. Sarah suppressed a cough, worried that she might actually have to buy a bottle of the stuff in order to gain an audience with this woman. She was unsure whether her budget would stretch to it and would resent having to pay for something that she would never wear.

The man lifted a ledger from the counter and retreated behind a curtained doorway.

'I can't talk to you here,' the woman hissed. 'We close in half an hour. I will meet you at the end of the street. Charlotte Square.'

Sarah paced up and down at the entrance to the gardens, gazing fruitlessly along George Street. She had been foolish in letting the woman out of her sight. She probably had no intention of keeping this impromptu appointment.

The pavement across the street was becoming increasingly crowded as clerks and office workers began making their way home: a few gentlemen in top hats, ladies in pairs, servants laden down with provisions. Sarah was uncomfortably aware that she was beginning to draw attention from passers-by: a young woman on her own.

She was about to admit defeat and make for home herself, when she saw the woman approach, revealed as a carriage clattered past. She lifted her skirts high to avoid a pile of muck that had accumulated in the gutter, stepped up onto the pavement and grabbed Sarah's arm, all but propelling her towards the north-western corner of the square, away from the crowds.

'Who are you?' she demanded. 'What do you want?'

'I don't want *you*,' Sarah said, which caused the woman to pause, dousing her temper a little. She let go of Sarah's arm.

'Then I ask again. What do you want?'

'I'm trying to find a woman who lives in Dickson's Close. And I think that you are trying to find her too.' Sarah looked at her, trying to gauge her response. 'Possibly for the same reason.'

This was all speculation now, thoughts coming to her and connections being made as she spoke. The look on the woman's face suggested that she had stumbled upon the truth.

'Perhaps we can help each other,' Sarah said.

The woman scoffed, though more in doubt than that it was undesirable.

'I am looking for a Mrs King,' Sarah explained. 'She takes in babies. And she sells them too.'

At these words the woman crumbled before her. Her chin wobbled, tears welled in her eyes.

They both took a seat on a nearby bench.

'I had a little girl,' the woman said, her voice faltering. 'I named her Lilian. After my mother. But she was not my husband's child.'

The information came out in pieces, slotting together to reveal the whole. A complicated picture emerged but not an entirely uncommon one. She and her husband were, on paper, a suitable match. He was a buyer for a large overseas trading company, a man with prospects who offered a comfortable life, security. What woman could want more? He travelled constantly, which proved to be a blessing as he had turned out to be a jealous and violent individual.

She had an affair, the details of which she did not divulge. She became pregnant with her lover's child and was able to conceal the pregnancy from her husband as he was in India during the latter part of it.

'You couldn't keep the child?'

'My husband was from home when I conceived. He pays little attention to women's problems, but he is aware of the normal duration of a pregnancy. Simple arithmetic would indicate that he could not have been the father.'

'So, what did you do?'

'I had little choice. I gave the baby away before he returned.'

Sarah found it hard to imagine such a thing: feeling compelled to part with your own baby. She had lost a child herself in early pregnancy, a complication that had almost ended her life. Sarah doubted that she had truly come to terms with this yet. She had been so fixated on the loss of Archie and all that had happened around that time, that she had not had the opportunity to grieve for what else she had lost. Her chance of motherhood was almost certainly gone for good.

Though she struggled to admit it to herself, the end of her pregnancy had also brought with it a degree of relief. Certain doors remained open that would otherwise have closed. Although after Grafenberg she was unsure if she would ever walk through them anyway.

Sarah saw that the woman was crying once more. She retrieved her handkerchief and handed it over, realising as she did so that since her return from her travels she had spent a lot of time comforting the weeping and bereft.

'I don't even know your name,' Sarah said.

The woman sniffed, wiped her nose. 'My name is not important, and I would prefer if you did not learn it.'

Sarah decided not to press the issue but was conscious that this one conversation might be all she was likely to get. She would have to extract as much information as she could.

'How was it all arranged?' she asked.

'Believe it or not, I answered an advertisement in the news-paper,' the woman said. 'In the miscellaneous section. "Married couple without family willing to adopt healthy child." It all seemed legitimate. I was told that they had a house in the country, that they were good Christian folk unable to have a child of their own. A meeting was to be arranged through an intermediary, who would make all the necessary arrangements.

'I met her – the intermediary – several times before agreeing to their terms. Her name was Mrs King. The rendezvous was always at a railway station, encouraging the notion that she lived somewhere other than Edinburgh. She gave the impression of respectability. I was confident my child was going to be looked after, and ultimately sent to a good home. Of course I had been convinced of that,' she added, as though still trying to justify her actions to herself. 'How could I have handed over my child otherwise?'

'Was it expensive, this service that she provided?' Sarah imagined it would have been.

'She took a lot of money up front,' the woman confirmed. 'Part of the fee, she said, was for "purposes of discretion". Effectively blackmail. She knew of course that I had something to hide. She asked for clothing too: as much clothing as I could supply. I gave all I owned and bought some more, as it was the last gift I might give my daughter.

'Then my husband died suddenly, of a stroke. My stroke

of good fortune, as I like to think of it. I decided to get my baby back. Lilian could now come and live with me and my new husband-to-be, her father. I tried to find the elusive Mrs King. My fiancé made some enquiries. He has an acquaintance on the town council who helped track her down. Well, her likely address anyway. Of course, I knew immediately that something was very wrong. You saw the place yourself. I have been back several times but there is never anyone there.'

She sighed deeply. 'I need to investigate further but how can I do so? Asking questions would reveal that which I must keep secret.'

Sarah realised then why she had confided so much. She saw in Sarah a means of protecting her anonymity while achieving her own ends.

As the woman walked back towards George Street, Sarah was struck by the enormity of what she had been drawn into. Tracking down one missing baby had already seemed a daunting task. Now she was charged with finding two.

TWENTY-THREE

s his cab emerged from the woodland and he caught sight of Crossford House up ahead, Raven noted the contrast with his previous visit. Gone were the crowds, the music, the smells and the atmosphere of conviviality. The lawns were deserted, the building itself looking lonely and grey, in keeping with the weather. There was an unseasonal chill in the wind as it blew a smirr of rain into the carriage. It seemed incredible that it was only a matter of days since last he was here. This felt like it could be October.

Another contrast was to be felt in his pocket, as he was having to pay for his own transport on this occasion, his journey being in service of his promise to Eugenie. He had not flattered to deceive McLevy: nothing he had discovered pointed at anything but Gideon's guilt. Nonetheless, he knew that Eugenie would only be able to accept the difficult truth of it if she knew his efforts had been exhaustive.

That said, his errand was not solely in service to Eugenie, but in part to his own curiosity. That Gideon should have reached out to Raven in his time of need, despite their mutual antipathy, remained a source of intrigue almost as compelling as the question of Gideon's guilt.

On that greater matter there remained only one outstanding

question, but it was a canker that continued to worry at him: Gideon's use of arsenic. Both Eugenie's father and McLevy suggested that Gideon would have acted without consideration for how he might be caught. Raven had been in enough tavern brawls to understand how rage drove acts of violence with no thought for consequence. He had seen drink and fury possess men, compelling them to attack without assessing the implications of their foe being bigger and stronger or having three nearby companions ready to weigh in. Poisoning, by contrast, was a planned and calculated act, carried out by those who wished to disguise their hand. Many were caught because they had not anticipated how their actions would become visible after the fact, unaware of how much could be revealed when a corpse was examined by the likes of Dr Struthers.

Had Gideon perhaps believed that his father's sudden death would not seem suspicious enough to merit such an examination? Raven doubted it. Something Henry said intrigued him too: that only a small trace of arsenic had been found. He wondered whether this tiny quantity was being read like the letters on the parcel: misinterpreted as the initials of Mary Olsen when there was a different, larger message to be found if you knew where to look.

There were two other carriages outside the house as his own pulled up. Climbing down onto the gravel, Raven saw a woman in black emerge from the front of Crossford House and make her way towards her waiting conveyance. He recognised her at once as Amelia Bettencourt, Gideon's sister. She had her son clutched to her chest, dressed in a pink frock, his chin resting upon her shoulder.

Raven anticipated that she would hurry past with a cursory nod, unlikely to tarry even if she did recognise him, but instead she stopped as he approached. She did not smile – nor did he expect her to under the circumstances – but her demeanour was far from cold.

'Dr Raven, is it not?'

'Mrs Bettencourt, ma'am.'

'I have heard that you and my dear friend Eugenie are to be wed.'

It was all Raven could do not to roll his eyes. He wondered whether there would be anybody left in Edinburgh who did not already know by the time they made an official announcement. Perhaps that was always the way of such things.

'News travels fast,' he replied.

'What brings you to Crossford today?'

This was not an idle question, he knew, and it would not serve him to shrink from it.

'Eugenie has asked me to take an interest, on behalf of Gideon.'

Raven calculated that Eugenie being Amelia's friend would get him a more sympathetic hearing than stating he was here entirely at Gideon's request. As the general consensus was that her brother had murdered her father, he doubted she would look kindly on anyone who might consider himself Gideon's confederate.

'She finds it difficult to accept that things are as they appear,' he added, in as neutral a way as he could put it.

Amelia did not respond, though she seemed deep in thought as she digested this. Her child was peering over her shoulder, his face coming in and out of view as she swivelled back and forth, quietening him.

'This is your son?'

'Matthew,' she said, her voice faltering just a little as she spoke his name.

Raven grinned at him. Matthew looked back with an expression of curiosity and confusion, which then resolved briefly into a smile. The provenance was unmistakable even in one so young. He looked very much like Gideon, apart from the happy expression and the air of sweet-natured innocence.

'The family resemblance is most pronounced,' Raven remarked.

Amelia nodded sagely. 'And I am endeavouring to ensure that is all he should inherit.'

It seemed a strangely unguarded remark, tinged with bitterness and hard resolve. It told Raven that neither of the Douglas siblings bore much affection for their father.

'Forgive me if it is inappropriate, but Eugenie would wish me to ask. Is it your feeling that . . . things *are* as they appear? That your brother should have poisoned your father?'

She adjusted her grip upon her son. Matthew gazed up at her, entranced. There was love in Amelia's face too, but it was quickly washed away by sadness and regret.

'Every opportunity was granted to my brother, every chance,' she said. 'It was not easy to watch him squander things that were never offered to me. Gideon was always as lazy as he was destructive. As a child, I recall spending hours building a house with little wooden bricks. He tried to do the same, but lacked the patience and the skill, and his walls would collapse. His response was to tear down mine so that I could not have it either. Gideon acts in anger and he seeks swift gratification, easy solutions.'

She gazed across the gardens as though this memory was playing out there in her mind.

'Knowing what he has done is a difficult thing to bear. I wish that it were not so. Such a wish drives me to deny it, as it has driven Eugenie. But there are many things I would wish were different when it comes to my family. That is what brought me here today, in fact. Dymock, my father's lawyer, is visiting to administrate his affairs. I am intent upon building a life apart from this family.'

'You are here to claim your share of the inheritance,' Raven stated.

She wore an odd smile: amused and yet resolute.

'Not exactly,' she said, then bade him good day.

TWENTY-FOUR

he rapid clump of feet outside the door alerted Sarah to the emergency before she was informed as to its nature. Dr Simpson stuck his head round the door, interrupting her tidying of Raven's consulting room.

'Where is Will?'

'He has gone out. I'm not sure where.'

'Come away then, Sarah. Someone is in need.'

Sarah wiped her hands on her apron, took it off and hung it on a hook beside the door. She looked around the room quickly for anything that she might require, threw a few things into a bag and followed Dr Simpson out to the street. They stood for a few minutes waiting for the carriage to arrive.

'A case of prolonged labour,' Dr Simpson said. 'Dr Paterson requests our assistance.'

She loved him for implying that she was an essential part of this. Sarah was fairly sure that Dr Paterson, whoever he was, was not expecting any help from her.

The carriage arrived and they climbed in, Angus the coachman giving her a smile and a nod.

'This is the patient's second confinement,' Dr Simpson continued. 'At her first, two different medical gentlemen failed in their attempts to effect delivery by the forceps.'

He did not say how the delivery was achieved on that occasion; a destructive operation, perhaps, using the implements that lay at the bottom of Dr Simpson's medical bag. She hoped that there would be no call to dredge them up today.

Sarah adjusted her position on the seat. Dr Simpson had already extracted a sheaf of papers from somewhere and was making notes in the margins with a stubby pencil. He insisted on making use of the broken and disjointed pieces of time that littered his days, maintaining that they were too precious to fritter away. 'Save up any odd moment and put it to use,' he would say, encouraging others to follow his lead.

Sarah sighed. She had not meant to. It just escaped, as though she had been holding her breath for some time. Dr Simpson looked up from his work.

'Are you alright, Sarah?'

'I am quite well.' A polite rejoinder. She did not feel well at all.

Dr Simpson stared at her for a moment. Sarah found that she could not meet his eye. She looked out of the window, noticed that they were heading south.

'It's just that it strikes me you have not seemed yourself of late. Not since your return from Europe, in fact. And it is conspicuous that you have not spoken at all about your meeting with Dr Blackwell.'

Sarah wondered if this was the real reason she had been brought along. Had she anticipated as much she might have refused, found a reason why she could not come. She willed herself not to cry.

'Am I right in assuming that it did not go as you might have hoped?'

She managed a tight-lipped nod.

Dr Simpson patted her gently on the knee. 'Whenever you wish to speak about it, I am here to listen.'

She was grateful for his solicitousness, but she doubted such a time would ever come.

The carriage continued through the town to Bruntsfield Place, far removed from the miasmic atmosphere of the more densely populated parts of the city. Sarah lowered the carriage window and took some deep breaths, trying to compose herself. The air here was clearer, the houses bigger, with gardens and trees and flowering shrubs, a world away from the cramped and dilapidated warren of the Old Town. But Sarah did not want to be here.

The work that she had previously enjoyed, which had given her so much satisfaction, was as nothing to her now. There seemed little point in her being part of it. She felt adrift, afloat outside of herself, as if she could not quite connect with what was going on around her.

She took another deep breath, determined to regain some control of herself. She had a job to do. Dr Simpson had asked for her help and it was incumbent upon her to perform her duties to the best of her abilities. She owed him that, at the very least. She owed Christina too, having promised to help find her child. Perhaps by focusing on the tasks at hand, on the more immediate things that she had to deal with, she would learn to cope with the greater calamity that had befallen her.

The loss of hope, the loss of her ambition. A little flame that had puttered out.

The carriage pulled up at a great porticoed door. There was a crunch of gravel underfoot, the smell of something sweet in the air. Jasmine or honeysuckle. The door was answered by a liveried footman, and a housemaid in a starched white apron took their coats. They were shown up carpeted stairs, Sarah aware of a strong smell of beeswax polish. She thought about what she would be required to do, rehearsing her actions in an attempt to quieten her mind and avoid costly mistakes. She was worried that the skills she did possess would somehow desert her.

They entered a bedroom of immoderate size that could have comfortably housed several families. It was crowded with furniture and there seemed to be a continuous flow of maids bearing basins of clean water and fresh towels. Childbirth was, however, a great leveller, mother nature no respecter of pocket-books. The afflicted woman looked much as any who had been in labour for a prolonged period: sweat-soaked and exhausted. Sarah immediately felt sorry for her. Fancy sheets and numerous attendants could do little to improve matters when the infant was stuck tight and no amount of maternal effort would shift it. Skilled assistance and obstetric instruments would be required.

Forceps, thought Sarah. Let it be the forceps. Not the cranioclast or the perforator.

Dr Simpson consulted with Dr Paterson, who looked about as worn out as his patient, the dark circles under his eyes suggestive of a long night without rest. As the men discussed the problem, Sarah readied the chloroform. She carefully decanted a dose from the larger bottle into a smaller receptacle fitted with a dropper, then folded a piece of lint into a cone.

Dr Simpson made his examination, the woman groaning and then crying out as he tried to ascertain what was amiss. The professor began to explain his findings to Sarah, which seemed to cause Dr Paterson no end of confusion. He looked about the room repeatedly, as though in search of the person Dr Simpson was addressing.

'The head is low down in the pelvis,' Dr Simpson said, 'but it is in the right occipito-posterior position and the forehead instead of the vertex is presenting. One orbit is easily felt behind the symphysis pubis.'

Sarah nodded. Dr Paterson's eyeballs seemed ready to pop out of his head. He looked from one to the other but remained silent. What could he say? He had requested the professor's assistance and was therefore not in a strong position to then question his methods.

If Dr Simpson was aware of the effect his behaviour was

having on his colleague he showed no sign of it, too intent upon what he was doing to concern himself with what Dr Paterson might be thinking. He then compounded matters further by asking Sarah to listen in for the foetal heart.

'It's there,' she said after a few moments of searching. 'Not as rapid as it should be.'

'Unsurprising,' Dr Simpson stated. 'I think the infant has been lodged in this position for some time.'

Dr Paterson looked as though he was about to interject but Dr Simpson cut him off.

'Grab the forceps from my bag, would you please?'

Dr Paterson retrieved the forceps as instructed, fumbling a little with the fastening on the top of the bag. Sarah began to administer the chloroform, watching with a small sense of triumph as the distressed woman subsided gently into sleep. Her groaning, which had accompanied all their efforts thus far, ceased completely.

Dr Simpson applied the forceps without difficulty, aided by the relaxation of the maternal muscles from the anaesthetic.

'I am turning the head a quarter of a circle into the occipito-anterior position,' he said.

He then proceeded to extract the child who, on account of its prolonged entrapment, required vigorous rubbing of its chest to provoke its first cry.

Dr Paterson finally found his voice. 'Extraordinary,' he said. 'Quite extraordinary.'

Sarah wished she could believe he was talking about the baby, but his flabbergasted gaze was fixed upon her.

As the coach pulled away to commence the journey home, Dr Simpson finished writing something then slid his notebook into his pocket. He looked at Sarah and smiled.

'Do not be dismayed by apparent difficulties on the road to professional distinction,' he said, as though reciting a prepared speech. 'Let them not enervate but rather stimulate you onwards. That is what I tell my students. Only the timorous and irresolute will be intimidated and daunted by them. And you, Sarah, are neither.'

Sarah returned his smile. She felt more relaxed, less tense than she had been. She realised that she had a few skills that she could rightly be proud of.

Despite that, the wider view had not substantially changed. There were certain things that she would have to acknowledge were beyond her control, and perhaps admitting to that would ease her mind. Sometimes it was important to know when a battle was lost. It helped to minimise the casualties. Fight the fights that are worth fighting. Fight the fights that you have at least some prospect of winning.

'Yes, but there is one difference that cannot be ignored,' she replied. 'I am a woman. I will never be accepted into the ranks of men. Even if I possessed the requisite qualifications, which at this time I do not, I would not be allowed to study medicine. I cannot *be* one of your students.'

Dr Simpson sat back in his seat.

For once, he did not have an answer.

TWENTY-FIVE

aven stood for a moment before the front door of Crossford House, wondering whether to ring, before deciding it would be better simply to let himself in. His experience of hospitals had taught him that if you appeared confident and intent upon your purpose, people would assume you had a right to be there. It was better to ask forgiveness than permission.

He opened the door and passed through the vestibule into the entrance hall, finding himself once again beneath the vaulted gallery with its glass cupola fifty feet above. The sense of scale was dizzying, the artistry breathtaking, the pillars intricately carved with creeping vines, leaves and flowers. Birds and creatures both natural and fabled peeped out from tiny nooks.

On his previous visit his thoughts had been on other things, but returning here it struck Raven that this was the house in which Gideon had grown up. He glimpsed how such a magnificent environment might inculcate a sense of one's worth and importance relative to everyone else. But equally, recalling what he had witnessed, he understood the burden of expectation that must come with it.

He heard footsteps upon the tiles and saw a figure striding towards him down a wood-panelled corridor. Raven recognised him as the man who had been serving drinks to Sir Ainsley, and to Sir Ainsley only.

As he looked at Raven there was a flicker of recognition on the man's face, but evidently not enough to place him.

'Are you with Mr Dymock?' he asked.

Raven seized the opportunity. 'Indeed,' he responded with a stiff, officious expression. 'You were Sir Ainsley's butler?'

The man gave a curt nod. 'I am Wilson. You will find Mr Dymock in Sir Ainsley's study, down there and to the right. Do you require me to escort you?'

'I will find it,' Raven assured him, wishing leave to explore on his own. 'I have visited before.'

Wilson seemed relieved. He had the air of someone with other things to be getting on with, even though he no longer had his master to work for. Raven wondered whether such a man served the house as much as its owner.

Raven found himself in a corridor he recognised. Eugenie had led him along it, though they had entered by a different route. He allowed himself a pleasant moment to consider how this place might now hold significance in his own personal history. Would it be a tale he shared with his children, of how he asked their mother to marry him? In a secret passage, no less, normally the preserve of discreet and furtive household staff.

As though summoned by his own memory, a housemaid walked towards him, her head bowed as she approached. It might have been the one who had emerged from the secret passage that night, though he had barely glimpsed her so could not be sure.

'Excuse me,' he said, to arrest her from hurrying past.

She looked like a frightened mouse, not expecting to be accosted by a visitor.

'Please don't be alarmed. I am Dr Raven, an associate of Sir Ainsley's physician, Dr Todd. We are attempting to ascertain the precise details of his demise.'

'I wouldn't know anything about that, sir,' she said. Her eyes flitted about, reluctant to meet his. Raven wondered whether she was unsure of the appropriate response or merely intimidated. 'He was dead when Wilson came to bring him his breakfast.'

'And what of his supper? I gather the plates and bedpan were cleared away. Did anything seem amiss?'

'I wouldn't have known what to look for, sir.'

'So you were the one who cleared them?'

She looked suddenly pallid at what she had unwittingly disclosed.

'Dr Todd felt these things were cleared away a little hastily,' Raven said. 'Did someone order it? You can tell me, it's all right.'

'It's my job, sir. To clear away the dishes and the bedpan.'

'Do you happen to know what he ate?'

'I can't recall. You'd have to ask the cook.'

'What of the contents of the bedpan? Was there vomitus?'

She was starting to look teary, afraid. He found himself wishing Sarah were here, the thought popping up before his pride could suppress it. It was true, though. She would know how to talk to the girl.

'You must excuse me, sir,' she said, hurrying away 'I have duties to attend.'

Raven knocked on the door of the study and strode inside without waiting for reply. Dymock was standing behind a large mahogany desk, upon which sat reams of paper and piles of ledgers: a prominent man's life reduced to mere numbers.

There were pictures on the walls, two of which caught Raven's attention. One was an image of somewhere verdant and exotic: the sun beginning to set upon a sandy shore, the vegetation lush and the sea a shade of blue Raven had never witnessed. He suspected this was Tobago, where Sir Ainsley had his plantation. The other was a painting of a tall gentleman with a posture and profile almost identical to Sir Ainsley's: Gideon's grandfather, presumably. He was depicted standing with a black child at his side, a proprietorial hand upon the boy's head.

Dymock stared at Raven with a look of confusion similar to that of young Matthew Bettencourt outside. Unlike the baby, his expression ultimately resolved into bemusement. Charles Dymock was even more ruddy-faced than he had been at the party and was sweating slightly given the stuffiness of the small office and the heavy wool of his waistcoat and jacket.

'Mr Dymock,' Raven greeted him, trying to project that sense of entitled confidence that seemed to work so well for others. He strongly doubted that the man would remember him.

'Indeed,' the lawyer grunted. He did not extend a hand along with the introduction. 'Who might you be?'

'Dr Will Raven. Assistant to Professor James Young Simpson.'

Dymock narrowed his eyes, trying to place him, but there was no hint of recognition. Raven was insufficiently important to have made much of an impression.

'I am investigating the circumstances of Sir Ainsley's death.'

'I thought that was James McLevy's remit. And I thought he had found all that he required.'

Dymock sounded as though any complication to this would be as welcome as a hungry pauper at his dinner table.

Raven paused a moment to consider his answer.

'Mr McLevy and I are working in tandem. It is incumbent upon the investigation to explore all possibilities so that we may be sure we have reached the correct conclusion. Indeed, I have come here direct from the police office after poring over the results of Dr Struthers' post-mortem examination.'

Raven derived some comfort from the fact that what he said was not entirely false, but that would not spare him from McLevy's wrath should he learn of it.

'I was under the impression there was nothing further to establish,' Dymock said. 'Arsenic was found, was it not? Gideon

Douglas poisoned his father in accelerated pursuit of his inheritance.'

'I spoke to Gideon in Calton Jail two days ago. He has a rather different perspective on the matter.'

Dymock scoffed. 'Aye, I'll bet he does.'

Raven glanced around, making a show of taking in the documents and the paintings.

'You know the family well?'

'I served Sir Ainsley for more than twenty years.'

Raven injected some regret into his tone. 'I am given to believe that Gideon and his father did not have a harmonious relationship. This outcome would not have surprised you, then.'

'As soon as I heard it was poison, I had no question as to who the culprit would be. The boy was always a wastrel. Irresponsible. A *roué*. Getting himself in trouble, getting . . . other people in trouble. That's why he was packed off to Tobago.'

Raven noted the pause, the course correction mid-sentence.

'As Gideon tells it, his father asked him to go to Tobago because he needed someone whom he trusted to oversee the plantation's recovery following storm damage. He said he was turning the place's fortunes around when his father summoned him home again.'

Dymock's face twisted into a snarl of derision. 'Sir Ainsley summoned him home again because of his incompetence. He had hoped that giving Gideon some responsibility might make him rise to the challenge. But instead his indolence, drunkenness and other familiar appetites prevailed.'

Dymock sighed, a grave expression upon his face. 'It is as well for everyone that he will not inherit now, for he would be the ruin of all this, just as he has been the ruin of everything else he has touched.'

He spoke with a certainty that Raven thought premature and wondered what underpinned it.

'He will not inherit if he is *convicted*,' Raven clarified. 'Though it would be the least of his worries at that point.'

'He would not need to hang to lose his inheritance. A reasonable suspicion of the heir's involvement in his father's death is grounds for what is known as "a corruption of blood". Not only is the tainted heir disinherited, but none of his issue would ever inherit either. His entire bloodline becomes forfeit, though that is moot in Gideon's case, for he has not married.' Dymock indicated the mess of documentation spread about the desk. 'It is in anticipation of such an outcome that I am forced to wrestle with all of this now.'

'Who would the inheritance then pass to?'

'There is normally a division between the heritable property, being the house and business holdings, and the moveable property, being Sir Ainsley's liquid assets. The firstborn male heir receives the heritable assets while the moveable assets are divided in three. A third is to be disposed according to the dead man's bequest: in Sir Ainsley's case primarily certain hospitals, the Church and the construction of a monument. A third goes to the widow and a third is further divided between the other children. It is simplified in this instance because there is no widow, so two-thirds of the moveable assets pass to Mrs Bettencourt. Or would do so, ordinarily.'

Dymock bore a look of frustration, the cause of which was not apparent.

'With Gideon corrupt, the law dictates that the heritable property should pass instead to the next male heir in the bloodline, which is young Matthew Bettencourt, Amelia's son.'

'And why wouldn't it in this case?'

'Mrs Bettencourt does not wish it. She stood before me not half an hour ago and indicated that she intends to refuse the inheritance on her son's behalf, as well as renouncing her own.'

Raven thought of her odd smile, her resolute manner.

Not exactly.

'Why would she do that?'

'I cannot begin to fathom it,' Dymock replied, sounding as though she had done it purely to complicate his task. 'Relations with her father have been strained at best since her mother died. Families can be baffling; rich families inexplicable.'

'But that she would give up so much wealth,' Raven pondered.

'She does not do it lightly, but she said she has seen what wealth can bring, and it is not always happiness. There is a weight of responsibility that she does not wish for her son.'

Raven thought of the entrance hall downstairs, the grandeur emblematic of the burden of expectation under which Gideon had twisted and buckled. He wondered what more Amelia had seen to make her wish to protect her child at such material cost.

Dymock did not seem about to volunteer it, so Raven pressed the obvious question.

'In that case, who would the inheritance pass to?'

'The next eligible male heir is Edward Hamilton.'

'Teddy?' Raven pictured the passionate and frustrated young man who had appealed in vain for Simpson's assistance in his argument with Sir Ainsley over the Poor Law and the rights of unmarried mothers.

'You know him?'

'I've met him. I think it is fair to say that he and his uncle were not of a mind on certain political matters. Sir Ainsley's proposed ordinance regarding contagious diseases seemed to be particularly contentious.'

Dymock paused at the mention of this, suddenly wary.

Raven recalled the aftermath of the discussion, Simpson saying how he suspected Austin Mansfield had been bought, and that he wouldn't have been the first. Raven wondered whether, as his lawyer, Dymock had played a role in such purchases.

'I gather Sir Ainsley's ordinance was initially opposed by none other than the provost,' Raven continued, 'but that he had subsequently changed his mind on the matter. I wonder what

changes Teddy might effect if he is able to wield the same level
of influence. Wouldn't that have Sir Ainsley turning in his grave?'

'You are not suggesting Mr Hamilton could have had a hand
in this?'

'Dr Todd did ask me who most stood to gain from Sir Ainsley's
death. Gideon suggested he was not his father's only enemy, and
far from the most ruthless.'

Dymock was now verging on anger. His face became redder,
beads of sweat speckling his forehead.

'Do not dare to speak of such things beneath Sir Ainsley's own
roof,' he warned, almost spitting the words. 'This tragedy has
brought not only hurt and loss, but unearned ignominy upon his
name. There are many who will not overlook it should you make
things worse by bandying about unfounded suspicion and innuendo. I cannot imagine James McLevy, for one, would countenance
such conduct. What exactly is your relationship with him, again?'

The name of his bête noir having been thus invoked, it struck
Raven as a prudent moment to take his leave.

TWENTY-SIX

Grafenberg, ten days earlier

arah stood in the doorway, watching as the young girl traversed the floor and approached a small group gathered in one corner. The space was vast, its dimensions more in keeping with a ballroom than a drawing room. It was painted in bright colours and hung with glass chandeliers, giving the impression of being part of a grand hotel rather than a sanatorium.

The girl delivered her card, the group breaking up to reveal the seated woman around whom they had been congregating: the famous Dr Blackwell. A bandage covered her left eye, announcing her reason for being there. She read the card – not blind, then – and spoke to a man seated next to her. They both rose and crossed the room towards Sarah, Dr Blackwell leading the gentleman by his hand.

'Miss Fisher? This is my good friend Mr Glynn, a fellow American. We are about to have tea. Would you care to join us?'

Sarah followed Dr Blackwell and her friend into an adjacent room filled with long tables bearing earthenware jugs of milk and plates of coarse-looking brown bread and butter. They sat at the end of a table, a short distance from an animated group talking loudly in another language that Sarah could not understand. German, perhaps.

Dr Blackwell cut a piece of bread for her companion and poured him a glass of milk.

'We have formed our own little set, our own little genus, haven't we, Glynn. Sight-impaired Americans.'

'Blind Yankees,' Mr Glynn replied, smiling.

'Speak for yourself, young man. I can still see. For now, anyway.'

Dr Blackwell offered Sarah a slice of bread, which she declined with a shake of her head.

'Have you come to take the cure yourself, Miss Fisher?' Mr Glynn asked.

Sarah shook her head again and then realised that he could not see her. 'No. But my travelling companion is very keen to do so.'

'It is most invigorating,' he said, laughing.

'That is certainly one way to describe it,' Dr Blackwell added. 'A half bath, a plunge bath, and then wrapped in a wet bandage. And as much cold water as you can drink.'

'Has it helped?' Sarah asked.

'It has certainly done me no harm,' Dr Blackwell replied. 'Although I suspect that being outside most of the day walking in the mountain air may have been more efficacious. And it has certainly been easier to bear than the initial treatment for my complaint.'

'Barbarous,' Mr Glynn said, shuddering.

'On the contrary. I was given the best care and attention; I can have no complaint on that account.' To Sarah she said, 'I had an unfortunate accident while working at the maternity hospital in Paris. I was syringing the infected eye of an infant. Some of the water sprayed into my own eye and I became similarly afflicted.'

'Cautery to the eyelids, leeches to the temples and vigorous purging,' Mr Glynn persisted. 'Sounds like torture to me.'

Dr Blackwell snorted. 'Without it I would likely be as blind as you are.'

'If you have not come for the cure, why have you come?' Mr Glynn asked Sarah.

'I have come to see Dr Blackwell.'

'Well, I suppose she is something of a celebrity,' Mr Glynn said, smiling again. A piece of the coarse bread had lodged between his front teeth.

'This young woman works with Professor Simpson,' Dr Blackwell added, as though this provided an explanation for why Sarah was there. 'The man who discovered chloroform.'

'Another celebrity. I am indeed honoured.'

Dr Blackwell removed an envelope from her pocket, the letter of introduction that Sarah had delivered the previous day. Sarah recognised Dr Simpson's elaborate hand and felt a sudden pang, an intense longing for home.

Her melancholic thoughts were interrupted by a sudden hubbub. A large group entered the room and several people stood to get a better view.

'Priessnitz?' Mr Glynn asked. 'Must be noon.'

'He arrives every day at the same time,' Dr Blackwell explained. 'You could set your watch by him.'

Sarah stood now, trying to see the man responsible for the existence of the spa and its world-renowned treatments. Son of a serf, with no formal medical training, and yet he had a list of patients any physician would envy.

Reputation and celebrity fostered notions of physical stature, bodily eminence. Priessnitz certainly did not conform to these expectations. He was small, compact, older than she had imagined, his complexion marred by smallpox scars.

Dr Blackwell stood up too.

'It is time for my afternoon walk,' she said and looked at Sarah. 'Care to join me?'

The air outside was wonderfully fresh: free from smoke, smog and dust. It smelled sweet, like freshly scythed grass, rather than replete with the foul aromas of the city. Sarah found herself taking deep breaths of it. There were wildflower-strewn meadows either side of the path, adding their fragrance to the air, and interspersed among these were clumps of alpine strawberries.

'Feel free to pick them,' Dr Blackwell said, noticing that Sarah was looking. 'They are terribly good.'

Sarah felt obliged to sample a few. They were indeed delicious. She scanned their surroundings as she ate, marvelling at the view. It was like a small piece of heaven. Little surprise then that invalids got better here. She wondered if these improvements were sustained when they had to return to their ordinary lives, although few of the patients fell into the category of ordinary. Aristocrats and minor royalty. The well-heeled of Europe and beyond.

'I shall take you up to the Priessnitz spring,' Dr Blackwell announced. 'It is a pleasant walk. Not too taxing.'

'I'm well used to walking,' Sarah said, matching Dr Blackwell's stride. They continued in silence for a while, the narrowness of the footpath forcing them to walk in single file. At the top of an incline the trail widened again. Sarah wondered how to begin. Now that she was here, she had no idea how to explain herself, her reason for coming.

'Is there any hope of Mr Glynn having his sight restored?' she asked. A tentative beginning.

'Unfortunately not,' Dr Blackwell said. She smiled. 'He has been like a brother to me in this concourse of strangers. He is one of the smartest fellows that I have ever met, bears his terrible misfortune with real heroism and has rendered me numberless little services.'

Sarah wondered if Mr Glynn considered his attentions to be brotherly. Dr Blackwell seemed to be entirely unaware of how attractive she was and oblivious to the fact that she drew male attention wherever she went, from the inebriated older gentleman in London, to the attentions of Monsieur Blot in Paris, to the blind American she had evidently become so fond of.

'It is most amusing to watch the people who come here,' Dr Blackwell continued. 'Grafenberg is all the rage in Germany and all classes are represented. As Glynn is unable to see for himself, he relies on me to describe everything to him.'

All classes. Does she mean me? Sarah wondered. She could not seem to shake the idea that her humble origins were in some way visible to others.

'I shall have to sit down,' Dr Blackwell said suddenly. She eased herself onto a low stone wall at the side of the path, obviously in pain. She placed a hand gingerly over her bandaged eye.

'The inflammation has returned,' she said, matter-of-factly. 'I plan to return to Paris soon to see Desmarres there. He is an oculist of some repute who has been recommended to me.'

'So, the water cure was not a cure after all,' Sarah said, almost immediately regretting it. It sounded harsh to her own ears.

'Well, I am stronger in myself and it has fortified me to cope with what is to come. It is not such a great disfigurement,' she said, pointing to her bandaged eye. 'But it has interfered in no small way with my plans. I wanted to become a surgeon, but if I lose the sight in this eye that ambition will have to be abandoned. Though my right eye remains strong and I can read and write without difficulty, so all is not lost. It could have been so much worse.'

'Did you always want to study medicine?' Sarah asked, sitting down beside her.

Dr Blackwell laughed. 'No, I did not. When it was first suggested to me, I found the idea abhorrent. I had no interest in the human body or the diseases that it fell prey to. I could not bear the sight of a medical book.'

'What made you consider it?'

'A close friend was ill. She suggested it to me. She said that her distress would have been less if she could have been cared for by a female physician. I could see the truth in that and so I began making enquiries about the possibility of pursuing such a course. It was unanimously decreed by all the medical men of my acquaintance to be impossible.' She laughed. 'That just made me more determined. Once obstacles were put in my way it became something of a moral struggle for me.'

'Do you have any regrets?'

'Given what has happened? No. None. Perhaps that is surprising to you.'

Sarah shook her head.

'And what about you? Why do you wish to pursue such a career?'

Sarah thought for a moment.

'I wish to be of use. I find the subject fascinating. I think that I am as capable as any of the apprentices that I have seen.'

'But that is the thing. In order to compete you must be better than they are: more than merely competent. You must avoid any perception of being inferior yet without seeming to be a threat. Like walking a tightrope. Perform poorly at any point and they will dismiss you. Outshine them and they will hate you for it. We are invading their territory here and you must be prepared for them to defend it.'

There was a pause.

'Are you in a position to apply to any institutions?'

'Well . . .'

'How is your Latin?'

'My Latin?'

Sarah felt a precipitous anxiety, akin to the rare occasions when she had forgotten to carry out a required task.

'Natural philosophy? Advanced mathematics?'

Sarah's blank expression said everything.

Dr Blackwell shook her head. 'It is a long journey that you wish to embark upon. You must ensure that you are suitably equipped before you set out on the road. Have you really considered what will be required? It is all very well having an interest. One that has been fostered, no doubt, by your work with Dr Simpson. But you will need so much more than an interest and rudimentary competence in a few nursing tasks. It seems to me that you lack the very basics required to get started. You cannot hope to compete if that is the case.'

'I can learn,' Sarah insisted. 'I know that I have the ability to do so.'

'But the commitment required demands more than merely a willingness to study. Have you considered the sacrifices that you will be forced to make? Marriage? Children?' She pointed to her eye, lifting the bandage to reveal the damage done – the iris and pupil obscured, clouded by the ravages of infection. 'Your own health?'

Sarah averted her gaze. She could feel tears forming and blinked them away. This speech felt like a rebuke, one that she felt she did not merit. She had been married and widowed already, there was little prospect of her ever becoming a mother, and she was well aware of the risks attendant upon looking after the sick. Medical knowledge offered little protection from infectious fevers; not all of Raven's medical school contemporaries had made it to the end of their studies, sacrificed at the altar of professional duty. She was not that naive. Even if her rudimentary knowledge of Latin was inadequate at present, she would learn. Of that she had no doubt. And surely Dr Simpson's faith in her had not been misplaced.

She had a sudden, horrible thought. Was this why he had encouraged her to take this trip around Europe in pursuit of this woman?

A dose of reality. A harsh lesson that he did not himself wish to deliver.

Sarah swallowed, forced herself to smile, and turned back to her companion.

'Perhaps you could tell me a little of your own journey. How you managed to achieve what you did. Give me some notion of what is required.'

'Well, it was far from easy,' Dr Blackwell said. 'I applied to several medical schools in Philadelphia and New York but was roundly rejected by all. The dean of one school admitted that his objection was on the grounds of female competition. He said, and I am quoting verbatim here, "You cannot expect me to furnish you with a stick to beat our heads with."' She raised her arm, brandishing an imaginary weapon. 'They cannot have it both ways. How can we be deemed incapable but threaten an unwelcome competition at the same time?'

She shook her head then winced, placing a hand over her eye again.

'I kept going and applied to some of the smaller schools. Geneva Medical College in New York state responded favourably. The students were supportive – largely because their opinion had been canvassed before I was offered a place. I kept my head down, worked conscientiously, gave no cause for complaint.

'I had hoped to extend my studies in Europe, and I was made welcome in London during my short visit there, though I was not seeking a formal position at that time. Once in Paris it quickly became clear that it would be impossible for me to study there as I wished to, as any man with an MD could easily have done. No one would grant me the slightest favour. I was eventually permitted to enter the maternity hospital but only on the same terms as any woman entering to train as a midwife.'

They sat in silence for a moment, looking out over the field in front of them. A few poppies swayed in the breeze around its edge, crimson petals obscuring a dark heart. *Papaver somniferum.* There were some things Sarah *did* know. She wasn't entirely ignorant.

'I learned a great deal there, at the maternity hospital,' Dr Blackwell continued. 'I will always be glad that I went, despite what happened to me. Because of my injury I have had to relinquish the idea of becoming a surgeon, but I still hope to pursue a career in medicine in some shape or form.'

She looked at Sarah.

'If I have learned one thing through all of this, it is that persistence is key.'

Persistence, yes, Sarah thought, contemplating the tortuous route Dr Blackwell had navigated, the obstacles thrown in her path, the sacrifices she had made, and the reduced version of her aspirations that even she had been forced to settle for.

But persistence had not been the only resource required to make such an arduous journey. It had also taken the right background, the right social standing and the right education.

Sarah was in possession of none of these.

TWENTY-SEVEN

arly morning found Raven awake and restless. Sleep had come in short stretches when it wasn't evading him completely, or was interrupted by intrusive thoughts about Gideon, Eugenie and Sarah. Eventually he gave up and got out of bed, washed and dressed. It was so much easier to do at this time of year when the daylight began creeping into his room just after four. He had to be up earlier than usual anyway because of the planned trip to Bridge of Allan. He would under other circumstances relish the prospect of a 'scamper into the countryside', as the professor liked to put it. It would usually provide welcome respite from the near-constant demands of patients at the Maternity Hospital and Queen Street, but right now he had too many claims on his limited time.

Raven went downstairs to his consulting room, relishing the quiet of the house at this hour. He made use of this peaceful interlude by dealing with the piles of correspondence that littered his desk and reading the latest edition of the *Edinburgh Medical and Surgical Journal*, or at least skimming through the articles that caught his attention. At breakfast-time he entered the dining room in urgent need of some strong coffee.

He found that Dr Simpson was already seated at the table,

his hand immersed in a wide-necked jar of clear fluid. The sweet smell of chloroform indicated what the jar contained.

'Good morning,' the professor said. He offered no explanation for the chloroform, as though this kind of activity at the breakfast table was to be expected. Raven had to concede that in this household it was.

The professor's parrot, perched by the window, was unusually quiet – it had the tendency to greet his entrance with a series of ear-piercing squawks – and Raven wondered if the bird was falling under the influence of the fumes. He walked to the window, intending to open it, then decided that a mildly soporised parrot would be preferable to a fully conscious one. He sat down at the table and poured himself some coffee.

'Experiment?' Raven asked.

'I still have that splinter in my hand. I have been trying, with some difficulty, to extract it.'

'And how is sticking your hand in a jar of chloroform intended to help with that?'

'I am investigating whether or not local application produces anaesthesia in the part exposed to it. If it does it would permit me to dig about in the palm of my hand with impunity.'

'And does it? Produce local anaesthesia?'

Simpson gave the jar a forlorn look.

'Not so far,' he said.

They took the early train headed for Aberdeen, disembarking at Stirling. A carriage had been sent to collect them, the horses stamping impatiently as though instructed to do so by their owner.

The carriage transported them from the station through the countryside to an imposing sandstone villa situated in a sprawling plot of land. Lady Mackenzie greeted them at the door herself. The house belonged to a friend who was travelling around Europe for the summer, she explained. Raven wondered if he would ever be in a position to afford such a residence or have such well-endowed friends. He doubted it. Lady Mackenzie kept referring to the house as a cottage. Raven wondered what her own home was like. A castle, perhaps.

She seemed delighted to see them, having finally secured a visit from the great Dr Simpson after so many years of trying. Raven marvelled at the professor's patience with such people: relentlessly demanding in spite of their evident good health.

No offer of refreshments was made despite their early start. Raven wondered about those who set such great store in decorum and appropriate behaviour, policing with vigour any perceived lapses in others but failing to see any deficiencies in themselves. He was grateful he had consumed a hearty breakfast otherwise his rumbling stomach would have interrupted Lady Mackenzie as she poured forth her litany of complaints, none of which Raven considered in any way serious or sinister.

'I have dispensed with the leeches but have persisted with the mustard baths,' she said, referring to the prescription made some time ago.

'It may be time to dispense with the mustard baths as well,' Dr Simpson suggested. 'If your symptoms have subsided.'

'Well, they have,' she admitted with an air of disappointment. 'But others have arisen in their place.'

The woman lacked attention, Raven thought. Or a sense of purpose, perhaps.

The lack of hospitality was starting to grate on him. Not even the offer of a cup of tea! Raven was beginning to think more fondly of his visits to Old Town slums. Those with considerably less seemed to be more ready in their generosity, offering to share what little they had. This woman was so self-obsessed she could spare not even a thought for anyone else.

Dr Simpson listened attentively for half an hour before insisting on examining her son, the purported reason for their visit. Evidently, he could find little wrong with Harry either, as after a brief examination he prescribed the white of an egg and some lime juice. Presumably as a tonic for the boy, as Raven did not think scurvy was a realistic possibility.

Lady Mackenzie accepted this prescription with good grace but became visibly upset when Dr Simpson then announced his intention to depart, complaining bitterly about the brief nature of the visit. 'When Sir Benjamin came to see my husband, he stayed for a full two days and gave four long consultations,' she admonished the professor, even as he was putting on his coat.

Raven had no idea who Sir Benjamin was, but if he had spent two days in this woman's company, then he deserved whatever exorbitant fee he had undoubtedly charged.

Half an hour later Raven was tramping through a muddy field behind Simpson, wondering where they were and what they were supposed to be doing.

'Not much further,' Simpson called back to him.

Not much further to where? Raven thought. He scanned his immediate surroundings but apart from some clumps of grass and the odd forlorn-looking tree there was not much to see. Whatever they were looking for, Raven knew that it had nothing to do with medicine or obstetrics.

Lady Mackenzie's complaints were still ringing in their ears as they had climbed back into the carriage. Raven had made some rapid calculations and concluded that, barring any unanticipated delays, they would be back at Queen Street in time for dinner. He was curious as to why they had travelled such a distance for such a short consultation, but all became clear when their journey home was interrupted by this impromptu excursion. Raven wondered if this had been the main purpose of the trip all along.

As they continued their expedition across this nondescript marshy field in rural Stirlingshire, Raven marvelled at Dr Simpson's ability to ignore his bodily needs. He frequently went for hours without sustenance and spent many a night without sleep but never seemed the worse for any of it. Raven had great difficulty functioning without food or rest, hence his growing grouchiness and lack of enthusiasm for whatever it was that they were supposedly about.

Dr Simpson stopped suddenly and spread his arms wide.

'Here we are,' he announced.

Raven looked around again. The landscape had not changed. There was nothing to see.

'You'll have to enlighten me, Dr Simpson. I have no earthly idea where "here" is.'

'Bannockburn.'

When Raven did not respond, the professor continued. 'Site of the great battle! Where Robert the Bruce defeated King Edward's army.'

Raven knew about the Battle of Bannockburn – what Scotsman did not – but the great battle had taken place hundreds of years ago and in 1850 they were just two men standing in a muddy field as the clouds gathered overhead threatening rain.

Dr Simpson removed an implement from his pocket, bent down and started scrabbling about in the turf.

'What are you doing?'

'Searching.'

'For what?'

'Things of antiquarian interest. Arrow tips and the like.'

Raven sighed, stuck his hands in his pockets and wondered gloomily how long this foraging was likely to take and whether the rain would stay off for the duration.

'It was my uncle Jarvey who got me started,' Simpson went on, 'collecting old bits and pieces.'

'Was it?' Raven replied, thinking it was useful to know who to blame for their current situation.

'He kept an inn in Bathgate which was full of old stuff.'

'Are they ever worth anything? The things that you find?'

Simpson looked up at him. 'They have value in what they teach us about the past.'

Raven could muster no energy for digging around for arrow-heads. This was not the sort of buried treasure that held any interest for him. As for the past, Raven felt that in general it was best left undisturbed. He found a large rock and sat down just as a fine rain began to fall.

Given the lack of anything else to usefully occupy it, Raven felt his mind drifting back to the many problems he was currently wrestling with – number one on this list being Sarah.

He had become concerned by her recent low mood but was convinced that it was not a result of his engagement. Not entirely. He felt sure that something was already amiss, hence her response to his news. He had thought that she would come back from Europe energised, consumed with ambition and inspiration, and that his new attachment would be of little concern. He wondered what could have happened to her.

He knew that he ought to ask, but he was worried about how she might respond. He was unsure if they could be friends any more; not in the way they had been.

The prospect of a growing distance between them gnawed away at him. He missed her. Her company. Her counsel.

He realised he had been foolish to think that their relation-ship could remain unaltered. Given that he intended to marry someone else, he would have to get used to Sarah not being such an integral part of his life. And yet the very thought of this made him unhappy. Much as he was loath to admit it, there were many ways in which Eugenie was no substitute.

Sarah, he knew, would have been a great asset at Crossford House. She would have wheedled more information out of that housemaid, and other members of staff too. In addition, she could probably help him find out more about Teddy Hamilton. As a young radical he was a writer of pamphlets and frequent speaker at meetings: the kind of gatherings that Sarah attended on occasion. She had recently joined the Edinburgh Ladies' Emancipation Society, a group of Quaker women who, having successfully campaigned for the emancipation of slaves, were now turning their attention to other oppressed groups. Women in particular, hence Sarah's interest.

Raven became conscious that Simpson's eyes were upon him, lively and inquisitive as he looked up from where he was rooting about in the earth.

'Where were you yesterday, late afternoon?' he asked. 'I saw you get out of a cab, wondered where you were returning from.'

'I was at Crossford House.'

He was aware that this answer would only further pique Simpson's curiosity, but he could hardly keep his activities secret.

'Gideon Douglas is held at Calton Jail,' he continued. 'Accused of killing his father with poison.'

'Yes, so I have heard,' Dr Simpson replied.

'Eugenie has asked me to look into it. She has known Gideon since childhood, Dr Todd having been Sir Ainsley's physician. She cannot believe this of him and wants me to investigate.'

'A difficult request to refuse. What have you discovered?'

'Little that would comfort her.'

Raven explained why Gideon was the sole suspect, why McLevy was convinced of his guilt. Simply put, he hated his father and stood to gain financially from his death.

'I must confess,' Raven said, 'given what I know of the man and what I have recently learned, I think it entirely plausible that he is responsible. But I have made a promise to Eugenie and will therefore pursue the few questions that I do have.'

Raven paused, bent down and rubbed at a scuff on his shoe.

'Gideon maintains that his father had greater enemies than himself. Do you think that is likely? How well did you know Sir Ainsley?'

Dr Simpson stopped his digging, thought for a moment.

'I know that no man procures or retains such wealth without leaving suffering in his wake,' he replied. 'Some men practise charity because they know they ought to atone, or because it helps them convince themselves they are good people. They tell themselves their benevolence retrospectively justifies their deeds. In Sir Ainsley's case, even his charity was a form of exercising control. He was a manipulative man. He enjoyed toying with people. I think he understood that money was not the only means by which one might wield power over individuals.'

'Do you mean his political manoeuvrings? The contagious diseases ordinance?'

'Indeed. I sincerely hope that idea died with him, but I fear it did not.'

'There can be no real harm in offering treatment to afflicted prostitutes,' Raven mused.

Dr Simpson scoffed and looked at him with something akin to pity.

'Forced examination of women, harsh punishments if they refuse, and who gets to decide who is a prostitute and who is not?'

Raven thought of McLevy's man Wilkie, persecuting Mary Olsen because she had refused his advances.

'Common in many a moralistic man, Sir Ainsley had a disproportionate interest in human weakness, in other people's vices. A prurient fascination, I would go as far as to say.'

Dr Simpson paused, looking around as though there might be eavesdroppers even in this deserted field.

'You know I have a discreet role in the fostering of unwanted children.'

Raven nodded. He recalled the professor's evasiveness and secrecy over the matter. He had once thought Simpson kept a mistress and child – a thought that he was embarrassed about now – but subsequently learned that the professor was engaged in finding homes for the illegitimate offspring of his wealthier clients. His former amanuensis Mr Quinton and his wife had taken one such infant. That relationship might have worked out better had a baby been the only thing they had taken.

'Sir Ainsley once approached me to let me know he was aware

of these activities. It was before his daughter was married and I wondered if perhaps she had done something foolish. Which would of course have been particularly embarrassing given Sir Ainsley's prescriptive pronouncements regarding chastity and abstinence. But his purpose proved far more shameful.

'He was attempting to ascertain whose children I had fostered, and to whom. In not so many words he let it be known that there would be financial emoluments if I complied. As if I could be so easily bought. He had heard a specific rumour which he hoped to have confirmed. I think he was also fishing speculatively for information that might be of use to him at a later date.'

Raven would have liked to witness that particular conversation. Sir Ainsley Douglas could hardly have chosen a less co-operative subject. Dr Simpson saw it as his duty to keep the secrets of his patients. It was something he repeatedly impressed upon students and assistants. *Whatever is communicated to you as a matter of professional confidence must ever remain buried within your own breast.* As for financial emoluments, Simpson was impervious to such things. There was once a wealthy lady in Brighton who wrote to him asking for consultations, offering ever larger sums to get what she wanted, eventually proposing a fee of a thousand pounds for a visit. Simpson refused to go, saying that there was nothing wrong with her and that he preferred to treat those who were genuinely unwell.

'Did he take your refusal with good grace?' Raven asked.

'On the surface, but I have it on good authority that he then had Sanderson digging around trying to find something on me that might force me to reveal what I knew.'

'Sanderson the newspaper editor?'

'Yes. Sir Ainsley's newspaper, remember. It is said of Sanderson that he has cumulatively paid as much for stories that were unfit to print as he has paid for those that have actually appeared in the *Courant*. Scandal is a currency like any other. Sir Ainsley understood that you must speculate to accumulate. The right titbit could provide the means to acquire more.'

The rain had become heavier and this mercifully brought their expedition to an end. Dr Simpson stood up and brushed the dirt from the knees of his trousers.

'Even Uncle Jarvey made for home once the rain started,' he said.

Good old Uncle Jarvey, Raven thought.

As they began their journey back to the waiting carriage, Raven thought about the pernicious nature of certain families. Not all were the nurturing environments that they ought to be. He knew that he had not been so blessed with his relatives as Simpson had with his. There had been no one to share passions and enthusiasms with, antiquarian or otherwise. Raven's primary concern during his childhood had been surviving it. His father had been a violent drunk, and Raven's fortunes had improved after he died. Some people have such a malignant presence that the world is undeniably a better place after they have left it. He wondered if Ainsley Douglas fell into that category. Was there a general benefit to his untimely departure? Did whoever perpetrated this crime have something more than money in mind? Was there more to this than merely a malignant conflict between father and son?

Although grateful that his own had departed this earth before he could inflict any more damage, Raven mourned his having grown up without a true father figure: a decent man to model himself upon. Then, as he tramped across the field behind Simpson, it struck him that to all intents and purposes he now had one.

Dr Todd's recent words come to mind: *Dr Simpson is to be family, as it were.*

This thought was some consolation for the claggy mud adhering to his boots, and the persistent drizzle soaking into his coat.

As they climbed back into the carriage he feigned interest in the few bits of mangled metal Dr Simpson had managed to unearth, presented on his handkerchief like jewels upon a cushion. Raven felt an unaccustomed contentment settle upon him. He sat back against the upholstery, closed his eyes, and began to dream of his dinner.

TWENTY-EIGHT

here was purpose to Sarah's stride as she crossed the North Bridge on her way back to Dickson's Close, but in truth she had little notion of what she would do if she again found no one home. Her conversation with the woman from the perfumier had been enlightening but she still had no idea of how she might track down her quarry if it turned out she was no longer at that address. There were several Kings listed in the Post Office directory, but Sarah doubted this woman would be formally advertising her whereabouts.

She had just turned on to the High Street when she glanced across the road and saw Raven on the other side, striding down from the direction of the castle. She stopped and considered turning back, then asked herself why she thought that she needed to conceal her activities from him.

Because she was on her own now. Fending for herself.

Her hesitation cost her any chance of escape. He had seen her and was now crossing to her side of the street.

'Where are you going?' he asked. His tone was light, friendly.

'Just walking.'

'Walking? Here?'

He obviously did not believe her, and she could not blame

him. Nobody would cross from the New Town to this place in search of fresh air and bracing exercise.

'Where are *you* going?' she asked, attempting to divert him.

'The Maternity Hospital,' he said. 'As I do most days.'

He seemed amused at her poor attempt at a lie. He knew her so well; it was almost impossible to hide anything from him. This was suddenly irritating to her.

'It's not really your business where I'm going, is it?' she said.

He raised an eyebrow at her. 'Well, if you're planning on wandering about the Old Town on your own then I would say that it is.'

'I don't need your help,' she retorted, immediately regretting it.

'Help with what?'

'It's nothing,' she insisted, her tone petulant, though it was herself she was annoyed with now. She really would have to learn to control her emotions better than this.

'Well, since you are here and have nothing specific to do . . .' Raven gave her an arch look that made her want to punch him. 'Why don't you come with me to Milton House? We have a couple of intriguing cases at the moment.'

She thought briefly about refusing this invitation but knew there would be less effort and obfuscation in complying. She also knew that her refusal would be made partly out of spite, partly out of sorrow: spite because it seemed that he still wanted her company and it was in her gift to withhold it, and sorrow because she had once enjoyed these visits to the Maternity Hospital and now felt there was no point to them.

Therein lay the crux of the matter, which lay beyond Raven, his engagement and the transference of his affections. She no longer knew what her purpose was or should be.

Raven shepherded Sarah up the steps of Milton House, his hand hovering close to her waist. She could feel the heat of him, could smell his shaving soap. She had a sudden urge to caress his face, to feel the smoothness of his cheek, the slight puckering where skin met scar.

She should not have come here. It was a form of torture.

'There are several patients here that are of interest at present,' he said as he pushed open the door. 'One in particular. A thirty-nine-year-old woman in the seventh month of pregnancy, admitted last week with increasing breathlessness on climbing stairs.'

Sarah tried to focus on what he was saying. He spoke to her as though she were a colleague, or a student he was instructing. Now she wondered why he did so, why he would encourage her interest.

'Much troubled by swollen legs,' he continued. 'Before you ask, her urine has been tested but showed no appearance of albumen on application of heat or nitric acid.'

He had barely closed the door when the matron appeared, a sense of panic about her.

'Dr Raven, thank goodness you're here. Come through to the kitchen. I think one of the patients is in danger of suffocation.'

Sarah wondered if someone was choking on the lumpy porridge that was foisted upon the patients several times a day, but when they reached the kitchen it became clear that the situation was considerably more complicated than that.

A woman was sitting on a chair beside the kitchen door, supported by another patient. She was breathing rapidly but ineffectually. Her lips were tinged with blue despite the heaving of her chest. Her eyes were wide and staring. She looked terrified.

'This is the patient I was telling you about,' Raven said as he knelt beside her.

'Oh, doctor,' she gasped. 'I can't get a breath.'

'Sarah, help me loosen her clothes,' Raven instructed.

Sarah unbuttoned the woman's dress and pulled at the ties on her stays, wondering why she was wearing such a thing. It was not tight to begin with and Sarah's unpicking of the knots made little difference. Her palms were damp with sweat, whether her own or the patient's she could not tell.

The woman was still struggling for breath and if anything appeared to be deteriorating. White frothy fluid began bubbling from her mouth.

'Let's get her into bed,' Raven instructed, and between them they partly dragged, partly carried her through to the ward, Raven asking the matron as they did to prepare some sulphate of zinc. 'An emetic,' he clarified, though Sarah was hardly likely to ask for explanations now.

Once in bed the patient looked no better. She sat upright, grasping at the sheets, her breathing laboured and noisy, a rattling sound emanating from deep within her congested chest.

The matron returned. The patient readily swallowed the draught given to her, but it seemed to do no good. Large quantities of frothy mucus were now pouring from her mouth, her complexion livid, her eyes staring. She flailed her arms, gasping for air, then grabbed at Sarah's sleeve, clutching at the material, fear in her face. After two further ineffectual inspirations she fell backwards onto the bed.

Sarah was struggling to comprehend what was happening. They had only just arrived. She could not be dead already, could she?

'Pull the bed to the window,' Raven ordered.

Sarah helped him to do this but wondered what he was planning. It seemed obvious that the patient was beyond all effectual aid. A bit of fresh air was hardly going to revive her. But this was not a time for questions.

'I can feel no pulse,' matron said.

Raven put his ear to the patient's chest. Frothy mucus was now running from both her mouth and her nostrils, her eyes wide open, unblinking, staring into the far distance.

'Give me a knife,' Raven demanded.

Without a word, Matron pulled a bistoury from a drawer

in a nearby cabinet. Sarah took a step back from the bed, her mouth dry.

Raven took the knife and cut through the thin material of the patient's dress, pulling it aside to expose the taut skin of the lower abdomen beneath. Without any further hesitation he made an incision. The uterus appeared, blossoming upwards between the cut edges of skin and muscle. He made a further cut, sticking his hand in through the opening, amniotic fluid spilling around his wrist and onto the bed.

He pulled the child out. It looked pale and clean, but also quite dead. Raven called for cold water, dashed it on the baby's chest, gave it a rub, then put his lips to the infant's tiny mouth and filled its lungs with air. He repeated this several times, rubbing the chest between breaths.

Sarah realised she was holding her own breath, willing life into the little body, though it appeared hopeless.

After several minutes, something miraculous happened. Sarah could see pulsations in the umbilical cord where it attached to the child. Raven placed his ear on the infant's chest and confirmed that he could hear the heart beating. He cut the cord and handed the child to the matron, who was standing with a warm towel waiting to receive it.

Raven stood for a moment, bloody fluid dripping from his sleeves, then bent over the prostrate woman again to complete his task. He worked less frantically, more methodically now. He removed the placenta and stitched the wound. When he was finished, he paused. He looked down at the patient as though only now becoming aware of what he had done.

Sarah handed him a towel and he wiped his hands. The bed was a mess, blood and fluid soaked into it. Raven reached forward, closed the woman's eyes and pulled the sheet over her. He murmured something. Sarah thought for a moment that he was praying. Then she realised that it was not a prayer but an apology.

'I'm so sorry,' he said.

Sarah suddenly felt light-headed. Dark spots began to appear at the periphery of her vision. She looked round for a chair and sat down heavily, taking a few deep breaths and hoping that she would not faint. As her own breathing slowed, her vision began to clear. She looked at the clock above the fireplace at the far end of the room. No more than twenty minutes had passed from the time they had walked through the front door.

Raven sat at the desk in the cramped room matron used as her office. He was bathed in the light from a small window, scribbling his notes in the little book he always carried with him. His hair was dishevelled and was becoming more so as he ran his fingers through it.

Sarah sipped from the glass of water that she had been given. She could still feel the drying sweat in her hairline, the patch of dampness at the back of her dress.

'How could you do that?' she asked.

He looked up from his notes, surprised at the question.

'There was no hope of saving the mother, so I had to try to save the life of the child.'

'You misunderstand me. I mean how could you remain so calm in the face of such tragedy? I know that I could not. I did not. But you did.'

He gave her a weak smile, finished what he was writing and closed the book. He looked at her, concern on his face.

'What is troubling you?'

'Apart from witnessing a sudden death?'

Raven sighed. 'You have not been yourself of late.'

Under other circumstances this statement could have unleashed a torrent of vituperation. Of course she had not been herself. What did he think was the matter with her? It should be obvious, shouldn't it? But she was too tired to fight. Too tired to explain. So, she said nothing.

In the absence of any explanation from her, Raven tried to justify his own behaviour, supply some reassurance.

'You learn how to deal with these things, little by little,' he said gently.

'They won't let me learn though, will they?'

Raven looked as though he was about to speak again but she forestalled him.

'I am thinking of leaving Queen Street,' she said.

'Leave Queen Street? Why? To go where?'

'There is no reason for me to stay.'

Raven looked alarmed and there was some comfort in that. A tiny piece of consolation.

'I will never be able to do what you do,' she said, 'and perhaps I was wrong to ever wish it. At most I can be half of something. Less than half of something.'

'What do you mean?'

He got up from behind the desk and began to move towards her, but she put her hands up to stop him. She feared she would collapse completely if he came too near.

'I have been deluding myself. It was all a foolish dream from which Elizabeth Blackwell helped shake me awake.'

'What did she say to you?'

He seemed angry now, but Sarah did not want his outrage.

'The specifics of what she said do not matter. What matters is that she was right. I am wasting my time. I would have made efforts to move out already were it not for Christina.'

'Christina?' Raven asked. 'What about her?'

He looked confused now. Bamboozled. Under other circumstances she would have found some humour in it, but there was nothing amusing about any of this.

She realised that she had said more than she intended, but it felt good to confide in someone.

'Christina had a baby before she came to Queen Street, a boy. She was forced to give him up but now she wants to find out what happened to him. There is a woman in Dickson's Close, a Mrs King, who arranged for the child to be adopted. That is where I was headed today when we met. I was going back to try to find her.'

'Going back?'

'I have been before but found no one at home. A neighbour thinks that she might have moved on. I thought, if nothing else, I might drag a bit more information from the neighbour. Perhaps she has heard something or can provide some clue as to where Mrs King has gone.'

'If there are clues to be had, they are likely to be in the house itself, don't you think?'

'Well, yes. But how do I gain access when there is no one there?'

Raven gave her a look that she recognised. Mischievous. Roguish. Dangerous.

'We break in,' he said.

TWENTY-NINE

aven followed Sarah into the narrow vennel of Dickson's Close. It was as gloomy and oppressive as before, even in the late afternoon, little light finding its way between the high walls. The ground beneath their feet was uneven, large stagnant puddles coalescing in places to form small lakes. Raven instinctively reached to take Sarah's hand as they negotiated their way between them, then restrained himself, unsure of how she might react.

He was relieved that she had allowed him to accompany her, alarmed by the thought that she had previously come here alone. That was Sarah, though. Not fearless in the face of danger, for only a fool could be truly so, but undeterred by it.

That was why it had been painful to see her in the matron's office looking so untypically unsure of herself, so wracked by doubt. Raven's perception of her was of someone formidable, of there being nothing she could not achieve once she had made it her purpose. There was no obstacle she could fail to overcome with her confounding intelligence and infuriating tenacity. Sometimes it seemed that her indignation alone could drive back an army. And yet there she had sat before him, Icarus bereft of his wings. She had been inspired by Elizabeth Blackwell's achievements, but having been confronted with the reality of the woman, it appeared all the fight had gone out of her.

A little voice whispered that if only he had waited, she would have become amenable to the idea of being his wife and assistant. In fact, she might have arrived at that point already, given her reaction to his news. But he could not bear the thought of her wishing to be with him only because her dreams had been crushed; of a lesser, chastened version of Sarah submitting to him. What kind of life would they have had together if they both knew that marriage to him had been a mere consolation? Surely she would resent him for taking advantage of her wretchedness, as he might come to resent her through knowing that he had been her second choice.

But was Eugenie *his* consolation, he wondered, *his* second choice? Raven thought of how his mother had married his father against her family's wishes and warnings. Was it better to know what you wanted and not be able to have it, or to get what you wanted and learn it was a mistake?

Raven would take the former, for in not having Sarah he had learned the value of Eugenie. What mattered was that he knew he and Eugenie could be happy together. They were a good fit, as Dr Todd put it, though Raven was still curious as to whether this remark had been entirely complimentary.

His feelings for Sarah had not changed. He knew that. He loved her but he did not wish to possess her. He wanted her to aspire, to dream, to always be more than she was yesterday. And right now, he wanted her to understand that just because you cannot reach the sun does not mean you cannot fly at all.

She showed him to Mrs King's address, clearly doubtful that he would be able to effect the entry he had suggested. The door looked imposingly sturdy, but often it was the frame that presented a weakness: hinges screwed into softening wood, rotted and warped by the weather.

Raven was considering whether he ought to kick or shoulder

it when he became aware of movement and glimpsed another door closing further along the close. Someone had been taking a curious peek at what was going on. Sarah had noticed it too.

'That's the neighbour,' she said. 'The woman I spoke to before.'

Raven was conscious that an act of noisy destruction was not going to go unnoticed. For what it was worth, he gripped the handle and gave it a twist. The door opened freely.

'I thought you said it was locked.'

'I didn't. I merely said there was no reply to my knocking.'

'And you didn't try it?'

'I am not in the habit of intruding into places uninvited and unauthorised.'

Raven gave her a sceptical look. 'Maybe not in the habit, but you can hardly claim you are entirely unaccustomed. Duncan and Flockhart's?' he reminded her.

He noticed her blush, and suspected it was not merely at the memory of breaking into the pharmacy on Princes Street. It was when they had first kissed, a moment that felt stolen and illicit, hiding in the darkness of a place they were not supposed to be. But Raven had fresher memories of kissing someone else, in darkness and in secret. There had been something stolen and illicit about that too.

They stepped through the door. What light there was in the alley did little to penetrate the gloom within. The smell of damp was overpowering. There was something sharper in it too, like ammonia.

'Can you see a window?' Sarah asked. 'Perhaps there are shutters preventing any daylight getting in.'

'I can't see anything,' Raven replied.

He took another cautious step into the darkness and jarred his knee against something. There was no point in proceeding – they were not going to find anything if they could not see.

'Perhaps you could ask if your acquaintance next door might oblige us with a candle,' he suggested, rubbing his knee.

'She didn't strike me as particularly obliging last time. Maybe you should try.'

Raven left her hovering at the entrance and hurried along the alley. He knocked on the door from which he had recently been spied upon. It was not opened by the woman Sarah had described, but by an old man. He stuck his head out into the alley and looked to where Sarah was standing.

'Looking for Mrs King, are you? She's not here any more.'

He regarded Raven with intense scrutiny.

'I know you,' he said, his expression softening. 'Aye. I saw you at Queen Street. I suffer terrible from my lungs. You gave me medicine. Donnie Mackay,' he said enthusiastically.

Raven smiled, feigning recognition. There were times when he felt he must have seen half the faces in Edinburgh inside his consulting room.

'Mr Mackay, that's right! I wonder if I might impose upon you for the loan of a candle?'

'Oh, for an associate of Dr Simpson's I can do you better than that.'

He disappeared into his dwelling and returned momentarily bearing a safety lamp, its wick enclosed in a cylinder of wire gauze.

'Thirty years a miner,' he said. 'This and a bad chest are all I've got to show for it.'

Sarah held open the door as Raven approached, clutching his prize.

'A Davy lamp,' she said, sounding impressed.

As he lit it, she asked: 'Do you know why it's so called?'

Raven could not resist. 'Probably because the alley doesn't get much sun.'

Sarah tutted, evidently in no mood for his poor jokes.

'It is named after its inventor, Humphrey Davy.'

She looked at him for signs of recognition.

'I've heard of him,' Raven said. 'And his experiments with nitrous oxide.'

'He was a man of many interests. He developed this safety lamp to prevent the explosions which could occur when a naked candle flame met with firedamp underground. The wire gauze absorbs heat and prevents the ignition of the gas.'

'Where did you learn that?' Raven asked.

'Where do you think?' she answered archly.

Simpson must have held forth on the subject. The man was a vast repository of arcane information. Raven wondered at his prodigious mental capacity. He seemed to be able to store enormous amounts of information inside his head. Raven struggled enough to cram in the knowledge that was immediately relevant. It seemed inconceivable to have any space left over for anything else.

Venturing inside, he thought it was as well they had illumination fit for the darkest pit. They were now able to ascertain why the place was so dim: an oilcloth had been tacked over the window.

'Why would you block out what little light there is to be had here?' he asked.

'To prevent anyone seeing inside,' Sarah suggested.

Raven pulled the oilcloth back, sending a shower of dust into the air. A thin light penetrated the dirt-streaked glass. Several of the panes were missing or broken. A slight breeze could be felt through the gaps, though the air it carried was far from fresh. Street smells mixed with the damp, mouldy odours of the room. Hardly an improvement.

The room was larger than Raven had expected, with a doorway to a second chamber at the far end. There was a range set into one wall, soot streaks above it reaching to the ceiling, and a pot resting on the hob with a spoon sticking out of it. Sarah took a tentative look, seeming relieved to find it empty. If any food had been left in it, Raven thought, it would have been consumed by the various pests that now inhabited the place. No one had been here for some time.

He observed with a frown that his knee had found the only freestanding article of furniture in the place: a flimsy table, its wood discoloured with dark patches.

Raven proceeded tentatively into the adjoining chamber, noticing as he entered that there were marks on the floor: circular impressions in the dust running parallel to the wall. They appeared to be laid out in a pattern: one, then three pairs, then one again.

'What could have made these?' he asked.

There was another oilcloth obscuring a smaller window. Raven peeled it away, covering his mouth this time, and as the light spilled in, he could see that there was an identical sequence of marks closer to the wall.

'Cots,' said Sarah. 'She had several babies staying here.'

Raven felt his foot brush something and shivered at the thought it might be a rat. Instead, he heard a clatter and saw that he had kicked an empty bottle.

He picked it up and showed Sarah the label. Godfrey's Cordial.

'Laudanum,' she said. 'So that's another reason the windows were blacked out. Keep her little charges asleep.'

As Raven returned to the main room, he saw that the table had an inset drawer in its centre. He pulled it open, but as he did so its very lightness told him he would find nothing.

'What are you looking for?' Sarah asked.

Raven paused. He had hoped to avoid sharing this with her, but she ought to know.

'White tape,' he said. 'There was a baby found in Leith harbour, strangled with white tape and wrapped up in parcel paper. I was present at the post-mortem.'

Even in the half-light Raven could see the concern on Sarah's face.

'Male or female?'

'A boy.'

'Did he have a birthmark?' she asked. 'On the left arm?'

'No. And there's no such tape here.'

Sarah nodded with relieved satisfaction, her expression indicating she had seen enough.

'It will be of little comfort to Christina,' she said, 'but I believe I know what happened to her son. This woman did not only look after babies, she found homes for unwanted ones. She would have collected a fee at both ends of the transaction.'

'Not passing them on, but selling them on,' said Raven.

'Christina fell behind on her payments, so Mrs King sold her baby to some childless couple. Sold *all* the babies, then absconded so that they could not be claimed back.'

As she said this, Raven realised he was wrong to imagine the dead child from Leith had been murdered in this place. Mrs King would not be so wasteful. The babies kept here had been valuable to her, though their worth was measured in pounds, shillings and pence. The wee boy in the parcel had been thrown away as worthless.

He wondered what answers McLevy might have found on Candlemaker Row and hoped the detective had not bumped into Charles Dymock in the meantime.

Raven watched Sarah as she looked the place up and down once more, checking for anything they might have missed. A smile crept across his face, which she noticed.

'What?' she asked.

'Nothing. You just look more like your old self.'

'How so?'

'I think it's the sight of you doing something you're not supposed to.'

Mr Mackay was standing in his doorway waiting for them as they re-emerged into the alley. Raven suspected he had been keeping a curious watch the whole time. He probably had little else to do.

As Raven handed over the Davy lamp with his thanks, the

man glanced in the direction of the Cowgate, from where a woman was approaching on unsteady feet, carrying a hessian bag.

'That'll be the missus,' he said.

Mrs Mackay eyed Sarah inquisitively, taking a moment to consider why she was familiar. Her eyes narrowed as recognition passed over her face, followed by a look of wariness. Then her features became animated as something seemed to occur to her.

'You were looking for Mrs King, aye? I think I saw her not ten minutes ago. I was cutting through Greyfriars on my way down to the Grassmarket. I saw her going into a haberdasher's, just down from the Covenanters' Memorial.'

'You *think* you saw her,' Raven said.

'Well, when I say that, I mean I didn't want to catch her eye, so I didn't stare. But I'm fairly sure it was her.'

'And what does she look like?' asked Sarah.

'She was wearing a blue shawl and a grey hat. Not but five minutes ago, really. If you hurry you might catch her.'

'Thank you,' Sarah said, before taking off at speed, altogether less mindful of the grimy puddles as she made her way out of the close. She turned right onto the Cowgate, Raven running to keep up with her.

'Do you know this memorial she mentioned?' Sarah asked as the crowded Grassmarket loomed ahead of them.

'Can't say that I do.'

Now Raven did take her hand for fear that they might become separated in the ebb and flow of bodies. The touch of her fingers sent a spark through him.

They made their way down the full length of the Grassmarket, then turned around and retraced their steps in case they had missed anything. They passed the Black Bull, the Beehive, the Clydesdale and the Market Inn in quick succession, the working men of these parts evidently fuelled by beer and whisky.

There was no sign of either a memorial or a haberdasher's.

Raven realised what fools they had been. *I saw her not ten minutes ago.* Then *Not but five . . . If you hurry you might catch her.*

'I think she just wanted rid of us,' he said.

Sarah rolled her eyes by way of agreement.

Raven still had hold of her hand. It felt awkward now. Wrong somehow. He let it go.

'I'm sorry,' he said.

'There is no need to apologise. I'm glad that you came along.'

'We didn't learn very much.'

'I know a little more than I did.'

He wanted to find some way to maintain the concord that had resumed between them.

'Perhaps you can do something for me in return,' he said, more in hope than expectation. 'I am frustrated in an endeavour of my own.'

Sarah smiled. It was like the sun coming out.

'How can I help?'

THIRTY

he care of the poor should not depend upon Christian charity. Poverty should not be seen as inevitable, an inescapable feature of the human condition. I believe it can be eliminated by the application of liberal principles: social equality and fairness, self-help and self-improvement through education and temperance. Let us use the powers of the state to improve the lives of all of our citizens: men and women, rich and poor.'

There was genuine enthusiasm in the applause as Teddy Hamilton concluded his address. Raven looked round the room. A wide range of people were represented here this evening: the haves and the have-nots; the well-to-do and those who had to make do. He had seldom seen so many ill-matched individuals congregated in one place. The closest had been in church, but even there parishioners were largely segregated according to wealth, from the polished pews at the front to the rough-hewn benches at the back.

It was the first such meeting he had attended, although Sarah had been to a few. She seemed to be a collector of radical pamphlets, soaking up the righteous indignation to be found in them. Raven was not averse to the concept of change, to improving the lot of the downtrodden, but he remained sceptical of those who proposed easy answers to complex and seemingly intractable problems.

'He thinks that the Church still has too much administrative power when it comes to dealing with the poor,' Sarah said, as though Raven was in need of schooling on the subject. 'The Poor Law makes provisions for the infirm but not the able-bodied unemployed; abandoned women with children receive no special consideration. Mr Hamilton favours a secular system of standardised state relief,' she continued, a little too much admiration in her tone for Raven's liking.

'He's brave if he thinks that he can take on the might of the Kirk and get away with it,' Raven said. He could feel his irritation building, like an itchy rash. He had not come here to listen to Teddy Hamilton's pontifications on the plight of the poor, of which Raven had considerably more practical knowledge. He was interested solely in what he might discover about the man himself, which was why he had asked Sarah if he might accompany her to the meeting. He had been explicit in his motives, filling her in on all he knew about Sir Ainsley's death, and his mission, at Eugenie's request, on Gideon's behalf.

He looked at Teddy again, gathering up his notes at the podium. He was handsome, articulate and – perhaps most importantly – blessed with the correct accent and consequent enunciation. Cut from a certain cloth and therefore not so easily dismissed as a rabble-rouser, he was the kind of man people listened to.

Raven realised that if Teddy's proselytising fervour was as real as it appeared, then it must have been a torment to remain silent and deferential in the presence of his uncle. Sir Ainsley's money, power and influence represented everything Teddy and his political allies were going to have to overcome.

'It's good that he is specifically highlighting the plight of women,' Raven suggested, hoping it would please Sarah.

There was a loud snort from the lady standing beside them.

'The plight of women requires more than Teddy Hamilton's proposals to remedy it. He talks of extending the franchise but do not be fooled. It is universal male suffrage he favours.'

She was an older lady, fashionably dressed. Raven recognised her but could not recall from where. Sarah had no such problem.

'How wonderful to see you again, Mrs Crowe. I so enjoyed the book you gave me.'

This did not help Raven at all. Sarah rescued him.

'Have you been introduced to Dr Will Raven, assistant to Dr Simpson?'

'I don't believe I have had the pleasure,' she replied. 'It's been a while since I attended one of Dr Simpson's dinners.'

Raven managed to piece it all together. Catherine Crowe. Author. Rather eccentric. Legendary imbiber of ether at Queen Street. Held literary salons at her home at Darnaway Street, which Mina attended on occasion.

Teddy had now stepped down from the podium and was shaking hands with a number of bewhiskered gentlemen while a group of ladies looked on admiringly.

'It appears he has won them over,' Raven said.

'He has the makings of a political leader, no doubt about that,' Mrs Crowe replied. 'He has charisma, passion and the ability to rally a crowd. But there is one thing he lacks: money. Speeches are all well and good, but you need a fortune behind you to get anywhere in politics.'

'I am surprised that finance is an issue,' Raven said. 'Given his provenance I would have assumed that money was not in short supply.'

Mrs Crowe looked at him as though he had said something profoundly stupid.

'His mother was Sir Ainsley's sister. They live modestly because all the family money and property went to Sir Ainsley after their father died.'

Raven was unembarrassed by his error. Indeed, it had been helpful. Did this mean that Teddy had a motive to want Sir Ainsley dead? Raven was still new to the laws regarding primogeniture and inheritance. Given his own situation, it was not something he had needed to take an interest in before – his own father had bequeathed him little more than a pocket watch and an occasional propensity for violence.

Raven realised that he had lost the thread of the conversation going on around him, too intent on trying to unscramble his own thoughts. He heard something about the lot of prostitutes and caught up fast: the contagious diseases ordinance that Ainsley had been so keen on.

'It wouldn't have got anywhere at all if it wasn't for the provost's sudden change of heart on the matter,' Mrs Crowe said.

'Why do you think Mr Mansfield reversed his position?' Raven asked.

'In the world of politics, who knows? But there are those who say you would be better asking Abigail Findlay.'

Raven remembered being briefly introduced at the soirée. She was the wife of Auberon Findlay, Dean of the Faculty of Advocates.

'There are rumours that she and Mansfield are lovers, despite both being married.'

Raven noticed Sarah's eyes widen at this revelation. Not at the information itself but at the manner in which it was being relayed. Mrs Crowe was being magnificently indiscreet.

'Just gossip, of course. If we had a means of proving it, perhaps we could have prevailed upon the provost to take our side in the matter. As it stands, Sir Ainsley's demise has made the problem go away. At least until someone else proposes it again, or something worse.'

Raven thought about what Dr Simpson had told him at Bannockburn: Sir Ainsley used means other than money to coerce people. He remembered Mansfield's stilted, reluctant contribution to their discussion at the soirée. He was obedient after a direct prompt, like he'd had his leash jerked by his master.

Then he recalled Mansfield skulking in the gallery that night, ducking out of sight the moment he was seen.

If an affair were to be exposed, it would be the end of him. Ruinous for his career, disastrous for Abigail Findlay, scandalous and damaging for the dean. Mansfield seemed a decent man, one who would not wish to precipitate all that. It stood to reason that if some manner of proof existed, then Sir Ainsley had possessed it, most likely through Sanderson. It was another instance whereby Sir Ainsley's demise made the problem go away.

Suspects were beginning to pile up. Teddy, Mansfield, Findlay and his wife. All had reasons to wish Sir Ainsley dead, but wishing and doing were quite different things.

Teddy had by now disentangled himself from his admirers and was making his way over to Raven's group.

'Mrs Crowe,' he said, making a great show of kissing her hand, 'what a delight it is to see you here.'

'Oh, Teddy. Save your charm for the younger ladies. I am impervious to it.'

Raven noticed a little reddening of her cheeks that suggested otherwise.

'Dr Raven, isn't it?' Teddy said. 'Dr Simpson's assistant.'

'Well remembered,' Raven acknowledged, thinking a memory for names and faces was another attribute that would serve a man well in politics. 'This is my associate, Miss Fisher,' he added, by way of introduction.

Teddy raised an eyebrow at 'associate', but Raven often struggled to find a suitable descriptor. What was he supposed to say? Friend? Acquaintance?

Teddy made a bow, smiled. It was Sarah's turn to blush a little.

Who was this man, with his uncanny ability to make women redden in his presence? Raven felt a pang of something, an uncomfortable twist in the gut. Was he jealous? If he was, he realised he was going to have to get used to that feeling. Where Sarah chose to plant her affections was now none of his concern.

'I was sorry to hear about the death of your uncle,' Sarah said.

Teddy paused before responding to her condolences. His polite answer when it arrived was an unenlightening one, full of the usual platitudes.

'It's very upsetting for everyone,' he said. 'I particularly feel for Mrs Chalmers, who was to be his new wife.'

'Do you think Gideon was involved?' Sarah asked.

Raven was surprised by her candour. Perhaps she was not as charmed by Teddy as he had assumed. It was the question he wanted to ask, but he had planned a cautious route to get there. Sarah had cut straight to it, spurred on perhaps by the presence of the forthright Mrs Crowe.

Again, Teddy was careful in his response.

'It's hard to imagine', he said, 'a son killing his father.'

He bowed again, graced them with a sad smile, and then resumed his circuit of the room. He was immediately swallowed up by a gaggle of young women. Mrs Crowe spotted someone she just *had* to speak to and disappeared too, leaving Sarah and Raven alone, marooned in a little island of calm amongst the excited throng.

'There is no denying his popularity,' Sarah said.

'Like a cult,' Raven replied. 'Or some form of demonic possession. Perhaps he induced one of them to slip some arsenic into Sir Ainsley's supper.'

'I think you are overestimating his powers of persuasion.'

'Really? It is not unprecedented: the idea that radicals and anarchists might turn to murder in pursuit of their goals.'

'Hardly the sans-culotte, are they?' Sarah scoffed.

She looked at Teddy again. 'I don't think that he had anything to do with it.'

'What makes you say that?'

'If the idea was to gain the Douglas inheritance for himself, how could he know that Amelia would renounce her son's claim?'

Cutting to the nub of the issue as usual, Raven thought.

'Depends how well they know one another, I suppose. If Teddy is an anti-establishment radical and Amelia believes that wealth and privilege are corrupting, it is not beyond the realms of possibility that they discussed what she did and did not want for her son.'

Sarah looked profoundly sceptical.

Raven put his hands up in an attitude of surrender.

'I admit that this is where the theory of Teddy's involvement falls down.'

'You ought to be careful, Will Raven,' Sarah said. 'You are allowing your attachment to Eugenie to cloud your judgment.'

She swirled off towards the exit, evidently having had enough of radical politics and Raven's disjointed theorising for one evening.

He let her go. He needed a moment alone to think. Was she right that his relationship with Eugenie was skewing his thinking? Was Gideon's guilt obvious? Much as he disliked the man, he still felt duty-bound to exclude all other possibilities.

Gideon said that Sir Ainsley had enemies more powerful than him. Perhaps what was significant was that Sir Ainsley had other enemies who were *weak* before him, as Gideon had been. People who did not have the means to go up against him directly and who might seek a subtler way to cut him down.

Who stood to gain most from his death? Dr Todd had asked.

Teddy would gain a fortune and, among other things, a newspaper. Together they represented a means to effect change, to wield real influence. The provost, Mansfield, stood to regain his autonomy by freeing himself from Sir Ainsley's leash.

And yet, even as he weighed all these possibilities, Raven could not ignore the fact that it was Gideon who had the most to benefit and the deepest reason to wish his father dead. Most importantly he had the means to do so. Not just the arsenic, but the will to use it, and this last part was crucial. Other people might idly wish a man dead, might even kill a man in the grip of rage, but to murder him in a premeditated and coldly deliberate way, you needed deep, lingering hatred. Raven had seen that in Gideon long before his father's death, on a night he could never forget.

Raven had been tutoring Gideon early one evening, following what had already been a long day preparing for a forthcoming exam of his own. As ever it felt like a losing battle, Raven struggling to imbue understanding into this singularly undisciplined student. So when Gideon had suggested they instead adjourn to a nearby tavern, Raven had acquiesced despite his instinctive misgivings.

Amid the tavern's raucous throng, it was not long before Raven remembered why he tended not to associate with Gideon beyond the university's walls. The fellow did not require much ale to become obnoxious, venting ignorant opinions and running his mouth off to people as though everyone present was there as his servant. Raven had been frankly embarrassed to be in his company.

Most of the clientele knew well enough to ignore such a blowhard, but there were a couple of men worse for their drink who took him to task. Unnerved by their vocal ferocity, Gideon had piped down, suddenly mindful that in fact nobody here owed him any deference. However, when he later noticed them making for the door, he was unable to resist barking out a parting shot.

'Back to the alley with you, you pair of mangy mongrels!'

Raven had recognised the cowardice of one emboldened only when he thought his enemy in retreat.

By the time he and Raven headed back into the night, Gideon had probably forgotten all about them. Unfortunately, the two men had not forgotten Gideon. They emerged from a doorway close to the tavern, blocking the way.

'You're in our alley now, your lordship.'

Raven assessed the situation as a matter of reflex. He saw that one of them carried a heavy bludgeon, the other a length of chain. They meant serious harm, of that he had no doubt. But they were drunk, they were old, and an evening in Gideon's company had put Raven in one of those moods that Henry so feared.

Things happened quickly after that. He remembered Gideon being knocked to the ground right away. He went down without a fight, curled up in the mud, arms about his head as his assailant whipped at him with the chain.

Raven quickly dispatched his man, wresting the bludgeon from him and driving it into his gut. The fellow lurched and listed, seeming as drunk as he was winded, before collapsing in a heap against the wall.

Raven then used the weapon to defend himself against Gideon's assailant, who came lashing at him with the chain. Raven let it wrap around the bludgeon, then pulled it from his opponent's grip before swinging the shaft two-handed between the man's legs.

Raven was watching him drop to his knees when he was blindsided by the first drunk roaring back. He launched himself into Raven with a leap, the two of them ending up rolling on the ground in a mess of gouging hands and shifting weight. As Raven wrestled and clawed with him, he caught sight of Gideon kicking and stamping the other man, who was helpless on the ground. Raven had seldom seen such fury, such viciousness. He could tell Gideon would not stop, utterly lost in his frenzy. Raven thus found himself in the absurd circumstance of having to defeat one drunk in order to save the man's companion.

Raven debilitated him with a blow to the throat, then scrambled to his feet and dragged Gideon away before he could inflict any further damage.

He still saw the man from time to time around the Old

Town. He was hard to miss these days, distinguished by his eye patch. He had lost the eye that night, Raven had little doubt; and but for Raven's intervention, Gideon would have surely killed him. As he kicked and stamped, blind in his rage, he had been screaming, 'I hate you! I hate you!'

It was clear even then that he was not addressing the man on the ground. At the time, Raven had no notion who Gideon really wanted to hurt.

But he did now.

THIRTY-ONE

fter the unseasonal chill of the past few days, sunshine had returned to remind Raven that it was indeed summer, even in Edinburgh. He spotted Dr Simpson marching along Castle Street towards the Caledonian Hotel and sprinted to catch up. Lady Furness was awaiting her consultation with the professor and Raven was pleased to have finished his morning duties in time to accompany him.

'Ah, there you are, Will. Beautiful day, isn't it?'

'Indeed it is.'

'A walk in the sun in Princes Street Gardens. That is my standard prescription for those prone to hypochondriasis,' Simpson declared, then added as a whispered aside, 'The place will be awash with valetudinarians today.'

He laughed as he said this, though Raven suspected there was likely to be some truth in it.

Simpson seemed to be in a jovial mood and Raven had no wish to spoil it, but he did have some questions he wished to ask. The professor always seemed to know a great deal about what was going on in Edinburgh at any moment – though given the amount of gossip Raven was sifting through, Mina might have been a better bet.

'I heard Teddy Hamilton speak at a meeting last night,' Raven said. 'It got me thinking about unmarried mothers and the fostering of their children.'

'Oh yes?'

'I know that is something you and Mrs Simpson have been involved in.'

'We try to find good homes for children whose mothers are not in a position to take care of them. Unfortunately, it is not an unusual situation, and often a complicated one. The consequence of seduction, adultery: there are many reasons but always the same outcome. Shame and dishonour if it should become common knowledge. And frequently the mother bears this alone.'

'So, if the child can be secretly spirited away the mother retains her good name?'

'That is the idea. Otherwise she is seen as tainted and her prospects limited.'

'That seems unfair. The father is never held accountable.'

'Some assist financially if they are in a position to do so.'

'But the child is never acknowledged.'

'Not in my experience. Reputation and good standing are of paramount importance in this world.'

Raven paused before proceeding, wondering if it was wise to share what he had learned from Mrs Crowe. There was no delicate way of putting it.

'I recently heard talk of an affair between the provost and the wife of the Dean of the Faculty of Advocates. Have you heard anything about this?'

Dr Simpson gave him a quizzical look. 'I did not think you one for such idle chatter, Will.'

Raven was about to protest but Dr Simpson continued, 'I have not heard anything of it, but it must be acknowledged that the fishwives of Newhaven trade less gossip than the great and the good of this city. That said, rumour and gossip emanating from such circles, in my experience, tend to have at least a whiff of truth about them. The remarkable thing is that more scandal does not seep out.'

'I just wondered whether perhaps it was this that Sir Ainsley Douglas held over Mansfield to force him to fall into line.'

'Quite possibly. As I said, this is a city where reputation is everything. They are all obsessed with status and posterity. How they will be remembered. It is as though they are in a hurry to lie beneath the turf, so long as there is a headstone grandly inscribed with glowing achievements.'

Dr Simpson, who was now getting up quite a head of steam, began gesticulating as he spoke, and Raven noted that his right hand was sporting a neat bandage. Sarah's work, presumably.

'They ought to be wary,' Simpson continued, 'for posterity is a capricious mistress. You might accumulate a lifetime of good deeds and noble achievements, but then be remembered for one weakness or failure, as long as it proves sufficiently conspicuous.'

He continued to wave his bandaged hand around.

'Beware any man who wishes to seize upon another fellow's weakness or failure as though it were his prize. It is often a sign of his own wretchedness: that secretly he knows he is worthless.'

'That cannot be said of Sir Ainsley Douglas, though, can it?' Raven said. 'He was a proud man of wealth and standing, his reputation untarnished by scandal.'

They were approaching the hotel entrance. Raven opened the door and stood aside to let Simpson go through. The professor stopped and looked at him before proceeding.

'A man can be all these things,' he said, 'and yet know deep inside that he is rotten.'

They crossed the hotel foyer, all chintz and ferns, and were on their way to the stairs when Dr Simpson was waylaid by a woman in black. So many people seemed to know him, and he always made himself available to them, despite time seldom being in abundance. From the grave look on this lady's face Raven could tell that this was not going to be a happy encounter. He resisted the temptation to check his watch. If Simpson dallied with this woman, they would be late for their appointment with the titled lady on the second floor.

'Oh, Dr Simpson,' the woman said, 'I have been in anguish since you saw my son. You must tell me: is he going to die?'

Raven knew nothing about the case, but could tell she was not some bored attention-seeker like Lady Mackenzie, and her son troubled by something far graver than 'queer sensations'.

Simpson looked her in the eye, his expression sincere, lacking all trace of its usual playfulness. He took her hand. 'Your boy knows,' he said. 'Nature told him as she has told you. And we doctors should leave such things for nature to tell. Her message comes softly to patient and friends when there is no more hope of life here.'

The woman nodded. She looked sad, but not surprised.

'Thank you,' she said. She gave him a sad smile, withdrew her hand and turned away.

They arrived at Lady Furness's room only a few minutes late, Dr Simpson rendered a little more sombre as a result of his encounter with the dying boy's mother. As they approached the door, a short, grey, dour-looking man, well known to them both, was taking his leave.

'What the devil are you doing here?' Professor Syme demanded, his words exploding from his mouth in a mist of ungentlemanly spittle.

'I could ask you the same,' Simpson replied.

'I have been providing a surgical consultation and can assure you, quite categorically, that the lady within does not require the services of a man-midwife.'

This last was said with an ill-concealed contempt.

'Need I remind you, sir, that I am a physician. As such, I deal with so much more than delivering babies.'

'Need I remind *you*, sir, that none of us should trespass into areas that are beyond our competence. Surgery should be left to surgeons, don't you think?'

Dear God, thought Raven. Here we go again. He wondered if Syme was alluding to a recent case where a patient had died after Simpson performed a minor surgical procedure. Rumours had spread that she died of haemorrhage as a result of Simpson's incompetence, rumours that were subsequently proven – largely thanks to Sarah's efforts – to be egregious and without substance. Had Syme also been involved in maligning Dr Simpson's good name? Raven had not suspected so at the time. All of the culprits had been identified. Or so he thought.

'Are you questioning my competence?' Simpson asked, a steely note in his tone now. 'I will not tolerate being slandered.'

'And I do not bear false witness,' Syme replied, unapologetically. 'I speak as I find.'

'How dare you address me in such a fashion. I have done nothing to merit such vilification.'

'That is a matter of opinion.'

Both men now looked to be on the point of detonation, thrumming with barely suppressed rage. Raven was beginning to think he would have to step between the two professors to prevent any further escalation.

Their raised voices had drawn the attention of whoever was behind the door. A young woman, the lady's maid presumably, peered out at them, unsure how to proceed given that two eminent medical gentlemen appeared about to come to blows in the hallway.

The two men continued to stare at each other. Raven held his breath.

A voice was heard from within: a lady's register, high and flighty.

'Is that Dr Simpson?' she trilled. 'The great Simpson of Edinburgh?'

The professor smiled. Wide. Broad. Unrestrained. This was perhaps even more provocative than his snarling retort only moments before.

Syme stood his ground for a moment, then rolled his eyes, turned and marched off down the stairs.

THIRTY-TWO

everal hours later, Raven had traded the lobby of the Caledonian Hotel for the lobby of the *Courant*, where a pimply youth manned the desk, if manned was the appropriate word for such a stripling.

'I'm here to see Mr Sanderson,' Raven told him.

The newspaper's premises were situated on the High Street, squeezed between the police office and the Temperance Hotel, and across the street from its competitors, the *Scotsman* and the *Caledonian Mercury*. A triumvirate of newspapers, keeping the citizens of Edinburgh appraised of world events. Raven resented having to be in such close proximity to McLevy's lair again. He was trying to steer clear of the detective since invoking his name during his tense interview with Dymock, the perspiring lawyer.

'Do you have an appointment?'

'I do not, but my business is urgent.'

'Mr Sanderson is too busy to see just anyone who walks in off the street,' the young man said. His tone was rather disparaging, and Raven did not care for it, particularly coming from someone several years his junior. He realised that he was unused to being addressed in such a disrespectful way, having become accustomed to the deference of the patients at Queen Street.

Resigned to the evident reality that someone so junior was not about to disturb the editor on behalf of some random stranger, Raven returned outside to ponder his next move. He looked to his right at the Temperance Hotel and thought it unlikely to be the preferred haunt of journalists and reporters. Sobriety was not an attribute for which they were generally known. He thought about where they were more likely to congregate, a plan forming in his head. His association with Dr Simpson might open Sanderson's door yet, just not in the usual way.

He was about to enter the Black Ram, a public house a few doors down, when he remembered a snatch of conversation from a dinner party some time ago, about Edinburgh newspapermen convening in a tiny howf in Fleshmarket Close. It was a place away from the prying eyes of ordinary passing trade, allowing them to conduct clandestine meetings or perhaps just to enjoy a drink in relative peace.

Raven found the place halfway along the close, a nondescript establishment unlikely to prove inviting to strangers. It was smoky inside, an old man on a stool near the door puffing away energetically on a pipe. Only a couple of the tables were occupied. Raven approached a man sitting on his own, nursing a glass of ale.

'Do you work for the *Courant*, by any chance?'

The man jerked a thumb at another table in the corner, where two men were deep in conversation. Raven wandered over.

'Gentlemen, I have some information that might be of interest,' he said.

'Oh, aye,' said one, barely looking up.

'Regarding Professor Simpson.'

'The chloroform man? Discovered something else, has he?'

'It's more of a personal matter.'

The man sat up a bit, his companion turning round. This was obviously of more interest than another scientific breakthrough.

'Take a seat,' the first man said.

Raven remained standing.

'The information I possess is of a sensitive nature. I will only disclose it to Mr Sanderson himself.'

'I can't go bothering the gaffer with any old rubbish. Who are you anyway?'

'My name is Dr Will Raven. I work with the professor.'

'A doctor, eh? Work at the Infirmary, do you?'

'No. Why?'

'That's a pity. A source of information there would be of use to me. People want all the details, you see. Unusual cases, the outcome of a brawl. That kind of thing.'

'Well, I can't help you with that.'

Raven had no interest in supplying medical gossip to reporters – or anyone else for that matter – whether they attracted emoluments or not. He agreed wholeheartedly with Dr Simpson that trust and confidentiality were sacrosanct.

He handed the man a slip of paper.

'If he's interested, tell Sanderson to meet me there. At the time specified.'

He tipped his hat then made his exit before the man had time to read the details.

There were streaks of red in the evening sky as Raven made his way to the rendezvous. He had little doubt that Sanderson would respond to his message. Given Sir Ainsley's interest in the professor, Raven knew that his bait was too tasty to pass up. His only concern was that, with Sir Ainsley gone, Sanderson might have lost interest, but it seemed unlikely. Information was power to whoever held it.

Crossing the High Street, Raven was unsettled to observe McLevy striding towards him. The detective raised his hand, whether in greeting or to halt his progress Raven was not sure. There was no way of avoiding the man, however much he would have liked to. Thoughts of his deceit towards Dymock loomed prominently in his mind.

'Dr Raven. I have some news that may be of interest.'

'Mr McLevy,' Raven greeted him in turn, touching the brim of his hat.

'That address you discovered on the parcel paper, in Candlemaker Row. Turned out to be that of an elderly bookseller who has his shop there. Says that he throws away such parcel wrappings every day. There was nothing to link him with the death of the child. Reckon the perpetrator lifted the paper from a common midden. So, what seemed to be a promising lead has proved to be worthless.'

'Worth something to Mary Olsen, I would wager,' Raven suggested.

McLevy frowned. He did not relish being reminded of his earlier certainty that he had found the woman responsible.

'What now?' Raven asked.

'There is little more to go on and I have no shortage of other duties to keep me occupied.'

He began to walk away as he said this, presumably to emphasise how busy he was.

Raven proceeded in the opposite direction, towards the Infirmary, hastening his steps to put distance between himself and the detective. He felt relieved there had been no repercussions regarding his interview with Dymock, but as he walked on, relief turned to disappointment. He would have preferred that the address had yielded something. A haberdasher, perhaps. Or a woman in a blue shawl.

Sanderson entered the mortuary at the Infirmary on tentative feet, as though trespassing. Which of course he was. They both were, in fact: Raven should not have been there either.

Raven had thought about offering to meet in a tavern but realised that such an environment would be precisely where

Sanderson was most comfortable. It was the kind of place a news-paperman did much of his business, and where he would probably have friends and colleagues nearby: possibly even unseen, just in case. Instead Raven had decided to host him in an environment where he could put Sanderson on the back foot.

He had arrived early and arranged a variety of surgical imple-ments on the table in the middle of the room: trephine, bistoury, amputation saw. There was also a fresh corpse under a sheet, though Raven had not arranged that. It was merely a happy coincidence. The place had its usual smell about it – nothing too terrible, but unnerving for those unused to it.

He offered his guest a seat, which was initially refused. Then Sanderson felt the full impact of his surroundings and thought better of it, settling himself down on a stool. Raven had forgotten how small the man was: a squirrelly little character, fastidiously neat in his appearance, wearing an exquisitely tailored suit and carrying a gold-topped cane. Very much the Edinburgh paradox: neat and clean on the surface but making his living rummaging in the dirt.

Raven wondered absently why everyone seemed to be so much better dressed than himself.

'Why did you bring me here?' Sanderson asked as he looked around, distaste writ large on his face. 'This of all places, like a dungeon at the heart of a bloody labyrinth. I am a busy man. I don't have time to waste.'

You came running quickly enough at the prospect of some-thing on Dr Simpson, Raven thought.

'You may remember that we were introduced at Sir Ainsley Douglas's soirée,' Raven began. 'I am Professor Simpson's assistant.'

There was no hint of recognition from Sanderson.

'The professor told me that your employer had been trying to wheedle information out of him regarding his discreet role in fostering children. The inconvenient issue of the well-to-do. I know that Ainsley Douglas deployed compromising information as a means of exerting influence on people. I also know that you provided him with much of that information. I imagine that even with Ainsley gone, you would be interested in something that might force Dr Simpson to be less—' He paused as though searching for the most appropriate word '—circumspect.'

'"*Sir* Ainsley" to you, young man. No one called him just "Ainsley".'

'Not to his face, anyway,' Raven suggested.

Sanderson looked round the room again, obviously uncomfortable.

'Well, what have you got for me?' he asked, impatient now.

Raven picked up the amputation saw and examined the blade.

'Nothing,' he answered. 'I have no information to give you regarding Dr Simpson and nor would I divulge it if I had.'

Sanderson's eyes bulged. 'Then what in God's name did you bring me here for?'

'I wanted your admission that it was you who supplied Sir Ainsley with this kind of information.'

'You knew that before I set foot in this ghastly place. Said so yourself. Is that all? Are we done here?'

'I do have a lead on a story. Potentially far bigger than anything Dr Simpson might disclose.'

'And what might that be?'

Sanderson sounded sceptical but curious nonetheless.

'That it was not Gideon Douglas who murdered his father.'

'What?' Sanderson spluttered. 'Of course it was! Poisoned him with arsenic to hasten his inheritance. Oldest story in the book.'

'Arsenic is a metallic poison. Do you understand the significance of that?'

'Chemistry and medicine are not my areas of expertise,' he said irritably.

'It is easily detectable in the body. Evidently you did not

know that, and why would you? But Gideon knew it, as would anyone who had studied medicine. Do you know who else would be unaware?'

Sanderson narrowed his eyes, suddenly less irate. 'Go on.'

'Austin Mansfield.'

'That is preposterous,' he huffed, striking his cane on the stone floor. The noise reverberated around the tiled walls, amplifying his rebuke. Sanderson was overselling his incredulity, and Raven knew why. This was the reason he had brought him here.

'Is it? He was there the night Ainsley died.'

'So were you. So was I. Why on earth would Mansfield want to murder Sir Ainsley?'

'I think you know.'

'Then you are mistaken.'

'It is rumoured that Mansfield was in an adulterous relationship with Abigail Findlay, but I believe Ainsley knew it to be more than gossip. He had hard evidence and he used it to command the provost's support for his contagious diseases ordinance. What proof did he have?'

'I have no idea. He was my employer. He wouldn't have shared that kind of thing with me.'

'We have already established which way round this works: that *you* were paid to procure such things for *him*. What if it was this particular piece of information that got Ainsley murdered? Everyone is fixated on Gideon, but he wasn't the only man with a motive.'

'You're havering,' Sanderson sneered, his lip curling. 'I didn't procure anything. This is no concern of mine.'

He stood up abruptly, turned his back on Raven and made for the door.

'I wouldn't be so sure about that,' Raven said.

Sanderson halted.

'Because if Mansfield was desperate enough to poison Sir

Ainsley Douglas over what he could reveal, he's hardly going to flinch from killing the man who passed him the information.'

Sanderson turned. He looked at Raven as though trying to formulate a response, something to refute what had just been said. He had nothing. If Mansfield was the murderer, and it was clear that Sanderson now believed this a possibility, it was in his best interests to reveal what he knew, for his own protection.

His shoulders slumped and he leaned on his cane, his defiance dispelled.

'There were letters,' he said. 'In Mansfield's hand, to Abigail Findlay. Intimate letters.'

'Stolen from her house?'

'I cannot disclose how I came by them.'

'And where are these letters now? Do you have them?'

'Sir Ainsley took them. They were no doubt safely stowed at Crossford, but are most likely back in Mrs Findlay's possession by now, as I would imagine Dymock will have discreetly recovered them.'

'Recovered them? Dymock?'

Sanderson looking surprised and amused at Raven's ignorance.

'Dymock is Mansfield's brother-in-law. He is married to Mansfield's sister.'

Raven thought of all the papers laid out on Sir Ainsley's desk, and of Dymock's flustered, sweaty look. He realised that the lawyer might have been searching frantically for something specific. Raven could see now why Dymock was not keen that he should look any further into Sir Ainsley's death, and why he was so quick to join in pointing the finger at Gideon. Dymock feared it was his brother-in-law who had murdered Sir Ainsley, and was content for someone else to take the blame.

Sanderson rapped his cane on the floor again, drawing Raven's attention back to the here and now.

'A word to the wise,' he said. 'Power does not lie only in the information one can reveal. It lies also in the information one can withhold. For instance, I know you have plans to marry.'

Raven scoffed. 'So does half the city, it seems. And your point is?'

'To Dr Todd's daughter, Eugenie.'

'Yes. What about her?'

'What indeed,' Sanderson said, and walked out the door.

THIRTY-THREE

he next day, Raven was shown into the morning room at St Andrew Square to discover that Eugenie already had a visitor. Amelia Bettencourt was sitting with her baby on her knee, young Matthew trans-fixed by a coloured refraction of light that was playing on the wall. The child was tightly swaddled, a blanket wrapped around him though the room was warm. Raven immediately thought about the little corpse with the white tape round its neck and hoped it would not be too long before such memories receded. Sometimes there seemed to be too many of them fighting for precedence. It was exhausting.

'Amelia, this is Dr Will Raven,' Eugenie said.

Raven thought he could detect excitement in her voice. Possibly even pride. Something in him warmed to the sound of it, and to the sight of her face. He had spent so long wrestling with his feelings over Sarah that he had forgotten how the mere presence of Eugenie made him feel.

'We have already met,' her friend replied.

'Of course. At the party.'

'And subsequently at Crossford House. Dr Raven was there making enquiries.'

Eugenie was brought up short by this.

'So you know then – that I asked him to. Are you angry with me?'

'No, I understand. You feel more affection towards my brother than I do, most likely because you have less experience of him. I hope you are prepared for disappointment. Your sympathy for him will not alter the facts.'

The baby started to girn.

'Teething,' Amelia explained. She stood and jiggled the child on her hip, which briefly quelled his complaints. She looked to the clock on the mantelpiece and began walking towards the door. 'If you will excuse me, it is time for our appointment with Dr Todd.'

Amelia left the room, the sound of the now crying child gradually receding.

'Is there something wrong with him?' Raven asked, thinking that the child looked perfectly healthy.

'I don't think so. She likes to have him examined regularly. She needs reassurance that all is well. He was poorly some time ago and she has never quite got over it. She fusses about every little thing. She dismissed the wet nurse as though she was at fault somehow. Insists on looking after him herself without any help.'

Raven could well imagine Sarah's response to such a statement. Most women looked after their own children without any help.

He began moving towards Eugenie, thinking that they might have some time together, but Amelia suddenly came back into the room and commandeered his intended spot on the couch.

'Your father wished to be left alone to conduct his examination,' she said.

Eugenie raised an eyebrow at Raven, underlining her previous remarks.

He retreated to the other side of the room.

'So,' Amelia said, addressing Raven now, 'what have you

discovered? I have heard all about your efforts last year, exonerating Dr Simpson when he had been wrongly accused.'

'It was primarily Miss Fisher who was responsible for clearing Dr Simpson's name. I merely assisted.'

He looked at Eugenie to determine her reaction. He was aware that he had deliberately not spoken much about Sarah, concerned as to how she might interpret their relationship. However, he did not wish to take the credit for Sarah's actions and was dismayed by how frequently her role was omitted from accounts of the case.

'I assume you are referring to Dr Simpson's female assistant, of whom I have heard much,' Amelia said. 'A woman giving chloroform and assisting in procedures. Quite unprecedented. Are these one and the same?'

'Indeed.'

'I am so admiring of any woman striving to venture beyond the bounds of what men will allow. I grew up with an avid interest in legal matters, and would have loved to pursue it further, but it is impossible for me to study the law, far less practise it.'

Raven could not help but think how chastened and reticent Sarah seemed of late regarding her own ambitions. He was beginning to understand why. If someone of Amelia's advantages could not proceed academically, what did that say for Sarah's prospects?

'Sarah has also been assisting in my investigations into the poisoning,' he said.

'You have known each other for some time then,' Amelia asked, somewhat pointedly.

'Do tell, Will,' Eugenie urged. 'Just how well have you *known* her?'

The innuendo in this question was clear and Raven was surprised by it. Eugenie was being risqué as a means of showing off to her friend, but there was an edge to it, more than a hint of insecurity and suspicion. Raven knew because he recognised it: the question of who else one's intended spouse might have lingering feelings for. And of course he did have intimate know-ledge of Sarah: just not in the way Eugenie might fear.

'Sarah is a widow,' he said, as though this in itself constituted sufficient explanation, but even as he said it he realised that it resolved nothing. Eugenie certainly did not appear to be reassured.

'A widow? And yet you refer to her as Miss Fisher,' Amelia said, demonstrating a particularity that would have served her well as a lawyer.

Raven was unsure how to answer. Sarah had reverted to using her maiden name shortly after Archie died. He knew it had some-thing to do with retaining her own identity, not being defined by her attachment to another person, but it was not a decision that he found easy to explain.

'Sarah is a very singular individual,' he said. It was the best he could do at short notice.

'And what have you discovered, the pair of you?' Eugenie asked, placing a telling stress on this last part.

Raven thought for a moment, conscious that he would have to be discreet.

'Gideon suggested that his father had many enemies. Unfortunately, I have found this to be true.' He looked from Eugenie to Amelia. 'I am not sure how appropriate it is to further discuss these matters here.'

'There is little about my father that would shock or disappoint me, Dr Raven,' Amelia insisted. 'Do go on.'

He paused, considering how best to share what he had unearthed.

'I have learned that your father had obtained damaging information regarding a certain gentleman in politics. That is not enough on its own to draw any firm conclusions, but Sir Ainsley's death certainly made things more comfortable and convenient for this person.'

'You said enemies plural,' said Amelia. 'Who else?'

Raven paused again. This was far more delicate.

'How well do you know your cousin Teddy?'

'Teddy Hamilton?' Amelia looked confused.

'He is the male heir should you renounce your son's inherit-ance, which Charles Dymock tells me is your firm intention.'

'We knew each other growing up,' she said. 'Family gatherings, weddings and christenings, but not so much in recent years. He went to London to study a few years ago, I believe. Eugenie probably knows him better than I do.'

Raven wondered if he was supposed to infer any deeper meaning from that statement. Sanderson's parting shot the night before bounced around his head. He realised that there was much about his future wife that he did not know, and he was becoming increasingly worried about it.

He looked at Eugenie. Did she seem anxious or was he merely imagining it? Suspicion could act like a slow poison, allowing doubt to creep into everything. Had she been involved with Teddy in the past? And if she had, did it matter now? It did if she still harboured feelings for him.

'Are you suggesting Teddy would poison his uncle?' Amelia continued. 'For money?' There was scorn in her voice, her scep-ticism starkly evident. 'That is an absurd notion. How could he anticipate that I would wish to renounce?'

'Did you ever discuss such matters?' Raven asked.

'Never directly. Only in as much as Teddy, like me, is not in thrall to wealth and status. There are more important things in this world than money.'

How easy it was to express such sentiments, Raven thought, without ever having suffered the depredations of poverty.

'Useful for the essentials, I find,' he said. 'Food, shelter. That sort of thing.'

Eugenie gave him a hard stare then turned to her friend.

'Are you permitted to renounce on behalf of the male heir?' she asked.

'I am his mother,' Amelia stated firmly.

That, although not strictly an answer to Eugenie's question, was one of the few elements in all of this that Raven could be sure about.

'What of the evidence against Gideon?' Eugenie asked.

'The main thing which casts doubt on his guilt is the arsenic,' he replied.

'I thought that it was surely proof of his guilt,' said Amelia.

'Gideon knows that it is easily detectable,' Raven explained. 'He argues that if he wished to poison his father, he would have used something else.'

Eugenie looked suddenly animated, as though Raven had solved the matter.

'Of course,' she said. 'He would not be so foolish as that.'

Amelia appeared to have been unsighted by this revelation. She clearly believed her brother was capable, motivated and ruthless enough to have committed the crime, and yet this represented a serious flaw in that hypothesis, a factor she had not considered. Perhaps for the first time she was feeling doubt that her brother was guilty.

Seeing this made Raven question certain of his own assumptions. Would he be disappointed if Gideon were exonerated? Did part of him *want* to believe Gideon killed Sir Ainsley? How much of that derived from Raven's relationship with his own father? How much of it came from his need for absolution? He was reminded of Sarah's remarks about his cloudy judgment and realised that he needed her input more than he had thought.

It struck him that the key to the whole thing was the poisoning itself, about which they knew so little. He needed to know more about what happened that night. He would have to go back to Crossford House: this time with someone who could get the staff to talk.

THIRTY-FOUR

s Sarah stood outside the front door of Crossford House she felt a sudden urge to take Raven's hand; an urge she suppressed, of course. She wondered what had prompted it. Perhaps it was the house itself. It seemed hostile somehow. Intimidating. And not merely because someone had recently died here.

They had come to question and to probe. To ask the staff difficult questions, no doubt upsetting people who were already distressed, their futures recently made uncertain. She felt a surge of gratitude, and not for the first time, that her own experience of domestic service had been with the Simpsons, a raucous family home, full of warmth and kindness. Crossford House seemed to be too big, too grand, to be in any way welcoming. Raven had told her of his ill-fated attempt to get one of the housemaids to talk to him. 'Terrified' was the word he had used to describe her. Sarah wondered if she would have any more success.

The door was answered by a severe-looking man wearing a uniform that seemed a little too tight. He seemed flushed, a high colour in his cheeks as though his necktie was effecting a slow strangulation.

Sarah very nearly reached for Raven's hand again.

Raven seemed unintimidated.

'Wilson,' he said loudly and with confidence, as though they were well acquainted. He brandished a piece of paper at the butler.

'I have here a letter from Gideon Douglas granting me permission to search the house and interview the staff.'

Sarah knew the letter was no such thing, just some random piece of correspondence picked up from the tray at Queen Street. Wilson did not look pleased (and more importantly did not look at the letter) but nor did he attempt to bar Raven's entry. He merely stepped aside and let them proceed into the entrance hall. It was an imposing space, with towering marble pillars and an intricately carved wooden staircase.

Raven wasted no time. He shoved the letter back into his pocket and started issuing demands.

'We need to speak to the staff who were present on the night the death occurred.'

Sarah noticed that he had not used the word murder and wondered if that was deliberate.

'I am particularly interested in speaking to the maid who cleared the bedroom after the fact.'

The butler looked as though he was about to speak. To complain, perhaps, or to refuse. In the end he said nothing, but scuttled off down a corridor, muttering under his breath.

He returned with a young girl who looked tremulous and on the verge of tears.

'Take us to the bedroom where the body was found,' Raven demanded. He had adopted a no-nonsense tone that he would never have used towards the staff at Queen Street: mainly because it would not have got him anywhere. Jarvis would most likely have laughed at him. It had the desired effect here, however, and the butler led them up the stairs, the snivelling housemaid following on a few paces behind.

The bedroom was as Sarah had imagined it: four-poster bed

(more carved wood) with matching armoire, chest of drawers, two armchairs, a small table between them, and a desk. It was tasteful, elegant. Almost regal. And exceptionally tidy. Not a thing out of place. It was hard to imagine how it would have looked the morning the body was discovered.

Sarah turned to the girl standing in the doorway.

'Handkerchief please,' she said to Raven, who hesitated for a moment then complied, handing his handkerchief to the housemaid. He looked less than happy as the girl blew her nose noisily into it.

'What is your name?' Sarah asked her.

'Meg, ma'am.'

'Can you tell me about the night of the party?'

The girl looked at Wilson.

'Tell the lady what she wants to know,' he said curtly.

The girl still seemed unsure, on the verge of tears again.

'Perhaps, Wilson, you could take me down to the servants' quarters,' Raven said. 'I need to speak to the housekeeper.'

Sarah smiled at him to convey her gratitude for this intervention. She was unlikely to get anywhere with the housemaid if Wilson remained hovering. She waited for Raven and the butler to leave before she tried again.

'This is much bigger than the house where I was a maid,' Sarah began, trying a different line of approach.

Meg looked at her, obviously surprised.

'It seems—' Sarah searched for the right word '—very formal.'

Meg nodded. 'Sir Ainsley was very strict about things.'

'Were you scared of him?'

She looked about as though reassuring herself that no one was watching, then nodded again, more vigorously this time. 'We all were. Well, all of us except Mr Wilson. Any mistake, the smallest thing, could get you dismissed. And it did happen. There was one girl—' She stopped herself, shook her head. 'But I can't talk about that.'

Sarah thought about pursuing this but decided to keep to the issue at hand.

'Can you tell me what happened after Sir Ainsley died? You were asked to clear things away, I think.'

'Mr Wilson told me to get rid of everything that was still on his supper plate and to empty the chamber pot.'

'What was in the chamber pot? Can you describe it to me?'

Meg winced at the memory.

'Vomit,' she said. 'And blood. A *lot* of blood.'

Raven followed Wilson along a carpeted corridor and down a set of unadorned stone stairs, a servants' route leading into the lower depths of the house. During their short walk they had discussed the butler's recollection of the morning in question, Wilson giving terse answers to Raven's enquiries.

'So, you sent for Dr Todd as soon as you discovered the body?'

Wilson nodded. Raven realised that this form of interrogation was of limited use as he could not see the man's face. Expressions frequently gave so much away, even when they attempted to give away nothing. Sometimes *because* they attempted to give away nothing.

'Why do you think Dr Todd suspected foul play?'

'You'd have to ask him that.'

'Did you suspect?'

'Me? No.' Wilson stopped and turned to face him. 'Why do you ask?'

'Because you told the housemaid to dispose of everything, before anyone had opportunity to examine it.'

Wilson's severity crumbled a little. 'I was concerned about who might be blamed. The staff in general, the cook in particular. I was worried about what had been served up on the supper plate. That there might have been an unfortunate accident,' he added hurriedly. 'No one in this house wished the master any ill. I was not thinking about murder or poison when I found him. We were all in a state of shock, not acting with good sense under the circumstances. I realise now I may have inadvertently had Meg dispose of important evidence.'

Inadvertently or deliberately? Raven wondered as they continued down the stairs.

'Do you remember who was in the house that night?' Sarah asked.

Meg seemed a little more relaxed as she grew used to her company. She had evidently decided she had less to fear from Sarah than perhaps she was used to in this household, and consequently had become more forthcoming.

'A few guests stayed late after the party, but none spent the night. And I would have known. I didn't get to bed until they had all left.'

'Which guests stayed on?'

'Mr Sanderson, Mr Mansfield, Mr Hamilton and the Reverend McLean. They had port and cigars in the drawing room overlooking the lawns.'

'What time did they leave?'

'Just after midnight. I took a tray up to Sir Ainsley before I turned in.'

'Was that unusual?'

'No. The master was often up late. He had trouble sleeping. Dr Todd made him take brandy for it.'

'What was on the tray?'

'A slice of cold pie, some cheese, some fruit. The brandy to help him sleep, and his medicine.'

'What kind of medicine?'

'I don't know the name. It was something for his stomach, I think.'

Meg wandered over to the chest of drawers and looked among the glass bottles arranged there in a neat line. She selected one and handed it to Sarah.

'Bismuth,' Sarah said. 'For dyspepsia.'

She was about to hand it back but decided to keep hold of it, worried that it might disappear like the rest of the evidence.

'How much of the meal was eaten?'

'He ate most of the pie and some of the cheese.'

'What about the fruit?'

'I don't think he had eaten any of that. I couldn't say for sure because I can't remember how many pieces were on the plate when I took it up, but I reckon most of it was still there.'

'What kind of fruit was it?'

'Some strange thing that came back from Tobago with Master Gideon.'

'Do you still have it?'

'No, Mr Wilson told me to throw all of it out.'

She looked furtive, and she knew Sarah had noticed.

'What?' Sarah asked.

'I tried a wee bit of it.'

'And?'

She grimaced, pursing her lips and shaking her head. 'Can't say that I cared for the taste at all. Burned my mouth like whisky.'

'Is there any of it left?'

'You'd have to speak to the cook.'

'Have you been working here long?' Raven asked.

They had entered the housekeeper's sitting room to find it empty and the scullery maid had been sent in search of her. Raven sat down in one of the armchairs beside the fire while Wilson busied himself polishing glasses from a tray.

'Many years, sir,' Wilson replied, once more conveying the bare minimum of information. Raven wondered if this was a practised discretion incumbent upon his job, or whether he had other reasons for his reticence.

'Were you fond of Sir Ainsley?'

'Fond of him? It wasn't my job to be fond of him.'

Raven rephrased the question. 'Did you have any complaints about his treatment of you?'

'It was a privilege to serve such an eminent man. He had achieved so much; few men in this city have done more to alleviate the plight of the poor.'

Raven was loath to let that remark go but knew now was not the time. In any case, it sounded as though Wilson was reciting a rehearsed speech rather than expressing his own feelings. A diplomatic reply if ever he heard one.

Wilson produced a kettle from somewhere and set it to boil over the fire. Raven wondered if he was going to be offered tea but thought it unlikely. He remembered Wilson at the party, being the only member of staff permitted to pour Sir Ainsley's drinks. He wondered if Ainsley had been worried about being poisoned. Had he suspected that his life might be in danger?

Raven tried to get his thoughts back on track.

'Did Gideon get on well with his father?' he asked. It was a question to which he already knew the answer, but reckoned it would be useful to gauge what could be detected beneath Wilson's next noncommittal reply.

The butler picked up a spoon from a pile of cutlery and began polishing it.

'Gideon was a disappointment to his father,' he said matter-of-factly. 'Things came too easily to him and so he valued nothing. He cared only for his own pleasure.'

He stopped polishing and stared at the object in his hand.

'Actually, that is not strictly true. There was one person Gideon cared for besides himself, but she is gone now.'

'His mother?' Raven suggested.

'Um— yes. Indeed. They were very close. He took her death hard. As did we all.'

Raven noted the hesitation.

'You didn't mean his mother, did you? You meant someone he cared for more recently than that.'

Wilson put spoon and cloth down, although why he was polishing the silver at this point Raven could not fathom. It seemed entirely unimportant given what else was going on. Perhaps going through the motions was the only way to maintain a sense of order and meaning.

'Gideon was involved with a young woman. An unsuitable girl. He got her . . . into trouble. That is why his father sent him to Tobago. To put an end to the matter. Gideon did not forgive him for it.'

Something cold passed through Raven as he recalled Sanderson's taunt, which continued to torment him, and Dr Todd's relief at his daughter finding a suitor. He could not help but wonder whether the unsuitable girl might have been Eugenie. Was this why she was 'complicated'? It would certainly explain her eagerness to exonerate Gideon – and Dr Todd's clear disdain for him.

'Who was she?' Raven asked, unsure whether he really wanted to hear the answer.

'That is not for me to disclose.'

Wilson picked up the spoon again – the same spoon – and recommenced his polishing.

'Sir Ainsley sometimes questioned whether or not Gideon was actually his issue,' Wilson went on.

Raven leaned forward in his chair. Wilson was suddenly providing information that he had not asked for.

'What on earth do you mean by that?'

'Gideon was such a disappointment to him that he preferred to think his wife had been unfaithful than that he had sired such a son.'

Sarah followed Meg into the kitchen, where a middle-aged woman in a starched apron and cap sat in a rocking chair by the range. She was knitting what looked like a scarf or a shawl, a great swathe of it piled up on her lap. The kitchen was quiet and tidy, everything scrubbed clean. Sarah realised that the house was largely empty now, with only a few members of staff present, their collective fate resting on the outcome of McLevy's investigation. How different it must have been only a week or so ago when there was a party to be catered for, guests to be served.

The woman spotted them and stood up, her ball of wool rolling and unspooling across the stone floor. She was very thin in comparison to Mrs Lyndsay, the Simpsons' cook, who Sarah presumed was better fed.

'It's alright, Mrs Morrison,' Meg said. 'This lady just wants to ask you some questions.'

Mrs Morrison gathered up her wool and her knitting, shoving them in a nearby drawer. She pushed a bit of stray hair under her cap and stood to attention.

What kind of house was this? Sarah thought. Run on military lines, perhaps. No questioning of orders, and harsh punishments for those who disobeyed.

Meg scurried out and closed the door behind her, clearly relieved that Sarah's questions would be directed at someone else.

'There is no need to stand, Mrs Morrison,' Sarah said. 'I am conducting some enquires at the behest of Gideon Douglas, trying to establish what happened on the night of Sir Ainsley Douglas's demise.'

The cook sat down again but did not seem reassured. She looked worried. Guilty, even.

'There was nothing wrong with that meat pie,' she said.

'I'm sure that you are right about that,' Sarah said, although in fact she could not be certain at all whether Sir Ainsley's final supper was implicated. She suspected the cook was far from sure either, despite her assertion. It had been Wilson who ordered everything be thrown away, which must have placed considerable doubt in the cook's mind.

Sarah pulled up a chair and sat down too, trying to appear

less intimidating. It seemed a house where the staff were used to being stood over, not sat down with.

'Meg tells me that you have worked here for many years. Since Gideon and Amelia were children.'

Mrs Morrison nodded, still uncomfortable.

'Not as long as Mr Wilson,' she said. 'He was here when I came.'

'He must have enjoyed working for the family to have been here so long.'

'I suppose.'

'Did he get on well with Sir Ainsley?'

'Well enough. Better in the past, I think. Things were never the same after Lady Douglas passed away.'

According to what Raven had told her, Margaret Douglas's death had been a decade ago, but evidently remained pivotal in the cook's mind. Sarah sought to know more.

'How did she die?'

'I don't rightly know. She became ill very suddenly. Dr Todd said that there was nothing anyone could have done. A tragedy. She was very young. And those two children left without their mother.'

'Was Sir Ainsley a good father to them?'

'Amelia was the apple of his eye. That's what he called her: my little apple. She was the firstborn but that makes no odds if you're a girl. Gideon was the one he placed all his hopes on. There was a lot of pressure on the boy, but he was never good enough, no matter what he did. I often felt sorry for him, truth be told. Tell someone they're useless often enough, they'll start to believe you.'

Sarah was surprised by the cook's sympathy and compassion for the dissolute and overindulged Gideon. Life with Sir Ainsley Douglas had obviously not been easy.

'Meg mentioned some exotic fruit Gideon brought back from Tobago. Do you still have some of that?'

'I do, as it happens,' she said, getting up from her chair and disappearing into the pantry. 'Not sure what to do with it, if I'm honest.'

Sarah wondered what manner of fruit might burn the mouth like Meg had described. There were none that she could think of. Such sensations were often nature's way of warning that something was not safe to eat. Could this perhaps be the cause of the poisoning, an important clue that they had missed?

Mrs Morrison emerged from the pantry holding a large pineapple. Sarah had seen one before: a gift to Dr Simpson from a grateful patient with a hothouse. She had not tasted it. In fact, she was not at all sure what Mrs Lyndsay had done with it.

'Do you want to try some?'

Why not? Sarah thought. She nodded and the cook cut her a slice. Sarah bit into it and some of the juice dribbled down her chin. The taste was both sweet and sharp, difficult to describe, and clearly like nothing Meg had ever encountered before. It was not unpleasant, and nor was it likely to kill anyone unless it was dropped from a considerable height onto their head.

THIRTY-FIVE

aven looked at himself in the mirror and tried to make an objective appraisal. He was wearing a new shirt and his jacket had been brushed until every last thread was clean. He was freshly shaven and his hair, for once, seemed to be behaving itself. He leaned in a little closer and examined the scar on his left cheek, letting his forefinger run along the length of it. A fine pink line. Fading nicely but still visible. An indelible mark that gave a little too much of his history away.

Was he a handsome man? He was far from ugly but lacked the kind of looks that drew attention; the right kind of attention, anyway. He was no Teddy Hamilton, but surely a reasonable prospect in terms of marriage. Added to that he was a man of some standing now, with the possibility of a lucrative career ahead of him. Was that what Dr Todd was referring to when he said that he and Eugenie were a good fit? Raven was still trying to convince himself, concerned that it was Eugenie's reduced status that made their match an appropriate one. And if so, what had brought her down to his level?

He was determined to find out. He had been invited to tea at St Andrew Square, where he planned to press Eugenie for answers. Awkward or not, he had to know.

He descended the stairs, concentrating on what he was going to say and narrowly avoiding a collision with Glen the Dalmatian and a snot-nosed child who seemed to be playing a game of some sort in the downstairs hallway. Something involving the coat-stand and an umbrella.

'Careful there, Wattie,' Raven said as he dodged out of the way.

Walter was a sweet-natured child but, as with all children of his age, he seemed to be permanently covered in an adhesive substance that defied definitive identification. Jam, perhaps. Raven was relieved that in his well-scrubbed state he had avoided any direct contact, but as he approached the front door, Walter's older brother, David, leapt out at him and jabbed him with another umbrella. Raven cursed his naivety for thinking Wattie would be alone. They tended to hunt in pairs. They also tended to be even more boisterous when their father was from home, and with the professor gone to London, he should have known to beware.

'We're pirates!' David yelled, prodding Raven again for good measure.

Jarvis appeared and handed him his hat. The butler wore the same inscrutable expression that he always did. Not even marauding pirates could dent his equanimity.

'I hear congratulations are in order,' he said.

'Yes. Thank you,' Raven replied, safely assuming that it was his engagement being referred to and thinking that there really would be no need for any formal announcement. There was nobody left to tell.

'When will you be moving out?'

Raven laughed, thinking that this was a joke, then realised that it was an entirely reasonable question.

'I haven't given it much thought,' he admitted.

Jarvis raised an eyebrow, which Raven interpreted as an admonition regarding his lack of proper planning.

As he descended the steps outside the house, it struck Raven that he was less concerned about where he would live than where he would not. The thought of leaving 52 Queen Street was not a pleasant one and perhaps explained why he had been slow to consider it. Not only because of what it had meant to him to live there, but also because of who he would be leaving behind. For once it was more than Sarah complicating his thoughts.

This family had become *his* family, Dr Simpson allowing him to experience the affection he imagined a father was supposed to provide.

His association with this adoptive family had also allowed him to rise in the estimation of his own true family – what was left of it. His mother had responded to the news of his impending matrimony with equal parts surprise and pleasure, but much as she was delighted at the prospect of her son marrying well, she seemed just as gratified that this might finally provide an occasion whereby she could venture across from Fife to meet the great Dr Simpson.

He knew well of her pride at his holding a position with such a man. She had even intimated that her miserable brother, who never expressed any pride in Raven himself, was nonetheless fond of casually dropping the Simpson name into conversation when in company. That, Raven knew, was as much acknowledgement from his uncle as he was ever likely to get.

Walking along Queen Street, with every step that took him closer to St Andrew Square he felt more burdened with uncertainty regarding the next family he was about to become associated with. Sanderson's words still haunted him.

What about her?

What indeed.

Dr Simpson's remarks regarding rumours in the city came to mind: that they tended to be true. He wondered if the professor knew something about Eugenie, something he was not telling him. Simpson's role in fostering children kept nagging at him, as if there might be a connection there. If so, surely he would tell Raven about it and not allow him to be deceived. Or would he? Dr Simpson's reverence for the inviolable confidentiality that shielded all interactions between patients and their doctors would put paid to that. It would be something that he would not, could not, divulge.

The thought made Raven confront what he feared: that Eugenie had got herself into trouble at some point and the evidence had been spirited away. To save face. To save her reputation. Was an illegitimate child the great secret? The shame that brought her down to his level?

He could not rightly say why this troubled him so much. He was not such a hypocrite as to demand a virgin bride. None of the lovers he had known had been any such thing.

Perhaps it was merely *not* knowing that was troubling him: not being trusted with the truth, and therefore not being able to trust the family he was about to marry into.

He recalled Wilson's words about Gideon, that he had been sent away for this very reason. Getting a girl into trouble. An unsuitable match. In a sober analysis there was no good reason to think this had anything to do with Eugenie. He counselled himself that it would be wrong to jump to conclusions. Perhaps it was his own self-esteem – or lack of it – that was posing the problem here. Maybe he really was good enough for a woman like Eugenie, and she did not need to be tarnished to accept him.

When he arrived at St Andrew Square, he was received in the morning room, Eugenie resplendent in an emerald green dress, white lace at the collar and cuffs. There was no need for clandestine meetings now, no more brief glimpses from behind glass. And yet he felt more distanced from her than ever.

A housemaid entered with a tray. She laid out cups and saucers and poured the tea. There was a rhythm to it, a pattern. The same movements in the same order each time. Eugenie watched it all with a calm contentment. Raven watched Eugenie.

He found that he was examining her, as if a close inspection would reveal what was being kept from him. She was beautiful, unblemished. The voice in his head made itself heard again, questioning his worthiness of her. He recalled something Henry had said: she had been sent away to protect her from a surfeit of suitors, and then suddenly Raven was good enough. It did not make sense. Something was missing from the story.

'You're very quiet,' she said. There was concern in her voice. She knew him well enough to sense his mood. 'How goes the investigation?'

'There is not much to tell. We went back to Crossford House and questioned the staff. I cannot say that it was particularly helpful.'

'We? You went there with Sarah?'

'Yes.'

She made no response, began fiddling with the seam on her sleeve.

'My friendship with Sarah troubles you, doesn't it?'

'No. Should it?'

'Of course not.'

'You said yourself that she is a widow and relatively new to widowhood at that. And I am the one who has your promise. I suppose that I am simply jealous.'

'Jealous?'

'She has known you longer than I have.'

'That could be said of any number of people. And anyway, it does not compare. My relationship with Miss Fisher has always been far different from the time you and I spend together. Much of it is spent butting heads, believe me.' Raven took a sip of his tea. 'What lies in the past with someone else need not prove any impediment to our being together. Do you understand what I am saying?'

She looked a little surprised at the turn the conversation was taking but said nothing.

'I don't see why you would feel the need to be wary of Sarah,' he said, then paused for a moment. 'Unless perhaps there is someone in *your* past whom I should be wary of. Is there something I ought to know? Is there something I *deserve* to know?'

Her expression hardened. A barrier had come down.

'I have no notion what you are talking about,' she said. 'I have kept nothing of importance from you.' She stood up. 'I do not know what you are insinuating but I tell you this – I do not care for it.'

He noticed that there were tears forming in her eyes. Her body betraying her. She rushed from the room, leaving him in no doubt that their conversation was at an end.

Raven did not follow her, thinking there was little to be gained by doing so. He was not reassured. Her response had been too vociferous, too combative. He was now convinced that she was hiding something from him and was beginning to wonder if it was indeed directly connected with Gideon as he feared. Gideon had been sent away for getting a girl into trouble. Eugenie had been sent away, ostensibly to protect her from ardent suitors, but there were other reasons young ladies might be sent away for a few months, as Dr Simpson could attest. Perhaps Eugenie had been sent away because of reasons pertaining to one suitor in particular.

Raven had just decided to take his leave when the door opened again. He thought it might be Eugenie returning to apologise for her behaviour or perhaps to explain it, but it was her father who entered the room. He smiled self-consciously at Raven.

'A lovers' quarrel? Eugenie can be stormy, but like any storm it will blow itself out.'

There was no doubt that Todd had seen her leave. His tone sought to make light of it, but he did a poor job of masking his concern.

'She is complicated,' Raven said.

He was beginning to lose patience. The whole thing felt like a charade. A trick. And he was the poor dupe in the middle of it.

'Indeed.'

'That is what you said of her yourself. How you chose to describe her. I wonder whether you would care to elaborate. Is there something I should know?'

'I really don't know what you mean.'

Raven could see the anxiety in Todd's expression and the faltering attempt at a smile to hide it.

'I had an interesting conversation with William Sanderson,' Raven stated.

'I hope you bathed afterwards. I would advise it after dealing with such a man who makes his living rooting in the gutters.'

If he expected a laugh or a smile in response to this, he did not get either.

'He spoke of the power inherent in withholding information,' Raven continued, 'and implied that there was something he was choosing not to tell me about your daughter. By further implication, something *you* are choosing not to tell me about her.'

Todd sought to wave it away as nothing. 'Sanderson trades in gossip, innuendo and rumour.'

'Your answer reveals more than you intend,' Raven said. 'Unless you believed there was reason why Eugenie should be the subject of any of those things, you would be telling me you had no notion why Sanderson might suggest anything about her at all.'

Dr Todd suddenly became severe, all attempts at humour and bonhomie abandoned.

'I would warn you not to dig too deep,' he said. 'There is nothing to be found that will profit you, Dr Raven. You already know the measure of my daughter. Take it as proof only of my esteem for you that I consider you a good match for her. Do not give me reason to reconsider my opinion, or reconsider my permission.'

Raven could think of no suitable reply and instead made for the door. All of his doubts were settling into something more solid.

He hoped that Dr Todd was never inclined to gamble at cards. He was as good a bluffer as he was a liar.

THIRTY-SIX

aven watched Sarah brush her hand over the brougham's red plush upholstery as it crossed Princes Street, a look of smiling approval upon her face. It did him good to see her looking pleased about something.

'So much better than walking,' she said. 'Especially in this weather.'

'It's only a bit of rain,' Raven replied. 'Although it was good of Dr Simpson to let us have use of the carriage while he is away.'

'While *everyone* is away,' Sarah corrected him.

Dr Simpson had departed for London some days ago, and Mrs Simpson had taken the children to visit relatives in Liverpool, where she would meet with Mina. Christina had gone with them, which Raven thought would impede Sarah's enquiries, but she maintained it would make little difference as the girl refused to reveal anything more than she had done already. Much as she wanted to find her missing child, there was evidently something or someone she was very much afraid of.

'I thought you liked walking,' Raven said.

'Not in the rain. I would like to see you attempt it in these skirts. They weigh you down when they get wet.'

'We're going to have to walk part of the way, at least,' he

said. 'It's market day. The carriage won't be able to get much further than the High Street at this time of the morning.'

Raven let his head rest back, pleasantly lulled by the movement of the carriage. He felt at his ease, even though his thoughts were so jumbled and contorted. The more he found out the less he seemed to know. Perhaps it was Sarah's presence that was calming him, a balm for his troubled mind. He was enjoying spending time with her again and wondered if that told him anything about his relationship with Eugenie. He had not felt this way around her of late, and speculation about her past was one of the reasons for his mental disquiet.

'Anyone who sees us today will assume that we are people of worth,' Raven mused.

Sarah scoffed. 'Only until we step out onto the street. Such things are illusory anyway. An image presented to the world rather than the truth of a person. Everything we are learning about Sir Ainsley Douglas is demonstration of that.'

Raven thought of Eugenie again and the elevation in his stature that an association with her father would bring. Setting up a practice as son-in-law to Cameron Todd would surely put him on the path to prosperity. But could he believe Todd genuinely esteemed him if he did not respect Raven enough to be truthful?

Perhaps it was not a lack of respect but rather the fear that Raven would take flight. That was why he had dangled the possibility of withdrawing his blessing. Todd had unwittingly revealed himself: he was the one afraid of losing something.

Maybe Raven ought to change tack: stress either to Todd or to Eugenie that they had nothing to fear from telling him the truth. But could he honestly say that? If it turned out she had borne Gideon's child – even if that child was now God knows where – he could not say for certain that he would feel the same about marrying her.

Had she borne Gideon's child? Was he truly contemplating this as a possibility? A dispassionate assessment of the facts would certainly support such a theory. And if this child existed, would it have a claim on Gideon's bloodline and inheritance? Were Gideon to be disinherited, if 'corruption of blood' was invoked, any such claim would be negated. Was that why Eugenie was so keen to clear him? Was she, as the mother of his bastard, protecting that child's future interest by preserving its right to inherit? In Scots law, marriage legitimised children born out of wedlock. If Eugenie were to marry Gideon and reclaim her child . . .

'Where have you gone?' Sarah asked, putting a hand on his knee. 'Come back to me.'

He looked at her hand and she withdrew it.

'Sorry,' said Raven. 'I have much on my mind.'

'Would it help to talk about it?'

Raven knew that it would, but he could hardly discuss Eugenie's possible past indiscretions with Sarah.

'It's fine,' he said. 'Just something I will have to work out on my own.'

The carriage pulled up on Market Street and he shook off his ponderings, lest they drive him mad. They disembarked, but there were few pedestrians to be impressed by their means of conveyance.

The rain had lessened to a fine smirr as they climbed the steps of Fleshmarket Close up to the High Street. Raven tried not to think of Sanderson as they passed the tavern where he had spoken to the journalists, but his surroundings were a constant reminder of the multiple problems he was wrestling with. There seemed to be no respite from them.

As they made their way across the High Street the crowds were thinner than usual on account of the inclement weather. They found what they were looking for in Hunter Square, beside Goldsmiths' Hall. Dymock and Paterson, solicitors-at-law, lodged in an ancient but well-maintained building giving the impression of a long-standing institution.

The front door opened onto an outer office, where a young

clerk was seated at a desk. Mr Dymock ambled out of his room just as they entered, carrying a sheaf of papers which he presented to his employee. He did not seem pleased to see them. He was perspiring less than when Raven had last encountered him, but he retained the same air of profound discomfiture.

'What do *you* want?' he demanded, abandoning all pretence of good manners. He scowled in the direction of the clerk, as though the lad should have known to eject Raven on sight. 'You were less than truthful with me when last we met,' Dymock continued, pointing a fat finger at Raven. 'I have been hearing about you from Amelia Bettencourt. You and . . .'

The finger now pointed towards Sarah.

'Miss Fisher,' she introduced herself, bright and pleasant in exaggerated contrast to his unwelcoming tone. 'And how was your meeting with Mrs Bettencourt?'

Dymock looked a little taken aback at Sarah's speaking to him in such a forward manner. Or perhaps simply speaking at all.

'Unsatisfactory,' he grunted. 'Neither of us was much contented with what we learned from the other. She informed me that you are not working with the police. I don't appreciate being lied to, Dr Raven.'

'I have not lied. I told you McLevy and I were working in tandem. I cannot be held accountable for any misinterpretation on your part.'

Dymock did not appear in any way placated by this. In fact, he looked like a pot about to boil over.

'And what did Mrs Bettencourt learn from you?' Sarah asked. Her voice was like an emollient on an angry rash. Dymock turned his attention from Raven to her, his expression softening.

'That the law dictates she may not renounce the inheritance on her son's behalf in the event that it should pass from Gideon. She was less than pleased, but surely there are worse problems to have in this life.'

Raven wondered if Amelia's attempt to renounce her son's

inheritance had anything to do with Gideon's suspected bastard, then reminded himself that there was no evidence such a child even existed.

'Anyway, I ask again: what do you want?'

Dymock's tone was even more hostile than before, causing Raven to wonder if the man had already shared more than he wished to.

'We should really speak in your office,' Raven suggested.

'I would rather speak here and get rid of you all the sooner.'

'Believe me, you will wish to discuss this in private. It concerns the letters you were looking for when last we met.'

The clerk looked up from his work as if to emphasise the lack of privacy in the outer office. He was a brawny lad with something of the countryside about him, as though raised on a diet of fresh air and mutton, more at home in a field than behind a desk. Raven wondered if they were going to be physically removed. Dymock he could handle. He was less sure about the young farmhand.

Dymock's expression betrayed the alarm of a man discovered. He ushered them into his inner sanctum, away from the big lugs of his young clerk.

'What do you know?' he asked defensively as soon as he had closed the door.

'That Sir Ainsley possessed letters proving Abigail Findlay and your brother-in-law were lovers. William Sanderson acquired them and passed them on to his employer.'

'Sanderson!' Dymock spat the name. 'Those letters have been restored to their rightful owner. Nothing more need be said about the matter.'

'They were being used to force the provost's hand, bend him to Sir Ainsley's will, and therefore provided Mansfield with a strong reason to murder the man. Given that I saw him that night skulking around upstairs, I believe there is plenty more to be said about the matter.'

'If you saw him where he should not have been, it was because he was looking for the letters. It is absurd to suggest Austin would murder Ainsley.'

'Not so absurd that you could not believe it yourself. That was why you were so eager to see Gideon named the culprit. You knew how desperate Mansfield was, and more importantly you knew what kind of man Sir Ainsley was. He was threatening ruin upon your brother-in-law and you stood idly by as he used this stolen proof of scandal to wield his power.'

Raven was pushing the man, trying to provoke him in the hope that in his anger he would reveal more information.

'You could have procured those letters,' he continued. 'You had easier access to Sir Ainsley's documents than anybody. But if they went missing, he would have known who had taken them, and that would have been the end of your association, wouldn't it? So, you swallowed all pride and principle merely to retain his patronage.'

If this was true, Dymock looked less than remorseful.

'I had my suspicions but not the proof, and both are necessary before making accusations. I only knew of the letters after Sir Ainsley died. I sought them out merely to prevent them falling into the wrong hands again. I wished to prevent my brother-in-law's infidelity becoming common knowledge and nothing more because I suspect him of nothing more. He could no more kill Sir Ainsley Douglas than you or I.'

He stood before them, bristling, his hands balled into fists by his side.

'And do not speak of patronage or currying favour,' he continued, 'nor saddle up your high horse to look down on me. Perhaps you should ask your future father-in-law, Dr Todd, what principles he has swallowed to retain that same patronage.'

He leaned in, eye to eye with Raven.

'You should ask him what he knows about the night Lady Douglas died.'

THIRTY-SEVEN

hey made their way back down Fleshmarket Close, the rain making streams of the gutters, washing away the worst of the filth from the narrow passage-way. As a consequence, the overwhelming smell of urine that usually pervaded the place was mercifully absent.

'Do you really think Mansfield did it?' Sarah asked, clearly sceptical of the notion herself.

'Probably not,' Raven conceded. 'I think Dymock is right when he said that Mansfield was searching for the letters when I saw him. It is less of an assumption than murder.'

'The explanation that makes the fewest assumptions is usually the correct one,' Sarah said. 'So said William of Ockham. That applies to murder as well as to medicine.'

Raven knew she was right. Gideon was still the most likely culprit. He wondered again if it was his obligation to Eugenie that had him chasing phantoms. Though Mansfield had a motive, that alone was not enough, and the case against Teddy was thinner still. As for the staff at Crossford House being involved, there was nothing to support it save the butler's over-exuberant clearing away of a supper tray in the interest of protecting his colleagues.

'What now?' he asked. 'Home to Queen Street?'

'Or perhaps we could take a little detour. I have a notion where else I could make some enquiries in my search for Christina's baby.'

'Where might that be?'

'You're not going to like it.'

He looked at her and smiled. 'Now I really am intrigued. Tell me.'

'Well, as Christina refuses to tell me any more than she already has, it occurred to me that Lizzie came to us via the Lock Hospital too. I asked her what she knew about her colleague and their previous shared profession.'

'You are a brave woman, Sarah Fisher. I would never be so courageous as to broach such a subject with Lizzie. What did she tell you?'

'She refers to Christina as "Teardrop".'

Raven laughed. 'She's the soul of warmth and tenderness, that girl. I am constantly surprised when I remember that she was a prostitute. She must have put the fear of God into her clients.'

'Maybe there are those who like that.'

'No doubt. I'd sooner bed her than fight her, I know that much.'

'I suspect there'd be little difference between the two.'

This caused Raven to laugh again. Really laugh. He could not recall doing so for some time.

'Lizzie said Christina did not work on the street, as she had herself. She plied her trade at an establishment called the House of Melbourne. It caters for refined tastes, apparently, and Christina with her exotic looks was a good fit.'

'There is something Continental about her features,' Raven agreed.

'According to Lizzie, Christina's mother was from Leith. She said it as though that was of significance, but I must confess I failed to grasp it.'

'She was implying that Christina's father was a sailor from foreign climes. One who did not tarry long.'

'Oh, I see. Anyway, that's where I plan to go next.'

'Leith?'

'No. The House of Melbourne.'

'Are you quite sure you wish to set foot in such a place?'

'Why do you ask? Do you think me too fragile? That sal volatile will be required?'

He saw the intensity of her expression, ready to leap upon what he might say next.

'I doubt that the salts will be necessary,' he answered. 'You're about as likely to faint as I am.'

She smiled but Raven tensed, suddenly aware of footsteps behind. He turned just in time to see a figure bearing down on them, a neckerchief pulled up around his face and a hat worn low over his forehead. Only his eyes were visible. There was a glint of silver against the swirling black of his coat. He was gripping a bayonet.

That flash of awareness in Raven saved him. He ducked and shifted just in time. *Almost* just in time. The thrust at his back would likely have penetrated to his chest. Instead it glanced off his shoulder. As he dodged and spun, the assailant's momentum took him forward, past them. The man tripped and skidded on the wet stone, unbalanced by his thrust, but he was soon righted again, coming at Raven once more. He could see the bayonet clearly, its edges finely sharpened as it tapered to a deadly point.

This time Raven had a moment to prepare. Putting himself between the attacker and Sarah, he rapidly hauled off his jacket and wrapped it around his right arm. As the man lunged and thrust again, he used the garment as a shield to deflect the blow, though it proved a more porous shield than he would have liked.

With his left hand he grabbed for the hilt. Pain was beginning to sting somewhere around his shoulder and his forearm, but he knew he could not afford to let go. It was one hand wrestling against his opponent's two, but with so much of his efforts fixed upon retaining his weapon, the man was leaving himself unguarded in other ways. Not a practised fighter, Raven sensed.

Without releasing his grip on the weapon, Raven turned and raked a heel down his attacker's shin, crunching into his instep with all of his weight.

The man grunted, suppressing a howl of agony. His grip loosened and his weapon clattered to the ground. The instant he realised the fight was lost, he hobbled away as fast as his injured foot would allow him, his descent hastened by his tumbling down the stairs at the end of the passageway.

Raven was about to pursue but was stayed by Sarah gripping his hand.

'I should go after him! I can catch him.'

She pointed out that he was bleeding from wounds on his shoulder and forearm, angry red blotches blossoming with frightening rapidity on the sleeve of his shirt. Sarah was visibly shaking but seemed primarily focused on him.

'We need to get you back to Queen Street.'

He nodded his assent and they made their way down the stairs together, each leaning on the other for support.

'Do you think this has anything to do with Mansfield and the accusations we made?' she asked.

'What makes you say that?'

'You had just pressed his brother-in-law on the matter, and now we are attacked. Almost as soon as we leave his office an attempt is made on your life.'

'It would surely take a little time to organise such a thing. Unless Dymock keeps a man in a back room just waiting for such an instruction. Anyway, I don't think you can assume he was trying to kill me.'

'What do you think he meant to do with the bayonet? Cut you for a stone?'

'No. What I meant was, how do you know he wasn't trying to kill *you*?'

THIRTY-EIGHT

ngus drove them back to Queen Street with all haste, leaping down from his seat to assist Sarah in getting Raven to the door. This was over the latter's protestations.

'It's nothing serious,' Raven insisted.

'The state of the seat would indicate otherwise,' Angus responded.

'Vinegar will prevent it leaving a stain,' Sarah told him, opening the front door.

'Is that a nurse's tip?' he asked.

'No, a housemaid's.'

There was an echo about the hall, the house unusually quiet. All the family were from home, the whereabouts of the staff unknown. Sarah led Raven towards the stairs.

'What about the consulting room?'

'You will be more comfortable in your own bed,' she said. 'I'll fetch what I need. You will have to rest for a while once I'm done.'

Raven scoffed. 'I'm not that badly injured.'

'You've already bled quite a bit.'

She tried to help him up the stairs.

'It looks worse than it feels,' he insisted.

Sarah was not convinced. He had developed a distinct pallor on the journey back and his hand as it gripped the banister was smeared with blood.

He made it to the bedroom where he collapsed onto the bed. Sarah left him there as she ran downstairs again to amass all that she required to deal with his wounds: lint, dressings, sutures.

She returned to find him exactly where she had left him. He had not moved an inch and his eyes were closed.

'Will?'

He opened one eye. 'Still here,' he said, and smiled.

She wrestled him out of his coat and bloodied shirt, Raven groaning as she pulled the latter over his head. She realised she was being a little rough in her haste to see what she was dealing with, how badly he was wounded.

The laceration on the forearm was deeper than the other. She started with that. She cleaned it carefully then stitched it neatly, relaxing a little as the edges came together and the bleeding stopped.

'If you keep this up, you're going to start looking like a patchwork quilt,' she said.

She expected him to laugh, or smile at least, but when she looked up he was staring at her with an intensity that made her feel suddenly weak.

She placed a lint dressing on his forearm and applied a bandage, aware of her own breathing in the silence. Short, shallow, rapid.

Then she began to clean the wound on his shoulder. It was superficial, little cause for concern, but in order to stitch it her head had to come close to his. She became unsettlingly conscious of his physical presence: the heat emanating from his body, the smell of him, the sight of his bare chest. She had to force herself to concentrate, and to blot out his stoic grimaces each time her needle penetrated the skin.

Sarah remembered the day she first met him. He had turned up at Queen Street looking like he had just been in a fight — which of course he had. He had fresh stitches on his face, his cheek swollen and bruised around them. Sarah had insisted he take a bath and had drawn one for him. She had helped to wash his hair. He had been embarrassed by his nakedness, something she had found amusing at the time. She had been attracted to him even then. She was still attracted to him, perhaps more than ever.

Sarah stitched the wound, aware of a very slight tremor in her hands. She finished, laid a piece of lint over it and looked up. He was still staring.

Their heads were mere inches apart, his lips close to hers.

She should have pulled back. Should have moved away, tidied up, busied herself with some small task. She leaned in further and kissed him.

She knew she should not. She knew it was wrong. But mostly she knew she wanted this, and would not be denied.

All other thoughts left her head.

THIRTY-NINE

arah dressed quickly, suddenly ashamed as their nakedness had been transformed from a source of comfort and pleasure to something altogether more troubling.

'There is no need to leave,' Raven said.

She looked at the carriage clock sitting on the table by Raven's bed. It was only two o'clock in the afternoon, which seemed impossible. Going to see Dymock, the attack in Fleshmarket Close: these things felt like they had happened a week ago rather than that same morning.

'Someone could return any moment. We can't be found together like this.'

Raven lay back, stretching his good arm. 'If I had known what you meant by resting, I would not have raised any objection.'

'Don't joke about it,' Sarah said. 'What just happened was unforgivable.'

'I can think of harder things to forgive.'

'I had no right to do that.'

'We *both* did it.'

Sarah ignored him. She was disinclined to allow Raven to share responsibility for what had happened. She was the one at fault.

'I feel as though I have stolen something: not only from you but from Eugenie.'

His hand found hers and squeezed. 'You have taken nothing from me, Sarah. Nothing that I did not wish to give. We have to face the fact that there is something between us, and always has been. I thought my relationship with Eugenie might drive it out, but the latest evidence would indicate otherwise.'

Sarah pulled her hand away. 'Why would you wish to drive it out? Am I still not good enough for you? Even now?'

Raven sat up. He was still bare-chested, which was distracting to say the least. She tossed a clean shirt at him, but he made no move to put it on.

'You are too good for me, Sarah. That is the issue: all that you are, and all that you *can* be.'

'What do you mean?'

She sat down on the bed. When he took her hand again, she did not withdraw it.

'After Archie died, I began to harbour hopes for us,' he said. 'I wanted to wait until it was appropriate, but in time I intended to ask you to be my partner, in work and in marriage. I was planning to set up in practice on my own and have you work beside me as my assistant.'

'But you told me none of this.'

'I would have, but then you expressed your intention to travel, to seek out Elizabeth Blackwell, to explore the possibility that you might study medicine.'

Sarah bit her lip. 'I don't understand.'

'I wanted you to be with me, to stay with me, but it would have been selfish, and love cannot be selfish. I loved you too much to stand in your way.'

'And now?'

'I have seen you laid low, but I know you are capable of getting up again.' He squeezed her hand once more. 'I have never known anyone so bloody-minded. Or so capable. There will be obstacles in your way but nothing that you cannot overcome. It is true that you do not have all of the advantages Elizabeth Blackwell enjoyed, but you are clever and you are resourceful. It will be harder for you, but I have no doubt that you can do it.'

'How did you know? About Elizabeth Blackwell, what she said to me?'

He smiled at her. 'I pieced it together.'

'And what about me? Don't I have any say in all of this?'

'You know how marriage can smother a woman's ambition. You have said so yourself. I cannot ask you to give it up for me.'

'But what if *I* want to?'

'I don't think that you do, and I would not be the one to hold you back. You would resent me for it.'

It was an uncomfortable truth. She did not like it, but she knew that he was right. Sarah loved him because of what he saw in her. What he made her see in herself. He had been prepared to sacrifice the life they could have had so that she might have the chance of a better one. Of rising higher.

She knew Will Raven. These were not idle words and his had not been actions lightly undertaken.

'And what about you? Is Eugenie the partner that you seek?'

He suddenly looked less assured.

'I thought so once but I am no longer so certain.'

'Because of what we have just done? You must forgive yourself, for I was the one who put temptation in your way. The past does not matter if Eugenie is your future.'

'That's just it. I am not so sure any more.'

'Of your love for her?'

'Of hers for me. I fear she loves Gideon.'

'Gideon?'

'I worry that is why she has asked me to intervene on his behalf. Wilson said he was sent to Tobago because of his involvement with an unsuitable young woman. Dr Todd believes the worst of Gideon, and I think that is why.'

'But Gideon had returned before she chose to marry you.'

'Yes, but what if they were forbidden to each other? Was I her second choice because she could not have Gideon?'

'She can still care for him. She doesn't want to believe he murdered his father, and nor does she want him to meet the rope. But that doesn't mean she sees her future with anyone but you.'

Sarah wondered at herself, defending her rival for Raven's affections.

'But while he is around,' Raven said, 'there will always be the question. That is what has me doubting my own judgment over the Ainsley Douglas murder. If I help exonerate Gideon, and we are married, will her mind still turn to him, with thoughts of what could have been? If I fail to save him, will she wonder whether I gave it my all? Will she blame me if he should hang?'

'If you marry her, will you still love me?' Sarah asked.

'Yes.'

'Can you love Eugenie and be a good husband to her while retaining that love for me?'

'I would endeavour to do so. My love for you and my love for her are not the same.'

'Then why would you not believe she can do that too? Marriage is never perfect, Will. God knows I can attest to that. But it's what you can share, the life you can offer each other and the love you can give that truly matters. If you both have people you love but cannot be with, then at least you should understand each other. It will be a marriage of equals in that respect.'

Sarah got up from the bed.

'You should go to her. Talk to her. She will listen.'

'What about you?'

Sarah reached for her coat.

'Appropriately, having just conducted myself as a jezebel, I am bound for a whorehouse.'

FORTY

s he strode along Queen Street, Raven was grateful that the rain had abated, for he had seldom been so much in want of air. Then again, he would have gone out in a storm if it helped make sense of what had just happened.

Once outside and in motion, he was surprised by the clarity of his thoughts. He had expected to feel more confused than ever after what had transpired, but there had been something cathartic not only about what they had done, but the conversation that followed.

It had pained him to tell Sarah she should pursue ambitions that would take her away from him, but in saying it he was bound by a commitment that lifted the strains of indecision and conflict. Having told her what he had, he could not go back on it, though a part of him might dearly wish to.

He knew that to do right by both the women he loved, he had to cleave to Eugenie and let Sarah go.

As he had done so many times before, he saw Eugenie at her window as he approached, though his arrival was unexpected on this occasion. She was looking out on St Andrew Square, lost in her own thoughts. He wondered if those thoughts were of the walks they had shared, and the possibility that they might share nothing further.

A coachman came hard along St David Street, bellowing his warning to a man crossing the road who appeared heedless of his approach. The sound was enough to break Eugenie from her trance, and at that point she noticed Raven gazing up at her.

In the past she would have beamed in response. Today, she looked anxious, as though his appearance was portentous in some way. He felt a tightness in his chest. To see her worried was to put worry in him.

He beckoned her down as he used to, offering an apologetic smile. His heart leapt to see it reflected.

Surely he could love Eugenie as a wife and Sarah as a friend. His feelings for Sarah, even as they were expressed physically this afternoon, did not diminish how Eugenie made him feel. He needed to have faith that Sarah was right: that the same would be true of Eugenie with regard to Gideon.

They walked together through Princes Street Gardens, the sun finally breaking through the lightening clouds. Raven recalled that this was the professor's prescription for those with illnesses more imaginary than real, many of whom paid the professor handsomely for it. He was not sure what it said that it was making him feel better.

Eugenie took his arm as they walked, Raven grateful to be walking on her right. Her grip would not have been so welcome had it been upon his other arm, where Sarah's careful stitches sat beneath the sleeve of his shirt, and he did not wish to have to explain himself if he were to wince at Eugenie's touch.

He could feel the heat of her hand through the material of his coat. He relished the sensation, officially sanctioned now that they were betrothed, but such pleasure also provoked a feeling of guilt regarding what he had just shared with Sarah.

Raven tried to clear his mind by thinking of what Sarah had

told him: that his past with her did not matter, only his future conduct with Eugenie. The worry was, it was hard to feel like it *was* the past when it had reached such a recent culmination.

Neither he nor Eugenie had said anything of substance since she emerged from her father's house. There was a sense of mutual comfort, the reassurance that they still wished to be in each other's company, but also a feeling of trepidation, of approaching something dangerous that would have to be broached for that comfort to mean anything.

Raven decided that he was not going to press her. He felt it was incumbent upon Eugenie to speak, even if it was to say that she wished to keep this matter private.

She slowed her pace and looked at him.

'I feel as though I am trapped between Scylla and Charybdis,' she said.

'How so?'

'I owe you the truth if I am to be your wife, but I am afraid that you will not want to be my husband once you know it.'

'Eugenie, there cannot be much that I have not already surmised, and yet here I stand. You are not diminished in my eyes. It is not as though I have never known the touch of another.'

'I speak of more than mere touch.'

'I understand.'

He squeezed her hand gently as he spoke.

'Your father said you were "complicated" but he did not elaborate on what this meant. I know he sent you away, and I was told that it was to deter suitors. But it was not for that reason, was it?'

Eugenie's eyes filled. He led her to a bench where they sat down, still close but no longer touching. He gave her a moment to compose herself, taking in his immediate environment. They were surrounded by trees and flowers, the combined scent of them heavy in the air. There were few that Raven was familiar with. Roses, a willow tree. The rest he did not recognise, would not be able to put a name to even if his life depended on it. Sarah would know, he thought, and immediately felt a stab of guilt, a disloyalty to the woman sitting beside him.

The sound of a train whistle cut through the quiet, a plume of smoke rising as an engine made its way towards the station at the far end of Princes Street.

'I had a baby,' Eugenie said eventually.

It was almost a relief to hear it, proof that he was not in thrall to some far-fetched fantasy.

'How could you still want me for a wife now,' she asked then, 'knowing what I have done? What kind of woman gives away her own child?'

Raven was all too familiar with the consequences of the body's reproductive urges. He was forced to confront them on a daily basis in his professional life and no one, irrespective of status, was exempt. He was surprised she would not anticipate his compassion as a result. But then the personal and professional were often quite separate spheres.

'What kind of woman? A frightened one. One who is unready for a life not of her choosing, for consequences disproportionate to her actions.'

He offered her a handkerchief. She wiped her nose and dabbed at her cheeks.

'What you say is true. I was terrified. I did not want a child. All throughout my pregnancy that thought persisted. *I do not want this.* I tried not to think of there being a child inside me, only of the life my father assured me I could return to after my confinement in the country. But when I held her in my arms, I did not want to let her go. I have never felt such love. My father took her, though, mere moments after. He told me to put her from my mind and look to the future this sacrifice allowed.'

She held herself straighter, looked Raven in the eye.

'I present myself as acerbic. Harsh, even. I am inappropriate sometimes, and often disrespectful to my father, as though I care nothing for trivialities or conventions. It is all a sham, to hide how much I do care. How much I hurt. I would like to tell you that not a day goes by without my thoughts turning to that little girl and where she might be now, but in truth many such days go by. It is how I live with myself. Father assured me she was going somewhere safe, somewhere she would be loved. But when one does not know . . .'

She hung her head again.

'Some nights I cry at the thought of her missing me, and some nights I cry because I know that she does not.'

Raven struggled to find something to say, some words of comfort, but could not summon anything that might ease this kind of pain. He reached for her hand and squeezed it once more, encouraging her to go on.

'There was a time when I begged him to tell me something of who her new parents were. He told me he did not know, only that she had been given to someone who would provide a good life. There had been an intermediary used to prevent such information becoming known. It was for the benefit of both parties, he told me, as well as for the benefit of the child. A clean break, he said. A chance to cauterise the wound.'

'Do you think that your child was given to Dr Simpson? I know that he discreetly arranges such things.'

She shook her head.

'No. It was arranged with someone from outside of the city. Clandestine meetings at a railway station where a substantial amount of money was paid for the services provided.'

She sniffed, dabbed at her eyes again.

'Sometimes when my father was angry with me, he would complain not only about how I had brought disgrace upon the family, but how much money it had cost him to hide it.'

Raven remembered what Sarah had told him about the woman from the perfumier who met with an intermediary at a railway station. A large sum had changed hands then too, *for purposes of discretion.*

Raven wondered why Dr Todd had not gone to Dr Simpson. The fostering services that he provided were no secret amongst the medical men of Edinburgh. Perhaps that was the problem. Edinburgh medicine was a small world, riven with rivalries and professional disputes. And perhaps Dr Todd wished to keep this from his colleagues, reluctant to seem diminished in their eyes, whether he trusted them to keep a secret or not.

Was this the information Sir Ainsley Douglas was hoping to wheedle from Dr Simpson? And if so, how was he planning to use it against his own physician?

Raven realised that there was a question he must ask now, or forever hold his peace. There might never be another opportunity.

'I hope you understand why I have to ask you . . . who was the father?'

Eugenie removed her fingers from his, clasping her hands together in her lap.

'I will not say. I would not say then, much to my father's anger and frustration, and I will not say now. If you still wish to marry me, you must reconcile yourself with not knowing.'

Raven sighed. 'What troubles me is that I think I do know.' He rushed on, not wishing to be interrupted. 'I believe it was Gideon, and that is why you requested I help him. I fear that you love him still and I worry that if I cannot save him, you will resent me for it. And if I do save him—'

Eugenie stopped him before he could finish.

'It was not Gideon.'

That gave him pause.

'Your father suspects that it was. I think that is why he was so quick to believe Gideon guilty of the poisoning. He already thought badly of him.'

'You have it backwards,' Eugenie replied. 'He assumed Gideon was the father because of our long association with the family and because he already thought him a scoundrel. I often suspected this was because privately my father did not think so highly of Sir Ainsley either, making it easier to believe the worst of his son. Not that he had the mettle to put his suspicion to the test. If he genuinely believed Gideon responsible, he should have challenged Sir Ainsley and insisted that his son do the honourable thing, but he was too cowardly. Sir Ainsley's riches and influence kept him loyal and obedient.'

'Are you sure your father said nothing? The butler at Crossford House told me that Gideon got a girl in trouble, a girl his father considered unsuitable, and that was why he was sent to Tobago.'

She laughed at that, relief and anger curiously mixed.

'Then you can be most solidly assured it was not Gideon. My confinement was almost two years ago. Gideon was sent to Tobago last summer.'

Raven felt a rush of relief, which only lasted until he calculated that there was no reason why Gideon could not have been responsible for both. If he was unconscionable enough to get one girl pregnant . . .

It was as though Eugenie read his mind. She took his hand again, looking him deep in the eye. She needed him to believe her, and he did, because he needed to believe it too.

'Will, it was not Gideon. I have never liked him in that way, nor he me. I knew him as Amelia's little brother. I asked you to help because I always felt for him. He seemed delicate and sensitive, and I saw how his father treated him. I know how badly he can behave, but I always thought there was something better within him; that the boy I used to talk to at the summerhouse might emerge if given the chance.

'I also hoped it would be a comfort to Amelia if she learned her brother was innocent, but I realise now that I was mistaken. I have come to appreciate that Amelia's opinion of Gideon was always closer to yours – and that perhaps you and she are right.

I thought her disdain derived from mere envy because he was the favoured one. But I have come to accept that, as the person who knew him best, she must have seen something in Gideon that made it possible to believe he would do such a thing. And I suspect you must have seen that in him too, long before you met me.'

Raven chose not to respond directly to this. It was not something she ought to be burdened with. But he realised, amidst another wave of relief, that she would not hold it against him should he fail to clear Gideon's name.

'Amelia's judgment would appear damning of more than just Gideon,' he said. 'She seems to wish to dissociate herself entirely from her family.'

'I witnessed a change in Amelia over the years,' Eugenie told him. 'A harshness of tongue and an air of indifference that I found myself imitating. But I know from my own experience that it is a mask, a hard shell to protect something soft and vulnerable inside.'

'She has suffered a great deal,' Raven suggested. 'The loss of her husband, and before that the loss of her mother. I can understand why she will barely let go of her son, as she came close to losing him too.'

Raven remembered what Dymock had said about Margaret Douglas, his implied accusation towards Dr Todd.

'Do you know what happened to Amelia's mother?' he asked.

'What happened? What do you mean? She died young, before her time. It was a tragedy that shook the whole family. I do not think they have recovered from it yet. But whatever changed in Amelia seemed to precede the loss of her mother. It began when we were both around twelve or thirteen. No longer little girls but beginning the transition to womanhood. I think that was when the reality of her situation struck her: the different roles allotted to the son who would inherit and the daughter whose only purpose was to marry and have children.'

'Does she know of your secret?'

'No. You are now one of a very select few. My father, his sister who I was sent to stay with, a midwife I never saw before or since. Some household staff in Perthshire who were told a fabrication about my husband being dead. No one else.'

She paused, as though deciding whether to reveal something further.

'Not even the father knows,' she said. She looked at Raven to gauge his response. She hurried on. 'In fact it suited me that my father blamed Gideon, because it kept him from suspecting the truth, and that in turn allowed me to keep it from the man responsible. He was engaged at the time. Though he loved me, the marriage was important to both families, and I would have been . . . yes, unsuitable. I could not betray him by revealing what had happened between us. I would not reveal it then and I will not reveal it now.'

This was more, far more, than Raven had anticipated being told. His fears had largely been confirmed and yet what he felt was not disappointment but admiration. He could see just how strong and honourable she was.

'He is married then?'

'Yes. With a child, and another on the way, I'm told.'

'What you did for him was an act of love.'

Eugenie saw the question in this acknowledgement.

'I will not attempt to deceive you, Will. I think of him still, as I think of that little girl. But I have thought of them less and less since meeting you. I no longer need to dwell on what might have been, the life I might have lived.'

She grasped both his hands in hers.

'Ours is what is here and now.'

FORTY-ONE

arah climbed North Bank Street, passing the Bank of Scotland building on her left, the New College of the Free Church off to her right. She had decided against taking the carriage out again. The rain had stopped, and she felt the need of some fresh air. She was deliberately keeping to the main roads and broad thoroughfares. There would be no shortcuts through narrow alleyways for a while.

She thought about what she and Raven had just done. Conventional wisdom would dictate that it was wrong, even sinful, but she knew that she did not regret it. Physical intimacy had forced an honest discussion that might not have happened otherwise. Everything seemed clearer now than it had been before.

Why was intercourse regarded as so precious, as though it were the greatest bond? She and Archie had made love, but it was not the sweetest thing they had shared. Equally she knew that in Raven's case, it was not mere lust for Sarah physically that was causing him conflict with regard to Eugenie. She used to wonder whether sexual congress changed everything between two people, or whether it was a sign that everything had already changed between them. Now she had lain with Raven, what was confusing was that it seemed to have changed nothing.

The great fears for most women after such a deed, out of

wedlock, were pregnancy and disease. She was afraid of neither. Raven's brave intervention during her recent pregnancy had saved her life, but in all likelihood had cost her the possibility of ever conceiving again.

After her initial embarrassment, Sarah had decided she would not feel guilty about what they had done, and nor would she entertain shame. Shame was a blunt instrument wielded by men to keep women in their place, and that they should be made to feel it when pregnant was particularly galling. The rounded belly, the indisputable evidence of indiscretion that women were forced to carry while the men responsible could retreat into the shadows, deny all knowledge and continue their lives undisturbed.

Though perhaps they were not always undisturbed. She thought of Gideon, accused of fathering a child and being sent to Tobago as punishment. Gideon was apparently as loose with his morals as he was with his money, so it could be any number of women who had succumbed to his charms and been left to bear the consequences alone. Did Raven think it might have been Eugenie? That would certainly exacerbate his concerns.

Having made this connection, she realised that it was not merely Eugenie's residual love for Gideon that Raven was afraid of.

Sarah stopped outside the denoted building on Melbourne Place, where she experienced the same feeling as when Christina had sent her to Dickson's Close. Had it not been Lizzie who supplied the address she would have assumed a mistake had been made.

She examined the building for signs of its use as a brothel but there were none. It was a three-storey townhouse, four steps up to a front door, all gleaming black paint and brass fittings. It looked as though a lawyer or a doctor might reside within – but that, Sarah assumed, was the point.

Hiding in plain sight. A respectable veneer concealing something sordid and debased.

Sarah was not as morally outraged as some by the concept of prostitution but in practice it seemed to be a form of enslavement, an occupation of last resort, whereby women were used, abused and then discarded when they became old or diseased. Raven had joked about how fierce Lizzie was, but Sarah could not but think how afraid she must have been as she took strangers, unknown and probably undesirable, to her bed; if even a bed it was. How much of that fierceness was the result of fear, the result of having been a prostitute?

While she was standing there, the door opened and a man emerged, straight-backed and surefooted. He was expensively dressed and immaculately presented, sporting neatly trimmed whiskers and a magnificent waxed moustache. He descended the steps, tipped his hat at Sarah and marched off down the street as though he had just concluded a satisfactory meeting with his bank manager.

Sarah looked at the door as it closed and wondered if she had the nerve to ring the bell. She was not sure what she would say to whoever answered. She did not have much option, however. If she learned nothing here, there were no further avenues of enquiry left to her and she was not ready to give up just yet. Raven's speech about her tenacity and resilience had put some fire in her belly.

She ascended the stairs and pulled the bell.

The lady of the house answered the door herself. She was extravagantly dressed for the time of day, with short sleeves and an abundance of décolletage. She looked instinctively wary. Sarah did not imagine it would be the first time an unexpected female visitor turned out to be an angry wife.

'Can I help you?' the woman asked, her tone suggesting that she would be strongly disinclined to do so.

'I would like to ask you some questions regarding one of your former employees.'

'Are you sure you're in the right place?'

'From the look of satisfaction on the face of the gentleman who just left, I would assume so. This is the House of Melbourne, is it not?'

The woman opened the door with much urgency but little grace. 'You had best come in,' she said tersely. 'I do not care to discuss business matters on the doorstep.'

Sarah stepped through the front door and instantly felt an edge of anxiety. The memory of the ambush in the alleyway was still fresh and she wondered if Raven was right that she was the one in danger.

She found herself in a grand entrance hall that reassuringly reminded her of a hotel: expensively furnished if a little gaudy. She was relieved to see that there was no one else present: no rough type with a cudgel, ready to bash her brains in. It was all rather opulent, in fact, with little to indicate the true purpose of the premises other than the imaginary landscapes framed on the walls. Although classical in theme, they all had a marked preponderance of nudes.

The woman stood with her arms folded, her mouth a firm line. She had a fine head of hair, thick black curls cascading around her face, an unnatural colour for a woman of her age. There was something familiar about her, but Sarah could not immediately identify what it was. She thought that perhaps she had seen her at 52 Queen Street but that did not seem at all likely. She could not imagine this woman seated around the dining room table.

'Have we met before?' Sarah asked.

'I very much doubt it.'

'I don't think I caught your name.'

'It is Bouvier. Madame Bouvier.'

Sarah had to stifle a laugh. Her accent betrayed her, suggesting she hailed from nowhere more exotic than Prestonpans.

'My late husband was from Paris,' Madame Bouvier added, sensing that some form of clarification was required.

'As I said, I am seeking information regarding one of your former employees, by the name of Christina Cullen.'

'I'm not sure I can help you. The girls here are seldom known by the names they use elsewhere, for purposes of discretion.'

It was then that Sarah realised why the woman seemed familiar. Partly it was the sound of her voice, but it was mostly her name that shook the truth loose. Her real name was not Bouvier, Sarah was sure, and it was indeed 52 Queen Street she knew her from. She had been there as a patient: an 'upstairs' patient at that, one of those who were better financially endowed and saw the professor rather than one of his assistants. She had presented herself less flamboyantly attired and without the wig, as an altogether different manner of lady.

'Perhaps if I describe Christina? I can't imagine you had many quite like her. Petite, black hair, olive skin, something of the Spanish or Italian about her. She would have been employed here around the early part of this year.'

'What did you say your name was?'

'Fisher. Sarah Fisher. Miss.'

'Miss Fisher, even if I were to recognise the girl to whom you are referring, it would not be my place to disclose anything about her. Privacy and confidentiality are paramount here. That applies to employees as well as to the clientele.'

Sarah paused, making a show of taking in her surroundings.

'Given the nature of your business here,' Sarah said, 'I fully understand the need for discretion. Confidentiality is of the utmost importance where I work too.'

Madame Bouvier was beginning to look a little wary now.

'And where would that be?'

'At 52 Queen Street, with Professor Simpson. One develops a good memory for faces – and other body parts – in such a place.'

Madame Bouvier's eyes widened briefly. She knew she was compromised and appeared to be calculating the implications.

'You work for Professor Simpson?' she asked, trying to place Sarah and perhaps to assess the damage. 'In what capacity? Are you a governess?'

'I work as an assistant to the professor. Preparing medicines. Tending to wounds. Administering chloroform.'

Madame Bouvier's eyes boggled more.

'Really?'

Sarah said nothing.

It was at such moments that people tended to scoff or be patronising. Madame Bouvier instead seemed genuinely impressed. She may have been the madam of a whorehouse, but Sarah would take credit where she could get it. It was so seldom forthcoming.

The woman unfolded her arms, placing her hands upon her hips.

'You have my respect, Miss Fisher. But do not confuse that with my good wishes. I do not appreciate being threatened.'

Sarah realised she had bluffed successfully. She had no idea what this woman's real name was and would never break a patient's confidentiality even if she did. However, Madame Bouvier did not know that.

'I mean you no ill-will,' Sarah stated. 'I am merely trying to help Christina.'

'What is your interest in her?'

'She works at Queen Street now, and she has asked me to help find the baby she was forced to give up.'

Madame Bouvier took a moment, weighing up her options.

'I will tell you what I can,' she said, 'on the understanding that you will remember my co-operation should I one day need a favour from you.'

Sarah nodded her assent, trying not to think of what form this obligation might take.

'I remember the girl,' she finally admitted. 'She left when she became ill. Ended up in the Lock Hospital. But truth be told, if you want to know more, I am not the one to speak to. She was friendly with another of my girls. Nora Burns is her name. You had better hurry, though. She's in the hospital too.'

'The Lock?'

'No. The Infirmary.' She gave a sad smile. 'Beautiful girl in her time, but I always said of Nora: if conceit was consumption, she'd soon be dead. I believe she's putting that to the test.'

FORTY-TWO

here was no doubt about it, Gideon Douglas looked rough. Unable to avail himself of his usual grooming regime, his appearance was dramatically altered. Although not completely broken, bodily or in spirit, he seemed humbled, shorn of his usual arrogance. He was the son Raven had seen cowering before his father, not the obnoxious fellow who had pretended not to remember him just an hour before that.

Just under two weeks had passed since Raven last stood here, but it looked like it had been longer for Gideon. He was unshaven, the beginnings of a beard sprouting from his chin, those fledgling bristles not enough to conceal bruising on his face. Fresh bruising this time, not the work of his recently deceased father.

'What happened?' Raven asked, as he took a seat in the cell.

Gideon, who had been lying on his bed when Raven entered, sat up and shrugged his shoulders as though it were nothing.

'Someone complimented me on my jacket.'

'How did that turn into a fight?'

'The compliment was an overture to something else. The short version is that the gentleman concerned now has my jacket and I have this bruise.'

'Did you inform someone? Given who you are . . .'

'Who I am?' Gideon wore a bitter smile. 'Who I am is why I am here. The son of a powerful man who died suddenly, and as a result, in less than a week I am to stand before Judge Arbuthnot. They say no butcher in Edinburgh has hung more meat.'

He looked at Raven with an expression in which hope was all but gone.

'Have you found anything?'

Raven had come here because he owed it to Gideon to tell him what he had discovered – or at least admit that what he had discovered did not add up to much. Following his conversation with Eugenie, he was feeling less pressure towards a preferred outcome and yet at the same time a stronger desire to get to the truth of it. Her accepting the possibility of Gideon's guilt allowed him to assess the evidence without prejudice. Unfortunately for Gideon, even as Raven laid it out, it was clear that none of it pointed to his innocence.

It was possible Teddy Hamilton believed he stood to inherit if Gideon was blamed, but this notion was contingent upon him anticipating that Amelia would renounce her son's claim, and that stretched all credibility. Furthermore, it had turned out that, much to her chagrin, Amelia had been mistaken in this assumption anyway.

Mansfield had a stronger motive, but not as strong as Gideon's, and the provost had other means to exhaust before he resorted to murder. He would surely have made further attempts to recover the letters, even despite his brother-in-law's cowardice. And though Raven did not say as much, he could not envisage any defence advocate introducing evidence that relied upon such a revelation regarding the wife of his faculty's dean.

In his growing despair, Gideon came back to the question on which he pinned the diminishing sum of his hopes.

'But can't people see that it makes no sense I should use such a detectable poison?'

'It makes no sense to me,' Raven replied, 'but McLevy insists that jails are full of men who thought themselves too clever to make a mistake. You were correct that other men might have reason to wish your father dead, but that is mere speculation, and none of them enjoyed the access you did.'

Raven paused, thinking there was not much more to say. The only other information he had uncovered had little to commend it. He decided to share it anyway. Gideon deserved that they explore all possibilities.

'The only others who had such access were the household staff. The butler was swift in instructing the maid to dispose of the supper remains. He told me this was because he was afraid the cook might get the blame for serving food that had gone bad. Might Wilson have any other reason to do this? It was my impression he was silently disapproving of your father.'

Gideon scoffed. 'Wilson would not dare go against my father in any way. Happy is the man who knows his place. Such men keep their own counsel. Wilson was loyal to my father regardless of what he might have privately thought of him; just as should I inherit, he would loyally serve me, his opinion of my character notwithstanding.'

'Wilson also told me you got a girl pregnant. Who was she?'

Gideon had endeavoured to maintain his equanimity up to this point, but this last piece of information seemed to fell him. His head dropped into his hands and he held it there for a few moments before looking at Raven again.

He looked crushed, revealing an aspect of himself that Raven had not seen before. There was affection and regret. Vulnerability. Anger. Contrition. And sadness.

Gideon rubbed his hands across his face, as though he could wipe away what Raven had already seen. He sat up, hands on his knees, ready to talk.

'On the morning I learned my father had died, I admit I did not mourn, I did not weep. And let me tell you why. I know you hate me because I am – I was – rich. So much was given to me.

But with that came demands that were impossible to satisfy. I did not want to become lord of a grand house. I wanted something simpler.

'At one time I thought if I became a doctor then I might have a career, a life that would take me away from my father. Unfortunately, as you know, I lacked the necessary discipline. My father's predictions of my failure became self-fulfilling. I had little confidence in myself. I was angry all the time, seeking comfort in hedonistic pursuits. And still I sought a simpler life. For a while I dreamed that I might have that with her.'

Gideon looked away for a moment, perhaps picturing the girl.

'She was beautiful. Apart from my mother, she was the only person who truly loved me, despite all of my numerous flaws. The only person who made me forget the anger that I felt. That I still feel.

'I know people would say I used her and then discarded her, but it was not like that. I realise how foolish it sounds now, but I genuinely believed that we might run away together.'

'And what did you imagine you would live on?' Raven asked. 'With no profession and cut off from your father's money?'

Gideon looked slightly ashamed. 'I did not think that far ahead.'

'I have heard that about you,' Raven said, wondering whether this also extended to detectable poisons.

'Yes, it was an impossible dream. Yes, it would be fair to say I did use her, because deep down I knew a relationship with her would never be permitted. If we had run away, we would have been found. We were undone before that, though, when it was discovered she was pregnant.'

'And that is the real reason you were sent to Tobago. Not as you told it the last time I was here.'

'What I said was partly true. I was exiled, but I was given charge of the plantation, ostensibly as a chance to prove myself. I enjoyed my time there. I managed it better than you might have heard. My father recalled me simply to demonstrate his power. I suspect he also recalled me because I was happy there, though not as happy as I would have been with her.'

'Who was she?'

The penitence and wistful remembrance disappeared. There was only bitterness and anger now.

'It does not matter, because she is dead. My father sent me off to Tobago and upon my return took pleasure in informing me of her fate: that her bastard was given away and she became the play-thing of many men before falling to disease.'

'All of this sounds like further reason for you to kill him.'

'But I did not. For in truth, Raven, I am too cowardly. Afraid of the consequences should I try but fail. It would take a stronger man than me to kill Sir Ainsley Douglas.'

'You cannot tell me you don't have it in you to kill someone. I was there that night in the alley, remember?'

'And I should belatedly acknowledge I owe you for saving me from myself on that occasion. I made that poor man a vessel for my rage, a surrogate for someone whom I had not the courage to challenge. I was kicking a man who was already down: put down by you, for I had failed to achieve even that on my own.'

Gideon thumped the tops of his thighs with clenched fists.

'My father ruined my life,' he said through gritted teeth. 'For a time, I believed that when he died, I would be free, but he continues to torment me from the grave. His death has become the instrument of my own end.

'My only consolation is the thought that somewhere my child lives yet. He or she will certainly outlive me.'

FORTY-THREE

arah climbed the steps to the Infirmary, passing a man as he descended, negotiating the stairs using a pair of crutches. He seemed well-practised in their use, suggesting some chronic affliction. He smiled at her, said hello, grateful perhaps to be able to walk at all.

As she approached the front door, she felt an unexpected reluctance to enter. The sights and smells of hospitals held no horror for her but the place was bringing back unpleasant memories. All that ghastly business a few months ago with a nurse who used to work here.

She made her way to the medical wards and had to enquire at several before finding Nora Burns. She drew stares as she walked down the corridors, her clothes indicating her relative affluence. The patients of the hospital were the poor folk of the town who could not afford to be treated at home. No one with any money to spare would allow themselves to be admitted here.

The patients were well cared for – supplied with regular meals, clean clothes and bedding – and for some that was all that was required to produce a cure. For others, the disease they suffered was beyond remedy.

Nora Burns was one of the latter. As Sarah approached, she saw her hoist herself up in the bed and begin to cough, expectorating copiously into a basin that she held in her scrawny hands. The bones of her skull were clearly visible through her skin. When the bout of coughing was at an end and she looked up at Sarah, there was a sheen of sweat across her brow, thin strands of hair plastered to it. She wiped her mouth on the sleeve of her gown, leaving a thin trail of crimson against the not-so white. Sarah could hear the rattling in her chest from the end of the bed.

She narrowed her eyes at Sarah, immediately suspicious.

'Come to save my soul, have you?' she croaked, clearly unenamoured by the prospect. 'You lot are all the same. Coming in here in your fancy clothes, spouting passages from the good book, trying to teach us the error of our ways.' She scowled at Sarah, as though doing so would force a retreat. 'You're not doing it for us,' she added, sweeping her skinny arm wide to take in the rest of the ward. 'You only do it to make your own selves feel better.'

She was a wasted, emaciated thing. Sarah tried to see the attractive girl that Madame Bouvier had described, but that required a fair amount of imagination. The girl before her was a ghost of what she must once have been.

'I'm not here about your soul,' Sarah said. 'I'm trying to help a friend of mine. Christina Cullen.'

Sarah could see the moment of recognition and curiosity.

'How is it you know her?' Nora asked.

'We both work for Professor Simpson. She's a housemaid.'

Nora looked Sarah up and down. 'I didn't take you for a housemaid.'

'I am not, but I used to be.'

Perhaps it was the admission that she had once been in service herself, but Sarah detected a diminution in the hostility emanating from the wraith in the bed.

'How did Christina end up there? Last I heard she was in the Lock.'

'Dr Simpson is a man who believes in giving people a second chance.'

'I don't think there'll be any second chances for me,' Nora said, before exploding into another fit of coughing. She spat some blood into a rag.

Sarah could see the truth of this and felt angry that nothing could be done for her; that this young woman's life would soon be over and all she had known was being used by men for their pleasure. She understood why Dr Simpson would defy the board at the Lock as Raven had described. She felt a renewed determination to help Christina, and Lizzie if she should ever need it.

'I'm glad for her,' Nora said. The last bout of coughing had left her breathless. She spoke in short bursts, pausing to recover herself between them. 'Christina was always good to me. She hadnae had all the kindness driven out of her yet. A timid lassie, though. Frightened. The patrons liked that, of course. Some preferred it that way. Liked to imagine she was intact. A virgin.'

She cast an eye at Sarah, gauging her response to this.

'I mean, they knew that wasn't the case, but at Melbourne it's all an act. Some men like you to be confident, in charge, like you cannae get enough. And some of them like a scared wee lassie that gives the impression she's never done anything like this before. Of course, in Christina's case they'd need to pretend they weren't seeing the belly she still had on her at first.'

'What do you know about the baby?' Sarah asked.

Sarah tried to make this sound incidental. Nora seemed happy enough to talk, but Sarah had feared that if she made her focus obvious, she might become evasive. She had a contingency for such an impasse, a suggestion made by Madame Bouvier, but it was a card she could only play once.

'What do *you* know about it?' Nora countered, vindicating Sarah's instincts.

'That it went to Mrs King.'

Nora eyed her for a moment, before nodding a disapproving affirmation.

'Aye. She and Madame Bouvier have an arrangement, sending business in each other's direction. Sometimes there's a pretty lass with a debt to pay off. Money owed to Mrs King. More often it's the other way round. We try to be careful. There's things we can do, a few wee tricks, but every so often somebody gets caught out and there's a bairn they cannae afford to keep.'

'But isn't it expensive?' Sarah asked. She thought of what the woman from the perfumier had said.

'Aye, it is. For those as has a reputation they need to preserve and the funds to preserve it. Mrs King will bleed them dry, wring out as much as she can. But most aren't looking to pay for discretion. Half the hoors in Edinburgh must have dropped off a wee parcel with Mrs King, and they've hardly tuppence between them otherwise they wouldnae be hoors.'

'And she looks after the babies until their mothers are able to do so themselves? What if that never happens?'

She thought of Christina's concern that her baby had been given away when she became ill and stopped making payments.

Nora wore a dark look, a combination of regret at what she was about to reveal and contempt at Sarah's naivety.

'The purpose isnae always for them to thrive.'

Nora pulled at a loose thread on the sheet.

'Those she takes in don't always get the best care, is what I'm saying. Not fed much, just a morsel of pap and a good slug of something to keep them quiet. They don't tend to last very long under those conditions. Christina knew that but told herself otherwise. Needed to hold on to a bit of hope.'

Sarah thought of the bottle of Godfrey's Cordial at the abandoned house in Dickson's Close.

'Everybody lies to themselves about it,' Nora continued. 'You cannae pay a pittance for the upkeep of a bairn, can you? Otherwise you could afford to keep it yourself. And the fine ladies who pay more arenae just paying for secrecy. They're paying to salve their conscience, spending on a fantasy. If Mrs

King charges so much, they tell themselves, it must be because she's moving only in the best circles and ensuring the children go to the finest homes.'

Nora continued worrying at the sheet, picking at a small hole in the fabric with a fingernail.

'Concealment of birth carries a prison sentence,' she said. 'And the killing of a child the death penalty. But if you give your bairn to Mrs King, and it doesnae thrive, then that's just what they call "marasmus".'

Sarah understood the term. A natural wasting away.

'Are you saying none of them are fostered?'

Nora coughed again. Spat again. A perpetual cycle.

'Of course not. Mrs King makes money selling them too. The healthy ones anyway. And it's just as important that she does because the women need to think that their bairn might be one of the lucky ones. See, I had a gentleman at Melbourne once, a military man. He told me how sometimes the soldiers have to execute one of their own men. Six of them in the firing squad, but one of the rifles has a wax ball in the barrel, and nobody is told which. It's so they can always tell themselves they might not have had a hand in killing their comrade.'

Sarah paused for a moment, trying to take all of this in.

'Do you know where to find this woman?' she asked.

Nora wore a bitter smile. 'Happily, I've never had the need. And I'm not likely to now.'

'But if you were to . . .'

'Christina told me she was in Dickson's Close off the Cowgate.'

'I've been there. It's abandoned.'

Nora nodded as though this came as no surprise.

'Aye. She comes and goes, I'm told. Wherever rent is cheapest. Madame Bouvier might know where she is now, but she won't be for telling.'

Sarah thought of their recent encounter and had no doubt as to the truth of this.

'Of course, you could always do as the childless do. Put a notice in the paper and she'll find you.'

Sarah realised that this was the most likely way to make contact and would arouse the least suspicion. It might take some time but it would be so much better than knocking on doors and asking awkward questions.

'Thank you, Nora,' she said. It was a gratitude sincerely felt.

She could think of no further questions to ask and was about to say goodbye when Nora spoke again.

'How is she doing? Christina, I mean. Is she well?'

For the most part Sarah had been met with evasiveness and obfuscation in response to her enquiries and had been prepared for more of that from this woman too. However, despite her hostility during the early part of their conversation, Nora seemed keen to continue it. Sarah realised that she was in want of company. Lonely and dying, and she knew it.

'Christina is well, though missing her child,' she replied.

'Is she pleasing her employers? Will they keep her on?'

'She's very conscientious. Obedient and deferential. We have all grown fond of her.'

This was largely true, though Sarah could not help but recall Lizzie's typically cruel nickname for the girl – Teardrop.

'It makes sense,' Nora said. 'She was a housemaid before.'

'Do you happen to know where?'

'She would never say. She was scared. I think someone had threatened her.'

'I had assumed her employer took advantage of her,' Sarah said.

Nora nodded sagely. 'The old story. Got her pregnant and then chucked her out. Except, it wasnae quite that way.'

Suddenly there was a glint in her eye, gossip to share.

'She told me she still loved him,' Nora said, 'and that he loved her. One night we got drunk and the whisky loosened her tongue. She said it was his father drove them apart.'

Sarah could feel her heart racing, her body reacting before

her mind had the chance to catch up. Disparate thoughts coming together, connections being made.

'Did she tell you his name?' she asked, her mouth suddenly dry.

'Not directly. She wasnae drunk enough for that.'

Sarah felt her hopes flag. Then Nora's eyes shone with that glint again.

'But she sometimes said it in her sleep.'

Nora paused. Sarah thought that she might need to be persuaded to reveal this last piece of information, and was about to reach for the bottle she had brought on Madame Bouvier's recommendation. It was brandy rather than whisky, which she hoped would be acceptable. But Nora did not require bribery or coercion. She shrugged her thin shoulders.

'I'll have no use for secrets where I'm bound. His name was Gideon.'

FORTY-FOUR

arah found Raven in his consulting room when she returned from the Infirmary. He was seated at his desk and had, as usual, a heap of paper in front of him, a medical journal opened at a particular page. He was not looking at it, instead staring into the middle distance, lost in his thoughts. Shafts of sunlight were illuminating the room, motes of dust swirling in its rays, still bright though it was gone seven. The room was warm, stuffy and oppressive but Raven was oblivious. Under other circumstances she might have left him undisturbed but what she had just discovered was too important to keep.

Sarah bustled into the room, made directly for the window and hauled it open. A welcome gust freshened the stale air of the room, rousing Raven from his introspection. He looked up at her in surprise, as though she had suddenly materialised in front of him.

'I didn't hear you come in.'

'Evidently.'

She took off her hat and gloves, putting them on top of his papers.

'It was Christina,' she told him.

Raven looked confused.

'The girl Gideon got pregnant. The unsuitable girl Wilson spoke of. The housemaid who was dismissed from Crossford House.'

She watched him as he took it all in, could almost hear the cogs turning in his head.

'There can be no doubt,' she insisted. 'It is our Christina. The two matters we are investigating are connected. Christina and the missing child. Gideon and his father.'

Raven leaned back in his chair and rubbed his eyes, then his expression resolved into a frown, which was not the response Sarah was hoping for.

'What?' she asked.

'The two matters are undoubtedly linked,' he said. 'But I still don't see how this helps us understand either of them.'

Sarah returned with a tea tray. She left the pot to brew for a while, thinking that perhaps a strong cup or two might assist them in their analysis of what they had uncovered thus far.

'What is unexpected,' she said as she poured, 'is that Christina professed to love him still, despite what has happened to her.'

She noticed Raven eyeing up the fruit cake she had also brought from the kitchen. She nudged a slice towards him, thinking that perhaps he had not eaten for a while and that hunger was impairing his cognition.

'Gideon apparently feels the same way about her,' Raven said. 'I have just returned from Calton Jail, where he seemed quite impassioned on the matter.'

'You sound surprised.'

'I am beginning to understand what Eugenie sees in him now. What struck me was not his despair, but his regret. He had deluded himself into thinking he and this girl, who he would not name, might run away together. Foolish as that sounded, I think it also serves to suggest he did genuinely care for Christina.'

'So, you believe him then?'

'I want to. But what still troubles me is that although Gideon could be foolish, he was never stupid. Perhaps he was acting a part to convince me of what he wishes me to believe.'

'If this is all some ingenious stratagem, he is leaving it extremely late to make his winning move, wouldn't you say?'

'He did not look like a man whose fate was in his own hands,' Raven conceded. 'Waiting for the perfect moment to turn the tables.'

'That said, if he cares so much for Christina, why has he not sought her out since his return from Tobago?'

'Ainsley told him she was dead. To prevent him doing just that, I would assume.'

The idea of this cut Sarah deep.

'What a cruel thing to do,' she said. 'Needlessly cruel.'

'That's not the end of it. Gideon told me that his father intimated that he had *used* Christina before sending her away. I suspect Ainsley intended it as a warning of what would befall her should she speak of any of this.'

'This would certainly explain the fear that has silenced her. Was there no end to the man's depravity?'

'And yet in time there will no doubt be a statue of him in some prominent place, looking down on us all.'

'Not if I have anything to do with it,' Sarah said, taking a sip of her tea. 'We need to find out what happened and expose his role in all of this.'

'Whatever Sir Ainsley Douglas is guilty of, it will not save Gideon.'

'None of this helps him does it?' she admitted.

'No, but it doesn't incriminate him either. And it does help me understand him a little better. I have never liked Gideon, and whether or not Eugenie is right about his gentler nature, I can at least now comprehend why he conducted himself as he did. What made him the way he is.'

Raven became pensive, wearing a troubled look Sarah was familiar with.

'Do you believe that he has inherited something evil from his father?' she asked. 'A taint in the blood?'

'Much as it is my own father's nature that I always fear in myself.'

'I don't know why you still hold on to that notion. You are not your father. "A tree is known by its fruit; a man by his deeds."'

Raven did not look convinced.

'Have you ever struck a woman?' Sarah asked.

'No,' he said with conviction. 'Nothing could compel me to do so.'

'Then there you have it. Conduct observed does not have to be imitated. Indeed, your father's action brought about an opposite *re*action in you. It made its mark, but not in the way you might imagine. The question is, what did it bring about in Gideon: a desire for love or an unquenchable hate? Did he wish to be other than his father, or was he inescapably shaped in his father's mould, his fate predestined by the damage long since done?'

Raven was quiet for a while. He sipped his tea, ate some of the fruit cake that had lain untouched on a plate by his elbow. Then something occurred to him.

'I meant to tell you,' he said. 'The case you witnessed at the Maternity Hospital – I know the cause.'

'Was it the heart?'

He smiled. 'Yes. The mitral valves were cartilaginous. The valve orifice scarcely admitted the point of a forefinger. Possibly the result of acute rheumatism when she was fourteen; her fate, as you say, predestined by damage long since done. If only Ainsley's post-mortem had been able to tell us as much.'

'Arsenic is not conclusive enough for you?'

'Well, there is no doubt that the presence of arsenic demands an explanation. But what we do not know is how it was administered and by whom. Gideon had the strongest motive and the easiest access, but there remains the question of fortitude.'

'Fortitude?' Sarah did not follow.

'Yes. Gideon claims he is too cowardly to do such a thing.'

'That sounds of a piece with his claim that he was too knowledgeable to use arsenic.'

'Nonetheless, much of what we have learned inclines me to believe him. So many people were afraid of Ainsley, cowering before his wealth and power. None among them dared defy him, so who would have the strength of nerve to risk all in killing such a man?'

Sarah was about to say that poison permitted the weak to fell the strong. The surreptitious administration of it was generally how women killed men, hiding it in their food or drink.

Or their medicine.

Then she remembered the glass bottle she had taken from Crossford House.

'Come with me,' she said.

'Where? Why?'

'Because it is just possible *nobody* poisoned Ainsley Douglas.'

FORTY-FIVE

hat do you mean?' Raven asked, following Sarah upstairs. She was moving at quite a clip, driven by one of the most powerful forces known to nature: Sarah's determination to prove herself right about something. 'Are you saying the arsenic was detected in error? Christison himself verified it.'

'Yes, but you told me that according to Struthers there was only a small amount in the stomach contents, and none in the liver or other organs. Have you considered that its ingestion could have been accidental?'

'Well, unless the man had taken to licking fly paper I don't think that's very likely.'

Unsurprisingly, she paid no heed to his churlishness. She led him into her bedroom, which looked more like a laboratory than a chamber of repose. There was a long bench beneath the window laden with test tubes, flasks and retort stands.

'What have you been doing in here? Distilling whisky?'

She ignored this too, handing him a medicine bottle.

Raven read the label.

'Bismuth. What of it?'

'I lifted it from Ainsley's bedroom. The housemaid said he took bismuth last thing at night.'

'So, he was dyspeptic. I'm fairly sure the man did not die of rampant indigestion.'

He had no idea where she was going with this. However, his growing confusion was in no way dampening her enthusiasm for whatever theory she had come up with.

Raven watched as she poured a quantity of the bismuth mixture into a glass flask and added another liquid to it.

'Muriatic acid,' she explained. She had a glow about her that Raven had not seen in a while. She started to describe what she was doing, the various stages of the test she was performing. Something about copper gauze, grey deposits, reduction tubes and arsenious acid. He was not entirely following. Raven did not share Sarah's enthusiasm for chemistry, far less her comprehension of it, which was probably why he struggled so much with it while at university.

'Where did you get all of this stuff?'

'Dr Morris. He lent me some of his equipment so that I could perform my own experiments. I've been working my way through Gregory's *Outlines of Chemistry*.'

Raven sat in an armchair in the corner, the book she had just referred to propped up on a table alongside. He thumbed through it, noticing its stained pages and the notes made in the margins.

'Was this before or after you went away?'

'Both,' she said.

Raven smiled. Something had been rekindled in her.

He put the book down again, the weight of it troubling his injured arm. He thought he might leave her to it for a while and was considering a tactical retreat to his consulting room to finish off what was left of the fruit cake when Sarah turned from her workbench, a rather severe expression on her face. Concentration. Disappointment. He could not tell.

She presented him with a flat dish containing a tiny mound of white crystals. It looked less than impressive given the time it had taken to produce.

'What am I looking at?' he asked.

Sarah smiled. 'Arsenic.'

'From the bismuth bottle? Someone put arsenic in his medicine?'

'Not necessarily. I was reading in a medical journal recently the report of a court case where a man had been accused of the slow poisoning of his wife with a metallic poison, either arsenic or antimony.'

She leaned towards him to retrieve her specimen, evidently not trusting him with it. She was flushed from her efforts, her cheeks tinged with pink. He noticed her eyes, aquamarine flecked with gold, the light dusting of freckles across nose and cheeks. She was in his head again, at the forefront of his mind, squeezing out all other thought and putting paid to the notion that what existed between them had been consigned to the past. He had to force himself to concentrate on what she was saying.

'Arsenic or antimony,' he repeated.

'Analysis of some of the evacuations from the dead woman demonstrated small amounts of arsenic but none was found in the liver. The woman had been exhibiting symptoms of dysentery before death and had been prescribed bismuth, acetate of lead and opium.'

Dysentery. Bismuth. Similarities with the Douglas case that helped to focus his attention.

'Several physicians who were called to give evidence for the defence stated that they had analysed ordinary bismuth in the course of their work and had on many occasions discovered that it contained arsenic. According to one of them, nearly *all* of the bismuth sold contains arsenic.'

Raven sat back, trying to absorb what she had just said. The small amount of arsenic discovered in Sir Ainsley's stomach could be nothing more than a contaminant of the medicine that he took at night to calm his irritable gut: a prescribed treatment for a long-standing gastrointestinal complaint. Not poisoning, not murder, but dysentery: as Struthers had first suggested.

Raven thought of Archie Banks and how his sudden death had been initially suspected as murder. Simpson had shown there to be an innocent explanation. A scientific explanation.

He looked at the bottle of bismuth again.

It was just possible that no crime had been committed here either.

FORTY-SIX

ames McLevy sat at his desk engrossed in his reading. He picked up his pen, made a great show of dipping it into his inkpot, and then began scribbling something. Sarah wondered if what he was writing had anything to do with their business there. He seemed to be enjoying keeping them waiting.

Sarah was aware of Raven shifting about on the chair beside her. It made her recall the rare occasions when she was called before the schoolmaster to explain some minor misdemeanour — usually her questioning his excluding her from lessons deemed only suitable for the boys. He had always kept her waiting, trying to instil in her a fear of potential punishment and inculcate a respect for his authority. It had achieved neither.

McLevy stopped writing but continued to pore over the document in front of him. There was a growing silence as they waited for him to speak.

Given his reputation, Sarah had expected him to be a brute of a man, but he was a little shorter and leaner than she had imagined. Nonetheless there was something quite formidable about him. A strong sense of will and a quiet purpose. The kind of man who seldom had to raise his voice because the mere threat of what he could dispense was often enough.

The day before, when they had first come to him to present their evidence – the bottle of bismuth taken from Ainsley's bedroom and a sample of the arsenic it contained – he had seemed an intimidating presence. He had looked less than delighted to be confronted by them at all, but by the time Raven had explained their business, his face resembled that of a dog eating nettles.

'The problem is, Dr Raven,' he had said, 'interesting as your little experiments may be, you are hardly an expert in the field of toxicology. Therefore I have to ask myself, just how reliable is this evidence that you have brought to me?'

Raven had made no attempt to dissemble but accorded Sarah the credit that she was due in having made the finding herself. That of course was a mistake.

'Miss Fisher has made extensive study of the subject and is quite certain of her findings,' Raven said.

Sarah had braced herself for the inevitable.

McLevy snorted and turned to face her.

'Begging your pardon, ma'am, but I can hardly put you forward as an expert witness.'

She could sense Raven tensing in anticipation of her reply. What he failed to appreciate was that, should she react with anger every time her credibility was questioned, then fury would be her permanent state.

'I am certainly not that, Mr McLevy,' she responded mildly. 'What is required here is corroboration. What if Professor Christison were to repeat my experiment and come to the same conclusion?'

'That, young lady, would be something that I could take to the procurator fiscal.'

McLevy thought for a moment.

'All right. Give me the . . . what was it?'

'Bismuth mixture,' Sarah said.

'Yes, the bismuth mixture. I will make my own enquiries as to the provenance of this liquid, confirm that it was prescribed by Sir Ainsley's physician, that it did in fact belong to the man in question, and then I will ask Professor Christison to analyse its contents. Though when I will get around to all of the above remains to be seen. It may have escaped your notice, Dr Raven, but there are more crimes in this city than the ones you take an interest in.'

On their way home Raven had predicted that, despite this note of petulance, the detective would expedite the matter forthwith.

'McLevy might talk about the law and justice, but primarily he serves the interests of wealth and property. He knows that if he is exonerated, Gideon will be a rich and influential figure, so McLevy will not wish to delay and risk antagonising him any further than he has done already.'

So it had proved. McLevy's message reached Queen Street less than a day later. They had ridden to the High Street in Dr Simpson's carriage, despite the professor having returned from his trip to London late that morning. Sarah had the impression that he was not looking his best. Raven suggested that perhaps he was simply exhausted from the journey, but his explanation lacked conviction and Sarah could see that he too was concerned.

Simpson himself would have none of it. He told them off for their fussing, saying there would be enough of that when Mrs Simpson and Mina returned with the children the next day. Despite that, he had taken to his bed. Sarah intended to check up on him the minute they got back.

A clock ticked loudly in the police office. They could hear the voices of passing pedestrians outside on the High Street. McLevy was definitely making them wait, toying with them for some reason. Sarah wondered if he was milking his moment of triumph or trying to establish his status ahead of an ignominious climb-down.

Raven seemed nervous, anticipating the worst. On the carriage ride here he had been pessimistic, certain that McLevy would only have summoned them to deliver bad news.

Sarah by contrast retained absolute confidence in what she had found. She recalled what Raven had relayed from Struthers' report: *There was a small amount of arsenic in the stomach contents, but none was found subsequently in any of the organs.* Someone meaning to poison a man as healthy and robust as Sir Ainsley Douglas would not have been light in their measures. Her theory was sound, and she had provided the evidence to support it.

McLevy finally put his pen down and sighed.

He held out a single sheet of paper, not looking either of them in the eye. If bad grace could be captured in a single gesture, then this was it.

'Professor Christison's report,' he said.

Raven snatched it from his hand as though wary McLevy would whip it away again.

'He concurs with Miss Fisher,' McLevy announced as Raven read. 'To his own surprise, I might add. You should have seen the man's face when I conveyed that it was a woman who had devised this hypothesis and carried out the initial test. I think he set about it all the faster to demonstrate how quickly he might prove you wrong. Nonetheless—' McLevy frowned, the result evidently having given him as much pleasure as it did Christison '—what I don't understand is, if not arsenic, what did kill him? He was healthy as a horse and just as strong.'

'We can never be sure of what will bring on dysentery,' Raven replied. 'There is often no obvious source.'

McLevy seemed dissatisfied with this explanation. 'It just doesn't seem to make sense that a man so high should meet his demise at the hands of nothing mightier than a manky pie.'

'So, you will release Gideon?' Raven asked.

Sarah knew he would be eager to give the news to Eugenie. He had yet to convey the possibility, lest it prove premature and Christison contradicted their findings. 'Hopes dashed at this stage are worse than no hopes at all,' he had said.

'I released him hours ago,' McLevy replied. 'As soon as Christison sent me his report.'

Of course he had, Sarah thought. As Raven predicted, he had acted to repair relations with the new laird of Crossford House before he would bother informing anyone else.

'He didn't come rushing to convey his gratitude?' McLevy added with a sneer. 'When you told me you had no interest in financial reward for your efforts, I hope that was true, because that's the way of the rich. Once they have what they want from you, you are quickly forgotten.'

Raven said nothing. Sarah knew it was not Gideon's gratitude he was primarily interested in.

McLevy wore his nettle-licking expression again. 'It is a small man who cannot admit when he is wrong. As much as it grieves me, Dr Raven, I must congratulate you for pursuing your instincts. But please tell me, why were you so convinced of his innocence?'

'I wasn't. I'm still not. It is more that I wasn't entirely convinced of his guilt, and that is a different matter.'

'Aye, there's the rub. That is why we have the "not proven" verdict. Juries are reluctant to hang a man on circumstantial evidence alone. But not proven does not mean innocent of the charges brought. It also means the matter is not closed. Gideon Douglas certainly won't be joining the Navy now, but I warned him not to travel far. There are still many questions to be answered over this business as far as I'm concerned.'

Just then, a young man burst through the door of the office.

'I have a message from Dr Littlejohn,' he announced breathlessly.

McLevy put his hand out. 'Give it here.'

The messenger looked at both men, one then the other.

'It's for Dr Raven.'

McLevy seemed more than a little affronted at being upstaged in his own office.

'I went first to Queen Street,' the messenger explained as

Raven opened the letter. 'I was told of your whereabouts by a housemaid, but I fear I may have somehow given her offence.'

'No,' Sarah said, thinking him sweet to be so concerned. 'That was just Lizzie.'

Raven stood up. 'Thank you for your invaluable assistance, Mr McLevy, but we must away. An urgent matter.'

He grabbed Sarah's arm and led her outside.

She waited until they were some distance from McLevy's door before asking what the letter contained.

'Henry has asked me to come urgently to Bonnington Mills.'

He handed the note to her.

'"It concerns a matter of interest to you,"' she read. '"Join me quickly while the news remains contained."'

'I will drop you at Queen Street. If it is something Henry has been called to, it will doubtless be unpleasant.'

On their way to the carriage, they saw one of McLevy's officers leaping down from a cab and hastening towards the office. Sarah thought this unlikely to be a coincidence.

'Henry said it was urgent,' she said. 'We should go there directly.'

FORTY-SEVEN

he carriage pulled up outside the flour mill close to Bonnington Bridge, the Water of Leith flowing beneath it. Sarah noticed that there was an odd smell in the air, presumably from the Bonnington chemical works further down the road. A group of men were standing beside some earthworks, great mounds of drying mud piled to the side of the river. There were hoists and rope lines, piles of timber. Beside them stood Henry.

'I heard they were widening a channel here,' Raven said. 'Dredging, perhaps.'

'They don't appear to be dredging anything today,' Sarah replied.

The men who should have been working were standing around looking restive. Something had halted their activity and they did not seem happy about it.

Raven and Sarah climbed down from the brougham and started walking towards the mounds at the edge of the water.

A man ran to intercept them before they could reach Henry.

'You can't come through here,' he insisted, holding his hands up in front of them. 'No one is to be admitted.'

Henry looked up, noticing the activity.

'It's alright,' he said. 'Dr Raven is here at my request.'

'And what of the lady?' the man asked. He looked appalled at the prospect of letting her through his cordon.

Henry regarded Sarah. 'You might prefer to remain where you are,' he said, 'but given what I know about you, I would not presume to bar your way. Whether you proceed is entirely your choice.'

Sarah knew that Henry would not be here were there not a corpse involved, but that held no fear for her. She had seen plenty of dead bodies in her time and knew that if she wished to pursue a career in medicine, she would see many more.

She strode forward at Raven's side. In a matter of seconds she was wishing that Henry *had* barred her way. There had been moments in Sarah's life the significance of which she did not appreciate until a long time later, their effects having continued to resonate down the years. And there were sights that even in that first moment of looking, she knew she would take to her grave.

As she approached the water, she saw a man huddled on his haunches close to the banking, pale and tearful. A man next to him had a supportive hand on his shoulder. The first man appeared to be in the process of assuring him all was well, but when he made to stand, he found that he could not and sank back down.

'The engineers diverted the flow into a tributary channel so that they could widen this section and strengthen the sides,' Henry explained. 'The water level dropped almost to the riverbed, revealing this.'

There were packages partially embedded in the mud, haphazardly arranged, driven by the flow of the water. There were dozens of them, some wrapped in sailcloth, some in bedsheets, and some in waxed parcel paper. Some were piled on top of others, some side by side. From Raven's description of what had been found in the water at Leith harbour, Sarah immediately knew what they were.

There was a sheet laid down on the banking a few feet from

where Henry stood, crenelated by several small shapes arranged beneath it.

Raven pointed to it. 'What's that?'

'The ones I have opened. I have barely begun to retrieve them. But each one I have unwrapped contained the same thing.'

He pulled back the sheet. Lying on the banking were a host of small bodies, pale and partially rotted away, bones visible.

'I think there could be two dozen at least. I sent for you because of those I have opened . . .'

They looked closer, Sarah pulling the collar of her jacket up to cover her nose and mouth. There was white tape looped around each little neck.

These were the ones she could not sell, Sarah thought. The ones that did not thrive. The ones she did not want to waste pap and Godfrey's Cordial on.

'They were probably thrown from Bonnington Bridge,' Henry said. 'All weighted down. The Water of Leith flows into the harbour where the first child was found. It was wrapped in parcel paper, presumably all there was to hand. The paper must have torn and the stone weighting it fallen loose.'

'Do you think Christina's baby is among these?' Raven whispered to her.

Sarah did not doubt it. Nora's words echoed in her head.

Everybody lies to themselves about it . . . They're paying to salve their conscience, spending on a fantasy.

This, laid out here and beginning to stink in the sun, was the brutal truth of it.

'Are any of them a boy with a birthmark on his upper arm?' Sarah asked.

Henry gave her a quizzical look. 'Not that I have seen, though it will be quite some time before I am able to examine them all. I take it that you are looking for a particular child. How long has he been missing?'

'A few months.'

'Then he might yet be identified. Some of these have been down here for quite some time. With the attendant deterioration in the tissues . . .'

His words tailed off as Sarah turned away. She was struggling not to cry. It was impossible to remain aloof, disconnected from the horrible reality of it all. She could not summon the professional detachment that Raven assured her she would learn to muster on such occasions.

When she looked at Raven, she could see that he was struggling too. She would not have expected him to be so moved on Christina's behalf and certainly not on Gideon's. Then she realised that his thoughts were with neither of them.

Henry seemed to sense that there was something personal in their responses. He replaced the sheet over the bodies and stepped away.

'Eugenie had a secret child, didn't she?' Sarah asked gently.

Raven nodded. Swallowed. When he replied, it was barely above a whisper.

'Two years ago. A daughter. Her father took the baby. He gave it to a woman at a railway station, just as the lady at the perfumier described. I think that Eugenie's child may lie here too.'

There was a commotion at their backs. Sarah looked across to see McLevy making his way through, accompanied by the officer they had seen rushing into the police office. Henry wandered across to greet him with the news of what had been uncovered.

Sarah thought of some of the terrible things she had borne witness to over the past few years. The dreadful crimes of the so-called French midwife that had never come to light, partly to protect the innocent, and partly to protect the values of a society not yet ready to confront them. Earlier this same year, the grim harvest of a murderous nurse had been suppressed to avoid a panic against a trusted profession. There would be no hiding this, however. Too many eyes had already seen it. News of this gruesome discovery would travel across Edinburgh faster than any carriage and would likely reach Queen Street before they did.

She heard McLevy loudly clearing his throat, clearly calling their attention. He was standing over the gruesome assembly of little corpses once again revealed beneath Henry's sheet.

'So, Dr Raven and Miss Fisher, what do the pair of you reckon? Am I missing an innocent explanation involving medicine and science, or can I call this lot murder?'

FORTY-EIGHT

he news was all over Edinburgh, seemingly the only thing Raven heard anyone talk about. The newspapers were referring to the perpetrator as a 'baby-farmer', and it appeared the practice was not new. It had proliferated in recent times all over the country, known about but never spoken of. However, as McLevy had put it, child neglect was one thing — children succumbing from want of proper care and attention — but this was something else again. Strangulation to hasten the end. This was murder.

Every patient at Raven's clinic yesterday had voiced an opinion about who was responsible, or about the women who had surrendered their babies in such a way. What troubled Raven was that they all gave the impression this horror had nothing to do with them. They were shocked that such a thing had been discovered here, but it was as though it had happened *to* their city, visited upon it by some unimaginable malefactor.

Raven was more of the opinion that it was something their city had done to the women involved. To his mind, the discovery at Bonnington Mills collectively shamed Edinburgh, and the more influence you had, the more shame you ought to bear.

He was sure that Mrs King would be lying low, if not already fled, while the likes of Madame Bouvier would be admitting no knowledge of the woman or her activities. McLevy's men were combing the city, and if they tracked their quarry down, she would surely hang, but Raven knew the true culprits would never be held accountable. It was men like Ainsley Douglas who created the baby-farmers, who proposed and helped devise the laws that made it impossible for unwed mothers to provide for their children, or to seek financial recourse from the fathers.

Upon those the scandal directly affected, the damage was considerable. If poor Christina had previously been deceiving herself about the fate of her son, she was not now. The news had reached her before Mrs Simpson's party had even made it back into the city. According to Mina, they had heard it read from the newspaper by someone who boarded their train at North Berwick, whereupon Christina had – inexplicably to her employer – collapsed inconsolably into weeping.

She had taken to her bed upon her return to Queen Street, where a strange reversal witnessed Mrs Simpson bringing her housemaid a bowl of soup in an effort to feed and comfort her.

Raven and Sarah had discussed telling Christina what they knew, wondering if it might lift her spirits to learn that Gideon had spoken of his love for her and had only failed to seek her out because his father had told him she was dead. Raven had counselled caution as he did not feel confident about how Gideon was likely to conduct himself should he learn that Christina was in fact alive. He was now a man of means and status, whether he liked it or not. His perspective on an affair with someone below stairs may have altered dramatically.

Perhaps significantly, Raven still had not seen the man.

Since Gideon's release two days ago, Raven had thought often of McLevy's scorn. He was not expecting tearful gratitude, but that there should be no word of acknowledgement didn't give the impression of a man humbled by the admonitions of his recent experience.

Eugenie had seen him, but only briefly, and he had barely registered her presence as he stormed in and out of the house on St Andrew Square. It had been far from the reunion she had envisaged, his conduct leaving her troubled.

'There was something coldly determined about him,' she had told Raven. 'He all but barged past me like I wasn't there, intent on speaking to my father, brooking no refusal. Then after they had spoken, he charged out again, barely looking at me as he went.'

'What did they speak about?' Raven asked.

'I don't know. My father would not discuss it, but he looked shaken. He had lost a button from his shirt. I think Gideon might have grabbed him.'

'Did you overhear anything?'

'They kept their voices low, deliberately so I would say, though it was clearly a heated exchange.'

There had been a time, only days ago, when Raven would have been relieved to learn that Gideon had not rushed straight to Eugenie's waiting embrace upon his release. But relieved or not, something about this did not feel right.

As Raven entered the dining room for breakfast, he saw that while Sarah, Mrs Simpson and Mina were already seated, there was once again no sign of Dr Simpson. He decided that, once he had eaten, he would go up and check on the professor whether he wanted him to or not. Thus far he had been refusing to let anyone except Jessie tend to him.

Dr Simpson's withdrawal was not unprecedented. It had happened on several occasions before, usually due to a profound depression of spirits or over-exuberant experimentation with various inhaled chemicals. Both usually responded well to a few days in bed but there was no sign of recovery yet and Mrs Simpson had mentioned a low fever that Raven did not like the sound of.

Raven had just finished off a bowl of porridge and was on his way to the stairs when the doorbell sounded. He postponed his ascent, conscious that it might be an urgent summons requiring his immediate departure.

There was no such emergency. Instead Jarvis opened the door to reveal Amelia Bettencourt, dressed as always in black. At the sight of her Raven remembered that today it was her father rather than her husband she was formally mourning: she must have stopped by on her way to the funeral. Following Gideon's exoneration – and despite McLevy's protestations that the case was not closed – the body had been released for burial.

Amelia was carrying her son Matthew, clutched tightly to her chest. He recalled Eugenie saying Amelia could not bear to be parted from him, as though constant vigilance would save him from succumbing to disease. She had even dismissed her nursemaid because she feared she had been insufficiently watchful. It seemed harsh to blame the woman for a child's illness when they went down with so many things, but it was testament to how precious the baby was to Amelia. A last remnant of her dead husband.

Christina had shared a similar maternal instinct, to protect her child at all costs, but she had lacked the financial means to do so and now mourned for the son she could not afford to keep.

Amelia nodded at Raven as she entered, the black feathers on her hat quivering as she did so.

'I must speak with you, Dr Raven. And Miss Fisher too.'

Raven led her upstairs to the drawing room, thinking that his rather messy consulting room would be inappropriate for an interview. She took a seat and settled the baby in her lap as Sarah entered.

Raven thought that Amelia looked wan, as though deeply burdened.

'Are you in need of refreshment, Mrs Bettencourt?' Sarah enquired.

'Thank you, no.'

'You are on your way to the funeral?' Raven asked. It was a banal question, but it felt polite to mention it, by way of tacitly acknowledging also that her detour via Queen Street was irregular to say the least.

Raven looked at Sarah, who seemed equally puzzled.

'It will be a relief, I hope,' Amelia said. 'Marking an end to this dreadful business.'

Raven waited for her to say more but she did not.

'How is your brother?' he asked. 'I have not seen him since his release.'

'Nor I. Indeed, that is what brings me here to speak to you both.'

She adjusted her grip on the child, shifting little Matthew in her lap.

'I know I should be grateful that you exonerated Gideon, because for all his faults, I would prefer not to live with the knowledge that he murdered our father. However, there is something that has been troubling me. Something that makes it difficult for me to accept that the matter is truly resolved.'

Sarah took a seat beside her, looking adoringly at the swaddled bundle in her lap. Raven could not but think of how she would now never bear a child of her own, and wondered at how that might weigh upon her.

Little Matthew seemed too old to be so tightly wrapped, Raven thought. His cheeks were flushed and his eyes heavy, his head nodding a little as he tried to fight sleep. Amelia, unusually for a proud mother, turned the child away from Sarah and shifted herself a little further too. Perhaps she feared that Sarah was a potential source of contagion.

'What is it that has caused you to feel troubled?' Raven asked.

Amelia paused a moment, then spoke.

'I must have cast the image from my mind while it was believed Gideon poisoned my father with arsenic. But now that you have proven arsenic was not the cause of his death . . .'

She sighed, the strain of conflict etched upon her face.

'I want to believe better things about my brother, but I know I will be unable to while there remains a question not merely unanswered, but never asked.'

'What do you mean?' Raven asked. 'What image?'

'On the night of the soirée, shortly before I left, I saw my brother go into the kitchen. He was carrying a hessian bag which he did not have when he emerged. He seemed furtive. I recall he had brought some exotic fruits home from Tobago, and I believe that is what was in the bag.'

'Yes, one of the housemaids mentioned that,' Sarah said. 'You may rest easy. It was merely pineapple. Quite harmless.'

'I know well enough what a pineapple is,' she replied. 'I have visited the Indies too. And that is not what he was carrying. The bag was too small. As I say, I discounted the significance of this while arsenic was believed to be the cause, but now . . .'

Amelia winced, as though tasting something sour and unpleasant. She turned to Sarah.

'Miss Fisher, I have heard much about you. You are clever and ambitious. I am told you have designs on becoming a doctor. I have always had an interest in the law, and would have liked to pursue a career myself. Alas, such a course is not open to my sex. I therefore know that to make any headway a woman needs to be twice as good as the best man. That is why I believe that if anyone might get to the truth of this, it would be you.'

Raven noticed Sarah blush at this unexpected praise. Unexpected but not unearned. Much as he was happy for Sarah, he could not help but feel overlooked himself, as though his efforts thus far counted for nothing.

'What is it you want me to find out?' Sarah asked.

'Gideon kept saying he is innocent because if he was going to murder someone, he wouldn't have used a detectable poison. Doesn't that prompt the question — what *would* he have used?

FORTY-NINE

rossford House loomed before Sarah as she stepped from the carriage onto the path nestled between two immaculate expanses of lawn. As she made her way to the front door, she belatedly wondered whether she was wrong to assume Gideon would attend the funeral, given his disregard for his father. If he turned out to be in residence at what was now his property, it would make explaining her purpose here considerably more awkward.

After the attack in Fleshmarket Close, Sarah felt wary of being on her own, but she knew that she would have to get used to it. There was often little choice in the matter. Raven had been called to an emergency at the Maternity Hospital almost as soon as Amelia left, and Sarah did not think that this visit could wait.

She understood now that whoever attacked them may well have had a lot to protect. It seemed most likely to have been someone connected to Mrs King, worried about what an investigation into her activities might uncover. She thought about Madame Bouvier and wondered just how many people were complicit in the baby-farmer's crimes.

Sarah felt sickened by the horror and tragedy that had been revealed. It had all started with her agreeing to help Christina find her baby. Even at that time she had not thought it likely the girl would ever be reunited with her child, but she had never imagined anything like this.

One thing she could be sure of was that it was not Gideon who had attacked them, as he had been locked up in Calton Jail at the time. But his innocence in the other matter seemed far from confirmed.

Sarah had thought herself so clever, but Amelia's question made her realise that the arsenic may have been a coincidental distraction. Christison had agreed that the amount discovered would be unlikely to cause such a sudden death, but just because Sir Ainsley Douglas had not been poisoned with arsenic did not mean that he hadn't been poisoned by something else: something that *wouldn't* leave a trace.

Therein lay the problem, however. If an organic poison had been used, how would they find evidence of it?

Sarah thought about how the killer's modus operandi might have been in front of them all the time. Gideon kept talking about the way he could *not* have done it. She was reminded of a conjurer she had seen in the Lawnmarket during a fair. He kept telling the crowd of all the ways that a feat was impossible, drawing their minds to the ways in which he couldn't do it. This was so that they paid no attention to the way he *was* doing it.

Raven had insisted that though Gideon might be rash and angry, he was no fool. In fact, it was possible he was the one who had fooled everybody.

Sarah pulled the bell several times but there was no answer.

She was reluctant to leave without getting what she had come for. She tried the door, and finding it unlocked, she stepped into the entrance hall.

'Hello?' she called out, her voice echoing down unseen corridors.

There was no response, so she walked in a little further.

She had forgotten just how dizzyingly vast the house was. Whatever the attendant pressures and responsibilities of inheritance, this place was a prize. She knew that she would not be comfortable living amongst such grandeur and thought of how Amelia did not desire it either. However, there were those who might be more than happy to live here.

Sarah thought again about the motive they had imagined for Teddy Hamilton: an inheritance of wealth, power and influence, owning land, businesses, a newspaper. But was it worth killing for? She knew that not everyone was capable of such a deed, no matter how great the reward. Teddy Hamilton had not seemed the sort of man who might contemplate such a thing, did not seem ruthless enough. But she had only met him very briefly and she knew that appearances could be deceiving.

She was making her way along the hall when a housemaid appeared, one she had not seen before. She expected to be challenged but the girl averted her eyes. Sarah was struck by how deferential she was, not asking any questions about what a stranger might be doing there. The right garb and an air of purpose and entitlement caused the girl to make all kinds of assumptions. Sarah wondered if this was what it felt like to be a man, everyone assuming you had a right to be wherever you were.

She made her way down to the kitchen, remembering the route without taking any wrong turns. She knocked on the door out of habit and politeness, then stepped inside, where she found the cook kneading dough at the kitchen table. Meg, the housemaid Sarah had spoken to before, was stirring up the fire in the range.

'Oh, hello,' the cook said, unperturbed by this unexpected visit. 'Back again, are you?'

'Is Mr Wilson here?' Sarah asked.

'He's at the funeral,' the cook replied. 'It's just us, though there's not much for us to do at the moment.'

'What about Gideon? He is the new master now, is he not?'

The cook gave her a look as if to say they were not quite sure.

'He has barely been here. Can't have been over the door more than ten minutes since he was released from the jail. He came to grab some of his father's money – well, I suppose it's his money now – and left again. Given the look on his face, I wouldn't have got in his way.

'You're not the first to be looking for him, either. There's been plenty others. Men he'll be in charge of now, needing decisions made, documents signed. I think he's dodging all of them. He's not ready for all that, if you ask me. I think he's holed himself up somewhere, probably getting drunk. Indulging his other appetites too, no doubt.' She pushed some stray hair away from her face with the back of a floury hand. 'Can't say I blame him when he's spent so many days facing the rope.'

She started shaping the dough, then put it in a baking tin ready for the oven.

'He's a lost young man,' she said. 'Lost and angry, and just because he's now lost and angry and rich doesn't change the first two things.' She wiped her hands on her apron. 'Anyway, how can I help you?'

'I've been sent to look for something. Some fruit that Gideon brought back from Tobago.'

'You mean yon spikey thing you tasted last time you were here?'

'No. This would be something smaller, in a hessian bag.'

'I'll have a look,' she said, heading for the pantry.

Sarah followed her in, Meg peering curiously at the doorway. As at Queen Street, she was struck by how much cooler the food store was, a place that admitted no natural light.

'I don't think I've seen such a thing, but to be honest I've not needed to hunt through the darker reaches of late. Not since the master died and young Gideon was hauled off to jail. Barely had call to cook anything, except for us staff, never mind replenish supplies with anything exotic or unusual. Normally there would be all manner of people passing through and needing fed: politicians, churchmen, businessmen, doctors.'

She pulled a crate forward on a shelf. Sarah could see jagged green leaves sticking over the top.

'Still a few of those pineapples left,' the cook said with a marked lack of enthusiasm. 'No, I don't recall . . . Oh here, hold on a wee minute. Here's the very thing.'

The cook reached into the pineapple crate and retrieved the bag that Amelia had described. She held it out to Sarah, who took it back through to the kitchen.

Placing it on the table, she turned the bag over and shook out a small and slightly desiccated green fruit.

'Does this resemble what you cleared from Sir Ainsley's plate on the morning he was found?' she asked Meg.

'Aye. Two or three of them, cut into halves.'

The cook's eyebrows knitted together, her expression defensive.

'I've never seen these before, and I certainly never put such a thing on the master's supper tray. I set out a slice of pie and some cheese, that's all. Always food he could eat cold because we never knew what time he would go to bed. Someone would take the tray up and leave it on the table in his room.'

'Who took him the tray that night?' Sarah asked.

'It wasn't me,' insisted Meg, looking worried.

'Could have been anybody,' said the cook. 'There was extra staff here for the party.'

'What is it anyway?' Meg asked. She was about to poke it with her finger but changed her mind.

'I have no notion,' Sarah said. 'But I know a man who might.'

FIFTY

aven walked out of the Maternity Hospital into the late morning sunshine having hauled another reluctant child safely into the world. It was a blessing of the job that he could so lose himself in it and banish all other cares while dealing with the problem before him: ultimately someone else's problem, for the patient was the one with the disease. However, as soon as each case was over, the immediate issue dealt with, his other problems came flooding back in, as though to fill the space vacated.

Chief among them, bustling its way to the front and demanding precedence like McLevy at the scene of a crime, was his concern over his mentor's illness. The professor's fever showed no signs of abating and before being summoned to the Maternity Hospital, Raven had insisted on a brief examination to try and establish the root of the problem. It did not take long. There was suppuration in the hand as a result of the splinter (long since removed) and an inflamed mass in the corresponding armpit. Raven had prescribed a febrifuge and dressed the hand himself but was worried that this would not be enough. He feared it might be appropriate to call in reinforcements, however much the professor might object.

At such times it was difficult to separate his perspective as a physician from his perspective as a friend; as a relative even, as he was coming to consider himself a member of the family. Sometimes family members were full of worry despite a physician's reassurance, and sometimes the physician was full of worry while the family failed to appreciate how dire was the situation their beloved relative faced. Raven's problem was that right now both the physician and the relative in him were concerned.

Dr Simpson was not well.

He was not an old man – forty or thereabouts – but even those who enjoyed robust good health could be quickly felled by disease. Raven had witnessed it often enough to be at least a little apprehensive. Fate could be cruel. Being a person of value was no defence.

Raven could not bear the thought of losing Dr Simpson now. He had plans to marry and had hoped the Simpson family would remain close, that the professor would still have a role in his life. He wanted his children to know him. The man had given him so much. He had not merely been like a father to him, he had shown Raven how to *be* a father.

Perhaps this was how it went when it was time to move on, to set up one's own practice and start one's own family. But if this was the cycle of life he heard spoken of, then it seemed an unnecessarily brutal trade. Edinburgh without Simpson seemed inconceivable. He loomed too large in the city's landscape to even imagine it. But Raven knew that the same had been thought of many men before. Two weeks ago, most people would have found it impossible to imagine a world without Ainsley Douglas.

Though perhaps there was one person who had been imagining it vividly.

Was it possible that Sir Ainsley's death had indeed been parricide, an act of vengeance and a means to rapidly obtain an inheritance? And had he and indeed Sarah been unwittingly instrumental in achieving that? Raven's elation at Sarah's findings being corroborated by Christison proved short-lived. The sheen had come off Gideon's exoneration troublingly quickly.

Raven was still caught between two visions of Gideon: one mercilessly kicking the man lying on the ground in that alley, and one who was tearful and contrite before him in the jail cell. One who was crushed and broken by the loss of the woman he loved, a lowly housemaid, and one who had barged past Eugenie as though she meant nothing.

His thoughts turned next to Eugenie. He had worried about her learning of the Bonnington Mill babies and assuming the worst about her own daughter. However, this was still Edinburgh, and she would be protected by its latest self-deception. The word spreading around the city was that the victims were merely the unwanted children of prostitutes. There was some truth to that, but it only formed the basis of a larger, comforting lie for people to tell themselves. It was not *your* baby parcelled up at the bottom of the river. The respectable woman you had paid all that money to would never have done *that*, unlike the monster these desperate whores had resorted to.

But Raven knew there were those who could not lie to themselves, those who knew too much to do so, and one of them was Eugenie's father. Cameron Todd must have known – or at least been aware of the possibility – that his own granddaughter lay at the bottom of the Water of Leith.

The thought prompted Raven to wonder what Gideon had spoken to Todd about, grabbing him so hard that he ripped the buttons from his shirt.

And then he saw it.

Todd had been Sir Ainsley's physician. When it emerged that Gideon had got a housemaid pregnant, Todd had proposed a solution. He knew a woman who could deal with it: the one he had paid to take his unwanted granddaughter.

Sir Ainsley Douglas knew about Simpson's fostering, but in those cases Mrs Simpson kept the mothers informed of who their children were with and how they were faring. The purpose here was for the child to disappear without trace, and like Todd, Sir Ainsley did not want anybody knowing about his connection to the child. Todd would have functioned as a go-between, a further remove between the Douglas family and the baby-farmer. He was the one who had arranged for Christina to have her confinement with Mrs King, and may even have delivered the child himself.

Gideon must have deduced this, and now he was searching for his child. Or rather, having learned the grim news from Bonnington Mills, he was searching for whoever was responsible for his child's death. And he had guessed that Todd knew where she could be found.

As he reached the top of the High Street, Raven remembered that the funeral was taking place this morning. He checked his watch, wondering if he had missed it. Wondering if Gideon would be there. Curiosity got the better of him and he decided to take a look himself, though only briefly. He knew he had to get back to Queen Street to see if his treatment had had any effect on the professor. It was always possible that things had improved, that his worst fears were unfounded.

He turned onto George IV Bridge, walking briskly towards the main gate at Greyfriars. As he approached, he passed many people in sombre dress proceeding in the opposite direction. It occurred to Raven to ponder whether Simpson's failure to attend had been noted in certain quarters. He knew that there were those who would make mischief of this apparent show of disrespect.

He entered the churchyard unsure which direction he should be heading. The place seemed deserted and he suspected he was too late. He noticed a man emerging from the kirk and asked him if he knew where Sir Ainsley's final resting place was to be.

'I think most of the mourners have already gone, but if you wish to pay your respects, the grave is up at the far end, beside the Martyrs' Monument.'

'The Martyr's Monument?'

Raven did not know it, even though he had been in this graveyard many times before.

'Yes, down at the end. You can't miss it.'

Raven was not so sure. Greyfriars was replete with monuments.

'Which martyr does the monument commemorate?'

'Not one but many. There are about a hundred Covenanters buried there. Or what was left of them.'

The Covenanters' Memorial, the one he and Sarah could not find.

Raven thanked the man and headed off down the pathway he had indicated, now less interested in paying his respects at the graveside than finding the monument they had failed to discover before. Mrs Mackay had not been lying to get rid of them. She said she had cut through the kirkyard on her way to the Grassmarket when she saw Mrs King going into a haberdasher's.

He passed what he assumed to be Sir Ainsley's grave. The last of the mourners had indeed departed, leaving a gaping hole that a pair of gravediggers were preparing to fill. Extravagant floral arrangements surrounded it, infusing the air with the intense fragrance of lilies.

The monument was at the far end of the graveyard. There was a gate set in the wall to the right of it, steps leading down to the street.

Raven quickened his stride as though there were hands at his back, then was brought up sharp as he emerged between the gateposts. Directly across the road was a haberdashery. A young woman was arranging a display in the window, laying out spools of coloured thread beside a large drum of dressmaker's tape. *White* dressmaker's tape.

He looked along the street. Signs hung from above several of the doorways. Engraver. Picture-frame maker. Bookseller.

Remembering what McLevy had told him, Raven noted that the bookseller's shop was immediately next to the haberdashery.

Reckon the perpetrator lifted the paper from a common midden.

That was when he realised which street he was standing on. It was Candlemaker Row.

FIFTY-ONE

arah entered through the main gate of the Royal Botanic Garden wondering why she had never thought to visit before. She passed the museum and the classroom, empty during summer months, and made her way to the gardeners' cottages, hoping to find someone who might point her in the right direction. If time permitted, she planned to visit the area reserved for medicinal plants on her way out.

She spotted a gardener wheeling a barrow full of manure and asked him where she could find the gentleman she was seeking.

'I'm sorry, ma'am, but I haven't seen him today.'

He called out to another fellow who was kneeling beside a flower bed, digging out weeds with a trowel.

'Last saw him up by the Palm House,' the kneeling man said.

The man with the barrow indicated a glass dome rising between the trees.

'Old Woody's pride and joy, that is,' he said.

'Woody?'

'Woody Fibre. The professor's nickname. Though I don't recommend you call him that.'

Sarah smiled, thanked the man and proceeded towards the Palm House, thinking that she was unlikely to forget herself and use such an informal style of address. The man she hoped to speak to was John Hutton Balfour, Professor of Medicine and Botany at Edinburgh University. She had decided to seek him out having consulted his *Manual of Botany* and failed to identify the small green fruit that had been found in the pantry at Crossford.

She knew that she was taking a risk in simply turning up and asking the man himself. Some did not like women asking questions, thinking that scientific curiosity was solely within the male purview.

She opened the door to the Palm House and was greeted by a gust of hot, humid air, the change in temperature noticeable despite the warmth of the day outside. Sarah stepped across the threshold into another world, somewhere equatorial and exotic, full of strange flora. There was a cloying smell of wet soil and mouldering vegetation. She looked up to the glass panels in the domed roof, condensation clouding the view of the sky beyond. The fronds of an enormous palm tree reached towards the top of it.

She had nearly made a complete circuit of the building before she found what she was looking for. The man was bent over examining some foliage with a magnifying glass. She watched him for a moment, so intent on what he was doing that he failed to notice her standing there.

She cleared her throat and he looked up, mildly startled but offering a smile as he noticed it was a lady before him.

'Are you lost?' he asked.

'Not at all, sir. I was looking for someone to help me identify an unusual specimen.'

'Were you indeed. And are you a student of botany, madam?'

'I have an interest in medicinal plants.'

'A utilitarian phytologist, eh? But there is so much more to the study of plants than that. They are endlessly diverse and fascinating.'

Sarah smiled, relieved. True enthusiasts were happy to share their knowledge with anyone who expressed an interest, meaning he was unlikely to interpret her questions as impertinent.

'You have something to show me?' he asked, indicating the small hessian bag that she was carrying.

She opened the neck of the bag to let him see what lay inside.

He took it from her, placing it on his palm so that the hessian fell partially away to reveal the item inside. Then for good measure he took a deep sniff.

'Hmm. I think I know what this is. Come with me.'

Professor Balfour led her through the forest of potted palms to a small office where a desk lay strewn with papers, illustrations, containers and plant pots. He gently moved some papers aside, clearing a space. Opening a drawer, he pulled out a pair of gloves and donned them before gingerly removing the specimen from the bag. He turned it around in his hand, scrutinizing it from every angle.

'I think I am correct in saying that this is the fruit of the manchineel tree. *Hippomane mancinella*. Native to the West Indies. Looks like a small crab apple but with a sweeter smell. May I ask how you came to be in possession of it?'

'An acquaintance brought it back from his travels to Tobago.'

'Bit of a dangerous souvenir.'

'Why?'

'Simply standing beneath the manchineel tree during rainfall can cause the skin to blister. The sap itself is corrosive. And as for the fruit, my goodness!' Professor Balfour grimaced and made play of turning away from what lay in his hand. 'The name derives from the Spanish for small apple. But the conquistadors had another name for it: *manzanilla de la muerte*.'

'I'm sorry, I have no Spanish,' Sarah said.

Balfour wore an expression of grim delight.

'It means "little apple of death".'

FIFTY-TWO

aven entered the haberdashery, little more than a single room crammed full of a haphazard jumble of contents: bolts of cloth leaning against walls; ribbons and buttons; skeins of yarn. He noticed that amidst all of this was a solitary shelf of finished garments: baby clothes.

The shopkeeper looked up from the pile of bobbins she had just finished arranging in the window. She seemed a little wary, probably unused to men coming in and inspecting her wares. Raven smiled and removed his hat.

'Is there a woman visits here by the name of Mrs King?' he asked, getting straight to the point. 'When last seen she was wearing a blue shawl.'

The woman laughed. 'Shops here? She does more than that.' She indicated the shelf Raven had noticed. 'Keeps us in baby clothes. Has done for years. A lot of fine garments.'

'Do you know where she lives?'

'Aye. Above the bookshop, door at the side. Took lodgings there recently. She used to live just along the row, then she moved away for a while and now she's back. Keen on her privacy, though. Doesn't like visitors.'

The woman began sorting through a box, pulling out balls of wool and arranging them on the counter.

'You're the second person asking for her today,' she added.

'A woman?' Raven asked, surprised that Mrs King would be continuing in her trade after the discovery at Bonnington.

'A gentleman. Finely dressed and well-spoken. Little good it did him, though. He got short shrift. Wasn't in there long. Saw him leave like the devil himself was after him.'

As soon as she said it, Raven knew who she was talking about. Gideon had wanted to know what happened to his son. Evidently, Todd had told him.

Raven found the door ajar, as though someone had left or entered in a hurry. He called out but there came no answer from within.

Raven pushed the door fully open and stepped inside. Down a short corridor he came to the main room, where two chairs sat on opposite sides of a table a few feet from a range with no fire in the grate. The air smelt stale, cut through with the sharp reek of ammonia. There was a dresser in the corner bearing a pile of baby clothing. Little cotton shirts, petticoats and napkins, all neatly hand-sewn, a few with initials embroidered at the hem.

The woman from the perfumier's told Sarah she had been asked to supply clothes for her child. She wouldn't have been the only one. It probably helped convince them that their children would be cared for, as well as providing the baby-farmer with an additional source of income.

The place was otherwise empty. Still. Raven stood in the middle of the room and listened but heard nothing. An open door at the far end led to another room. As he crossed towards it, the smell became much worse.

He saw a row of cots lined up against the wall.

Raven assumed they were empty but upon approach he saw that he was wrong. Each contained an infant, and each infant was quite obviously dead, white tape looped around every tiny neck and pulled tight.

Mrs King must have realised that the game was up, that all

trade must immediately cease. Given the story was all over the city she could not afford to be discovered with several babies in her home. She could not even afford to have anyone hear them cry. And with Bonnington Mills discovered, she would have needed to find somewhere new to dispose of them. That she had not done so yet was because she had been interrupted.

She was lying on the floor behind the door, her eyes bulging, the skin of her face purple and congested. She too had been strangled with a length of dressmaker's tape.

Raven checked the tiny body in each cot for signs of life; a forlorn hope but he felt it was something he ought to do. He then knelt down beside the body of the baby-farmer and felt for a pulse, unsure what he would do if he found one. There was none and he was released – thankfully – from any obligation to act. She was still warm. Whoever had done this had not been gone long.

He knelt beside the body for a moment, thinking that there would be many people in this city relieved that she could not spill their secrets or speak of their complicity. But there would be no comfort now for the dozens of women asking why and how: women anxious to know whether their child had been sold on to a good home or disposed of at Bonnington Mills.

Mrs King would not be providing them with any answers. She had answered only to the vengeance of Gideon Douglas: a man eminently capable of murder after all.

FIFTY-THREE

aven entered the drawing room ahead of the house-maid whose job it was to announce him. Dr Todd was sitting in an armchair by the fire reading the *Scotsman*. He looked over the top of it, frowning at the intrusion. The housemaid began to apologise but Todd got up and shooed her away, waiting until she had closed the door before addressing his visitor.

'To what do I owe the pleasure?' he said, though his tone was far from friendly.

'I can assure you, sir, that there is no pleasure to be had in this business.'

Todd folded up his newspaper, putting it down on the table in front of him.

'Whatever do you mean?'

'I know that you were involved in getting rid of Christina Cullen's baby. That is why Gideon came to see you as soon as he was released.'

'I have no idea—' Todd began, but Raven cut him off.

'Gideon had deduced that you were to blame, that you were the one who came up with the solution, because you had disposed of your own daughter's unwanted child through the same channel.

Gideon's son lies in the mud at Bonnington Mills, and most likely your own granddaughter lies there too.'

Todd looked for a moment as though he would continue to deny his involvement, but Raven already knew too much and could see the older man's resolve disintegrate.

'Eugenie spoke to you of this?' he asked quietly.

'There is a bond of trust between us. She is a complicated woman, as you said. But she is also honest and honourable. It is a pity that I cannot say the same for her father. What other mistakes and inconvenient truths have you covered up? What happened on the night Margaret Douglas died? Dymock said I should ask you that.'

Todd now looked wounded, but he was not yet ready to surrender.

'I don't owe you any explanations,' he said. 'You should tread carefully lest I reconsider your future.'

Raven decided to call his bluff. He no longer had anything to fear from this man.

'You are the one concerned that your daughter will never find a husband. If you still want her to marry someone who cares about her, then you will show me some respect, and you will start by being honest with me, sir. What did you conceal? The staff said you were called to Crossford House on the night that Lady Douglas died and that only you were admitted to the room.'

'She became ill most suddenly,' Todd said. 'I am the family physician. There is nothing suspicious about my being there that night.'

He was still trying to brazen it out, but as he spoke Raven remembered what Gideon had said in the stables, causing his father to strike him.

My mother's only weakness was her blindness to what you are. But in time the scales fell, and that was why . . .

'She killed herself,' Raven stated. 'She took her own life and you concealed it.'

Todd's eyes widened with alarm. He seemed to know now that he was undone, that further resistance would be futile.

'It is true,' he said, sitting back down in his armchair with an air of defeat. 'She died by her own hand. Swallowed the best part of a bottle of laudanum.'

'Why?'

'I don't know.'

'I think you do.'

'I can only speculate. Why does anyone do such a thing? Because she was unhappy, I suppose, and as you are no doubt assuming, it was most likely Sir Ainsley who made her so. But I did what I did as an act of mercy, to protect the children as much as Sir Ainsley. It would have been an appalling scandal had it been known she committed self-murder.'

So there it was. Another man prostituting himself before Sir Ainsley's power and wealth. But Ainsley had been wary of the leverage this knowledge might grant his physician. That was why he had been pressing Dr Simpson, trying to wheedle out evidence of a scandal that he could hold over Todd.

'There are things you can hide from wider society,' Raven told him, 'but within a family you cannot hide the sins of the father. Amelia knew. Eugenie told me her manner towards her father changed irrevocably following her mother's death. Gideon knew too.'

'I suspected as much, and I understand that the nature of his mother's demise may have contributed to his behaviour. But that does not mean I can forgive him for what he did to my daughter.'

Raven shook his head. At least there was one charge Gideon appeared to be innocent of.

'Gideon was not responsible for Eugenie being with child. She let you believe that he was the father so that you would not pursue the truth.'

Todd looked taken aback. 'If not Gideon, then who was it?'

'That is for neither of us to know. If Eugenie does not wish to speak of it, then I will respect that as her right.'

'And knowing all this, you would still marry her?'

Raven looked at him in his fine clothes, with his persistent haughty demeanour, as though he was still the better man despite what he had just admitted.

'How absurd that it should be her honour that is somehow in question. That you should fear she might never marry if people knew her secret. In this house, she is the one with the least to be ashamed of. If I were to fear the stigma of a tainted association, sir, it would be with you.'

FIFTY-FOUR

aven was seated at the kitchen table while Sarah made tea. More tea. He seemed to be running on the stuff of late. He remembered something Sarah once said: *The higher ranks of society used tea as a luxury while the lower orders made a diet of it*. It was from *Buchan's Domestic Medicine*. Sarah could quote from it like some Christians recited tracts from the Bible.

He put a hand to his forearm, probing delicately at the site of the larger wound. It was smarting less by the day, Sarah having done an exemplary job. Never mind learning about it, she could be teaching this stuff.

The kitchen at Queen Street was one of his favourite rooms in the house. It was always warm and usually full of inviting smells, which could certainly not be said of the consulting room upstairs. He had already told Sarah about Mrs King and the circumstances in which she was discovered. Hence the tea-making.

'What did you do after finding her?' Sarah asked as she emptied the kettle into the brown enamel teapot Mrs Lyndsay favoured, and which was never permitted beyond the confines of the kitchen. Only china for the upstairs rooms, despite the old brown pot doing a better job of brewing tea.

'I alerted McLevy and pointed him in the direction of Mrs

Mackay, who was able to identify the body as the same woman who rented the premises on Dickson's Close.'

'Who do you think killed her?'

'McLevy suggested it could be any of the dozens of women who gave her their babies. I did not get the impression he would be looking too hard. He seemed satisfied that she had been dealt with; the whole city will be satisfied simply that she is dead. Everyone can put the matter behind them and forget about it.'

'Until another Mrs King sets up in business.'

Raven took a sip of his tea.

'I think it was Gideon,' he said. 'He went to see Cameron Todd immediately after his release. It is my guess that Gideon suspected Todd had been involved in dealing with Christina's pregnancy and what happened thereafter. Presumably, Todd told him about Mrs King and where he could find her.'

'Did you share your suspicions with McLevy?'

Raven sighed, rubbing his hands through his hair. 'No,' he admitted. 'I could not. To do so I would have had to reveal how I knew, which would expose Dr Todd's connection to Mrs King, and through that Eugenie would learn the likely fate of her daughter.

'I want to be the one who confronts Gideon with this,' he added. 'I fear that if he is revealed by McLevy as the man who killed Mrs King, he will be hailed as some kind of avenging hero, not a mere murderer.'

'I have no doubt he is that,' Sarah said, placing a small hessian bag in the middle of the table.

'What is this?'

'It's what Amelia saw Gideon carrying into the kitchen the night Sir Ainsley died. This is the fruit of the manchineel tree. I took it to Professor Balfour at the Botanic Gardens. He told me it is also known as the "little apple of death". Highly poisonous. Tastes sweet initially then burns your insides. Meg said that she had tasted a piece of the fruit on Ainsley Douglas's tray that night and it had burned her mouth.'

'But Ainsley did not eat the fruit on his tray. Or have I misremembered?'

'No, you are correct. The burning would likely have alerted him to the poisonous nature of the fruit before he consumed enough of it to cause any real harm. The taste would need to have been disguised in something else.'

'Like what?'

'Most likely the brandy he drank to help him sleep.'

'If it was put in the brandy, why then leave the fruit itself on the plate?' Raven asked.

'Perhaps Gideon intended that it should appear to have been served up and consumed, so that a kitchen mishap looked to be responsible for Ainsley's death. Accidental rather than deliberate.'

'But why even leave any such clue, particularly if Gideon could be revealed as the source, having just returned from Tobago?'

Sarah looked as though she was about to suggest a reason when they heard footsteps on the stairs. Raven was surprised to see that it was Mrs Simpson who entered. She looked distraught.

'Will. Sarah. Thank goodness you are here.'

Raven was immediately on his feet. 'What is the matter?'

'He has taken a turn for the worse.'

Raven was off up the stairs before she had time to finish her sentence. Sarah was hard at his heels, Mrs Simpson following on behind. He burst into Dr Simpson's room without knocking and could immediately see why Mrs Simpson was worried. Simpson was flushed, delirious, muttering to himself. Hot to the touch and his pulse rapid.

Raven had a look at the axillary abscess he had spotted before. It had increased in size and was tense with pus.

'That abscess will have to be drained. He needs a surgeon.'

'A surgeon?' Mrs Simpson asked. 'Can't you deal with it?'

Raven could certainly attempt it – surgical drainage of an abscess was not a technically difficult procedure – but there was too much at stake. Was he being a coward by not taking responsibility himself? He had, after all, performed a particularly risky procedure on Sarah a few months before, but that had been done out of necessity, and had an alternative been available then, he would happily have taken it. If things went badly here, he was not sure he would be able to live with himself.

'A surgeon would be better,' he stated.

'I will ask Professor Miller,' said Mrs Simpson. 'He's only next door.'

'Professor Miller left to see a patient across the Forth this morning.'

It was Jarvis who spoke, coming up the stairs carrying a jug of water and some towels.

'He is not expected back tonight.'

Mrs Simpson looked at Raven and Sarah in turn. 'If not Professor Miller, then who? Who is the best?'

'Syme,' Raven said. It was out of his mouth before he could stop himself.

'Then that is who he must have,' Mrs Simpson declared.

'Syme?' Sarah repeated. 'Are you sure?'

Raven knew that she was not questioning the surgeon's ability but expressing her concern about the personal relationship between the two men. Simpson and Syme. Notable adversaries. Always on the opposing side of an argument.

'I'm sure,' Raven said. 'He's the best. I'll go and fetch him.'

'I've already asked Angus to bring the carriage round,' Jarvis said, having evidently anticipated the need for reinforcements.

Raven ran down the stairs, grabbing his coat on the way. He called out the address to Angus and climbed aboard the carriage.

'It's urgent,' he added as he slammed the door. The coachman pulled away without a word, well used to such demands.

As the carriage crossed Princes Street and began its journey to the south side of the city, Raven wondered about his choice of Syme as their saviour in this situation. In the heat of the moment it had been the first name that had come to mind. He hoped his mentor would not regard it as some kind of betrayal, given that he might end up owing the man his life.

They had just passed the toll on Leven Street and were approaching the junction for Millbank when the coach veered left and picked up speed.

Where the hell were they going?

Raven leaned out of the window to tell Angus he had missed the turn.

But it was not Angus who was driving.

FIFTY-FIVE

arah was doing all that she could. Tepid sponging, an open window for ventilation, spooning in the mixture Raven had left to help bring the fever down. None of it was making much difference. Dr Simpson was still fiercely hot, though the muttering had subsided, and he was a little less restless.

Quiet. Still.

Was he going to die? She could not conceive of a world without him in it. Her life had been transformed by her association with him, with this family. He had encouraged her in her reading, pushed her to consider a life beyond domestic service, urged her to see how much more she might do, what she could become. Even as she had come to doubt herself, his faith in her had remained unwavering.

Sarah removed the cloth from his head, shocked by the heat in it. She rinsed it in cool water, replaced it. She thought about praying but could not bring herself to do so. She wished she had a stronger faith, something to comfort her at such times of uncertainty, when she felt that there was little she could do to effect a particular outcome.

She looked over at Mrs Simpson, sitting on the other side of the bed. She did not seem to share Sarah's difficulty.

Her eyes were closed, her head bowed, lips moving in silent supplication.

Suddenly their peace was disturbed by a noise from downstairs, a commotion in the hallway. Was Raven returned already? She knew that he could not be unless he had fortuitously encountered Syme along the way.

Sarah left the room and looked over the banister into the hall. She could see Angus, his head bleeding, being assisted by Jarvis.

She ran down the stairs, Mrs Simpson close behind, and helped the butler get the coachman into a chair.

'I was leading the horses out through the lane at the back,' Angus said. 'Fellow came up to me. I thought maybe he was lost and was going to ask for directions. He drew a pistol: told me he would shoot if I so much as raised my voice. Had me take the carriage out onto the road then led me back into the lane and whacked me on the napper. I came to lying in the gutter, water soaked right through my britches, a swelling the size of a hen's egg on the back on my head. He's made off with the coach!'

Sarah thought that this was the most she had ever heard Angus say. He was a quiet man who seemed to prefer the company of horses to people.

'Can you see to him, Sarah,' Mrs Simpson said.

Sarah went into the consulting room to retrieve a cloth and a dressing for the coachman's head, wondering as she did so why Raven had not come back in to announce that the coach was missing. A chill ran through her as she realised – Raven was inside it. And it was not headed for Millbank.

'Raven has been taken!' she announced as she returned to Angus's side.

'Taken?' Mrs Simpson asked. 'By whom?'

There was only one name in Sarah's head, only one man who

would have done this. The problem was that a more pressing matter needed her attention first. There was nothing she could do to assist Raven right now, as she had no idea where he was. She only knew where he most certainly wasn't, which meant that she would need to go and fetch Syme herself.

FIFTY-SIX

storm of implications billowed around Raven's head like the wind in his face as he leaned from the carriage and saw who was staring back at him from the driver's seat.

Wilson. Sir Ainsley's butler.

He suddenly apprehended the ways in which the fellow must have been in conspiracy with Gideon, though it had been before him all along. The man who had served Sir Ainsley drinks all night, and who must have brought him his supper tray. The man who had commanded the maid to throw away the remains of his final meal and the bloody contents of the bedpan.

I realise now I may have inadvertently had Meg dispose of important evidence.

'I would warn you to sit back in the carriage, Dr Raven,' Wilson told him, raising his voice above the thundering of hooves and the burr of the brougham's wheels upon the rutted road.

'Where are you taking me? I have urgent business back at Millbank. Dr Simpson is gravely ill and I need to fetch Professor Syme!'

Even as he spoke, Raven understood there was nothing he could do for now without risking mortal injury. Wilson was driving like the devil, and he knew where they were bound. He would wait until they reached their destination and then wrest control of the brougham. He only hoped the horses would do as he asked. He had never driven before.

The carriage raced into the Crossford estate, but a quarter of a mile past the main gates, instead of proceeding towards the house, it veered off at a fork in the road and headed deeper into the woods. As the narrowing track wound between the trees, Raven spied the shimmering of a river in the late afternoon sunshine and got the first inkling of where they might be headed. Soon enough he made out the looming shape of the summerhouse: the place Eugenie had spoken of, to which Gideon had often retreated in search of solitude and simple comfort.

Was this where he had been lying low?

But as the butler brought the carriage to a stop, he deduced another reason Wilson had brought him here, and under such means of subterfuge. There were staff at the house, but here there would be no witnesses.

He thought of what McLevy had said about being quickly forgotten by the rich once they had what they wanted from you. What if it was worse than that? With a jolt it struck him that Gideon might have learned that Sarah had visited the house that very day and discovered the manchineel. It was not only himself who was in danger.

Raven stepped down from the carriage, which had come to rest in a clearing before the summerhouse. He could see empty bottles on the porch of the wooden structure. The new laird was in residence.

He watched Wilson climb down from the driver's box seat, calculating when to make his move. Raven's practised eye took in two things that gave him pause. The one of more immediate concern was that Wilson was carrying a pistol, but it was the other that truly had him reeling. The man was moving gingerly to protect his left foot.

It had been Wilson who attacked them in Fleshmarket Close: the masked man with the bayonet.

Raven walked slowly towards the summerhouse, his thoughts a blur as his assumptions were once again turned on their heads. It did not follow. What reason would Wilson have to attack him and Sarah if they were working to exonerate Gideon?

Then he saw that he had it wrong. Gideon's exoneration was the very thing Wilson wished to prevent, because Sir Ainsley's wayward son had been set up to take the blame.

Had it been Wilson all along: the butler murdering his master? That did not feel right either, not least because there seemed no strong motive. Was it the death of Lady Douglas? Sir Ainsley feared she had taken a lover, and perhaps that lover had been his own butler. But if so, why would he wait so long to take his revenge?

More practically, Raven could not envisage how Wilson might know what a manchineel was. Even Sarah had needed to seek out the Professor of Botany to identify the fruit and describe its deadly properties. A person would only know such information if they had encountered the deadly fruit personally, and that wasn't going to happen during a lifetime working in a mansion at the foot of the Pentlands.

Then Raven realised that there *was* somebody who must have encountered them first-hand.

I know well enough what a pineapple is. I have visited the Indies too.

Amelia had been to Tobago. Gideon said he and his sister had wintered there after their mother died.

Raven could vividly imagine the scene: a moment of panic as someone shooed the unsuspecting girl from beneath the branches of a deadly tree lest its sap burn her skin. The dire warning of how lethal its fruit was.

He was stopped in his tracks as everything finally became clear, and this time all the pieces fitted. Amelia had told people she wished to renounce the inheritance, but this was merely to dispel suspicion and disguise her true intentions. She had a keen interest in law, so she had always known that as a woman she could not renounce on behalf of a male heir. She had merely pretended otherwise.

This was why the fruit was placed on the plate, though the poison was delivered via the brandy. The fruit was *supposed* to be found, in order to incriminate Gideon. But then the arsenic was discovered, and though she could not have anticipated this, she had been happy to let events play out because they were leading to the same end. That was until Sarah had proven the arsenic came from Sir Ainsley's bismuth, and Gideon was released. Suddenly Amelia had to revive her original plan. She had planted the remaining manchineel but needed someone else to discover it, and had identified Sarah as the perfect conduit, flattering her into doing so.

If anyone might get to the truth of this, it would be you.

FIFTY-SEVEN

arah had to walk all the way to Charlotte Square before she found a cab for hire, several occupied carriages passing on either side of Queen Street as she hastened along it. Once she had finally secured a conveyance, she had to ask the driver several times to hurry, requests that he seemed happy to ignore. Eventually she offered to supplement the fare and they made much faster progress thereafter.

She wondered what had happened to Raven but tried to put it from her mind. She had to see to Dr Simpson first. She knew that she could not afford to lose either of them. Certainly not both.

The cab covered the distance in less than twenty minutes, but it felt considerably longer than that. They pulled up outside Millbank, a grand, ivy-clad house set back from the road, where the door was answered promptly and she was asked to wait in the hall. All was quiet. She could not imagine children or pets running amok here as they did at Queen Street.

Sarah had retained a small hope that upon arrival she would be told that Professor Syme had left already, that a young man had come for him with an urgent request, but nothing had been said.

As she stood in the hallway, she wondered what kind of reception she would receive. Again, she allowed herself to be optimistic, indulging in the fantasy that Professor Syme would appear from behind a closed door, bag in hand, Raven at his back, but when the surgeon did descend the stairs he was stern-faced and alone.

'Whatever it is, I hope that it is of the utmost importance,' he said. 'I do not like to be disturbed at home.'

'Dr Simpson is gravely ill,' Sarah told him, unintimidated by his severity. 'Mrs Simpson has sent this note kindly requesting that you attend.'

She proffered the letter, hastily scribbled just before she left.

Syme opened it and read. Would he refuse to come? Sarah recalled Raven describing a recent argument at the Caledonian Hotel, how he had thought it might come to blows.

Syme looked up and frowned. 'Mrs Simpson has communicated her concern but has failed to supply any detail as to the nature of the complaint.' He eyed Sarah sceptically. 'I don't suppose there is much point asking you, is there?'

'Dr Simpson has a large axillary abscess, the result of an injury to his hand. He is febrile and his condition has worsened over the last few hours.'

Syme raised a bushy eyebrow. 'You have a carriage?'

'I have a cab waiting.'

'Then we had best be off.'

And that was it. No further discussion. No hesitation.

He called for his bag, which a young girl brought to him. Black shiny leather, as though polished every night before being put away. Dr Simpson's bag was a scuffed brown thing, flung about with abandon unless there was a bottle of chloroform in it. And sometimes even when there was.

They climbed into the cab, Professor Syme instructing the driver to make haste, which this time he did without question or the promise of an enhanced fare.

The return journey to Queen Street was made in silence, which was a blessing as Sarah felt incapable of making polite conversation. She imagined that it would have been difficult to exchange pleasantries with Syme at the best of times. These were not the best of times.

When they arrived, Sarah jumped down from the cab hoping to see Raven at the door, but it was Jarvis who answered the bell.

'Is he back?' she asked.

Jarvis shook his head.

Syme, who Raven had always described as a dour and irascible fellow, was kindness itself when dealing with Mrs Simpson, a woman who was no stranger to family tragedy. She had already lost two children to the rapacious clutches of infectious disease. She was fragile and Sarah worried what kind of toll any further catastrophe might take. Mrs Simpson already spent an unhealthy number of hours shut up in her room with the Bible and improving tracts for company; and sometimes, if Lizzie was to be believed, the chloroform bottle.

Sarah escorted Syme to Dr Simpson's room. It felt stuffy despite the open window.

Syme wasted no time. He asked a few questions – how long Dr Simpson had been this way, what remedies had been attempted, what medicines administered – then conducted his examination with surprising gentleness. Simpson himself was still delirious and did not seem to recognise his medical attendant as the man he had locked horns with on so many occasions.

'You were right to call me,' Syme said. 'This requires immediate surgical drainage.'

He pointed to the ruby red swelling in Dr Simpson's armpit. It seemed to pulsate, blinking like an angry beacon in time with the patient's rapid pulse.

'I'll get the chloroform,' Sarah said.

'There's no time for that,' Syme declared. 'And there is no one to give it.'

'I can do it,' Sarah told him. She could not abide the thought of Syme cutting into Dr Simpson's flesh without the aid of an anaesthetic. It seemed grossly unfair that he should not receive the benefit that his discovery had bestowed upon so many others.

Syme looked at Mrs Simpson, who nodded by way of confirming what Sarah had said.

'Very well, but be quick about it. If you are not back by the time I am ready to start, I shall begin without you.'

Sarah fetched the chloroform bottle while Syme made his preparations. She was well versed in the technique, having been taught to administer it by Simpson himself, but still her hand shook as she sprinkled a small quantity onto a handkerchief and held it to his face. It was hard to imagine the stakes being any higher. If something were to happen, if the professor did not survive, would she be held accountable? Chloroform, or at least the administration of it, was often blamed in similar circumstances. Almost immediately she thought about Hannah Greener, the young girl who had died within three minutes of it being administered and was purported to be the first chloroform-related death.

She dismissed the thought as being singularly unhelpful, but it was replaced almost immediately by an account she had read of a public demonstration at the Royal Institution in London. It had been intended to reassure those present regarding the safety of chloroform and ether. The lecturer had chloroformed a guinea pig, promising to revive it after a few minutes, but at the end of the demonstration the animal was found to be dead.

She forced herself to concentrate on Dr Simpson's breathing, which was now slow and regular.

If Syme shared any of Sarah's apprehension he showed no sign of it. He pointed at the chloroform bottle.

'I wasn't convinced at first,' he said. 'Certainly not by ether. Its effects were too unpredictable, and I was wary of using it despite the unbridled enthusiasm it seemed to engender. The first time I saw ether used by Professor Miller at the Infirmary, there were so many Free Church ministers present that I thought I had intruded upon a meeting of the Presbytery.'

Sarah smiled at this, despite her tension.

'Alright to go?' he asked, brandishing his scalpel.

She nodded and Syme made a large incision in the abscess. Sarah could see that it took a boldness born of experience to make a large enough opening to evacuate all of the pus: to attack the thing rather than gingerly poke at it. Being tentative would not do. Being tentative courted disaster.

A considerable amount of foul-smelling pus poured forth, the stench mingling with the sweeter chemical tang of the chloroform. It produced a noxious and thoroughly unpleasant combination.

Syme squeezed the edges of the abscess, encouraging the disgorgement of more of its evil contents until satisfied that he had got it all out.

'We'll need to apply a poultice,' he said.

'I'll see that it is done,' Sarah replied.

Syme smiled and nodded, seemingly satisfied that she knew what she was doing. Sarah withdrew the chloroform and watched with some satisfaction as her patient continued to sleep, breathing regular, pulse rapid but strong.

'That's as much as can be done for now,' Syme said, wiping his scalpel before putting it back into his instrument case. 'With a bit of luck, he should start to improve.'

Luck. Was that what it was going to come down to?

Syme packed up his things, declined an offer of tea and requested Jarvis summon a cab to take him home, vowing to return the following day.

As the door closed behind him, Sarah felt the urge to pray again, to request some divine intervention. She knew better than to expect miracles. There was a limit to what a surgeon could do, even one as revered as Syme. She made do with applying the poultice he had requested and bandaging it into place.

She sat by the bedside after Syme had gone, monitoring the patient for any signs of change: for better or worse. She felt conflicted. She wanted to stay but also desperately needed to leave: to find Raven, wherever he was, and help bring him home.

FIFTY-EIGHT

aven heard the creak of a door opening and saw Gideon emerge onto the porch, little resembling a man who had inherited a fortune. He looked like he had slept in his clothes, if he had slept at all. He was bleary-eyed, slow and confused in his movements.

'What are you doing here?' he asked in the croak of a voice that had not spoken in some time.

Raven observed that Wilson was holding the pistol by his side so as to keep it from Gideon's sight, and in that moment he saw the answer. The butler meant to kill them both.

'Get back inside, Gideon,' Raven called out, 'and bar the door!'

Wilson raised the pistol, pointing it at Raven. It was a flint-lock, so there would be a slight delay between Wilson pulling the trigger and the charge firing. Raven took in the ground between them and estimated how fast he could cover it.

Wilson took a step away as though reading Raven's intentions. He swung his arm back and forth to aim the pistol at each of them in turn.

'Both of you stay where you are,' he said. It was intended as a command, though his voice was faltering.

Gideon ignored both entreaties, moving slightly closer to the edge of the porch. His daze looked less the result of alcohol than of a man punch-drunk from too many blows. Nothing was making sense to him.

He distilled all of this into a single word, less a question to either of them than to the whole world for what it had been doing to him of late.

'Why?'

'Because he is in league with your sister and fears her original plan has fallen apart,' Raven answered, keeping his gaze on Wilson, oscillating his focus between the weapon and the man's eyes for notice that he was about to shoot. 'She poisoned your father and intended you to take the blame. If he makes it appear that we killed each other, perhaps in a fight, then your father's inheritance will fall to Amelia's son.'

Raven could tell Gideon saw the truth of it, but he looked less like it had ignited a blaze of anger than that it had dealt one more devastating clout to someone with little stomach left for the fight. He turned to face Wilson, his expression a mixture of hurt, accusation and disbelief.

The butler, for his part, looked like a man unravelling, his expression contorted with desperation. Irrational and unpredictable. He only had one shot, but at this range it would likely prove mortal for whoever it hit.

Then in a burst, faster than Raven would have believed he could move, Gideon hurled himself from the porch, his hands grappling for Wilson's arm. As they collided, the pistol fell to the grass without discharging.

Raven seized it but by the time it was in his grasp he saw that there was no fight to be had. Wilson had dropped to his knees and broken down in tears, making no attempt to defend himself.

'Forgive me, Master Gideon.'

His arms were open as though to invite Gideon's rage. However, there was no echo of that night in the alley.

Gideon stepped back, his face a study in turmoil and hurt.

'Does my sister despise me so much that she would see me hang for something I did not do?'

Wilson shook his head, his tone sincere and imploring.

'That was never her intention. She reasoned it would be impossible to prove that you administered the poison, only that you had motive. A "not proven" verdict would be enough to invoke a corruption of blood. She wanted the inheritance to pass to Matthew. She feared you would squander it.'

Raven watched Gideon's hackles rise and felt glad he had control of the pistol. Wilson's explanation bore a harsh truth, one that was unlikely to ameliorate Gideon's outrage. But to Raven there remained a deeper question still, concerning the conduct of this man who had been so loyal and dutiful towards Sir Ainsley all his days.

'You conspired with Amelia to murder her own father?' Raven asked him.

Wilson looked distraught, a man in need of absolution.

'It wasn't like that,' he insisted.

Raven gestured idly with the gun, in case the man's need to confess proved insufficient.

'Then tell us what it was like.'

Wilson swallowed. 'On the night of the soirée, Amelia left early, you may remember. But I saw her return. No one else did, because she had dressed herself as a housemaid. She must have passed a dozen people without them giving her a second look, but I have known her since she was a child. I recognised her at first glance.'

As he spoke, Raven realised that it had been Amelia he saw emerging from the secret passage, the one who had seemed tantalisingly familiar. It was because they had been introduced less than an hour before, when she was dressed very differently. She had turned and scurried away as soon as she saw that the room was occupied. He now knew that it was because Eugenie would have recognised her immediately.

'I had no notion what she was about,' Wilson went on. 'People can do queer things at such parties, so I thought no more of it. But the next morning, when the master was found dead and I saw the blood in the bedpan, I knew he had been poisoned, and I knew it had been Amelia. That is why I instructed Meg to clear everything away.'

It struck Raven that while Wilson's conclusion was correct, his deduction process was missing a few steps – as was the reason for his subsequent conduct.

'How could you know so instantly that Amelia had done such a terrible thing? And why would you so swiftly act to protect her?'

Wilson winced. He looked to Raven and then to Gideon.

'Because I failed to protect her before.'

Gideon's gaze became more intent, both curious and wary.

'Do you know why your mother died?' Wilson asked him.

'We were never allowed to know, but I am certain she killed herself.'

'I did not ask *how*. I asked why.'

Now Gideon's face was intent, as rapt as he was anxious.

Wilson grimaced again, a man reopening a wound.

'After Amelia turned twelve,' he said, 'your father began going to her in the night.'

He let this hang in the air until they perceived its enormity. All that it did not say, and yet all that could be understood from it.

'I witnessed comings and goings. Things I failed to deduce the significance of, or perhaps things I refused to *accept* the significance of. I told myself it could not be what it appeared, but it was convenient to my cowardice to believe that.'

'Lady Douglas knew too?' Raven asked.

'One morning I saw her standing over Amelia's empty bed. There was a smell off the sheets, something unmistakable. A smell of seed. A smell that should not, could not be upon a young girl's bed.

'I overheard their argument. Sir Ainsley said: "What would you have me do? Would you rather I visited the whores in the town and risk disease?" It was as though to his mind this was a lesser sin.'

Gideon sat down on the edge of the porch, a defeated look in his eyes as he took this in. It was as though he had been drained of his outrage.

'I was a coward too,' he stated. 'I recall seeing my father enter Amelia's room in the night. I heard strange noises, but I was too young to understand what they meant. And maybe that was true at the time, but I understood later, and I lacked the strength to accept it. I have always been a coward.'

'We were all cowards before him,' Wilson said. 'Which is why Amelia had nobody with the courage to protect her. It took Lady Douglas's death for him to stop. Amelia had far more reason than you to hate your father, and that was before she had to watch you squander all that was given to you and denied to her. Which was why she devised a plan, and once she had a son, eligible to inherit where she was not, she set it in motion.'

Raven remembered Sarah telling him how Ainsley had called Amelia the apple of his eye. He marvelled at the dark poetry of it. She had avenged herself upon him with the little apple of death.

'You confronted Amelia with what you knew,' Raven said. 'That she had killed her father.'

'Yes. My knowledge was too much to bear alone. Too much for her to bear too, for she told me all. She needed someone to understand her, why she had done this.'

'And she promised to reward you for your silence.'

Wilson nodded. 'I was to be kept on as butler and given a generous pension when I chose to retire.'

'Did she send you after Sarah, after me?'

Wilson looked appalled at the suggestion. 'No! It was I who feared that you would be her undoing. I knew that she had suffered so much, and I wished to see the house thrive under her stewardship. It has sat ill with me down the years and I owed her a debt of protection that I would have gone to any length to redeem. I plead for your forgiveness. I have done terrible things in search of redemption.'

As he said this last, anguish in the man's expression, Raven realised that Wilson was not merely talking about Fleshmarket Close, or even his actions here. The woman in the haberdasher's had described a finely dressed gentleman. Well-spoken. It had not been Gideon.

But if Wilson's aim was to protect Amelia, what threat did the baby-farmer pose to her?

Raven stood over him where he knelt and looked him in the eye.

'Why did you kill Mrs King?'

The shock of being discovered animated the butler's face like a flash of lightning, but the moment lasted just as long. Once it had passed, his visage was one of sternest resolve.

'I will take what is due me, but I will say no more. I have told Master Gideon all that he deserves to know. The rest I will take to my grave.'

FIFTY-NINE

arah had maintained her vigil at Dr Simpson's bedside for as long as she could. He was still hot but sleeping peacefully – because he was improving or as a result of the residual effects of the chloroform she did not know. As Mrs Simpson continued her silent prayers for the man she loved, Sarah's thoughts turned to Raven. She was sure it was Gideon who had taken him. But taken him where? She knew that she had to do something to help him but was toiling to think what that might be. Then she thought about the irony of Syme being called upon in Simpson's time of need and realised who she ought to turn to for assistance.

Eugenie.

Sarah ran the last part of the way, hitching up her skirts and ignoring the bemused looks of those she raced past. She felt guilty, conflicted, as though she was being made to choose between the two men she loved most. But she could not continue to sit by Dr Simpson's sickbed while Raven was in danger. And yet, what if it was a deathbed rather than a sickbed? She had left him before she could be sure. How would she feel if Dr Simpson succumbed and she was not there? What if she missed her chance to say goodbye?

She picked up her pace as she reached St Andrew Square.

She wondered at her course of action, why she had decided to appeal to Eugenie. Ultimately it came down to the fact that she had no one else. Usually it was Raven she turned to, no matter how pig-headed and annoying he had been.

It was a warm and bright evening, a surprise after the gloom of the sick room. The Scott Monument looked resplendent against the evening sunshine, Edinburgh oblivious to her despair. It looked as though everything was well with the world. Right then, it felt as though nothing was.

The address was easy to identify, a brass plaque beside the door stating 'Dr Cameron Todd MD'. Sarah pulled the bell and waited, catching her breath.

A maid answered, and after she gave her name, led Sarah up to the drawing room. Eugenie stood up as she entered, which was when Sarah observed that she was not alone. Amelia was sitting on a chaise longue beside the window.

'How fortuitous,' Amelia said. 'We were just talking about you. What did you discover at Crossford?'

'Crossford?'

Though she had been there only this morning, it felt like a month ago.

'Yes. I asked you to make further enquiries.'

Sarah realised that there was a lot of information she had yet to share.

'I found a deadly fruit that I think your brother may have used to poison your father.'

Amelia shook her head, a look of grim satisfaction on her face.

'I knew it,' she said. 'I understand his nature too well.'

'I am here because I believe Gideon knows he is discovered and has taken dire action. Our coach driver was attacked, and Raven driven off to who knows where.'

Eugenie looked horrified. 'Will is in danger?'

'I need to know where Gideon might be,' Sarah said. 'Where Raven could have been taken.'

Eugenie's face became unexpectedly thunderous. 'Come with me!'

She took Sarah by the arm and led her out of the room while Amelia remained seated, wearing a concerned expression, as though unsure what she should do.

Sarah followed Eugenie down a long corridor towards a room at the back of the house.

'It is time my father spoke honestly of what he knows,' Eugenie said as they went. 'I am tired of his evasions, his *lies*.'

Eugenie barrelled through the door into what appeared to be her father's study. Dr Todd was seated in an armchair reading a book. On the floor in front of him, lying naked on a blanket, was young Matthew. Freed from his habitual bindings, he was kicking his little legs in the air and gurgling softly to himself.

'What are you doing?' Eugenie asked, taking in the scene.

'This child requires no medical attention from me apart from releasing him from the excess clothing and tight swaddling that Amelia insists upon employing,' Dr Todd replied quietly. 'She has him wrapped like an Egyptian mummy. I have told her many times that it is not only unnecessary but possibly harmful. Much like you young women and your insistence on restrictive corsetry. Impedes the action of the ribcage and impairs the function of the lungs. Anyway, why the interruption?'

He looked past her, suddenly anxious that perhaps Amelia might be hovering in the doorway ready to pounce. Sarah wondered at the man. An eminent and respected physician hiding what he was doing from his patient. It made her wonder what other secrets he might be party to, what he might have done to avoid confrontation with his most wealthy patron.

Eugenie gazed down at the child, frowning.

'What is that?' she asked.

Dr Todd looked at what she was pointing to.

'It is a congenital naevus.'

'How long has it been there?'

He scoffed at her. 'Congenital means that he was born with it. From the Latin *congenitus* meaning "generated together".'

'How can it be a birthmark? I have not seen it before.'

'You mean you did not notice it,' Todd said, happy to dismiss his daughter's doubts.

'I have seen this child naked before,' Eugenie insisted, 'and I assure you he did not have a birthmark.'

'But Christina's baby did,' Sarah said.

Sarah approached the child as Todd made a move to cover him up. He was not quick enough. Sarah had seen all that she needed to: an oval birthmark on the child's upper left arm, just as Christina had described.

Eugenie looked confused but Sarah was beginning to see things clearly.

'Matthew died, didn't he?'

She addressed this question to Dr Todd but did not wait for an answer.

'That is why the nanny was dismissed,' she continued. 'So that a substitution could be made. So that Matthew could be replaced.'

It was as though, after many attempts, the correct key had been placed in a lock, all of the tumblers falling into place.

'That is preposterous,' Dr Todd replied, his tone suffused with condescension. If it was an attempt to disarm her, it did not have the intended effect.

'You knew, and perhaps Amelia did too, that her brother's son had been given away to the self-same woman you had previous dealings with. You, Dr Todd, were the linchpin in the whole scheme.'

Todd looked from one to the other, assessing his options – continue to lie or tell the truth. He narrowed his eyes at Sarah, trying to work out how much more she knew, how certain she was about what she had just said.

She held his gaze. She did not look away. She did not blink.

Todd sighed with resignation, casting another wary glance towards the door before he spoke.

'I was called to the house the night Matthew died. I arrived in time to witness his final throes. It was a pitiful sight. Amelia was distraught. She had just lost her husband and now she had lost her son. She made a request that I could not refuse.'

He spoke as if what he had done was the most natural thing in the world, something entirely reasonable. Passing off one child as another.

'She knew I had been instrumental in dealing with the problem of Gideon's housemaid. Though Amelia no longer lived at Crossford, Wilson kept her informed of what went on there. Through him, she knew that the girl had given birth to a son, and that he was being kept by a woman, for payment.'

Sarah had to bite her tongue. She had no wish to interrupt his confession but his manner of referring to Christina as Gideon's housemaid — as though she were a mere bit player in the whole thing — was infuriating.

'Amelia asked me to procure the child,' Todd continued. 'She considered it fitting that she should replace the son she had lost with one from the same bloodline. One unwanted, undeserved by her brother. Thrown away like he had thrown away so many other gifts.'

But Sarah saw that there was more to it than that: so much more than the consolation of a bereaved mother. Sarah now understood what should have been plain to her and to Raven had they not been following the misleading trail of breadcrumbs Amelia had laid.

Amelia had another reason she could not do without her son. Without *a* son.

She needed a male heir for her plan. Christina's child was around the same age, and even bore the family resemblance. Only the nanny would know the difference.

Everything had been given to Gideon and nothing to her. But

if Gideon were to be blamed for their father's death, the entire Douglas fortune would pass to her son, and control of it to her until he reached maturity. Talk of renouncing the inheritance was a ruse, designed to disguise her true intentions.

When Matthew had died, it had thrown her plans into disarray. But what better way to rectify things than to replace her own son with Gideon's unwanted offspring? There was a sense of natural justice to it, if not for the fact that someone had to die, and her brother blamed.

Just then Amelia appeared in the doorway, immediately sensing from the silence that something was amiss. She spotted the child still naked on the rug.

'What on earth is going on,' she asked.

She strode across to pick the child up, looking about the room for his clothes.

'Dr Todd, have you taken leave of your senses? If Matthew takes a chill . . .'

She began to dress him.

It was Sarah who spoke first.

'She named him Jamie.'

Amelia stopped what she was doing and glanced at Sarah.

'Christina, the housemaid at Crossford, now at 52 Queen Street. Gideon's lover. She named the child you are holding Jamie.'

Amelia's self-possession deserted her. She seemed suddenly panic-stricken. She clutched the half-dressed child to her bosom.

Sarah was aware she could prove nothing, but Amelia did not know that and she was getting better at bluffing.

'I know what you have done,' she said. 'But what concerns me right now is who else is involved, and where they have taken Raven. If you do not speak up and any harm befalls him, you will be answerable to me.'

Eugenie moved to stand alongside Sarah, her face hard-set, sternly resolute.

'And to me,' she said. 'What is going on? Where is he?'

Todd let out a laugh, a sudden bark that seemed entirely inappropriate to the circumstances. Then Sarah noticed his expression of relief as he pointed out of the window to the square below.

'You may set your minds to rest on that score. Dr Raven is alighting from a carriage outside as we speak.'

If his words seemed to comfort his daughter, his next statement had the opposite effect upon Amelia.

'And so is Gideon.'

SIXTY

'm sorry, but the professor is not at home.'

The words fell hard on Raven as he stood on the doorstep at Millbank, calculating how much time had already been lost.

'Do you know where I might find him? He is needed urgently by Professor Simpson.'

The housemaid looked confused. 'He already attends Professor Simpson. There was a lady came by earlier to request him. A Miss Fisher?'

Raven felt the relief flood through him. Sarah had been alerted that something was amiss. Simpson was in the best hands now.

He walked quickly back to the brougham, impatient to reach Queen Street. He would not rest easy until he saw how the professor fared.

Wilson was at the reins, a faraway look in his eyes, perhaps contemplating what he had done and what might lie in his future. That, like so much else, was yet to be decided. Every time Raven looked at the man he felt the tingle of the stitches in his arm, but he found it difficult to summon much anger. There was no question who the true villain of this piece had been. It was nobody present here, nor Amelia, and nor even Mrs King.

Its resolution had brought forth an unlikely hero too. As

the carriage began to move once again, Raven placed a hand on Gideon's shoulder.

'Several times I have heard you call yourself a coward. What you did for me today took great courage.'

'You do me more credit than I am due,' Gideon replied. 'Part of me reasoned he would shoot the one he did not wish to fight hand-to-hand. Another part of me did not believe Wilson could bring himself to kill someone he had watched growing up. And so it proved, for he did not fire.'

'What matters is that you threw yourself in front of a loaded pistol. You are a better man than you permit yourself to believe, Gideon. A stronger man than your father *made* you believe.'

Gideon offered an apologetic smile, as though he was not ready to accept this.

'I am remiss in not having thanked you for getting me out of jail.'

'In truth it was Sarah who demonstrated the source of the arsenic.'

'I have heard much about her. Eugenie wrote to me in prison, and I gather my sister was rather impressed by her too. Is it true she used to be a housemaid?'

'It is true, yes.'

'I am sorry not to have expressed my thanks to you both sooner, but in truth I was not feeling much gratitude or good will towards anybody. Following my release, I learned about the squalid discovery at Bonnington Mills, and I was aware what fate my father had intended for my child. I went to Todd. I knew that as my father's physician he must have played a part. He confirmed what I feared. He delivered the child at some hovel in the Cowgate. I had a son, but the boy had been given away. Todd said he believed the woman found good homes for such children. I suppose a lot of people believed that. Or told themselves they did.'

Raven thought of the comfort Eugenie clung to.

'It is true that some – many – of the babies were given away,' Raven told him. 'Or sold, to be more accurate. Your child might yet survive. Though you will never know with whom, and thus never find him.'

Gideon nodded. 'I have made my peace with that,' he said. 'Better for him that he be brought up by someone more fitting. I had a lot of time in jail to think about how I had lived my life, and found little I was proud of. I ruin everything.'

Raven could see now that Gideon had truly changed. The humility he witnessed in the jail cell had not been a sham.

'You told me you successfully managed the plantation's recovery. Was that a lie?'

'No. The lie was what my father told people. It was hard work and I made mistakes, but I truly gave myself to it, perhaps the first time I have ever done so. I liked the people I was working with. We were making progress.'

'So you do not ruin everything.'

Gideon scoffed. 'It was but one small corner of my father's domain. When McLevy showed me to the gate at Calton Jail, he told me: "Congratulations, you have your freedom back." I found myself asking what kind of freedom I truly had. All my life I have been burdened not only by my father's expectations but by the knowledge that one day I would have to take on his mantle. Amelia was right. I am not fit for any of it.'

He put his head back and sighed. He did not merely look chastened. He looked tired, older.

'Amelia,' he said, as though all of his cares could be distilled into one word.

The carriage slowed at a crossroads. They were approaching Salisbury Road and Raven could hear the sound of an approaching carriage, voices of people on the street. Edinburgh quietly getting on with itself, heedless of other people's dramas.

Gideon turned to face him.

'You were once my tutor, Raven, and I did not have the sense to pay attention to what you were trying to teach me. But I will listen if you will grant your wisdom now.'

Raven doubted he had much wisdom to impart, though he kept this to himself. He was wishing the professor were here: hoping he would be well enough to dispense more wisdom for years to come, whether Raven wished to hear it or not.

'My father deserved to die for what he did,' Gideon said. 'I do not wish to lose my sister too. But that is not for me to decide, is it?'

Raven knew what he was asking, and realised that in this instance, he did have wisdom, or at least experience.

He recalled the sound of water slapping the sides of a boat, saw a body wrapped in sailcloth. His father, dead at Raven's hand that his mother might live. As he hefted the dead weight, he had shouldered a kind of manhood, though he was a mere twelve years old.

'The hangman is not punished for executing the guilty,' he told Gideon. 'As far as McLevy knows, your father died of dysentery and the suspicion of poisoning has been cleared. No one need know anything else. The question is, can you forgive your sister for what she would have done to you?'

Gideon swallowed so that his words were not choked.

'There is nothing to forgive. She has delivered us both.'

Raven glanced out of the window. They were passing the Royal Infirmary on the right-hand side, the university to their left. It was where he had first encountered Gideon. Contrary to Henry's joke, Raven now knew that Gideon had not chosen his parents well at all.

Raven calculated that they would be at Queen Street in fifteen minutes. Before they arrived, there was something Gideon ought to know. A decision he needed to take.

'The summerhouse,' Raven said. 'Where Wilson knew you would be. Eugenie told me you retreated there as a child. It was where you went with Christina, wasn't it?'

'Yes. We used to meet there, where we knew we would not be disturbed. That was where we dreamt our foolish dreams, of being together somewhere far from all of this.'

Then it struck him, as Raven intended it should.

'How do you know her name?'

'Because she lives yet. Your father lied.'

Gideon sat straighter, a sudden anxiety upon his face as though he did not dare believe it lest he be crushed again.

'She is a housemaid at 52 Queen Street, where we are bound. However, you should know that some of what your father said was true. She was forced into prostitution. She became ill and was admitted to the Lock Hospital. But there she was noticed by Professor Simpson and given a position in his house.'

Gideon's eyes filled. 'She lives yet?'

'I tell you this now because before we reach our destination, you must decide whether you wish to see her.'

Gideon was incredulous. 'Of course I wish to —'

'She has been through a great deal,' Raven interrupted. 'She does not know you have returned from Tobago, nor do I imagine she has any expectation that you would seek her out. I would not see her hurt further by impossible dreams.'

Raven watched the implications pass over Gideon's features like a shadow.

'I understand. It would not be fair to raise hopes of something that cannot be met. I have a mountain to climb in proving myself to Edinburgh society, and I can only imagine how it would be received should I be associating with a housemaid, one about whom sordid rumours are bound to spread.'

'I once faced the same dilemma,' Raven told him. 'And the stakes are far higher for you.'

Gideon said nothing throughout the remainder of the journey, deep in contemplation as he gazed from the carriage.

Then, as the brougham turned on to Queen Street, he broke his silence.

'Do you regret it? Do you think about her still?'

Unbidden, Raven's mind pictured Sarah in a thousand ways, but it also summoned a memory of the blow he had suffered in the moment he learned she had married.

'Every day,' he answered. 'But that is the burden you must bear, the sacrifice you have to make.'

Gideon nodded. He looked resolved but not resigned. Perhaps for the first time, there was a calm about him.

SIXTY-ONE

he little chapel was warm, the sun slanting through the stained-glass windows, tiny jewels of colour illuminating the polished stone floor.

Sarah was grateful that they were here for a wedding and not a funeral, despite her reservations about the marriage itself. Dr Simpson had ignored his summons from the grim reaper and, although still weak, was gaining in strength every day. Not as rapidly as he would like, of course. And whether the truce between himself and Syme would last was anyone's guess.

Sarah looked at Raven, resplendent in his new suit. Not one borrowed from the professor, for once. He looked handsome, distinguished, respectable. And he looked happy. For all his doubts she knew that he had made the correct decision. They both had.

Over the past few weeks there had been many choices to make, none of them straightforward; none a simple choice between right and wrong. The hardest had concerned Christina and what the outcome of all this meant for her. The girl had been gushingly grateful for everything that Sarah had done, but she felt awkward receiving Christina's thanks because of what else had been denied her.

Sarah had told Christina that none of the babies found at Bonnington Mills had a birthmark. Christina took this as proof that her child had been given to a loving family, that he would be looked after. Fortunately, that much was true. Her son's future was assured in ways beyond Christina's imaginings. He would be brought up to want for nothing, by someone who loved him. But she would never know where or by whom.

That was a choice she and Raven had made together and a burden they would both have to carry from now on. They had reasoned that telling Christina the whole truth would only bring pain, because nothing could be proven. If it came down to the word of Amelia Bettencourt against a housemaid and former prostitute, there would be no contest. The only other person who could testify to the truth about Matthew was Dr Todd, but to do so would require him to publicly reveal his involvement with the baby-farmer, and quite possibly his daughter's secret too.

That was the genius of Amelia's plan. Absolutely none of it could be verified. It was difficult enough to prove murder with arsenic, and that was a detectable poison. The manchineels left no trace, far less any means of demonstrating how they had been administered or by whom.

Sarah, little as she could condone Amelia's actions, was nonetheless admiring of her cunning and determination. The lengths she was prepared to go to. If women were to progress in this world, they would need more like her. To take down a bigger, more powerful enemy, you had to use underhand strategies. Sometimes you had to fight dirty.

Upon the altar, the minister said the final words: 'I now pronounce you husband and wife.'

Sarah felt her eyes moisten as Gideon and Christina kissed.

She had seldom seen two people look so happy.

Soon enough, she would have to watch Raven and Eugenie stand before a minister too. She did not believe she would feel the same joy that day. Sarah had previously believed that she and Raven having lain together changed nothing, but if that was true, why did she think about it every day? And why, despite knowing how wrong it would be, did she feel so absolutely certain that she wanted it to happen again? That it *would* happen again.

Raven leaned closer to her on the pew.

'I would not have thought someone could look so pleased after giving up a fortune.'

Gideon had renounced his inheritance and his title, letting them pass to the next male heir. He had given up status and fortune to be with the woman he loved. But he had also come to an accommodation with his sister. He would retain the plantation in Tobago that he so loved. He and Christina would begin their journey there today. They would have a life together, far from all that they wished to leave behind.

'He's hardly destitute,' Sarah replied.

Raven rolled his eyes. 'Where is your sense of romance?'

Sarah would have to concede that she did not see how else the whole sorry episode could have ended, what different conclusion might have been more fitting. McLevy was satisfied that the baby-farmer had been dealt with. He maintained that his enquiries were ongoing as to who had killed Mrs King, but Sarah wondered if that truly meant anything. Privately McLevy admitted that the perpetrator had merely saved the hangman a job. Justice had been served; the punishment fitted the crime, even though it had not been officially sanctioned.

As far as the authorities were concerned, Sir Ainsley Douglas had died of dysentery, carrying the worst of his secrets to the grave. And it was a grave he would be turning in if he knew that the child of his scorned son and a lowly housemaid would ultimately command his fortune.

Of the other main players, Gideon and Christina were married and about to start a new life together; Amelia had a child she would love, and Gideon's son would inherit all.

Perhaps it was the best that could be hoped for.

★

The wedding breakfast had been set out on tables on the lawn before the summerhouse. There was an elaborate selection of food: salmon, lobster and ham, as well as fruit jellies, blancmange and wedding cake. Sarah stood a little distance away as she watched Raven and Eugenie fill their plates.

'They look happy,' a voice said.

Sarah turned to see Amelia standing beside her. She had not been aware of her approach, but she was learning that stealth was very much to be expected of the woman. This was the first they had seen of each other since that evening at St Andrew Square, and there was a palpable tension between them. Amelia was now a woman of power and property, but Sarah knew her secrets. Which one was consequently the greater threat to the other remained unclear.

'Gideon and Christina,' Amelia clarified, signalling that she knew it was not the bride and groom who had caught Sarah's attention.

'Yes. Yes, they do,' Sarah replied. Caught on the back foot and struggling for something to say, she echoed Raven's recent words. 'I would not have thought someone could look so content after giving up a fortune.'

'He surprised us all,' Amelia replied. 'And I admire him in a way I never thought I could. But please remember that he got what he wanted from the accommodation. Gideon exercised a choice, one that we women do not enjoy.'

Amelia then made play of gazing towards where Raven stood, underlining that she had caught Sarah staring.

'You love him, don't you?'

Sarah looked at Amelia, trying to fathom a response. Amelia was still dressed in black: mourning her late husband but inviting people to assume it was for her father. An affectation hiding the truth.

'He loves Eugenie.'

'Not an answer to my question.'

'She will be a better wife to Raven than I ever could. She can give him things that I cannot.'

'What manner of things could a woman of your gifts fail to provide?'

Sarah glanced at Eugenie as she answered.

'Children. The willingness to put all of his ambitions first. The sacrifice of allowing my own aspirations to wither.'

Amelia said nothing for a moment as she took this in. She appeared to be considering Sarah's words carefully.

'What next for you then, Miss Fisher?'

'Work and study,' she replied. 'I will continue to work for Dr Simpson but plan to take a course of lectures to make up for the deficiencies in my education.'

'Deficiencies?'

'I had a parish-school education: a *girl's* parish-school education. Many of the things I require to know were never taught to me – Latin, Greek, natural philosophy, chemistry.'

'How will you manage both?'

'I'll make use of bits and pieces of time,' she said. '"Do not wait for ideal circumstances to arise, act as though they are already here."'

She smiled, realising she was quoting Simpson, reciting his own philosophy. And she would need to do all of that. The lecture course she was referring to extended over a period of four years. It was a considerable commitment but one that she was prepared to make.

'It will be expensive,' Amelia stated. She paused for a moment then said, 'I could perhaps assist.'

Was this payment in kind for Sarah maintaining her silence? She could not say, but if Amelia wanted to make amends of a financial kind, then Sarah had no shortage of suggestions.

'I have the funds to pay for my own education,' Sarah replied. 'But there are plenty who do not. You are someone with the means to pay for the education of many women like me.'

'Like you?'

'Women with ambitions to study as men do, those of us who are not content with sewing, knitting and making bread.'

Amelia smiled, nodding her approval; and, Sarah inferred, her assent.

'We will need more than a few fortunate individuals,' Sarah continued. 'We will need a battalion. For the more of us there are, the more of us there will be.'

HISTORICAL NOTE

n writing any historical novel, the fun is in weaving true elements into a wider fiction, leaving the reader wondering which parts of the story really happened and which are the products of our combined imaginations.

Sir Ainsley's infectious diseases ordinance was based on legislation enacted in 1864 – the Contagious Diseases Act – whereby women suspected of being prostitutes could be arrested and subjected to intimate examinations in an attempt to contain the spread of venereal disease. No provision within the act was made to prevent men from consorting with sex workers.

Elizabeth Blackwell was the first woman to obtain a medical degree (1849) and the first woman to be registered with the UK General Medical Council (1858). She graduated from Geneva Medical College in New York before travelling to Europe to extend her training and experience. She developed an eye infection while working in the maternity hospital in Paris and lost the sight in her left eye. On her return to America she experienced difficulty in setting up in practice. When she could not secure a position as a doctor in any hospital or dispensary, she set up her own. With her sister Emily she opened the New York Infirmary for Women and Children in 1857.

Unfortunately, infanticide and baby-farming were not uncommon in the nineteenth century. There are several women whose crimes were amalgamated into our version, including Amelia Dyer, who strangled her victims with dressmaker's tape and disposed of dozens of them in a canal, and Edinburgh's Jessie King, who was the last woman to be executed in the city in 1889.

Dr Simpson is of course a real historical character. He discovered the anaesthetic properties of chloroform in 1847 and as a result became world-renowned. He and James Syme were constantly in dispute and did almost come to blows outside a patient's bedroom.

In 1850, after returning from a trip to London, Simpson became dangerously ill with an axillary abscess and Syme – despite being Simpson's nemesis – was called in to deal with it. It is not clear why Syme and not another surgical colleague was asked to assist. Whether chloroform was administered or not is unknown.

ACKNOWLEDGEMENTS

armest thanks to those who have made this book and the series possible.

To everyone at Canongate, especially to our editor, Francis Bickmore, ably assisted by the eagle-eyed Megan Reid. Thanks to Jamie Norman, Vicki Watson and Jenny Fry for keeping Ambrose's profile so high, and all the wonderful people in the foreign rights department who have seen the books translated into multiple languages.

Our ongoing gratitude goes to Sophie Scard, Caroline Dawnay and Charles Walker at United Agents for their invaluable feedback and support.

A special thanks to Eugenie Todd, our copyeditor, who kindly agreed to let her name be used for one of the characters in the book.

And to all those responsible for digitising archives – what a godsend you are.